**William Corlett** was a successful children's novelist. He also wrote widely for television and the theatre for both adults and children, and twice won the Writers' Guild Children's TV Writer of the Year Award. His second adult novel, *Two Gentlemen Sharing* is also published by Abacus. William Corlett died in 2005.

'Not a word is misplaced in this subtle exploration of middle-class inhibition' *Independent*

*Also by William Corlett:*

TWO GENTLEMEN SHARING

# WILLIAM CORLETT

# *Now and Then*

ABACUS

First published in Great Britain by Abacus in 1995
This paperback edition published by Abacus 1996
Reprinted 1996 (three times), 1997 (twice), 1998, 1999, 2001, 2003, 2005,
2007, 2009, 2011

A CIP catalogue record for this book
is available from the British Library.

ISBN 978-0-349-10775-2

Typeset by Palimpsest Book Production Limited,
Polmont, Stirlingshire
Printed and bound in Great Britain by
Clays Ltd, St Ives plc

Abacus
An imprint of
Little, Brown Book Group
100 Victoria Embankment
London EC4Y 0DY

An Hachette UK Company
www.hachette.co.uk

www.littlebrown.co.uk

# Now and Then

# *Now*

The room he died in smelt of Dettol and bonfire smoke. It was a warm September afternoon and the french windows had been opened to let in some air. It was the room he had used as his study, though what he had actually studied there was never quite clear to any of us. It had been converted to a sickroom when his lungs had finally packed in and he had stopped being able to move. His bed was squeezed in between the desk and the wall, with the bedhead flanked by rows of books that he had never, to my knowledge, read. The desk had been cleared and spread with a blanket, to protect the mahogany, and a white linen cloth, to give a sense of hospital sterility. The protection suggested a future he would not share and the sterility a present that he did not recognise.

He had lain in a gloaming world of heavy rasping breath and frail movements for many months and it was uncertain how many of the tiny day-to-day occurrences were noticed by him. Did it irritate him that his study, that private sanctuary and only room in the house that no one entered without first knocking and awaiting his bidding, had become the casual thoroughfare of doctors and nurses, women who sponged him and women who cleaned around him, of bearers of food he couldn't eat and of news that he couldn't comprehend? Was he even aware that Laura now used the room as a short cut to the garden, a route which would have been unquestionably forbidden while he was still in control? She

1

could of course have used the drawing room, but that would have meant mud on the carpet, and although there was a garden door it was situated at the side of the house and was inconvenient for the terrace and the herbaceous borders beyond. In this and in so many other ways were his last months spent in a state of permanent frustration and unexpressed rage? Or did he, as we all chose to believe, pass 'quietly away' sometime between the hours of two, when Laura had removed his untouched lunch tray, and five, when she came in from the garden to discover him lying across the bed, with his arm outstretched in a gesture of surprising abandon for a man who had never shown the least sign of abandonment during his previous seventy-four years?

Later we discovered his spittoon lying in a far corner of the room. Perhaps he had used the outstretched arm in this final act of anger and protest. If so, it does not suggest a quiet passing but rather one of disgust. Thus may all our goings be registered, not, as the living like to comfort themselves by believing, with a joyful surge of wonder at the life to come, but rather with the shock of recognition of the futility and the waste of the life that has gone.

I was preparing a chicken casserole when the telephone rang. I thought perhaps that it might be Catherine. Although she was expected later, bringing Bill to be introduced to me – the reason for the casserole – she was quite likely to have phoned for a gossip. Catherine and I have an almost perfect telephonic relationship. In many ways we get on better with the airwaves between us than we do face to face. Like safe sex, a phone call once terminated leaves no unwanted traces and even while it is in progress one can get on with other things, the odd clue of the crossword or making a shopping list, things it might seem rude to do if the person were actually present. Bill was Catherine's latest man and, although it had been going on for some time, I had not so far met him. She made him sound rare and wonderful, but I was reserving

2

judgement. There had been a number of Bills; some I had liked and some I had tried to like and one or two I had openly disliked. The new one had the distinction of being half her age and a yachtsman and, consequently, a degree of nautical terminology had recently crept into Catherine's vocabulary as well as an interest in the shipping forecast. This was actually a great relief after the stockbroker period in the shape of a balding man called Terrence during which all the bits of the Sunday papers that I automatically throw away had had to be saved for her, and nothing, I would swear on oath, could ever rival the ghastly Mick who gambled the shirt off her back, treated her like a beast, was violent when drunk and whom she still misses when the moon is in the seventh house. So, all in all, the yet-to-be-met Bill sounded harmless and I was looking forward to the evening.

But, of course, the phone call wasn't from Catherine. It was Mother, speaking from Sevenoaks, telling me that Father had finally died.

Protracted illnesses are difficult for the next of kin and others closely associated with the dear departed because they lack the element of surprise that can stimulate grief and a sense of loss. Mother sounded terribly calm. But then, why wouldn't she? Father had been dying off and on for three years, ever since a stroke had rendered the right side of his body immobile and his speech slurred beyond comprehensibility. He had also recently escaped death via pneumonia which had left the added complication of emphysema, and really his life hadn't been worth living for some time. In fact it seemed more than likely to me that he would be glad it was over. Some if not all of this I said to Mother and then, almost as an afterthought, I asked her if she would like me to come down. Did I detect a trace of disbelief in her voice when she replied that yes, she thought that would be a good idea and that Angela was already on her way from Canterbury? If so it was soon past and she was hurrying on to explain that she had called Angela first because she was nearer. I said I quite understood – which I did. Not to have done so would have been rather like an actress arguing about her billing before signing the contract. I added that I'd have to try to cancel my evening appointment and then I'd be on my way.

'I'm sorry, Chris,' Mother said, apologising as though she were in some way responsible for ruining my social life.

I told her not to be silly and we had a brief discussion about what to do with the uncooked, but browned and ready for the casserole, chicken.

'Couldn't you take it round to Catherine on your way here?' Mother suggested. 'It seems a shame to waste it and she will still have to eat this evening – unless, of course, you were expecting other people as well. In that case, couldn't Catherine come round to the flat and play hostess for you?' Mother has wanted to get Catherine into my flat as 'hostess' for almost as long as she has known of her existence, which must be all of fifteen years. Mother approves of Catherine wholeheartedly without knowing the first thing about her, simply on the grounds that she is a woman. For Mother that single virtue is all that is required as a suitable companion for her only begotten son. Not that Catherine and I haven't discussed it ourselves. Older generations always believe that they see solutions that have not occurred to the young, while the young have been through and discarded the suggested possibilities long before. While I am not certain that I, close approaching fifty, and Catherine, also in her forties, could possibly be called 'young' any more, we have nevertheless discovered for ourselves one of life's great truisms. We have realised the strength of friendship and companionship that can never survive the strictures of cohabitation and the deadening effect of family life. People who live together all seem to lose the ability to talk to each other. Catherine and I survive on talking. If that went, what

4

possible grounds could there be for staying together or for wanting to?

Catherine was still out. I knew that she was spending the afternoon helping a girlfriend move into a new flat but had thought that she might have got home. Her answerphone asked me to speak clearly after the bleep. I hate speaking to a machine at the best of times, which this obviously wasn't, and it was difficult not to make the message sound lugubrious. I tried a breezy, bright delivery:

'Hello, it's me. I'm afraid we'll have to cancel the soirée, darling. I've just heard from Mother that Father has died – so I'm going down to Sevenoaks. Give my apologies to Bill and tell him that my seal of approval will have to wait until another time. I'll phone you if I get a chance. 'Bye.'

Then I wrapped the chicken in silver foil and put it in the fridge, bolted the windows and remembered to double-lock the door as I was leaving. The flat below me was burgled earlier in the year and there has been a great deal of neighbourhood watching and patent alarm installing going on ever since.

The car was parked further down the crescent. As I edged it out from the kerb and was caught up in the traffic that increasingly uses the road as a short cut for Kensington High Street and the M4, I felt the familiar gloom that descends whenever I set out on the journey home. Does everyone experience this familial angst, I wonder, or is it peculiar to me? Today, perhaps, there was more justification. You can only lose your father once. And yet, if I were honest, I'd never really known him in the first place, so it was hard to be precise about what I actually felt I was losing. I don't think he liked me and I didn't particularly like him. Catherine's close relationship with her family is a source of endless fascination to me. When she speaks of them and of the bond of love and support that she obviously feels for them, it is as though she is trying to explain to me the higher reaches of quantum maths or, to be honest, just plain old multiplication and division – so utterly innumerate am I.

I took the Guildford road and then turned on to the M25. The car could have done the journey on automatic pilot. Not because I have been a dutiful son, forever going home for visits, but because I had fallen into the habit of swift, brief half-days rather than longer stays. Even at Christmas time I was more likely to drive home to London and back for Boxing Day than stay a night in the house. Even now, as I changed down and took the filter for Sevenoaks, I half expected that I would return to London to sleep. This phobia for independence went far back into my past. It was as though my freedom, which had been so hard won, was still precious to me and I was afraid that even one night under my parents' roof would in some way trap me back into the turmoil of my adolescent self.

My parents' home, for I had not considered it my own since I was in my teens, is a large, rectangular house of mellow bricks in the between-the-wars mansion style that the Midland Bank adopted at one time for its high street branches as though it somehow thought that a mock-Georgian façade would instil confidence in its customers. Perhaps Father bought 'Rosebank' for much the same reason – the chosen customer being Laura, to whom he gave the place as a wedding present. Laura was at that time eighteen years old and he was in his mid-twenties. He was already on the board of the family business and he had just inherited a considerable amount of money from his paternal grandmother. I'm sure that he believed he was being generous, lavishing upon his new young bride the five-bedroomed, two-bathroomed house, set in its three and a half acres of prime English countryside with views across the wide and verdant Weald of Kent, but it is worth remembering that he was going to live there as well, so could it really be counted as a present? A simple diamond might have been more personal, though to be fair, such tokens were to be forthcoming on future anniversaries. In fact, Father was more generous with tokens than he was with himself. I don't think I can ever remember seeing my parents embracing or there being any outward shows of emotion between them. This demonstrative frigidity brushed off on to their children, and the thought of kissing my sister Angela as a sign of welcome or of parting always brings me out in a cold sweat.

As I pulled up at the side of the drive, parking behind Angela's estate — bought to accommodate the menagerie of infants, dogs and lesser animals that she and her husband, Dick the Prick, had surrounded themselves with over their sixteen years of scrupulously planned marriage (one child every two years then a vasectomy for the Prick and an exercise bike for her) — drifts of bonfire smoke hazed the evening sky and the late sun cast long shadows on the immaculate lawns. It all looked so ordinary, so as it had always looked, that I half expected Father to appear round the side of the house, stepping towards me with a diffident smile and a formal greeting: 'How was the traffic?' or 'You're a bit late. Kingston bypass still being repaired?' The first quarter of an hour was always spent discussing the route from London. Neighbours' alternatives via the City, or the horrors of the Dartford Tunnel. And then we would lapse into awkward silence, punctuated by a few vain attempts on both sides to establish some basis for conversation. 'The roses are looking wonderful.' 'Pretty good. Pretty good. That's your mother's department.' 'The tennis has been a bit of a washout.' 'Absolute washout . . . Help yourself to a drink. I'll just go and . . .' and he would go, without ever once finishing the sentence.

Angela met me in the hall. I was surprised to see that her face was red and bloated from crying. She was holding a sodden handkerchief, gripped tightly in one hand, and she spoke in the hushed voice that the bereaved use in the near presence of the deceased, as though they actually believe the euphemism about 'going to sleep'.

'Here you are at last,' she said, managing to sound tragic and cross at the same time. Then she shook her head several times, screwed up her face and started to sob.

'Where's Mother?' I asked, hoping that conversation might bring her back to her usual state of crisp authority.

'I don't know. Lying down, I think. You'd better go in.'

'In?' I asked, genuinely confused.

'To see him. He's still in the study. The undertaker was out on another call.'

'Oh dear. Father would be furious. You know how he hated queuing.'

'Really, Chris. I don't think this is the time for jokes, do you?' Although Angela is eight years my junior, she has always seemed to me to inhabit an adult world that has remained just beyond my reach. Now she gave me a severe look through her tears and walked into the drawing room.

The study was in semi-darkness. Someone had half drawn the curtains across the french windows, emphasising the not-dead-but-sleeping story. As if party to the conspiracy, Father was lying on his back, with his eyes closed and the covers neatly drawn up under his chin. I realised that Mother or Angela must have laid him out and was surprised by the act. I stood, rather foolishly, at the foot of the bed, not sure how to behave or even what I was supposed to be thinking. Having rarely had much to say to him during his life, it wasn't likely that I would find anything now. Lacking any form of religious bent, I was unable to pray for his departed soul, yet I recognised the need to do something to punctuate his passing and I regretted not at least being able to implement some well-learned but long-forgotten ceremonial gesture, the kind that must forever be embedded in the memory of a Catholic, a Jew, or, so far as I know, a Hindu or a

Buddhist. The Church of England, that secular faith and political club, is sadly lacking when it comes to comforting symbols or reassuring nods from the Almighty.

Instead, I stared at his empty body, for that is how it seemed; like a house only recently abandoned by the occupant, with a trace of smoke still at the chimney and an empty milk bottle on the step. Perhaps, I thought, there is such a thing as a soul; perhaps it is the soul that fills us out and makes us lively. If not a soul then an energy, a life force, an essence . . . but any descriptive word sounded inadequate and I soon tired of wrestling with the semantics of the situation. As a fiction editor I acknowledge without rancour that someone else must first come up with the words, before I am able to assess whether they are the correct ones.

I walked over to the french windows and, opening them, went out on to the terrace. The evening was drawing in and the warmth of the day had been replaced by a chill little breeze that was buffeting the branches of the trees and tousling the seed heads in the borders. The last of the light clung to the Japanese anemones and to the white blotches of chrysanthemums. Deep, sea-green shadows seeped out from the edge of the spinney, and a late blackbird flew, with agitated twittering, towards the sanctuary of the beech wood. I found the air refreshing after the antiseptic cleanliness of the sickroom and I continued down the steps on to the lawn and across it to the shade of the trees. Here, in the spring, bluebells turn the ground into the sky and later, with the summer, hedgehogs grub in the warmth. A path leads from the lawn in a gentle meander through the trees until it reaches a low stone wall. Beyond, the land, no longer ours, drops steeply away with a wide view out over the Weald. Mother, who was responsible for reshaping the spinney and for having the wall constructed, christened the place 'The View of Eternity'. She took the name from a psychoanalytical game that was in vogue at the time the work was completed. Now, coming out of the deep gloom of the wood, the last of the sunlight, flooding the land below, made me pause and an unexpected tear escaped my eye and trickled down my cheek. I wiped it away hurriedly and, sitting on the low wall, with my feet dangling over towards the view, I contemplated if not Eternity, then at least life without Father.

Suddenly, in that unexpected way that 'life' has of altering the status quo, I was the last of the line. There were no other male Metcalfes. *Après moi, rien*. It was not a comfortable thought. Of course, there were Angela's three boys. But they belonged on Dick the Prick's branch of the tree, where they would no doubt flourish like their father and become brain surgeons and Nobel prize winners and be the sort of grandchildren who would have made Father proud. I actually think that his idea of 'life after death' depended solely on the continuation of the family name. In that case, I'd finally done for him. Thanks to me he had just passed into outer darkness. There would be no more Metcalfes. The family business had already gone, and now I alone was left holding the family name. It was probably a bit late in the day to say 'sorry'. Not that I particularly felt it. But there is always a certain desire to be well thought of . . .

The angst was getting into top gear when Mother emerged from the spinney and saved me.

'There you are. We've been searching. The undertaker is here.'

'Oh, Lord,' I said, climbing off the wall and feeling guilty. 'Sorry. D'you want me to come?'

Mother shook her head.

'Angela is dealing with him. Aren't you cold?'

'I suppose I am a bit.'

We walked back together through the darkening wood. Neither of us offered any sympathy to the other. I felt I should, but she didn't give me the opportunity.

10

'Cremation on Wednesday. Will that be awkward for you?'

'No. I expect I can manage that.'

'Oh, I think you must come, Chris.'

'Of course I will.'

'It'll just be us. Unless, of course, the Cutlers and Plates people insist on coming.'

'You don't have to have them if you don't want to.'

'Then there's the Rotary and all those people.'

'We could take Wembley Stadium.'

As we were letting ourselves in through the garden door, the undertaker drove off and we met Angela in the hall. She was no longer tearful. But she was still cross.

'Where were you?' she asked, glaring balefully.

I decided not to answer.

'I found him at the View of Eternity,' Mother said, leading the way into the drawing room. 'Who'd like a drink?'

'Not for me,' Angela said. 'I'll have to start back quite soon. You're sure you'll be all right, Mother? Chris will stay with you over the weekend.'

This was news to me.

'I'll come back to see you on Monday,' Angela continued, speaking as if she was ticking off a list. 'Unfortunately Rupert has a friend staying, and I can't see Richard coping on his own. He said he would, of course, but I don't think it would do, really. Rupert's friend is the youngest of the Lavell children.'

She left this piece of information dangling before us as though it were an explanation and a justification. Mother seemed hardly to listen. She poured herself a brandy and then indicated the tray to me with a nod of the head.

'Help yourself, darling,' she said and walked out of the room.

As soon as we were alone, Angela hurried to close the door.

11

'How do you think she is?' she asked in a low, urgent voice.

'Fine,' I told her.

'Well, obviously she isn't fine, Chris. She's just lost her husband . . .' As she said the words her voice broke and I thought she was going to cry again. 'You'll have to stay with her till Monday, then I'll take over. Unless, of course, you can get time off from the office. Do they let you have time off?'

'Of course. But is this really necessary?'

'I knew you'd make it difficult. I can't just leave home. I've got a family to look after.'

'And I'm on my own?'

'Well . . . yes. Oh, that reminds me, that woman called. While you were missing. You know, your friend.'

'Angela, you know perfectly well that she's called Catherine, so why do you always refer to her as "that woman"?'

'I don't. Good heavens, I hardly ever mention her. She simply wanted to know if you were all right. And she sent her condolences. She sounded rather nice. Well, I thought so anyway.' She made it sound as though no one else did. 'Mother had better take a sleeping pill. I've brought some. There's one for you, if you want it. I'm dreading telling the boys . . .'

'Angela. Father's been more or less dead for three years – don't you think you're making this all a bit too tragic?'

'I'm sure you do,' she replied witheringly. 'But then I don't think you have a scrap of feeling in you.' Her eyes were beginning to moisten again.

I turned my back on her and poured myself a gin.

'We'll have to decide what to do with her,' I heard her say behind me. She made the statement sound like a *fait accompli* – as though whatever it was that had to be decided had already been done.

'Do? With whom?' I was on my guard now.

'Well, Mother of course. Obviously she can't go on living here, on her own.'

'Has she said this?'

'She's in a state of shock, Chris! Of course we haven't discussed it. But in time it will have to be talked about.'

'And what had you in mind for her? An old people's home? She's quite young, you know.'

'Of course not. I would never put my mother into one of those places. I thought she could live with you.'

Perhaps she was nervous. That would explain the note of defiance that had crept into her voice. But I should have seen it coming a mile off. I didn't, of course. It still came as a complete surprise and knocked me sideways. In the silence that followed I added more gin to my already copious glass and she blew her nose.

'We'd have her like a shot,' she said after the pause became overlong, 'but I don't think it would be right for the boys. And you, of course . . .'

'I have my own life, Angela,' I told her, firmly. Then I took a deep breath to stop myself shaking, followed by a long gulp of gin and tonic.

'Have you?' she said, blowing her nose again. 'We never quite know what you're up to. For all we know, you could be a queer.'

'Is that a question or a statement?' I could feel the anger rising but I didn't want to lose my temper.

'I'm not prying. It doesn't matter to me what you get up to. At the moment my only concern is Mother. I just hoped you'd feel the same.'

She was standing midway between the sofa and the door, gripping her handbag as though her life depended on it, and making little bobbing movements up and down from the knees, like an athlete preparing to do a standing high jump. She should have looked ridiculous. I should have found the whole thing absurd and funny, but the effect was actually rather touching.

'I must go,' she said when it became obvious that I wasn't going to be goaded into further argument. 'Will you at least stay the weekend with her?'

Before I had a chance to reply, Mother came back into the room. She seemed serene and normal, and smelt of newly applied scent.

'I must be off, Mummy. You are sure you'll be all right, aren't you? I hate leaving, but you know what that drive's like. Still, Saturday evening, it shouldn't be too bad. It's going to be worse if they ever actually open that wretched tunnel . . .'

Angela, it appeared, subscribed to our father's theory that arrivals and departures had of necessity to be accompanied by an endless flow of road and traffic information. It was a bit like living with the AA, which prompted me to take another gulp of gin.

''Bye, Chris,' she called, as though we were the best of friends. Then Mother and she went out into the hall, leaving me alone.

The drink was going to my head and I realised that I hadn't really eaten. Glancing at my watch, I saw that it was coming up to nine. Father would be insisting on the television news – and would then get irritated that it was on at a different time on Saturdays. I wondered how long the dead hang about to haunt us with habitual memories and whether this was the basis of ghost stories. I found an opened packet of stale nuts in the drinks cupboard and was chewing some when Mother returned.

'Poor Angela,' she said. 'Even as a girl she was prone to histrionics. But I'm not at all sure it hasn't got worse since she became a mother. One of the boys has only got to stub his toe and she behaves as though he'll never walk again.'

'How are you, Mother?' I felt I was seeing her for the first time as a widow. She looked, if anything, tired.

14

'I'm all right, Chris,' she answered, then sat down in one of the fireside armchairs. 'It is a shock,' she continued after a moment's consideration. 'However much one knows it is going to happen; however much one tells oneself it will be for the best; when it does . . .' She shrugged. 'Well, it's a shock. I didn't think he was sleeping. I knew at once. But I hadn't been expecting it – any more than one did each day. He didn't eat his lunch. He never eats his lunch. He was beastly about it, actually. He pushed it away with his good hand. I used to tell myself he couldn't help it, but I really wished he wouldn't do that. When he had his stroke, that young doctor – the one who used to stand in for Maxwell – he told me that in many ways he would become childlike. I said to him, "That is far from reassuring. I was never a natural mother!" What he meant was that, like a child, there would be fewer areas of light and shade, his particular character traits would be emphasised, he wouldn't cover them up. Well, of course, the doctor – oh, what was his name? – was quite right – so much wisdom in one so young. John became impossible.' She paused, staring blankly into the hearth, then she shook her head, as if dismissing a thought. 'Well, well,' she said. 'All over.'

She turned and looked at me, a strange, cool, almost distant expression on her face. I smiled, hoping that I was showing loving concern and support and anything else she might be searching for in me. She didn't return the smile, I'm not sure that she even saw it.

'Would you like me to stay the night?' I asked her, in a tone that suggested that I was making the ultimate sacrifice – which, in some ways, I was.

'Oh, yes, darling. Of course,' she rejoined, as though there had never been any question about it. 'I've prepared your room.'

I hadn't even brought a toothbrush.

I cooked us some scrambled eggs, but she didn't really

want anything. Then, early, before ten, we both took one of Angela's sleeping pills and went to our rooms. On the landing, as we were saying good night, she unexpectedly put her arms round me and kissed me on the lips.

'Thank you, darling. I feel better, knowing you're here.'

My room is one of the smaller bedrooms and faces out over the front drive. It hasn't been decorated since I was a child. The same magnolia wallpaper overlaid with a raised white linear design of leaves and the same off-white paintwork has been regularly dusted and cleaned so that it has all faded into a pale sepia sameness. The carpet is a dark blue Axminster that once reached out on to the landing and down the stairs into the hall. But outside the door two different carpets have replaced each other with the passing of time. Only in my room have the years stood still. The bed is still covered with the same blue candlewick spread. There is even a stain on one corner of the mahogany chest of drawers where I once spilt a bottle of ink.

As I climbed, naked, into the bed, I wondered when she had made it up – or whether it was always waiting in readiness for me. Angela's sleeping pill was beginning to make me drowsy. I regretted having taken it. I don't know why I did. Perhaps because it was unusual to do so; perhaps because I instinctively knew that I would want to blot out the bedroom.

I reached out, to turn off the lamp, and it was a boy's arm that I saw. The switch always used to stick as it was slipped across; my fingers remembered the secret as though it were only a moment ago. Even the darkness was familiar. Even the silence was unchanged.

And the morning light shone through a chink in the blue cotton curtains and woke me as it always had and for a moment, before the day began, I was seventeen again, and the pain was appalling.

Mother was still sleeping, or at least her bedroom door

was shut and there was no sound of movement. The sleeping pill had left my head feeling fuzzy as though it were full of cotton wool. I went down to the kitchen and made myself some tea. It was much later than I expected; after ten o'clock. The Sunday papers were lying on the back step. Father had insisted that they should never be delivered to the front door. Perhaps having made a fortune out of trade had left him oversensitive to the distinction between the types of traffic that passed up the drive. Though he had never managed to stop the postman from using the, nearer, front door and consequently while tradesmen used the back, circulars still thudded on to the hall mat along with the more acceptable bills and letters. So far as I know there are no hawkers left in the Sevenoaks area.

An hour later Mother still hadn't come down. I flirted with the idea that she might also have gone to permanent 'sleep' in the night and that I was now, therefore, an orphan. But, going upstairs to wash, I met her coming out of her room, already dressed.

'Those beastly pills,' she said. 'At least with a hangover one gets a bit of enjoyment first. There's a razor of Dick's in the bathroom cabinet, darling, and a spare toothbrush.'

I pulled a face. I didn't fancy Dick the Prick's razor, I told her.

'Oh, don't be silly. He's the cleanest man I've ever met. Angela once told me that he washes both before and after he makes love to her.'

'Do you really have that sort of conversation with Angela?'

'Not very often. In fact there was a reason for it – I don't remember what now. Personal hygiene, I expect. At one time, just after Roger was born, they were both obsessed by germs. First babies can do that to parents.'

'Did I?' I asked, with a grin.

She looked at me and smiled.

17

'You were never a baby. You were born intelligent.'

'Would germs know the difference?'

'Oh, then there was a war on. We were far too obsessed with Germans to worry about germs.'

She was bright and more cheerful than I had seen her for ages. Maybe she's forgotten what's happened, I thought; or, more likely, she remembers precisely and that's why.

When I returned downstairs the study door was open and she was leaning on the side of the desk.

'I was dreading the golden wedding,' she said. 'I think, probably, we'd just have ignored the event. But Angela was already making plans. Would you have come?' She looked at me, accusingly, as though she knew the answer.

'I shouldn't think so,' I replied, and she smiled. 'Don't you want tea or anything?'

She shook her head.

'I want to clear this room. Will you help, Chris?'

'Why don't I do it?' I told her. 'You read the papers.'

But she shook her head and for a moment I thought she was going to cry. I pretended not to notice and walked over to the bed. I pulled the two blankets off and bundled up the sheets and pillowslips and handed them to her.

'D'you want to put these in the washing machine?'

She took them, relieved to have something to do, and left the room.

By the time she returned I had dragged the divan out through the french windows on to the terrace and the room was already beginning to take on its former identity. Together we started to go through the drawers and cupboards of his desk. He had kept everything very neatly. Files for business; files for family. Bank files, accountant's files, investment files, tax files. We didn't bother to read any of it. For the most part we put everything back where it came from. It was turning into a ridiculous, time-wasting exercise. Maybe Mother believed that by touching things she was claiming

18

back the space, or maybe it made her feel closer to him. Maybe she was missing him? I didn't know the answer to any of the questions that presented themselves to me and she remained silent, working quietly and methodically from drawer to drawer.

On either side of the knee-hole, there are two cupboards. I suggested that I should attend to them and so I was kneeling on the ground beside her chair when I found the box.

A plain cardboard carton. The kind that might once have contained a dozen bottles of wine, or a piece of expensive electrical equipment. The top flaps were tied down with string, and a sticky label, yellowing slightly with age, was covered with his neat pen strokes.

'Christopher. Blandfords.', the legend read.

'What is it?' Mother asked, looking down and speaking for the first time in an age. Then, after reading the label, she reached out as though she wanted to lift the box away from me.

'I'll deal with that, darling,' she said.

But I had already broken the string. In a way it was addressed to me. I felt I had the right. Perhaps I knew I would find it, or if not it, something similar. Mother was watching me as I opened the flaps. The contents were as neatly packed as the drawers of the desk had been. The school reports, tied together in a bundle. Accounts, all paper-clipped at one corner. Some letters, probably from the headmaster. Three school photographs; long rolls of thick card, coiled like springs that, once released, revealed images of five hundred boys and assorted elders and betters – masters and matrons and wives – spread out, four rows high – cross-legged, seated, standing behind the seats and standing on a row of benches, with the grim Georgian façade of Blandfords as a backdrop. And, at the bottom of the carton, lying flat, the four house photographs from the four long years I spent there, each in a thin black frame, with 'Ely House' in Gothic above and the name of every boy printed neatly below. Seventy or eighty earnest faces: hair short and slicked down into side partings; collars and ties stiff and formal; smug, bored expressions, with only one or two smiles.

Four pictures of my former self. Each year a little older, a little taller, a little more muscular. Four outer shells, revealing no more than Father's dead body had revealed in this room last night. In the earliest I look like a little angel. In the last I am almost invisible, standing behind a tall, scrubbed youth with a shock of golden hair.

'Let me take them, Chris. No point going back over old ground.' She is pleading with me, her voice agitated, her face creased with concern. But I shake my head and carry the box away from her, out of the room.

'Don't worry,' I say, in a bright voice. 'I'm OK. It's interesting after all this time. I'll just . . .' and, like Father, I don't finish the sentence.

But once in the comparative privacy of my room I take the photographs out of the box once more. It isn't my own image I am searching for along the rows. Nor do I have any difficulty in finding the person I seek.

Thirty years of carefully controlled emotion trembles for release.

I walk over to the window. I turn my back on the smiling face. I used not to be able to remember exactly how he looked, and then I schooled myself not even to try. Now, in a chance moment, like an unexpected encounter on a railway station or in a crowded street, I've seen him again. He's back, lodged – perhaps for ever? – in my mind.

Outside, on the drive, the sun is shining. There is the distant hum of traffic from the bypass. But I can hear the tarantella and the sky is dark beyond the windows.

# *Then*

'The tarantella, boy. I don't suppose you can already dance the tarantella, can you?'

'No, sir.'

One or two of the others laugh and I can feel a blush burning my cheeks.

'Speak up, speak up. Projection is the most vital lesson you'll have to learn. Well?'

'No, sir,' I say, louder.

'No, what?' TG is enjoying every moment.

'I can't dance the tarantella, sir.'

Glossop crows with laughter. I don't know him very well. He's a prefect in Lincoln House and he's playing Dr Rank.

'Shut up, Glossop,' TG spits. 'Is there something funny about the tarantella?'

'I don't know, sir,' Glossop replies, his voice still smirking.

'Well, there won't be in my production. Metcalfe, you will have four sessions with a dancing teacher from Ipswich. Her name is . . .' TG refers to a pad on the desk in front of him, 'Miss Bingley.'

'Can we all learn, sir?' Heslop, senior prefect of my house, Ely, asks with a grin. He's playing Torvald and I'll have most of my scenes with him.

But then, I'll have scenes with all of them. I'm playing the lead, the title part almost; Nora, in *A Doll's House*.

'Good idea, Heslop,' TG retorts. 'It would be as well if you had a knowledge of the dance, as you are supposed to put Nora through her paces. Yes, you can report as well.'

'You lucky dog, Heslop!' Glossop exclaims.

TG simpers.

'I'm sure, Heslop, that you will enjoy the experience. Miss Bingley claims to have been taught dancing by the great Karsavina herself!'

'Who, sir?' Heslop asks.

'Karsavina. One of Diaghilev's girls, or some such pansy group. She'll be just up your street, Heslop, she must be eighty if she's a day.'

'Oh, no!' Heslop groans, to the enjoyment of the others. 'I think I'll skip the dancing, sir.'

'Right. For a first reading that wasn't too bad. But there's a hell of a lot of work ahead. Rehearsals Tuesday, Wednesday and Friday evenings after preparation. And later, of course, we'll have to do Sunday afternoons as well. Duff, have you got a lisp?'

'Sorry, sir?' Nigel Duff stammers, surprised by the sudden attention. Nigel is my best friend. He also is in Ely House. But then most of the actors are. TG is housemaster of Ely, and there are often complaints that the other houses don't get fair treatment when it comes to casting the school play.

'A lisp, child. You know what a lisp is. Get rid of it. I can't have Mrs Lind with a lisp. Walker, that was a good first reading. Krogstad must be satanic and handsome. Every woman in the audience must long to be abused by him . . .'

Glossop and Heslop both stifle guffaws, making TG slam his notes down on the desk.

'What is your problem, Glossop?'

'Nothing, sir,' Glossop replies, still giggling.

'All right, all of you. Have a good laugh and get it over. Because I don't want any more of it. After tonight, I am going to treat you like professional performers – and all the smutty little jokes will only waste time. All right? Yes, Metcalfe and Duff will have their faces made up for the performances, as will you all. My wife will be in charge of that. And yes, Glossop, have a good laugh now, Metcalfe and Duff will be wearing false bosoms ... and you may have to embrace them and kiss them on the cheek. Go on, boy, laugh. What's the matter with you? What's the matter with you all? Bloody well laugh. Because there won't be any laughter after tonight, of that I can assure you.'

The tirade ends in stunned silence. None of us is laughing now. I daren't look at Nigel to see how he's reacted. I stare at the script in front of me and wish I hadn't put my name on the list for auditions. I only did it as an excuse to get out of the boxing tournament. Boxing and rehearsals compete for extramural activity time.

'Right,' TG says after a sufficient silence, 'have any of you any questions? No? Then to work, to work. Starting tomorrow with a blocking of the first scenes of the play. Mr Martineau will bring the model of the set and Thompson, you and your stage management team will tape out the stage area in Hall and the tape will be left down unless we are informed that Hall is required for other functions. Yes, Thompson?'

He, Thompson, a rather thick fifth-former from St Edmond's House, is stage manager and has raised a hand for attention.

'What are the dates of the performances, sir?'

'Wednesday, Thursday, Friday and Saturday of the last week of term. Then you can all go home and stuff yourselves full of Christmas fare and forget all about it. Yes, Glossop?'

'It isn't very Christmassy, is it, sir?'

'Christmassy?' TG thunders his revolt. 'Christmassy? *A Doll's House* is a classic, child. Just because the school play is annually performed immediately prior to the so-called

23

of goodwill" does not mean that we should descend
excruciating plethora of bad taste that usually
accompanies that feast. Does it, Glossop?'

'No, sir,' Glossop mumbles.

'Make no mistake, any of you, this play changed the world,
because it changed society's view of women. When the door
slams before the final curtain and it is clear that Nora has
walked out on Torvald, her husband . . . there was a riot
in the theatre on the first night. That, Glossop, is how
powerful the play is. That, Metcalfe, is what you must do to
our audience. Now out, all of you. Start learning your lines.
The sooner we have no books in our hands, the sooner we
can get down to the real work.'

Pale, white-grey clouds across a bleached sky. The leaves
on the stunted trees turning from greens to browns and
russets but still not into their full autumn colours. A soft
late-September afternoon. Returning from an exercise run;
five miles along the beach towards Dunwich and back
through the soft boglands that lie behind the flat, featureless
coast. We do these runs two or three times a week; sprints,
followed by bouts of exercises – 'on your backs, down',
usually in the mud, as a junior prefect works out his sadistic
instincts on us. Then more sprinting and more exercises.
The fast runners get rests while they wait for the dawdlers
and the less athletic. I, as in all areas of school activity,
come in somewhere in the middle; neither fast nor slow,
not a winner nor a loser. After the last exercises, usually
out on the sea marshes among the waders and the geese,
where the water is deep and cold and your shorts and shirt
cling damply to your body, there is a long dash back to the
school grounds. The quicker you get there, the warmer the
shower water is and the longer you have to yourself before
afternoon school. As I turn off the main drive and follow
the path towards Ely House, Walker appears ahead of me,
walking towards the library. He is Krogstad in the play, we

have several difficult scenes together. He is also a prefect and is in the English Sixth. He is down for Cambridge and is expected to do well in the exams. I like him. He's more civilised than most of the others and he doesn't abuse his power. But I don't know much about him. I have just entered Middle Five and the Sixth seems a long way off.

As we pass, we hardly acknowledge that we've seen each other. Then, almost as an afterthought, I hear him call:

'Oh, Metcalfe . . .'

I turn, surprised.

'Tomorrow afternoon, after games,' he says, 'come to my study, will you? I want to go over those lines in Act One. I made a complete balls of it on Wednesday.'

He doesn't even wait for a reply. I watch him walk away from me, not on the path but on the grass and with his hands in his pockets; two privileges allowed to the prefects and denied to all of us, the lesser mortals.

Walker's study is up under the eaves of Ely House. It shares a narrow landing at the top of a steep flight of stone steps with the Junior Games Room. It is situated at the corner of the building, and has two dormer windows. From one you can see a distant glimpse of the sea and from the other the roofs of Blandford House, which houses all the main school buildings. It is a two-man study. He shares it with Morrison, another prefect, who is in the First XV and the shooting team.

The following day is a Saturday. The evening rehearsal the night before had gone on half an hour longer than was scheduled. There are two little children in the play and TG has borrowed Mr Pearson's brats. But, because they are babies, they obviously can't be called to evening rehearsals and two of the chaps doing stage management have to stand in for them. It is hideously embarrassing having to act motherly love with two strapping fourth-formers. Particularly as there aren't actually any lines in the script for the children and they will be expected to ad lib. The fourth-formers find the whole thing hilarious and giggle a lot, which only makes me more tense and TG more exasperated. We go over and over the scene and each time it gets worse. I can't see the point of it. We will only have to begin all over again once the real children start rehearsing – although it appears that their mother, Mrs Pearson, a sexy woman with red hair, known to the Junior Common Room as 'The Peach', is already preparing them for their moments of glory in the privacy of their own home. It is the scene that leads into my first scene with Krogstad, the scene that Walker wants to go over with me. The rehearsal has dealt with the opening scenes of the play and we are meant to stop at Krogstad's entrance. All the rest of the cast have been dismissed, except for me and my stand-in children. We go over and over the few lines until I am beginning to hate them and the play and everything about it.

'No, no, no, Metcalfe. You're a mother – not a gallumphing idiot . . . You love the beastly creatures, Metcalfe. What do you do when you love someone?'

'Ugh, sir!' one of the fourth-formers protests, when I try, desperately, to kiss him on the cheek.

'Oh, for heaven's sake, Wetherspoon Minor! It's just flesh touching flesh. It isn't exactly carnal, you know. In France the men do it all the time. Now get on with it. You will simply have to stay here until it works.'

'But sir,' the benighted Wetherspoon Minor wails, 'I'm only on stage management!'

'You'll be on Death Row if you don't shut up. Now get on, Nora. Get on.'

Calling me Nora sends both the boys off again, and Thompson, who has come in to see why the lights are still blazing in Hall, believing that the rehearsal should have finished twenty minutes ago, laughs out loud and punches one fist into the palm of his other hand in a rather sinister fashion.

'Oh, shut up, Thompson. Shut up all of you,' TG yells, beside himself with rage. 'Go to bed, all of you. Go away. Pray for your immortal souls. Not you, Metcalfe. I want you. All right, Thompson, we won't forget to put out the lights . . . "And then, put out the light".' As he says the final words, TG raises his arms in a dramatic gesture and rolls his eyes. 'What's that from, child?' he asks me.

'I don't know, sir,' I reply, feeling that my world is falling in pieces around me.

'You don't know? Shame on you. *Othello*, boy. Othello, the Moor. Look here, you're going to be bloody good in the role, Metcalfe.'

'Thank you, sir.'

'Oh, do shut up. I haven't called you here to flatter you. Flattery, you will not have failed to notice, isn't my style. Is it?'

'No, sir.'

'It's only a part you're playing, Metcalfe.' He sounds almost kind and gentle now. 'Don't get too deeply involved in it. You're not being ribbed by the school? Are you?'

'No, sir.'

'Try and do well at games, or something – anything, really. Boys like a boy who's a boy. You understand my drift?'

I don't. I haven't the vaguest idea what he's talking about. But I nod, because I think it will keep him happy and because I want to get away.

'All right, then. Off you go,' he says, with a wave of the hand.

'Good night, sir.'

'What? Oh, yes. And speak up when you're with Duff. The boy's got a lisp and you mumble. It's like trying to listen to the Home Service in a rainstorm.'

The following afternoon, Saturday, there was an away

match. When the First XV was away all the other teams moved up a pitch and Walker, in the Second XV, had a practice game on the School Field.

I'm down to play squash with Hart, a drippy boy whose father was rumoured to have been a British spy during the war. As the rumour was started by Hart himself, I've never given it much credence. However, I enjoy playing squash with him, because he is worse at the game than I am. We finish at three thirty and the court is taken by two senior prefects, who make us hang up their blazers and collect bottles of pop from the tuck shop before they'll let us go. It's nearer four o'clock by the time I've showered and collected my copy of the script from my locker in the Junior Common Room.

I see Walker returning from the practice match, covered in mud, from the Common Room window. I hang around, until I think he will have finished showering and dressing, and then climb the stairs to his study floor. I'm not particularly looking forward to going over the lines. The rehearsal the previous evening has had a bad effect on me. I feel insecure in the part and also a bit ridiculous. The two fourth-form stage management boys will no doubt have told all their year about what happened, and I'm beginning to get a complex that people are talking about me. In fact, I don't think they were at the time, but soon after this one or two of the boys started to call me 'Nora'. I suppose that was inevitable.

I knock on Walker's study door and wait. There's no summons to enter from within. I knock again, then, realising that I must be too early, I walk into the Junior Games Room, to wait for him. This is a big square room, lit by three ceiling lights which open on hinges on their upper edges and are supported by curved metal bars that slot into pegs on the bottom edge of the frames. The centre of the room is taken up with two full-sized table tennis tables. There isn't much other furniture. In fact, there isn't really room for both the tables and, when they're used at the same time, the players bump into each other and get hopelessly embroiled in the next match. Along one wall, under the ceiling lights, is a row of school benches. I stand on one of the benches and open the light immediately above me. Cool air blows in, coming off the sea, with a scent of salt and seaweed. There are so few opportunities to be alone at Blandfords that whenever it happens it's like being given a present.

I don't hear Walker come up the stairs, but I have left the Games Room door open and he catches sight of me as he's passing.

'Ah, there you are,' he says. 'Come on.'

As I turn, he has already gone along the corridor and I hear him unlocking his study door. I hurry to follow him.

He's waiting for me, holding on to the open door. His dark hair is still wet from the shower, and he has a towel over his shoulders, as though he has hurried. He's wearing an open-necked shirt and his grey flannels, part of the school uniform, are belted and not braced, another perk of becoming a prefect.

'Sorry to keep you,' he says. His voice is breathless, as though he has run up the stairs. 'Come in.'

I go past him into the study, and he closes the door behind us.

'Sit down,' he says. He seems nervous.

There is an old sofa facing the fire and a battered armchair beside it. I sit on the edge of the sofa, expecting him to sit in the armchair. But he walks over to the window.

'D'you want a cup of tea?'

'No thank you, sir.'

'Oh, you don't have to call me sir. I think I'll . . .' he picks up an electric kettle and shakes it, 'make a cup of tea all the same. I'll just . . . go and get some water.'

He goes out of the room, and I hear his steps going swiftly down the stone stairs to the floor below, where the prefects' kitchen is. I open my script and try to concentrate on the scene we are about to rehearse.

'Excuse me, the outer door was ajar; I suppose someone forgot to shut it,' he says, coming back into the room, replacing the lid on the kettle. Then he smiles. 'There,' he says. 'I do at least know the first line!'

I glance down at the script. Actually, his first line is 'Excuse me, Mrs Helmer.' To which I am supposed to reply, with a stifled cry, turning and getting up on to my knees from the crawling position I have adopted while playing with the dreaded children: 'Ah! What do you want?' But I haven't the heart to correct him.

He, meanwhile, has plugged in the electric kettle and is getting cups and saucers and a bottle of milk from a cupboard. He sniffs at the milk.

'I think it's all right. It should be. It was fresh this morning. Oh, damn. That isn't my first line, is it?'

I shake my head and he bursts out laughing.

'God! Why did I ever put my name down for the school play?' Then he looks at me and smiles again. 'What is it?'

'You're supposed to say, "Excuse me, Mrs Helmer"'.

'Oh, bugger!' he says. 'Excuse me, Mrs Helmer.'

'Ah! What do you want?' I find it difficult actually acting the words, sitting down, waiting for the kettle to boil.

'Excuse me, the outer door was ajar; I suppose someone forgot to shut it.'

'My husband is out, Mr Krogstad.'

'I know that.'

'What do you want here, then?'

'A word with you.'

He leans towards me, as he will in the play, and lowers his voice. I can smell the soap from the shower room masking the sweat from the rugger field.

'With me?' I say, with more truthful fear and agitation than I've ever managed before.

We stare at each other. I wait for him to speak. I can't remember what happens next. He is still leaning towards me, looking into my eyes.

'Is it me?' he says, in a whisper, and we both suddenly laugh at the foolishness of the situation.

'Oh, no, it's me. Sorry,' I say, checking in the script. 'I have to get rid of the children.'

'Oh, those bloody children,' Walker says, and laughs again, moving easily away from me and attending to the kettle which is coming up to the boil.

'You can say that again,' I say, hoping I sound as relaxed and as adult as he seems.

'Yes. I gather you had quite a time of it last night,' he says as he brews the tea.

'You heard?' I say, trying to make it sound unimportant, but wishing that he hadn't.

'Thompson.'

'Oh, of course. He's in your team, isn't he? Did he find it very funny?'

'Fairly. I think you'll find "Nora" will stick for a bit.' He glances at me, and smiles. "Oh, don't look so glum. It doesn't really matter, does it? And besides, you're going to be brilliant in the part.'

I'm pleased that he thinks so, but:

'That'll only make it worse, won't it?'

'By the time they see it, it'll be the holidays. Next term it'll be a thing of the past. You've no idea how quickly they forget here. Sugar?'

'No, thank you.'

'There are some biscuits somewhere.'

I shake my head.

'No, I'm not hungry, thank you.' Why am I so nervous, I wonder? I couldn't eat a biscuit. It'd stick in my throat.

'We'd better get on then. We don't have to act it, do we?'

31

'No,' I say, surprised that he's asking me.

He sits down on the sofa beside me, blows on his mug of hot tea, and then we continue with the lines. Until, after a lot of going back over difficult bits, we reach:

'You must be a very poor lawyer, Mr Krogstad.'

'Maybe,' he replies, and he is sitting so close to me that I can feel his breath on my cheek, 'But matters of business – such business as you and I have had together – do you think I don't understand that?' Then, he hesitates. 'Damn, it's still me. What do I say next?'

I glance down at the script, open on my lap.

'Um.' I can't find the place. 'You say . . .' My heart is beating too fast and it makes my voice sound unsteady. He is leaning over the book beside me, so that our cheeks are almost touching. 'You say, "Very well, do as you please."'

'Oh, yes. Of course. I'd probably have remembered if we were doing it with the moves.' He starts again. 'Very well, do as you please. But let me tell you this – if I lose my position a second time, you shall lose yours with me.'

When he finishes speaking, there is a long pause, just as there is in the play after he has gone from the room. I take a deep breath, not daring to look at him.

'Nonsense,' I say, trying to appear as if I'm still concentrating on the lines, 'trying to frighten me like that. I'm not so silly as he thinks! . . . And then the children come in again.'

'No,' Walker says, quietly. 'You've forgotten your best line.'

'Oh, yes,' I say, almost sadly. And then I try to act again. 'Trying to frighten me like that. I'm not so silly as he thinks. And yet . . .? No, it's impossible.' And it is, I don't want to go on. But I feel that he's waiting for me to finish. 'No, it's impossible,' I repeat. And I finish, in a whisper: 'I did it for love's sake.'

He puts his hand on my knee.

I smile shyly and close the script.

'And then those awful children come in,' I say, in a shaking voice.

'Now what should we do?' Walker asks me and, as he speaks, he slowly moves his hand up my leg until it is resting in the warm crease between the thigh and the crotch.

I think we're both scared by the move; he as much as I; both waiting for the other to come to the rescue.

'We mustn't,' I say at last. I'm surprised that any sound comes out at all. I'm shaking inside.

'I know,' he says. But he doesn't move his hand.

'We would be expelled if we were caught,' I say, hoping that reason will help.

'Yes,' he says, nodding his head too vigorously. 'But, you want to – don't you?'

'Somebody could come in,' I tell him, the agitation making me plead.

'Morrison is in the away team. He won't be back for hours.'

'Someone else.'

'I can lock the door.' He speaks in a quiet, reasonable voice.

'If you were expelled now – it would ruin your chances of going to Cambridge. You can't, Walker. I mean – we can't.'

'But you do want to, don't you?'

'I don't know. No, not if it means ruining both our lives.'

'How old are you?'

'Nearly fifteen.' My birthday is early the following month. But I don't tell him that.

'You'd better go, then.' He gets up and walks over to one of the windows. With his back to me he says, 'If you tell anyone about this, I'll be expelled anyway.'

'Of course I won't tell anyone.' I'm shocked that he should think it of me.

33

'Why not? If it means nothing to you.'

'I didn't say that.' I'm hurt that he seems to be disappointed by me.

'Then you do want to?' he asks, turning to look at me. 'But not enough to take the risk, is that it? Well, I don't blame you.' He leans against a cupboard, his hands in his pockets, one leg crossed over the other.

'I think I had better go,' I say, getting up.

'Yes, of course. Sure. Well, at least we did the lines.'

I turn and hurry from the room, closing the door quietly behind me.

As soon as I'm outside, I start to shake violently. I go into the Games Room and over to the window light, which I had left open earlier. I stand up on the bench and lean with my hands gripping the steep slate roof outside and I gulp great draughts of the cool air.

The sky is turning from pale blue to grey. A pigeon flies past me and settles on the gabled roof of Walker's study window. I know without any doubt that I have done the right, the sensible, really the only possible thing. I have behaved correctly and therefore I should at least feel some degree of satisfaction. But I don't. I feel desperate. That strange, pent-up sensation, when you want to cry, but can't.

All around me the house stretches away in silence. Most of the boys will be out on the playing fields or pursuing their hobbies. It is Saturday afternoon. He's right. There is no one here to discover us. It would be safe. But is that the only reason why I refused him? What about morals? What about religion, for heaven's sake? What about what it does to you? I never believed all that nonsense about going blind and growing hair in the palm of your hand, but all the same, doing it with another boy is unnatural, and there must be consequences.

I wonder what he's doing next door. He seems much more ill at ease about it all than I have been. It's almost as though

I have somehow been responsible for making him suffer. I didn't want that. Maybe I should go back to tell him. Maybe we need to talk it out more. Yes, that's what I should do. Go back and reassure him that I won't say anything. And maybe, if he really wants to – if it will make him feel better – then we could do it. Just once. To see what it's like. If I have to do it with anyone, then Walker is a pretty good choice. He's about the most handsome chap in the house and quite a few of the younger boys have crushes on him. In fact, it's rather flattering that he should have chosen me. Or is it just because I'm playing Nora? Is he getting fact and fantasy confused? I don't know.

I don't know any of the answers. I only know I want to go back. I want to find out what it is that is so forbidden, that is so sinful. I want to feel his hand on me again.

When I knock on the door, his voice sounds low and surprised.

'Come in,' he says.

I open the door. He is standing where I left him, leaning against the cupboard, his hands in his trouser pockets, his legs crossed, half turned towards the window, as though he also has been looking out at the same view as I have. Now he turns, and seeing me, a look of surprised relief comes on to his face.

'Walker,' I say.

He crosses quickly behind me and closes the door. I hear the key turn in the lock. Then, as I turn to look at him, he puts his arms round me and hugs me to him.

'Thank you,' he whispers.

I can feel the warmth of his body. His cheek against mine is so hot that it almost burns me.

Still holding me to him, he gently pushes me backwards, so that we are doing a strange, ungainly dance. Then I feel the edge of the sofa pressing into the back of my legs. He lowers me gently on to it and climbs on top of me.

He puts his legs on either side of mine, so that they are gripping me. I can feel his hard cock pressing against me. Mine also is hard. Our two cocks are pressed against each other, separated by Y-fronts and flannel. He puts his hands on my cheeks and stares for a moment into my eyes.

'Thank you,' he whispers again. Then he kisses me hard on the mouth, with his lips closed.

He starts to move his groin, pressing from side to side. His hands tear at my shirt, pulling it out of the waistband.

I am copying everything that he does. But it seems natural that I should do so. I pull his shirt out of his trouser waist and feel his bare back beneath my hands. Low down, by the waist, he has hair growing. I explore this new discovery.

Then he is holding himself away from me, supported on his outstretched arms, so that his body forms an arc, pinned to mine at the hot, moving crotch.

I close my eyes as the familiar tension starts to mount.

We come together in a wave of short stabbing breaths and a convulsion of muscle spasms.

Then the familiar warm, damp stickiness and the mess.

He sinks exhausted down on top of me, his cheek still scalding when it touches mine.

'Oh, shit!' he whispers.

# *Now*

The crematorium was packed. When Mother and Angela and I entered, rows of faces turned to look at us. It was a bit like a sombre wedding, with all the men in their best suits and the women in dark colours and hats.

I had gone to London the day before to get clothes from the flat. Catherine had come round, bearing a bottle of Sauvignon and some smoked salmon sandwiches. She was looking tired, which with Catherine was usually a good sign. It meant she was using the nights.

'How goes it?' I asked, settling down to a happy gossip in my own home. I was amazed to discover how much I had missed it and I'd spent the half-hour between phoning Catherine and her arrival walking from room to room, just enjoying being there.

'Heaven,' she replied and then started to tell me how ghastly all the new Bill's friends were.

I said in that case she should concentrate on the sex and that I hoped she was getting plenty. Which looks prurient in print but I don't think it sounded so. Catherine and I employ a sort of banter sometimes, which helps us to relax. She told me to mind my own business and said I should remember she had a lot of lost time to make up and that:

'Anyway, it probably won't last – so I may as well make the most of it.' Then she started to cry.

I thought maybe I'd read the signs wrong and that it was

over already and started to make the appropriate noises, but it wasn't that.

'I'm so afraid I won't manage to keep him, Chris. He's so young. I think he's younger than I've ever been. And he's eager and ambitious and . . . Oh, I don't mean work ambition. But . . . He wants to go everywhere and do everything.'

'And you don't?'

'Yes, of course I do. But I can't just take off. There are the cats. And what would happen to the business?'

Catherine and I first met when she had, briefly, worked in publishing and we were on a committee together. But she had got out of that rat race around the period that time-and-motion experts started appearing in all our offices and cash flow became a girl to be reckoned with, and now she manages a small bookshop in the Portobello Road. It doesn't pay very well, but it gives her enough freedom to take the odd long lunch hour, or to leave early for special weekends.

'So what's the problem?' I asked, pouring some more wine. 'He wants to go round the world and you can't find anyone to look after the cats?'

She smiles.

'The problem, my darling, is that if he wants to go round the world, as you put it, he may not necessarily want me to go with him.'

'Seriously?'

'Yes – well, not exactly. I don't think he wants to go round the world. In a way that would be easier. At least eventually he'd end up back here. No. He wants "space".' She says the word with exhausted distaste.

'Has he just said so?' I ask, suspecting that this has been a fairly recent revelation.

'Last night.'

'Before or after the fuck?'

'After.' She smiles. 'I know what you're thinking; that I'm

rushing things. But I don't want to marry him, Chris. I just want him there when I come home. Or, better still, to be at home and to know that he'll be in soon.'

'How very suburban! Slippers and a pipe?'

'Why not?' She sounds almost defiant.

'Because you'd be bored within a week.'

She shakes her head.

'I wouldn't. Not with the right person.'

'Bill?'

'Why not? Why shouldn't Bill be the right person?' Then she suddenly changes her tone from defiance to self-pity. 'You don't know how lucky you are.'

'I am?' I wonder how she has arrived at that conclusion.

'Yes. You like living alone. You don't need people.'

Later, driving out of London in the early rush hour, I thought about what she had said and I decided that she was probably almost right. But it wasn't that I didn't need them, it was more that I didn't like them; not enough. I have a lot of friends; good friends, of whom Catherine is one of the best; but I wouldn't want any one of them living in, trying to get under the skin, trying to change and alter and share me. I'm with Bill all the way. I need my space.

Dick the Prick and the three younger Pricks were sitting in the row immediately behind us. We're in front because we are 'principal mourners'. This rather grand title suggests exotic African customs, with a lot of wailing and mud-stamping. In the event we were disappointingly circumspect, although Angela shed a few tears at one point and Dick leaned forward and put a comforting hand on her shoulder.

The boys all looked very scrubbed and neat. Dick could only have sired male children – like Macbeth. I often wondered what character trait was revealed when he, or maybe it was Angela, or both of them after careful debate, decided that all the boys would share their father's initials. Like Lyndon B. Johnson and all the other LBJs. Richard

Dowland and his three sons, Roger, Ralph and Rupert. Angela should have changed hers by deed poll to Rachel or Rebecca or Rose. All RDs together. 'Kiss me, RD', to make a very bad pun. No, come to think of it, don't, RD. Well, certainly not RD the Prick. The thought of his thick, moist lips touching mine makes me feel nauseous. I suppose it is common for people to wonder at the pairing of the sexes; but what Angela ever saw in Richard utterly confuses me. And she waited so long for him. At one time I actually thought she might be lesbian. She had a rather jolly schoolfriend called Elspeth who had more than a touch of the Vitas about her. But no, all the time she was keeping herself pure . . . for Dick the Prick. She once told me that the first time she saw him she thought, 'That's the man for me.' Dick the Prick? All six foot two of his pink, shiny body with the thin fuzz of yellow hair on an almost balding head? I mean, I know looks aren't everything, but . . .

'We are gathered here today to remember our brother, John . . .'

That was when Angela started to sniff and Dick's hand reached out to her across the ether. Mother, on my other side, was ramrod straight and staring at the coffin on its sliding table. She looked wonderful in a black coat-dress and a black hat, with dark feathers curling down one cheek. She betrayed nothing of what she was feeling or thinking. I admired that. I admire her. All but fifty years of her life was contained in the plain oak box in front of us. But she voiced no complaint. She was there as she'd always been, serene and capable. Back at the house everything had been prepared by her for the receiving of mourners. The food had been ordered, with people to serve it. The drink had been checked. Nothing would go wrong. She, who had run John Metcalfe's life like clockwork for as long as I could remember, was continuing so to do until the very end.

The electric organ didn't quite disguise the sound of the

motor as the mortal remains disappeared into the dark and the curtains closed on another play. I, even I, who profess to feel nothing, gasped and looked away, unable quite to accept the banality of the scenario. Though what else, for heaven's sake, are they supposed to do with the body; the empty shell; the husk? Just not this, I think. Better to have left him lying there and for all of us to have gone out into the light.

The family were conveyed back to the house in a long black limo like the ones sheiks use to carry all their wives on shopping expeditions. The hired help was already in the hall. Two cheerful girls in black dresses with starched white aprons. They wore expressions of suitable compassion and I had the feeling that they kept a wardrobe of looks to suit any occasion.

All the RDs were given a swift lecture by Angela about not hogging the food. Mother went upstairs to take off her hat and I into the drawing room to pour myself a stiff drink. D the P followed me and saw what I was doing, which made me feel slightly apprehensive, as though I were an alcoholic. I offered him something, but he smiled and shook his head.

'Never during the day,' he said, using that smug voice that people can't help employing when discussing habits that they themselves have kicked.

'Heavens!' I exclaimed. 'During the day is the best time.' I find it difficult not to be petty when I'm with him.

He asked me how the publishing world was getting on, with about as much enthusiasm as a vegetarian would ask a butcher about the meat trade. Which isn't surprising. Dick is on record as saying, the first time we met, that books were something he was really going to get stuck into when he retired. I suggested, at the time, that I should draw up a list for him; rather like the book marketing people submit a selection to Balmoral for Queenie-bags' hols. I have often since enjoyed a quiet half-hour's variation on the *Desert Island Discs* theme by choosing 'Dick's Books'. Sometimes it includes the whole of Proust and on other occasions it leans more towards *L'Histoire d'O*, *Emmanuelle* and a revolting little horror called *The Eye of the Cat*, which I once found wedged under the mattress in a cheap hotel in Chartres, of all places. Perhaps it's true that religious fervour brings on the raging hots.

Guests started to arrive. Guests? Mourners? I wasn't quite sure what to call them or how to treat them. One couldn't be too hearty, but at the same time sepulchral tones didn't seem to go with the clinical little service that we had all just attended.

Far more people remembered me than I remembered them. They spoke to me as though I were a distant cousin from a foreign land. Angela circulated valiantly and the three boys, I have to admit, behaved perfectly and were very popular. The English middle classes regard the young with unstinting approval so long as they are clean, quiet and white. And the three Rs certainly are all of those, although Rupert, the youngest, rather endeared himself to me by hiding a lump of fat off a piece of ham in the pot of a hydrangea.

When the hired help began pouring drinks everybody perked up no end and were soon merrily chattering and hooting with laughter, each within their own circle of friends, quite forgetting why they had all gathered there.

There were the Cutlers and Plates brigade. These are the people to whom Father sold the family business, Metcalfe's China and Cutlery – 'Nothing but the best, our slogan.' I suppose at one time he must have hoped that I would stay in the firm and carry on the tradition, started by his grandfather as a stall in Cheapside selling tin trays and mugs. By the time Father inherited, it had grown into a string of small shops in the Kent and Sussex area, still mainly dealing in cutlery. Father built up the china department, introduced other household goods and was obviously hoping that I would go on to even giddier heights. But lacking either the imagination or the conviction, I stayed as a shop assistant for three years after leaving school and having failed to get anywhere near the university I was intended for, then got the hell out and went my own way. Consequently, I could find nothing to say to the Cutlers and Plates representatives and got into a hopeless muddle over Rat Tail and Classic Queen Anne with a man who turned out to be an accountant who wouldn't know one end of a spoon from the other.

Father didn't have friends, but he was a staunch supporter of the Rotary Club, probably because it was good for business. I think at one time he was also a Mason, for the same reason. But he would never divulge anything about it and it remained a mystery to me, spiced by once finding a sinister little bag filled with regalia, which included a gaudy apron that looked as though it was meant for the Dame's Walk-Down costume in an Egyptian pantomime. Did Father actually wear it? Naked, I liked to imagine, except for his apron? The mind still boggles at what grown men will do to ensure a comfortable living. At least the Rotary was more straightforward. And the Rotarians here present seemed a jovial bunch, pleased to meet the only son, but obviously thrown that he had never married.

'And is your wife with you, Mr Metcalfe?' they would each ask in turn.

'No,' I'd reply. 'No, I'm not married.'

'Oh dear,' they'd say and then flounder about trying to think of some further conversation.

Gradually in dribs and drabs they began to depart, shaking Mother by the hand and murmuring words of condolence, and issuing invitations to 'come and see us whenever you feel up to it.' Knowing that she wouldn't, which gave them the courage to ask. And finally we, the family, were left and the hired help discreetly withdrew to the kitchen to get on with the washing up and to leave us to our grief.

I suppose I must be blamed for the ensuing unpleasant-ness. But I merely observed that the whole thing had been a terrible farce. I didn't mean it in a derogatory way. It was just a thought, in passing. But it acted on Angela rather like lighting the blue touchpaper does on a firework. She exploded. As usual, it took me totally by surprise. I thought she'd been having rather a jolly time chattering away to Cutlers about cutlery and Plates about plates and Rotarian wives about all manner of subjects. But, apparently, the whole thing had been a ghastly experience for her and she didn't know how she'd got through it, nor did she know how she was going to face life without the thought of Father being there, and if I didn't feel the same, then there was obviously something wrong with me.

My immediate reaction was to blink and look startled. It wouldn't have been so bad if she'd done it quietly in some corner, but we were surrounded by all the Pricks and Mother, who had just decided to pour herself her first drink of the day.

Richard leapt to his wife's support, putting an arm round her shoulder and patting her, as though she were a baby with wind. The boys all hung their heads and stared at their feet. Mother, after a moment's hesitation, continued to pour whisky.

'Come on, old love,' D the P murmured gently. 'Bit strung-up, are you? We should be getting home ourselves.'

'Oh, we can't leave now. We can't leave Mother with him,' Angela literally blubbed into Dick's shoulder.

I felt that this called for some reaction on my part, but unfortunately the only one that surfaced was irritability.

'Oh, for God's sake, Angela. What's the matter with you? I simply meant that the service was a bit mundane. Good God, they were queuing up with the next coffin outside. It lacked dignity, that's all I meant.'

'Leave it, old chap,' the P said, rather sternly.

For some reason we were all being dubbed 'old' now. Angela blew her nose loudly and Mother told the boys to go out into the garden; which they did, with slightly too much haste.

'I'm sorry, Mummy,' Angela said, when we were alone.

'Darling, that's perfectly all right. You have a good cry. You're going to miss Daddy.' Her emphasis made it clear that she didn't think I would. Again, I felt I must state my case.

'He has been a living vegetable for three years. He hasn't been here. It is pure hypocrisy not to admit that. You should have cried three years ago.'

'How would you know whether I did or not?' Angela spat at me. 'You're never here. I'm surprised you came today. Well, I'm not going to go on being responsible for everything on my own. You're going to have to pull your weight as well.'

'Responsible for what, Angela? D'you mean me, darling?' Mother's voice was sweetness itself, but there was a hint of danger in it. If Mother was about to lose her temper, a rare occurrence, then we were in for a glorious barney. But Dick came to the rescue, pouring oil from his unlimited supply.

'I don't think this is the time to talk about these things, do you?' he said.

'No, absolutely right, Dick. Time you were all off. The boys will be going back to school tomorrow, will they? So sweet of them to come. Your father would have been so pleased . . .'

She must immediately have wished she hadn't said it, because Angela started crying again.

'Now come along, darling. Upstairs and wash your face . . . then off you go home . . .' Mother continued, guiding her out of the room while she was speaking.

'Pity about that,' Dick said after a long, awkward pause.

'My fault. I shouldn't have made that stupid remark. I didn't realise she was in such a bad way.'

'Angel feels things very deeply . . .'

Angel??

'. . . She's worried stiff about how your mother will cope on her own. We were rather hoping, that is to say, well, as you're on your own, we just thought . . . you might . . . keep an eye on her.'

'Does she need keeping an eye on?'

'Well, leave it for now. We'll see how things go, eh? I've brought some more sleeping pills and what about some tranquillisers?'

'Who for?' I was genuinely flummoxed.

'I've brought enough for both of you?' He made the statement sound like an apologetic question. I felt almost kindly towards him and refrained from telling him what Mother and I thought of his sleeping pills.

'We'll probably rely on a few stiff drinks,' I told him, confirming once and for all his opinion of me as a lush.

Then Mother came back into the room and said that Angela was ready and Dick rushed off to rally the troops because he didn't want to keep her waiting. Whatever I may personally think of the Prick, Angela certainly fell on her feet when she met him, I decide. He seems to actually like her. Mother and I went out to the drive to watch them all embus in the estate car. Angela kissed Mother and hugged her and said that she'd phone the minute they got in, but that the traffic might be a bit of a nuisance because they were doing repair work on the M26. Then she turned shyly to me and I patted her awkwardly on the arm.

'Sorry,' I said.

She clenched her teeth and nodded stoically.

'Nice to see you. Chris. Don't forget, if you're ever down our way . . . Well, you never know. Canterbury is the sort of place that an author might live.'

'Probably more the area for biography,' I said, wanting to humour her. 'I might persuade Runcie, d'you think?'

'Oh, don't mention him!' she responded brightly. 'None of our friends can stand him. What has the Church got to do with politics? I ask you. Say goodbye to Grannie, kids,' then she looked sad again, obviously remembering that the goodbyes would from now on be halved. And, to a chorus of farewells, the P drove off.

I glanced at my watch and was surprised to find that it was already four o'clock. I was in no hurry to get back, but it certainly never occurred to me that I should spend another night here.

Mother went to speak to the food girls, who were packing their boxes into the back of a small van which was parked by the kitchen door. On the van's side was painted the legend: 'Kent Kousins. Food for every occasion'. I wanted to copy-edit it. But instead I strolled out on to the lawn and a few moments later Mother joined me.

'Let's go for a walk,' she said. 'Does it matter about your shoes?'

'A walk?'

'Not far. I've been in all day.'

'Shouldn't we change?' I was wearing my best suit, bought for the post-Booker wake when Marianne Lauder didn't win, although everyone with any taste knew that she should have.

'Don't be such an old maid, Chris!' Mother told me, but she said it with a smile. 'Come on.'

We walked in silence through the spinney, towards the View of Eternity. Then we took a narrow path along the edge of our land to where it meets the bridleway that runs along the side of the hill. It was another clear afternoon, and the view was miles deep. A lark fluttered somewhere out of sight above us and, distantly, a dog was barking.

A girl on a horse passed us, looking back as she trotted

away. I suppose we looked incongruous, dressed in our best black clothes.

'Was I awful to Angela?' Mother said after a while.

I was surprised and told her that if anyone had been awful, it was me. But she shook her head.

'I hurried her away. I shouldn't have. I usually do. I try not to, but . . .' She shook her head again and fell silent. I thought it probably best to let the subject drop, but she wouldn't.

'Actually, she's better when she's on her own. And of course she and your father did have a special relationship, for all the obvious reasons.'

They weren't obvious to me, I told her.

'Oh, surely, Chris? Almost as soon as you were born he was away fighting. He hardly knew you. But Angela was his little present for after the war was over.'

'I've never thought about it like that,' I said.

'No, well, why should you have?' She looked at me and smiled. It was a beautiful smile, in a beautiful face. It always pleases me to be told I take after her. I can even see the likeness myself, which is not always the case. We have the same straight, narrow bodies, the same oval faces, the same dark brown hair.

She was speaking again.

'I was a child when I had you,' she said. 'Where did it all go? No, it's all right! I promise that I won't become maudlin!'

'I don't mind. Be maudlin if that's what you want.'

But she shook her head and smiled, looking away from me, out over the countryside.

'I was pregnant when we married,' she said, in a voice so quiet that I almost didn't hear it.

But this was no surprise to me. It had always been a possibility. Either that or I was the premature present of the marriage night. Which was, more or less, the authorised version.

'I always knew I was a bastard!' I joked.

'Oh, it doesn't affect you. And, of course, no one even bothers about it nowadays. But then . . . I was just eighteen and your father was in his twenties. There was so much talk of war . . .'

'What are you trying to tell me, Mother? That I am the result of a panic fuck?'

'Perhaps I wouldn't have put it quite so crudely.'

'Sorry.'

She shook her head.

'I rather approve of the word when it is used in its correct context. It has a good Old English ring. And after all, the act of copulation has to be called something.' She walked on in silence again and then, reaching a farm gate, leaned on it, still staring ahead of her, but perhaps not really seeing the golden and green autumn orchards.

'This is how it all began,' she said. 'Just the two of us. Alone together. No sooner were John and I married than he was called up. I think he enjoyed playing soldiers. No, that isn't fair. I think he was scared a lot of the time. They all were.'

Hoping that she wouldn't notice, I glanced at my watch again.

'Should you be going?' she asked.

'Not if you'd rather I stay.'

'No. You must do what you want. You have a life . . . Have you?'

The peculiar question deserves some glib reply, but it catches me off guard and I say only:

'Yes, of course I have, Mother.'

'How would we know? You never tell us. I'll have to stop using the plural in the present tense. Told us.' She emphasises the words. 'You never told us what happened.'

I knew, of course, to what she referred. But I felt only

anger. It had nothing to do with her. With any of them. It never had.

'Maybe you should have tried asking me at the time,' I said, aware that my voice was shaking. Really, all this emotion suddenly; after years of safe, boring equanimity. I must get a grip on myself, I thought.

'We couldn't. We couldn't even speak about it to each other.'

'Even now you're dodging the issue, Mother. Even now you're skirting round it. Maybe I don't even know what you're talking about. Maybe it's all obscure to me.'

She turned and looked at me for a long time; a look that betrayed none of her feelings. Then she smiled and patted my hand, which was resting on the gate beside her.

'You're a very handsome fellow. I should think you have the girls falling over each other trying to get to you. And, of course, you are quite right not to confide in me. So long as you're happy, that's all that concerns me. I don't at all mind you having some raging affair with a *femme fatale* that honour forbids you to talk about. But I don't want you lonely and unloved.'

And, secure once more in that fantasy world that perhaps all parents inhabit, she walked slowly back towards the house with me.

She asked me if I wanted to stay for supper. She seemed quite prepared for me to be leaving. I explained that I had some proofs to read, which was only half a lie. I had, but they weren't urgent. But I wanted to get away and yet I didn't want to hurt her feelings.

I went upstairs and collected my clothes. The room had been tidied as it had been each day since I'd arrived. The box containing the Blandfords mementoes had been put away somewhere earlier, and I hadn't liked to ask her where.

She was waiting for me in the drive beside my car. I saw her from the stairs window as I was on my way down. She looked slim and youthful, the black of her dress contrasting with the thin haze of the evening light. I realised that, when I went, she would be alone and that she had probably never been alone for more than the odd night in all of her fifty years with Father.

As I was getting into the car she appeared to remember something that she wanted to ask me. Her face lit up. But then she seemed to edit the thought, to cross it out.

'What was that?' I asked her, innocently.

She shook her head, and smiled. For a moment I almost thought she was afraid and I felt myself being drawn protectively towards her.

'Tell me,' I said, not liking to drive off without being sure that she was all right.

'Oh, it was nothing. The school photographs. Do you want to take them?'

'Good God, what would I want those for?'

She looked relieved.

'I'll keep them here, then. You look so innocent in them. So young and vulnerable.'

'Well,' I said, 'that's how I was.'

Innocent? Young, certainly. And vulnerable. But innocent? Why not? If not innocent, of what was I proved guilty?

I put the car into gear and was on the point of driving off when she leaned in at the window again.

'That boy,' she said, 'the one you had to stay. What was his name? I was trying to find him on the photographs.'

'Oh, heavens. I don't remember. It was centuries ago. Another lifetime.'

But as I drove off, I knew I'd done a stupid thing. She would see through my lie and she would wonder why I had bothered. Even now, thirty years on, was I still in hiding? Or was it that I didn't dare to say his name? Would saying his name bring it all back? Would just saying his name start it all again?

'Stephen Walker,' I whispered.

And as I heard the sound I was breathing, I knew that my safe, comfortable shell was beginning to crack and I found the knowledge appallingly exciting. Is this how the imago feels, coming out of the chrysalis, I wondered? Or the snake as he sheds his skin?

'Stephen,' I said again.

# *Then*

'Nora, you revolting little pansy, is there a book under those covers?'

It is Dixon who has entered the dormitory, switching on the light and crossing the room with a great deal of noise, waking one or two of the other boys, who have already gone to sleep.

I have immediately put my torch and book under the covers, although I know it is a pointless move.

'I saw you, Nora. Through the window from Three Dorm. Naughty Nora!'

One or two of the others snigger, but not really maliciously, just relieved that they're in the clear.

As Dixon speaks, he grabs hold of the covers on my bed and whips them off, leaving me lying in my pyjamas, still holding the torch and the copy of the script.

'Oh dear, Nora. Is that a book I can see?' Dixon is this year's sadist. There is always one among the prefects. He is a short, round tub of a boy, who already looks middle-aged. He probably compensates for his physical inadequacies by being as vile as possible to the younger school.

'Can't you speak, you revolting fairy? Is that a book I see?'

'Yes,' I reply, trying not to let my contempt show in my voice.

'And is that a torch?'

'Yes,' I say again.

53

'Yes – what?' he screams, enjoying every minute of his power.

'Yes, sir.'

'That's better. Give.' He thrusts out his hand, and I put the script in it.

'Oh dear. Nora – listen to this, kids.' He reads very badly, like a ham actor. '"We have been married now eight years. Does it not occur to you that this is the first time that we two, you and I, husband and wife . . ."' He can scarcely say the word 'wife' for the glee in his voice, and, as people do who relish things, he says it again: '". . . husband and wife, have had a serious conversation." Who is your husband, Nora?' he asks, taunting me.

'Torvald Helmer,' I reply. I'm not being brave. I just despise him.

'No, you horrible little snot. Which one of the men?'

'Heslop,' I reply, and I see him squirm. Heslop is his senior prefect as well as mine. People like Dixon keep on the right side of their superiors.

'Call me sir,' he rasps, gaining ground by attacking again.

'Sir,' I say, still staring at him. Does he, I wonder, know how much I hate him? How willingly I would allow my look to kill him if only I had the power? Perhaps he does because he can't hold my eyes. He looks away and catches sight of Nigel Duff, lying in the next bed to mine.

'Are you in this poxy play as well, Fluff?'

'Yes, sir,' Duff replies quietly.

'And what's your name, Fluff?'

'Lind, sir,' Duff replies, wisely leaving out the 'Mrs'.

'Right, Nora. Just because you're playing the lead in the frigging play you think you can get away with things. Well, you can't. See me after prayers tomorrow night. All right, the rest of you, go back to sleep,' and he goes out, taking my copy of the script with him.

After prayers is punishment time. Perhaps we are meant

to pray for our safe deliverance before we go to the Prefects' Common Room. Knowing Blandfords, we are probably also expected to pray for the souls of the prefects who will later mete out the punishment, on the grounds that they are only inflicting the pain for our own good.

Walker and I have avoided each other since the day in the study. Apart from seeing each other at rehearsals there has been no reason why our paths should cross.

The feeling of guilt and remorse and loathing that accompanied our mutual orgasm has, for me, worn off, leaving only a sense of sadness, I don't know why. But I think Walker is still suffering. Probably because he believes that he was the instigator of the episode. But this isn't strictly true. I went back to the study. I chose to go back. I knew what would happen. Could it not, therefore, be said that I seduced him? For that is what I know took place. A seduction. Can you have a mutual seduction?

Evening prayers in Ely House take place in the large entrance hall. Here there is a grand piano, on which Mrs TG plays the hymns. Mrs TG, it is rumoured, was intended for the concert platform as a solo pianist. But she met TG and abandoned all thoughts of a career in order to devote her life to him. As a story it is almost the equal of Hart's one about his father being a spy. But she did marry TG, which is the oddest bit, so maybe the rest is true. Now she is a vague, nervous woman, who hides when she sees the boys coming and stays in the background as a shadowy figure in the house photograph or at the keyboard during evening prayers. Tonight she has chosen 'Who would true valour see . . .' which seems uncannily apt – as though she is playing it specially for me.

Fortified by the prospect of becoming a pilgrim I go, as soon as prayers have ended, to the Prefects' Common Room and wait outside the door for them to arrive.

Morrison, who shares a study with Walker, is the first to

come. He goes in without looking at me, making me feel somehow unimportant. Then Heslop appears, walking with Wickstead. Heslop smiles:

'What are you waiting for, Metcalfe?'

'Dixon told me to report here, sir,' I tell him.

Heslop shrugs and goes in, saying:

'He's just coming.'

I turn, expecting to see Dixon, and am confronted by Walker. Our eyes meet and he frowns. But before he has a chance to say anything, if indeed he was going to, Dixon appears behind him in the corridor, walking with Van Burghen.

'Ah, Nora!' he says, making Walker look back over his shoulder in surprise.

'You know what this revolting little fairy was doing last night, Walker? Reading after lights out. Wait there, Nora,' he says to me as he sweeps past and follows the other prefects into the room and closes the door.

I don't have to wait long. There is supposed to be a discussion before the sentence is passed and carried out. If so, they all must have been in agreement that my crime demanded scant debate.

The door opens and Dixon appears.

'Come in,' he says curtly.

The centre of the room has been cleared of furniture and two chairs have been placed back to back at one end. The prefects are all standing at the other end of the room, near the fireplace, in which a coal fire burns. Heslop, as head of the house, is in the judgement seat. He sounds almost bored with the proceedings.

'You know why you're here, don't you?'

'Yes, sir.'

'Tell me.'

'I was reading after lights out.'

56

'And you acknowledge that that is a flagrant flaunting of the house rules?'

'Yes. But . . .'

'But?' he says, his voice becoming harder. 'But? But what?'

'I was learning my lines.'

'You can't use the fact that you're in the school play as an excuse for everything, Metcalfe. Now while I'm prepared to admit that reading after lights out isn't the worst sin on earth, we are all agreed that the fact that you are playing the lead in this wretched play is going to your head. You're a horrible little boy puffed up with conceit. What are you?'

I cannot bring myself to reply.

'I said, what are you? Metcalfe. Be a good chap and tell me. You're puffed up with conceit, aren't you?'

'No,' I say defiantly, again, not because I'm brave, but because I don't think it's true.

One or two of the other prefects tut at this. Dixon turns slowly from looking at me to Heslop. I can't bring myself to look at Walker.

'Oh dear, Metcalfe!' Heslop says, as though he is actually experiencing regret on my behalf. 'Your attitude only confirms what I have said. Puffed up with conceit. I'm afraid we're going to have to beat it out of you.' He indicates the two chairs with a nod of his head. 'Go on,' he says. 'Kneel on the first chair, with your body over the back of it and your hands resting on the seat of the other chair. Go on. We don't want to do this, so let's get it over.'

I walk towards the chairs. My legs feel weak, but I don't think it shows. I kneel on the chair, as I was instructed, and bend my waist over the back of the chair.

'No, no, you nasty little poofter,' I hear Dixon snarl. 'Get your arse up,' and, as he speaks, he crosses swiftly to me and grabbing a handful of my hair pulls me up over the chair, pushing my head down towards the seat of the second one.

'That's what we mean, child. So that the arse is nice and exposed. Now, stay still.'

I am bent double over the back of the two chairs with my backside uppermost. The flannel of my trousers is stretched tight across the seat. I am perspiring. It's difficult to breathe in this position. The waiting seems endless. I hear footsteps as Dixon returns down the room.

'That's better,' I hear him say. 'What an inviting little fanny, don't you agree?'

Then I hear Heslop say:

'You understand, Metcalfe? We don't want to do this. We are doing it for your good. We are of the opinion that playing Nora has gone to your head. Each prefect will give you one stroke of the cane. The punishment shall begin.'

As he finishes speaking I hear the sound of footsteps running swiftly towards me. They stop, there is a moment's pause, and then, with a whistle of wind, the cane is lashed down across my buttocks with such strength that it almost knocks me off the chair back. Pain fizzes up the nerves of my body. I clench my teeth.

The footsteps retreat and then a moment later the process is repeated all over again.

The second lash seems to find exactly the same narrow line as its predecessor. I imagine the wound opening, like a knife cut. The third stroke lands wide of the target, cracking down on the base of my spine, connecting with the bone. A knife-like stab of pain surges up my back and into the front of my head between my eyes.

'Shame! No score, Wickstead!' one of them says.

The next blow is precise and stinging and makes me gasp, but somehow I manage to clamp my mouth closed and no noise escapes my lips.

'Nice one, Walker!' I think it's Morrison who says it. I don't feel disappointed. It all seems part of the system. If I turned round now and told them what happened last week in his study, they'd probably congratulate him and punish me more.

The final lash of the cane is administered by Dixon, because it is his punishment that is being carried out. He also misses the mark, catching me low down across the back of the thighs, which is clever of him because the arse is numb with pain now but the thighs are untouched.

'Get up,' I hear Heslop say.

I wonder if I will be able. I force myself to climb off the chairs. My shirt has come untucked from my waistband and is sticking out beneath my pullover. But I don't bother to adjust it.

'You can go now,' Heslop says, turning away towards the fire, as though the incident has all been rather boring.

I walk unsteadily towards the door, my legs and backside stinging. Then I remember that Dixon still has my copy of the script. I have to get it back from him. I hesitate.

'Well go on, idiot child,' Van Burghen says. 'You surely don't want it all over again, do you? What are you? A masochist? Have we been entertaining you? Giving you pleasure? Go away, child!'

I can hardly speak. I am trembling all over.

'But, please,' I say, willing myself not to cry.

'Now what is it, Nora?' Dixon snarls, with gleeful cruelty.

'Please, Dixon, you've still got my script,' I say in a quiet voice.

'It is confiscated. Now get out.'

'Oh, don't be stupid, Dixon. He's got to learn his lines,' Walker says in a low, intense voice.

Heslop is banking coal on the fire and doesn't look round. Perhaps he's ashamed of what has taken place. Now he says:

'Give him the script, Dixon.'

Dixon crosses to a shelf, picks up the book and throws it at me. It lands at my feet and I have to bend to pick it up. I think the skin across my buttocks may split open. I kneel down to retrieve the book.

'Now get out,' Dixon tells me.

I hurry away out of the room and manage to reach the privacy of the junior bogs before the nausea and the pain engulf me. I stay locked in the cubicle until I hear Nigel Duff calling my name.

'I'm here, Nigel,' I say, and I flush the toilet before coming out as though I want even him to believe that I haven't been hiding.

'I was looking everywhere for you. Are you all right?'

I pull a face and nod. He must have noticed that I've been crying, but he doesn't mention it. I'm grateful for that. He washes his hands at the basin, looking at me in the mirror.

'Dixon should be reported, you know.'

'For what?' I ask, washing my hands in the basin next to him.

'He picks on people. I looked up "sadist" in the dictionary. It says it's the gaining of pleasure or sexual gratification from the inflicting of pain and mental suffering on another person. That's him.'

I grin. For some reason I almost want to giggle.

'So – you're going to report him for being a sadist? Who to? TG? Besides, they all beat me. It wasn't just Dixon.'

'Did it hurt?'

'No, Nigel. I loved every minute of it.'

'I looked up "masochism" in the dictionary as well. That's the gaining of pleasure from physical or mental cruelty. D'you suppose we'll all grow up masochists because we've been here?' He looks genuinely worried.

"Pends how much you enjoy being beaten, I suppose. I happen not to. In fact, I hate it. And them for doing it.'

'Maybe you'll turn into a revolutionary, like Lenin. I can imagine you leading the mob against the Masters' Common Room!'

'Will you be in the mob, Nigel?' I ask with a grin.

'God, no. I can't wait to be a prefect myself. Then I can get some of the younger bastards and make them squirm!'

Nigel is like that. He makes jokes that aren't all that far from being the truth.

'D'you want some of my cocoa?' he asks, drying his hands.

Greater love hath no friend than to offer his cocoa, and he knows I haven't any. I grin and nod. Well, he had most of mine anyway.

There's always a prefect on dormitory rounds, to see the younger house into bed and switch off the light. At least I know it won't be Dixon, he was on last night. That's how he caught me. Our dormitory juts out in a wing. He had seen my torch light from a window in Three Dorm, which is along the main front of the house.

I return from the showers and am getting into my pyjamas. We usually have about ten minutes' grace between the prefect in charge coming in and lights being switched off. I think originally this time was used by boys for their personal prayers. Kneeling at the side of the bed like Christopher Robin. But that has rather died out in the godless days in which we now live. Actually, I did once go through a religious phase. But I was too embarrassed to pray in public and I did so in bed after the lights were off. I stopped when I realised that the saying of the prayers – the Lord's, followed by one for my parents, sister and the world's population and ending with a quick list of apologies to the Almighty for any misdemeanours of the day together with an occasional request, if I thought it worth the risk – when I realised it was becoming a superstition. If I didn't say my prayers bad luck would follow. They became a quick gabble to ensure a safe tomorrow. Quite what I would have said to God on the evening after Walker and I had been together, I'm not sure. Probably a simple 'Sorry, God' and then wait for the thunderbolt.

I am pulling on my pyjama trousers when Walker comes into the room.

'Come on, you lot,' he says as he enters. 'I'm late, so no hanging about. Into bed.'

'Oh, Walker,' someone protests. 'I haven't been to the toilet.'

'Lavatory,' Walker corrects him. 'Toilet is an unacceptable euphemism. Go on then. But hurry.'

The boy bolts for the door, grinning.

'Into bed, the rest of you. Go on, Duff — move.'

Nigel scrambles for his bed and, as he does so, he inadvertently kicks me on the thigh. I can't help reacting. He has hit the spot where Dixon's cane stroke has cut a thin blue and red line across the flesh.

'Ow!' I say, under my breath.

'Sorry,' Nigel says.

I'm finding it difficult to move. The bruising has become very swollen and tender. As I'm climbing into bed, trying not to lie on the buttocks, I see that Walker is watching me from the other end of the room.

We hold a look for a moment. It is the first time our eyes have met since the study. I smile at him. Just to let him know that it's all right. That there's no problem. But he frowns and walks away, and asks one of the other boys a question about his target score on the rifle range.

It's a horrible rebuff. I don't deserve it. I don't know why he's done it. Unless, of course, there are rules that I don't understand. Maybe last Saturday in the study was just some minor event in his life that he's forgotten about. Or maybe it was something so enormous that he's still suffering from the guilt. But for me it was neither of those things. It was special, not so much because of what we did but because of how we were when we were together. I suddenly realise that

I thought he was my friend. And I'm hurt and disappointed that he is proving me wrong.

As soon as Jenkins, the boy who'd the sudden urgent call, returns, Walker goes to the door. He has to pass my bed, of course. I determinedly stare at him, willing him to look at me. But he keeps his eyes averted.

'Good night, everyone,' he says and snaps off the lights and goes out of the room, closing the door with a bang.

We have a strict rota for morning showers; a dormitory at a time, starting with the youngest boys, who were first to bed and who anyway have to be up to get on with their fagging duties. In this way the shower room is meant not to get jam-packed at the last moment, causing a mad scramble through the school grounds to the dining hall for breakfast. The prefects, of course, have a more leisurely time and can if they wish get their fags to make them breakfast in their studies. The fag's life is a miserable one, which I have happily escaped. It only lasts for the first year and is supposed to humiliate you into obedience or some such balls. The prefect for whom I fagged was called Snaith. I always had trouble laying his fire and, in the end, he used to buy me firelighters out of his own pocket money, not out of kindness, I think, but more because he grew tired of finding the study full of smoke and freezing cold. The prefects also have the added privilege of warm showers in the morning, if they want them. Most of the hail and hearty ones pretend that they still have the ice-cold douches that are obligatory for the rest of us, but in very severe weather they all add a bit of warm to take away the agony.

The shower room is crowded with fourth-formers when I go in. They giggle and whisper and have probably heard in elaborate detail about the kissing session with Wetherspoon Minor and his chum. The three showers are in use and there are a couple of boys waiting in line. One of them is called Hobbs. He is a muscular boy with a shock of corn-coloured hair. Last term he was quite short, but he has suddenly started growing and none of his clothes ever seem to fit him. I have a particular feeling of wariness about him. He's always staring at me, and if I look at him he giggles as though he knows some secret about me. I can't think that there is any – or, at least, there wasn't until a week ago – but he makes me uncomfortable. Particularly today. I keep my towel round my waist and lounge against the wall, waiting for the others to finish. One of them is running hot water in his shower. He looks round, guiltily, as I enter, but seeing that I'm not a prefect he continues to shower, almost arrogantly, challenging me to pull rank, which I could do, being a year senior.

The other two showers quickly become free. Cold water in the early morning doesn't encourage lingering.

Hobbs takes one of them; as he does so, he glances sideways at me then looks away, giggling and blushing. I think he may be a lunatic. I don't know anything about him, but his behaviour is certainly not normal.

Then the door opens and Walker comes in.

The atmosphere in the shower room immediately changes. The boy in the warm shower switches off both taps and steps aside, making room for Walker to take his place. The other fourth-formers hurry to get away.

Walker hangs his towel on a peg and walks across to the shower. He has his back to me, and even in the dim electric light I can see the fuzz of dark hair at the base of his spine that I had discovered with my hands.

'Pringle,' he says to the boy who has just vacated the shower and who is hurrying through the door.

'Yes, sir?' Pringle says, sounding far from arrogant now.

'You're supposed to have a cold shower, aren't you?'

'Yes, Walker.'

All the time he has his back to us, as he adjusts the taps to a satisfactory temperature.

'Do me a hundred lines by tonight. "I must have a cold shower in the morning." Best neat writing, Pringle – nice straight lines.'

'Yes, sir,' Pringle says, and departs.

Hobbs vacates the shower next to Walker and, as I am the only person waiting, I am forced to take off my towel and hurry to it. As I move I notice my cock is in a dangerous mood. I swear it has a life and a will of its own.

Then the boy in the other corner shower switches off the water and a moment later Walker and I are alone together in the shower room, standing naked, side by side, he in the warm and me in the cold. We keep our backs to each other. I am nervous and have to struggle to breathe. The cold water is sharp on my face, it runs rivulets of ice down my back. I rub with my hands on my shoulders, not just to keep the circulation flowing, but also to seem busy and unconcerned.

Then, just as I think I have been under the stream for long enough and that I can retreat to safety, I feel his warm, strong hand on my shoulder. I daren't look at him. My cock is getting hard. Oh, Christ, my cock is getting hard.

'Last night,' I hear him say. 'At the punishment. I'm sorry, I had to. I'm sorry.'

'It's all right. I understand. It's all right,' I gasp.

The water is so cold that I'm beginning to shake. His hand reaches out and he switches off my shower. I turn and look at him over my shoulder. He is so near to me that I could touch him with my entire body. He is tall and lean, with dark hair on his chest. I daren't look down although I want to. He reaches out towards me, with his hand, like he did in the study, just touching my cheek and all the time staring solemnly into my eyes. I am gasping for breath. I slowly turn towards him, but this movement seems to shock him into activity. He switches off his shower and hurries to where his towel hangs on the peg. I remain standing with my back half to him, hiding my shameless penis. I can't move. I must wait for him to go away.

As he is drying himself, he looks up at me. His face looks haggard, as though he's in pain.

'It isn't safe here,' he says.

Although he is holding his towel in front of him, I can see that he also has an erection. I'm ridiculously pleased. It makes me feel less stupid. But then I suddenly get frightened. It all seems so complicated. I can feel the blood surging round my body; it makes a singing sound in my ears.

I want to cross to him; to touch him. And, almost as though he can read my thoughts, he takes a step towards me.

'Walker?' I gasp, not quite sure why it sounds like a question.

But he shakes his head and fastens the towel round his waist, covering his hard cock with a gathering of cloth.

'No,' he says. 'This is mad. Anyone could come in. Leave it to me. I'll think of something,' and, turning, he goes quickly out of the shower room.

# *Now*

Catherine left at about twelve thirty, after a rather miserable evening. The affair with Bill was not going well. As far as I could make out, he was more than happy to know her, both socially and biblically, but he didn't want to sign an exclusive contract. I still hadn't met him and the way things were going I doubted if I ever would. The main problem appeared to be age: there were almost twenty years separating them. Not that that in itself should matter, but Bill sounded a very young twenty-four going on the dreaded thirteen and three quarters that we all loved to hate, we who hadn't published the *Mole Diaries*. Maybe, I suggested to Catherine, we could do *The Sexual Diaries of Bill: Size Nine and Three-quarter Inches*. But she was in one of those moods where she was determined to remain cheerless. I therefore tried the 'let's all be reasonable about the boring child' approach, and hinted that, if he was only twenty-four:

'Good God, darling. He hasn't hit the big time yet. You've got to give him a little leeway.'

But that didn't go down very well either.

'What "big time"?' she demanded.

When Catherine is depressed her mood can turn ugly as quickly as an electric light can be extinguished at the switch.

'It's just a figure of speech. You know . . .' I answered lamely.

'No, I don't know. You tell me.' She seemed determined to pick a fight.

67

'Look, there's no point taking it out on me. I haven't done anything.'

'No. Exactly. I'm going to have that put on your gravestone. "He didn't do anything." That just about sums you up.'

'Oh, for Christ's sake! If you're going to pick a fight – go home.'

'I'm sorry,' and she started to cry again. She had been crying on and off all evening.

The trouble is that it appears Bill has another girlfriend. There is someone else whom he's also poking. Someone of his own age and probably sharing his same 'free spirit'. Some other kid who thinks that affairs of the heart are as abundant as the fruits of the earth, there for the picking whenever they feel hungry. He was being open about it and, therefore, I'm sure he felt free of any guilt. Personally, he seemed to me to have been an idiot to tell her. All he'd achieved was a soggy-hearted Catherine, forever fretting about her rival. Perhaps he had also realised the error of his ways and that could explain his trying to reassure her by telling her that this other girl was no more important to him than Catherine was. The fact that he chose to express this sentiment from the negative direction seemed to have escaped Catherine's notice and I didn't help matters by drawing her attention to it. But then, to be reasonable to all parties, I could remember Catherine telling me, early in the relationship, that it was all a glorious game; no strings; just the fun of companionship and a great deal of biblical bliss.

'So, what changed?' I asked her, as she sat on the floor beside the coffee table drinking far too much red wine and smoking cigarettes.

'I did,' she replied. 'I changed. I know that. But it doesn't make it any easier. I changed.' She stubbed out her cigarette and immediately lit another. 'I don't want to share him. This isn't some game we're playing. This is real life. My life. I don't care what I said, Chris, so I'll thank you not to throw it in my face.'

I hadn't been going to; only a fool would do so twice in her present mood. No, I was going to remain silent and let her talk. I actually felt sorry for her. Mainly because, once again, she seemed to have chosen a real jerk for a lover. But I couldn't tell her that. I wished very much that she could get over the dreaded Bill. We had a much happier time when she was between affairs and we could talk about books and go to the theatre and out to dinner with mutual friends. On such occasions we were a near-perfect couple, which confirms once and for all that it is sex that is the fly in the ointment. Perhaps the two should be kept scrupulously apart; there should be friends and fucks. But, of course, that wouldn't work because of the little monster; Cupid. Falling in love. That was ever the problem. That's what scuppered Catherine's perfectly happy arrangement with sailor Bill. She fell in love with him. Am I turning into a cynic, I wonder? Or have I always been one? Or is it that all my life I have been waiting to be in love again and I despise Catherine for getting it so hopelessly, totally and constantly wrong?

Meanwhile, she seemed to have reached a familiar plateau of misery. One where the grass seemed greener anywhere but in her field. And so:

'I wish I could be like you,' she sighed, taking another drag of the cigarette, followed by a gulp of wine.

Catherine usually makes rosy assumptions about me and my lifestyle when her own life isn't working out too well. She sees me, I think, as a happy celibate; a monk without an order or a religion. And maybe she's not so far off the mark at that. I do prefer my own company. I don't think I could live with anyone else; not now. But, of course, there is still sexual frustration and awful longing. I am not nearly so secure as I must seem to people. There is an unfilled gap for me also, only I don't go on about it. A monk, one has to assume, has his belief and his faith to support him in his hour of doubt. Lucky old monk. I can't help but envy him. Of course, he probably wanks like the best of us, but he wanks to the glory of God. Me, I wank into a handkerchief and am left with a feeling of emptiness and of peculiar, bleak relief. Let's face it, it doesn't sound exactly healthy, Catherine! No, I wouldn't take my life as a blueprint for survival. Not of course that I would say any of that to her. We talk endlessly about her sexual problems, but never about mine. Not that she wouldn't like to; not that she doesn't care, doesn't want to be of help. But I couldn't admit her to my interior world. It is too private. Another fault of mine, I'm sure. And of course, by denying her this final intimacy, I am also denying the friendship the possibility of greater depth. It is as one-sided as all my adult relationships have been.

Perhaps I wasn't the best person to advise her about her love life, but the solution did seem horribly obvious to me.

'Leave him,' I told her, when she seemed to be failing to get to that point on her own.

'I can't,' she replied, after a moment's bleak realisation of what that would entail.

'Then put up with it the way it is.'

'I can't do that either. I can't bear to think of him with her.'

I presumed, although it was not actually stated, that that's where he was this evening.

'Isn't it a bit risky?' I asked, slightly changing the subject, which was getting bogged down in alcoholic lethargy.

'Risky?' She seemed perplexed by my question.

'Having a promiscuous lover? With the dreaded Aids stalking the streets?'

'Oh, that.' She used the bored expression of the ignorant. 'We take precautions. Besides, he isn't promiscuous. He just has two mistresses.'

'What do we know about the other one?'

70

'Penny? He's known her for ages. They more or less grew up together. She works in a shop in South Molton Street.'

'I don't think the Aids virus is designer-selective.'

'Only temporarily, until she can get a proper job. She's got a degree in modern languages.'

'I'm sure that must come in handy with all the foreign visitors.'

We looked at each other and she smiled.

'Which shop?' I asked.

'I don't know. Bill won't tell me. I think he's afraid that I might go there and cause a scene.' She smiled, blearily. 'Don't think I haven't walked up and down wondering, though. I imagine she's thin and trendy. I hate her, Chris. Isn't that awful? I hate someone I don't even know.'

'I wasn't entirely joking,' I said, sticking to my point. 'If he's sleeping elsewhere, you have a right to know about her. She might be a tart.'

'I'm sure she's a tart. He doesn't see her all that often, so who's she with the rest of the time?'

'That's what I'm getting at. It's a terrible risk, Catherine.'

'Yes, all right. Don't go on about it. It's a risk I have to take.'

'Oh, darling, don't be silly,' I said. 'I don't want to sound prudish or sanctimonious but – is it worth it?'

'Yes!' She shouted the word. 'Don't you see? He's all I've got, Chris. There isn't anyone else. And I'm so bloody scared of ending up on my own. I'm so scared of that,' and she sobbed as she said the words. Then she shook her head and rubbed her face. 'Oh, God! Too much wine. I must go home.'

I ordered a taxi for her and when it arrived I went down to the street with her. The wind was fierce, tearing at the trees in the communal gardens opposite. I gave her a hug as she got in.

'Sorry,' she said. 'I've been a terrible bore.'

71

I told her she hadn't and that I loved her. Which I do.
She smiled and said:

"'I have been faithful to thee, Cynara! in my fashion . . .'"
What's that from? I don't remember.'

Neither did I.

I felt depressed after she'd gone. I cleared up the remnants
of our supper and stacked the dishes beside the sink. Then I
went and looked up Cynara in the dictionary of quotations
and discovered that it came from *Non Sum Qualis Eram* by
Ernest Dowson, 1867 to 1900, and that another line from
the same work is: 'And I was desolate and sick of an old
passion.'

The following day, Friday, I was going to have a long and
difficult session with an author telling him we weren't going
to publish his new book. I had decided against a coward's
lunch at L'Escargot to sugar the pill and was going to break
the news in the office. He would, of course, demand that
another editor see it; but they all had. Unfortunately, they
were in agreement with me. I would encourage him to take
the manuscript to another publisher, but I doubted if he'd
get much joy from any of them. It was a good book; well
written, subtle and sensitive. But I couldn't see anyone selling
enough copies to cover the advance, let alone costs. In a way
the publishing world is 'life' in microcosm. Fewer and fewer
books are attracting bigger and bigger sales. Megabucks on
the shelf for three days, then pulped to make way for the
next one, and God help all the other hopefuls with their
works of genius. If the analogy holds then Catherine is a
slim volume of feminist poetry and I am a Serbo-Croatian
phrase book: neither of us would make the best-seller list
or a review in the *TLS*. We are both 'worthwhile', which
is, in present-day publishing terms, to kill stone dead with
faint praise.

Later I realised that the wind, which had been strong when
Catherine was leaving, had increased to what seemed like

hurricane force. The noise it made was terrifying. I stood at my bedroom window in the dark, staring out into the street. One of the trees in the gardens opposite was bending so that it brushed the ground. Then, as I watched, it was uprooted and thrown across the railings as though it were no more than a twig. I was, for once, glad that my flat wasn't on the top floor. The house is in a poor state of repair and I doubted if the roof tiles would survive the night.

I got back into bed, but I couldn't sleep. The turbulence outside seemed to mirror my inner state. Since Father's death I had been unable to throw off a nagging depression, which was surprising considering that we had had so little in common and hadn't even liked each other. I hadn't been back to Sevenoaks since the cremation service, but I had been good about speaking to Mother on the phone. She seemed to be managing and I knew that Angela was making periodic, dutiful visits, so there was really no need for me to go as well. I presumed that Mother would adjust to her new life without too much trouble. Indeed, I could only think that it would be a relief for her not to have an invalid on her hands any more. Perhaps I don't make enough allowances for other people's emotions, but, for me, the incident of his death was a thing in the past, and seemed of little relevance now. My depression had therefore to be due to some other reason.

I got up again and went into the sitting room. The wind was howling down the street, sweeping away dustbins. I thought I should go to see if the car was all right. But what would I do if it wasn't? Besides, we don't get hurricanes in Britain. It couldn't be happening. It was just some freak event that would soon go away. I picked up the dictionary of quotations from the armchair where I had dropped it earlier and read again the Dowson quote:

'And I was desolate and sick of an old passion . . .'

And it was as if Stephen had come into the room and was standing in a dark corner, watching me.

73

'Go away,' I pleaded. 'Please.'

It wouldn't be true to say that I hadn't thought about him, or about us, over the years. Of course I had. But the thoughts were neatly filed away in a corner marked 'might have been', and had only been brought out on occasions of total indulgence when I was feeling particularly sorry for myself, which, at the moment, didn't seem to be the case. In fact I was recently coming round to Catherine's opinion that I had discovered the divine secret of life; namely that being alone meant being content. Yet from the moment I had come across the school photographs in Father's desk, this spurious equilibrium had been under threat.

It would be psychoanalytically neat to connect Father with the episode, and therefore to relate his death to my renewed fascination in those events of so long ago, but it wouldn't be true. Father never knew any of the real story. He knew of course what happened to me, and he was probably disappointed in me, although we never once talked about it or anything else relating to the episode. He was a staunch Old Blandfordian himself, with fantasy memories of his time at the school. Perhaps my subsequent behaviour had sullied these for him. But of one thing I am certain; he didn't know why what happened happened. The fact that he stored all my school mementoes in a box, out of sight, is easily explained. He didn't want to remind me of the place, for fear it should trigger more disturbance. He was a man who liked order and discipline. My emotional mess must have seemed appalling to him.

I had put the dictionary of quotations back in the bookcase and was returning to bed, when the phone started to ring. I glanced at my watch and thought it must be a wrong number. No one in their right mind would telephone so late, or so early, depending upon one's attitude, an hour. I reached the receiver on the table beside my bed just as it stopped. Thinking that it was perhaps the wind getting the wires in a twist – my mechanico-scientific knowledge being equal to that of the Stone Age tribesman – I left the receiver off the hook and put a pillow over it to shut out the buzzing. I then fell asleep to the sound of the hurricane and had vague and threatening dreams, the kind that leave a flavour of despair and no specific memories of content.

We had, it appeared the following day, lived through the worst storm winds that have swept across Britain since God knows when. Roads were blocked by fallen trees, cars were displaced. London looked as it had done during the Blitz. I gave up trying to drive through the chaos and decided to walk to the office, which is in Mayfair.

Hyde Park was a battleground. Great trees were scattered like children's pick-a-sticks, craters had been formed by the tearing roots, a terrible calm hovered over everything.

Half the staff didn't arrive. The receptionist phoned in to say that no trains were running on her line. I hoped that this would mean I would get my reprieve and that my author would be unable to keep his appointment. But I was forgetting the nature of the beast; a writer would willingly cross the Arctic wastes, barefoot, to talk about his work, and so he was only a few minutes late.

He's a nice man. We have published two previous novels by him. Neither of them set the Thames on fire, although they picked up one or two goodish reviews and a television company flirted with the rights on one of them for a time. I rather suspected that the present offering was autobiographical. The break-up of a marriage from the man's point of view. It could have been a good idea, but it was too small and too delicately handled and, dare I say it, too boring for the bodice-ripping marketplace that was its natural outlet. I tried to be constructive; but it's hard when the message is a rejection. He took it stoically. But he lives by his writing. I was probably putting the mortgage into jeopardy. I said I'd fix him up to see a colleague who was editing a series of armchair travel books because I knew he'd been to Swaziland, which had potential, and I didn't want to send him away empty-handed. I walked down to the street with him. I felt desperately sorry. We shook hands on the pavement and I watched him walk away with his head bent, looking at the ground.

When I got back to my office the phone was ringing. It was Mother.

'Oh,' she gasped, 'I've been trying to get you. I think your phone must be out of order at the flat.'

I remembered that the receiver was still under the pillow beside my bed.

'Are you all right?' I asked. Her voice sounded tense.

'Darling,' she said, 'it's the most ghastly mess down here. The garden is ruined. The spinney is all down. Every tree. I tried to get hold of you during the night. It was absolutely terrifying. D'you think . . . I mean, could you come down, Chris? Would it be an awful bore? It's just that . . .' and she started to cry.

'Mother?' I must have sounded surprised. I can't remember ever before hearing her upset. 'Of course I'll come. I'll have to go back for the car, and I'm not sure what the roads will be like . . .'

'Thank you, darling,' she said. 'Sorry, I got a bit worked up. There is something so unstoppable about acts of God.'

After we'd finished speaking, I telephoned Catherine at the shop. Her flat is just off Westbourne Grove, so she doesn't have far to walk to work. We marvelled at how all the fallen trees seemed to have missed the buildings. I told her about Hyde Park and she told me that she'd heard on London Radio that Richmond Park had also taken a hammering. I said I was going down to Sevenoaks and she said that it had apparently been particularly badly hit. I asked her what she was doing for the weekend and she said she'd just spoken to Bill and that they were going down to Chichester. She sounded jaunty and cheerful, as though the previous evening hadn't occured. I knew Bill had friends with a boat at Bosham and I said I hoped she wasn't thinking of going sailing in these hurricane conditions. But she pooh-poohed the idea and said that lightning never strikes twice. I told her that was mixing the metaphor and she said, not at all, that the metaphor was the weather. We were just about to ring off when I remembered Ernest Dowson and *Non Sum Qualis Eram*. But she hadn't a clue what I was talking about. She must have been more drunk last night than I thought.

As soon as I arrived, Mother took me out on to the terrace. It was as though the house had been picked up by the Genie of the Lamp, like he did to Aladdin's palace, and put down in a different place. Nothing was the same. Where yesterday the view had been of banks of trees, sheltering the garden and creating an impression of a cultivated clearing in the forest, today there was nothing between it and the vast horizon of the Kent countryside.

We picked our way as best we could through the great mounds of debris and tree trunks to the View of Eternity. One of the oaks had fallen across the wall and smashed it, sending the rubble scattering down the steep hillside. In front of us the familiar countryside was littered with fallen trees. Turning our backs on the view we surveyed the unaccustomed sight of the house, surrounded now by space. It was a miracle that it was still standing.

'It must have been terrifying,' I said, putting an arm round her shoulder. Her body felt taut and thin. She moved in towards my embrace and leant her weight against me. She was wearing a blue three-quarter-length jacket and had her hands in the pockets. One fist, clenched like a fighter's, pressed against my thigh. She remained silent, staring at the devastation that had once been the garden.

'It seems incredible that the house was spared,' I said.

Still she didn't answer.

'And that the forecasters failed to give us any warning. Though what you could have done I'm not quite sure. You could hardly have tied the spinney to the ground.'

She took my hand that was resting on her shoulder and drew it down round her waist, holding it in both of hers and snuggling in to me, as though she were cold. Then she rested her head back against my shoulder. I could smell the clean, washed-linen scent of her perfume.

'Are you all right?' I asked her eventually.

She nodded, but she wouldn't speak. The light was beginning to fail and a thin breeze was blowing. I extricated my hand from her grasp and she allowed me to lead her back, scrambling over the fallen trees, towards the house.

When we reached the lawn, she hesitated, looking round her again, and shook her head.

'Your father used to escape to the study and I to the garden,' she said. 'Forty years of work, ruined.'

I looked round. She was exaggerating. It was mainly the trees that had suffered. The shrubs and the plants, being whippy, had bent with the gale and would soon readjust.

'It will be all right, once it's tidied up,' I told her. 'You'll see. Mills will help you. You could get him in full time for a while. He'll be glad of the money. The fallen trees will need clearing and then – just think, a virgin canvas! You can start creating all over again.'

She looked at me and smiled. Then she shook her head.

'I couldn't,' she said, and turned to walk into the house.

I collected my case from the front door and took it up to my room. She had hung the four house photographs in a neat group on the wall opposite the bed. It came as a shock. I didn't know what had prompted her. I stood in the fading light, staring at Stephen's smiling images. How strange, I thought, he's always smiling. The same smile in an increasingly mature face. He is only in three of the four, of course. Because he had left before my final year.

I turned my back, abruptly. Was it chance that was making her force me to remember? I heard her calling from the foot of the stairs.

'Is it too late for a cup of tea? Or too early for a drink?'

I selected alcohol and she called out:

'Good! Will you pour me a gin and french?'

'You on the hard stuff, Mother?' I chided her as I went down to join her in the drawing room.

'Tonight, I think, the harder the better! I need it for my nerves. Besides, Angela is on another health jag and when she's here I have to secretly tipple in the kitchen. It will be rather pleasant to be able to drink my own booze in my own drawing room for a change.'

I poured her a gin and french and decided it smelt so good that I'd have one as well; which would probably be the beginning of the end. They are lethal and lovely and I've never yet managed to have the prescribed two. Any more and the world turns upside down. I once had five and ended up engaged to a German publisher who was already married to a skiing instructor and had three children.

As I handed her the glass she looked up at me with sad spaniel eyes.

'I hate it here, Chris,' she said. 'In a way that gale did me a good turn. It's shown me the way out.'

'Out?' I asked, fetching my drink and sitting in the armchair opposite her.

'I want to sell the house.'

'Well, it is rather big. Good idea. You shouldn't have any trouble. D'you want me to get on to an estate agent? What are you thinking of instead? Somewhere smaller round here?'

'I don't want to stay in Sevenoaks,' she protested.

'But, Mother, all your friends are here. It's where you belong.'

79

'I wouldn't mind if I didn't see any of them again. And I don't belong here. I hate this house. I always have. Your father chose it. He gave me the key in a little box.'

'I expect he thought he was doing the right thing.'

'I'm sure he did – for him. Well, he's gone now. And so have the trees. I liked the trees. I liked the spinney. I liked the View of Eternity. It's all gone.'

'All right,' I said, treating it lightly. 'Where would you like to be instead?'

'With you,' she said, and to give her her due, she didn't look at me as she said it.

I was so surprised that I said nothing. An awkward silence ensued. I began to doubt if I'd heard correctly. It was so unlike her. She never made demands, and besides, it was such a ridiculous idea. It could never work. We'd be at each other's throats within a week. She'd hate living in London. Which is where I had to be, because of the office. And anyway, all my friends were there, and my life . . . I glanced at her, uneasily. She was sitting back in the chair, her arms stretched out and supported by the padded sides, her glass balanced delicately between two fingers. She was wearing a white blouse and black trousers. Her hair looked different. It seemed lighter. I must ask her about it. But this didn't seem to be the moment. I think she knew I was looking at her, but she didn't at once raise her eyes.

'And answer came there none,' she said, quietly.

I was embarrassed and this made my tone brusque.

'Sorry,' I said, 'I didn't know you'd asked a question.'

'Perhaps I didn't. Let's forget we had this little conversation, shall we? You're absolutely right, I can get Mills in full time and the garden will soon be tidied up. Are you hungry?' she asked, and only then did she look at me.

We stared at each other across the room, almost like strangers. I didn't want to hurt her.

'Mother, it wouldn't work,' I told her. 'You'd get bored in no time.'

She got up and poured herself another drink, slopping the gin into the glass and waving the Martini bottle somewhere near it.

'That's neat gin,' I said, smiling.

'You do that to me. I tried neat gin to terminate your arrival; and hot baths and jumping off the kitchen table. I also went to a sordid little house in Pimlico that a girlfriend told me about, but I was too scared to ring the bell.'

'I'm sorry that I caused so much trouble.'

'I don't suppose I can really hold you responsible, Chris!' she said, and smiled at me. 'The night I told your father I was pregnant he asked me if I had done it because of his recent inheritance! He'd just been left all that money by his grandmother. He asked me if I had done it. Me! Where was he supposed to be while it was happening? I was a child, of course, and I was scared. I thought he might at least share the responsibility. And yes, I had been a virgin, and so, I expect, had he. One was, in those days. Or rather, we were – our sort of people. The gay young things were probably doing it all the time, but not us. Not in Kent. I wasn't in love with him, you understand, or anything like that. I don't think there was much "loving" in Kent. We were too respectable. Though, of course, we had no idea then what the Nicolsons were getting up to! We knew they were keen gardeners and that she had an independent spirit but we thought that was all part of the upper-class mystique and we rather admired it. Have you ever wondered where it happened? Your conception? No, I don't suppose you have for a minute . . .'

She wasn't waiting for any replies. I might just as well not have been present, although she kept darting me looks, so perhaps I was necessary, as a sounding board.

'It was all very Betjeman, really: "By roads unadopted",

that sort of thing. A Saturday afternoon spin in his new car, the first purchase from his recently acquired personal wealth, and fifty years of marriage were contracted. I suppose, now he's dead, I wouldn't be betraying a confidence if I were to tell you that he was hopelessly in love with the barmaid at The Oast House in Tonbridge at the time. A fantasy, of course. He was very young for his years. Do you know that he used to go back, every autumn, to the reunion weekend at Blandfords? I thought that so strange. Even after the war, when everything was getting back to normal again – off he would go, every autumn, singing the old school song and straining his muscles in the Old Boys match. I don't know why he actually chose me. We weren't even particularly good friends. I rather suspect that he was worried that he still hadn't done it and he was coming up to twenty-five. Losing one's virginity was a bit of an obsession in those days; like getting a degree, or having had mumps. Something better behind you. I remember why I let him, very clearly. I thought it would seem rude not to. Does that seem feasible? I promise you, it was the reason.'

'It's not doing much for my ego, all this, you know!' I said, rising and pouring myself another drink. Mother waved her empty glass at me. 'You're drinking them too fast, Mother. And that last one was huge.'

'Oh, don't be such an old maid. That's why we should live together, so that I can shock you into the land of the living. You're a terrible old stick-in-the-mud.'

I poured her a small one and handed it to her as I returned to my seat.

'It's a thimble measure,' she said, rising unsteadily and sloshing more gin into the glass. Then she turned and leaned against the table.

'Have you noticed my hair? Tinted! It is a step towards the full works. I didn't have it done all at once, because I couldn't face Angela's disapproval. Poor Angela. She never really had a chance, you know. Not where I was concerned. You see, no sooner were you born than off he went to fight for King and Country. It was heaven. I hadn't wanted to have you, but having got you, I absolutely adored you.'

'Thanks!' I said, raising my glass.

'Well, you were so beautiful and so quiet. When Angela arrived she did nothing but howl, morning, noon and night. Anyway, he went off to the war and got captured and all that . . . I watch those films set in prisoner-of-war camps, where they're all digging tunnels and longing to get out and back into the fight . . .' She shrugged and raised her eyebrows as though trying to clear her vision. 'He never did. Once he was captured, he stayed put and taught himself shorthand. So I had you all to myself. Until the war was over. You slept in my room, usually in my bed. You were my man. But then he came back. And soon after Angela was forced on me. And you couldn't stay in my room any more. God, I feel awful.'

I helped her upstairs to her room. I felt irresponsible. I shouldn't have let her drink so much. She said she could manage to undress herself, which was a relief, and I left her leaning against the basin in her bathroom.

I went down to the kitchen and fixed myself a chicken sandwich and a glass of wine.

Later I heard her calling my name. I hurried up to her room and found her lying face down on her bed in a dressing gown. She had been crying and her make-up had smudged round the eyes.

'Let me help you get into bed,' I said. 'Then I'll get you some water. You must drink plenty of water. Alcohol dehydrates you.'

I supported her as I pulled back the covers, but then she pushed away from me and went and sat on the dressing table stool and started to put cream on her face.

'God, I look awful, and I deserve it.' She slammed down

83

the cream jar and took tissues from a box. 'What d'you think of the streaks? I'll tell you. They make me look old. "Like an old peeled wall." God, God, God. I hate old age. You won't believe this, Chris – but I'm a young woman inside. Still waiting to start living. How pathetic! Still waiting – when the whole thing is practically over. And you . . .' she nodded at me through the mirror, 'you are exactly the same. Wasting your life. Why? Why, Chris? You never would tell me. I think you never will. But whatever happened, was it really that bad? So bad that you would throw away your entire life for it? We're two of a kind. And maybe you're right. Maybe we can't help each other. But we could try. I've wanted to talk to you for years. You wouldn't ever let me. I wanted to ask you if I could leave your father. I felt you were the only one who could give me the right. I wanted to be with you, like it had been at the beginning. I wanted . . .' She stopped and rested her head on her hand, then tilting it sideways she looked at me and began to cry quietly.

I couldn't help her. I felt embarrassed and trapped. I wanted to get away. There was too much emotion, an indecent amount. She had to be stopped. If not, things would be said that would be forever there between us. I felt angry and vengeful and now I wanted to hurt her. She was using my life for her despair and she was trespassing.

'Get into bed, Mother. You're drunk,' I said, and hurried from the room.

I thought of driving back to London, but I had had too much to drink as well. So, instead, I poured myself a large glass of brandy and took it up to my room. But I didn't want it after the first sip, nor could I bear the smell of it in the room. I took it to the lavatory and poured it away. As I was doing it I remembered Stephen at some time saying that 'toilet' was a suburban euphemism.

This sudden memory of him caught me unawares as I was lifting the lavatory seat and, to my utter amazement, it made

84

me cry. I don't cry. I have no tears left to shed. I stifled back the rush of feelings and tried to swallow them, as if they were bitter bile.

I tiptoed back along the landing, passing Mother's bedroom door. The light was shining under the crack at the bottom. But I didn't go in. I went back into my bedroom and opened the window. I needed air in my lungs and on my face.

I'm a good editor, I thought. I handled today's rejection with sensitivity, but I pushed it through. I was tough. No point flannelling people – giving them false hopes. I am good at my job. I have a flat that is worth a fortune and for which I long ago gave a pittance. I have several loyal and loving friends; people who care more about me than I do about them, really. I am intelligent. I am still good-looking. I don't look anywhere near my age.

I wish Stephen were here.

People rely on me. I am good with their problems. I listen. I care what happens to them. I want only the best for them. I do not make waves. I am civilised and cultured and enjoy the best of the arts.

I wish I knew where he was.

I like my own company. I don't need relationships as some people seem to. I am not afraid of being alone. I like travelling alone. I am content on my own. I need to be on my own. I am reclusive.

I am not sixteen any more.

# Then

The library at Blandfords is situated on the first floor of the main school building and is one of the few rooms to have survived in its intended form from the original house. It is a long, tall room, like a shoe box on its side. There are fine mahogany bookcases from floor to ceiling and there is a narrow wooden gallery running along the upper shelves, approached by a spiral staircase. One wall is entirely taken up with sash windows. The room is in the centre of the main façade and the view is down the main drive to the ornate iron gates. On either side of the drive, chestnuts droop almost to the well-cut lawns, and beyond these trees, iron railings separate the lawns from a pair of meadows in which a small and judiciously culled herd of deer graze. This gracious view is no doubt intended to reassure the families of the five hundred or so young men who at any one time pass their formative years at the school. Although for at least half the number a nice suburban semi would probably make them feel more at home.

The entrance to the library is through a door in the centre of the back wall where a short tunnel pierces the bookcases. To the right of the door is a flat-topped desk, with card index files and rubber stamps. The only other furniture is a circular library table, which takes up the centre of the room, and a number of sets of library steps to admit easy access to the lower shelves.

For the most part the contents of the library comprise

sets of huge tomes, donated by Old Blandfordians and destined never to be opened by any present members of the school. The most popular shelves are devoted to a small number of newer books which are replenished at the beginning of the autumn term with the pick of the year's publications. The library prefect, upon taking up his task, submits a list of suggestions to the Masters' Common Room. The list is vetoed by all the teaching staff and the final selection is purchased by letter from Foyles in Charing Cross Road and dispatched by special delivery.

The most popular book while I have been at Blandfords is *The Cruel Sea* by Nicholas Montserrat. Not, I think, for its literary merits but because of the passage where the man returns to find his wife in a dressing gown, having just left her lover on their bed of lust. Looking at the telltale stain on her gown he observes that she 'seems to have spilt the milk'. The Blandfords copy of *The Cruel Sea* falls open automatically at this scene and the cleanliness of the previous pages suggest that no preamble is required to add to its enjoyment. The phrase, 'spilling the milk', would appear to excite the younger school to a frenzy and certainly results in periodic bouts of further, personal, staining. One of my greatest problems for quite some time has been the passing off of these very stains that Mr Montserrat so acurately describes. 'Splashes of toothpaste' is a good stand-by; though how toothpaste always lands on pyjama trousers would not, I think, stand up to intensive laboratory testing.

The library is open for half an hour each afternoon, Monday to Friday, immediately after final school, and on alternate Sunday afternoons between two thirty and four. The library prefect can call upon any fifth-former to do library duty. This lasts for a week and is greatly resented, because it interferes with free time, a rare commodity at Blandfords. Not that it's very demanding. The library is seldom used except by sixth-formers requiring reference books and frustrated fourth-formers who have only just been alerted to the joys of *The Cruel Sea*.

Walker is the library prefect this term and he has put me down for a week's duty, including a Sunday afternoon. We haven't started rehearsing on Sundays yet and I had planned to spend the afternoon walking up the coast towards Dunwich with Nigel Duff. Which isn't exactly thrilling, but at least it gets you out of the school grounds for a while and gives you a sense of freedom. Nigel is a keen ornithologist and carries binoculars. He gets fearfully excited at the sight of a grebe or a lapwing and tries to enthuse me. But all birds look the same to me, except that some are big and others are small.

It is a dank, dreary November afternoon and I don't really mind not being out in the cold air. I thought that perhaps Walker had put me on library duty in order that he could see me. But I've spent each afternoon here without him coming anywhere near the place and I've rather given up hoping. His behaviour is erratic to say the least. Since our encounter in the showers we have hardly seen each other apart from during rehearsals for the play. At these times he is civil but he doesn't make any attempt to communicate with me by so much as a look, let alone a chance encounter. Which would be perfectly possible. I have arrived early for rehearsal each evening in the hope that he might be there. And I always leave last, half expecting to find him waiting for me somewhere along the winding path that leads through the nighttime grounds from Hall to Ely. Never once has this come about. He usually strolls back with Heslop and I hear them laughing and talking somewhere ahead of me in the darkness.

A couple of sixth-formers come in to borrow copies of the complete works of Christopher Marlowe. *Tamburlaine* is one of the set books this year, but they all want to read *Edward II* and there is only one copy left. I stamp it and they go off, leafing through the pages as though it were *The Cruel Sea*. A man from St Edmond comes in to return *Ben Hur*, which he says is so dull that it should be banned. And, earlier, soon after I opened, a first-year brat came in to see if we had any Zane Grey. Zane Grey? He said he'd once read *The Roaring UP Trail* and he thought it was the best thing he'd seen in years. I told him to try Nevil Shute instead – not that they're remotely similar. Apart from that it has been a quiet afternoon. I'm afraid Blandfords won't go down in the annals as a school with any great literary reputation, however hard TG tries with the school play. We're not particularly best at anything – but we certainly veer more towards physical pursuits than intellectual ones. Reading isn't considered manly. Rugger is. That being the case, I dread to think what they'll make of *A Doll's House* at the end of term. Apparently quite a few of the staff are already questioning the wisdom of the choice. Mr Tollmun-Jones, housemaster of Lincoln, and my maths master, told me that anything by Ian Hay would have been far more suitable. But then, Mr Tollmun-Jones would despise anything I am associated with, because he can't stand me. I can't blame him; I'd loathe me if I had to try teaching me algebra – but I would start by telling me what the point of it is. He never has and I'm not very enthusiastic about pointless subjects.

I am sitting at the desk reading *Orlando*, by Virginia Woolf, which I have to admit I find impossible, when Judd, the senior prefect from Lincoln, comes in. Judd is also deputy head boy and I like him because he plays the violin and is going to the Royal Academy of Music. It's a relief to have an artist in a position of power, here where science and games usually gets one to the top of the tree. He is returning three books. I get their tickets from the index and cross to the shelves, to replace them. Judd meanwhile goes up the spiral stairs to the upper level, to where the specialist subjects, including a music section, are stored.

I have my back to the door when I hear it open. I turn and see Walker standing in the doorway. He looks round and I can tell that he thinks the room is empty apart from us. He closes the door and I hear the key turn. Then he crosses quickly towards me.

Desperately, I call out to Judd:

'Can I help you, Judd? Is there a particular book you're looking for?'

'What?' he says, leaning down over the gallery balustrade. 'Oh, no thanks. I was just looking something up.'

As he speaks, Walker hurries back to the door and I hear the lock snap back. Then he saunters over to the shelves and stares at the lines of books.

Judd comes down the steps.

'You're library prefect, aren't you, Walker?'

'Yes,' he replies easily.

'The books up on the music shelves are in a hopeless muddle. There doesn't seem to be any system of cataloguing. Are they meant to be in categories or simply alphabetical order? What's your name?'

This last question is fired at me.

'Metcalfe, sir,' I reply.

'Well, instead of sitting reading, you could do some tidying up.'

'Yes, sir,' I say.

'I'm taking *The Mozart Letters* again,' and, leaning over the librarian's desk, he picks up the rubber stamp, breathes on it, and stamps the front page. Then he walks out of the room, closing the door behind him.

'Bloody hell!' Walker says, when we are alone. 'I didn't see him.'

'I'd better do those shelves,' I say nervously, moving towards the spiral stairs. As I pass him, he reaches out and catches my arm, gripping it so that it hurts.

'I have to speak to you,' he says.

I look at him, waiting. He is wearing the school uniform of grey flannels and a grey V-necked sweater. But, instead of the striped school tie, he wears the cricket XI cravat, tucked into an open-necked shirt. His black hair is longer than I am allowed to have mine. He wears it with a side parting and it falls forward over one eye like a crow's wing. As he looks at me he runs a hand nervously through this lock of hair, pushing it back away from his brow. He has dark blue eyes, and very black eyebrows, and his clear, unlined face has a dark shadow of stubble on the top lip and round the beard line.

He is still holding on to my arm and his nails are digging into the flesh just below the elbow.

'You're hurting,' I say.

He lets go at once. He is extremely agitated. He pushes the hair back with his hand again and walks over to the window so that he has his back to me.

'It's bloody impossible, this place,' he says, almost as though he's speaking to himself. Then he turns and looks at me. 'There's nowhere to go. For us, I mean. I've tried to think of somewhere, but I can't. Not during the day.'

'It's all right. Don't worry,' I tell him. I feel he's making apologies to me, as though he thinks he's letting me down.

'I can't bear the rehearsals. Being near to you and yet surrounded by other people.'

'I thought . . .' I start to say shyly, nervous about making a suggestion.

'What?' he asks.

'Sometimes we could walk back together. After rehearsal. I hang back, thinking maybe you'll meet me . . .'

'Do you?' He seems surprised.

'Every night. And I always get to rehearsal early,' I continue, growing bolder, 'in case I get to see you.' He is staring at me from across the room. He makes me feel embarrassed and I lose courage. 'But that's not much

91

use, really, because you can never be sure when stage management will turn up.'

He stares at me thoughtfully for a moment longer, after I finish speaking, and then he crosses past me towards the door. I think he's going and part of me is relieved because his presence makes me so tense that I think I may snap. But he doesn't leave. Instead he turns the key once more in the lock and then he leans with his face against the wooden door and I see that his body is trembling.

'There's nowhere for us to go,' I hear him say in a muffled voice.

'But we can't here,' I say, panic beginning to shake my voice. 'It isn't safe here. Anyone could come in. Please. Please, Walker. You must go.'

He looks at me over his shoulder, a frown on his face.

'I don't understand you,' he says. 'One minute you seem to want me and the next you're telling me to go.'

'I do. I do want you. Only I don't want to get caught,' I tell him. I'm gasping for breath now. I don't know why. The tension, I expect. Or maybe it's because he's so near to me and I want to touch him and I daren't.

He turns, still leaning against the door, and opens out his arms towards me. I cross to him and he puts them round me, holding me to him, burying his face in my hair. I can feel his heart beating and his body trembling. He holds me close, with one hand supporting my head. It's different to the day in the study. It's more painful. Even though nothing is happening, it's more desperate. In the study, it was just like tossing off. But this is like . . . like the edge of hell. It's as though I want to become part of him, to merge with him and yet at the same time I know that that can never be possible. And I think that that's how he feels as well.

Then the doorknob beside us suddenly moves and a moment later there is a thump on the wood that sends us darting across the room, breathless and guilty. The panic that has been in me since he came into the library erupts and makes me blind. I bang into a set of library steps, making them scrape along the floor.

The knocking on the door is repeated, and a voice is heard calling:

'Hello? What's going on in there? Why is this door locked?'

Walker looks at me and puts a finger to his lips. Then he straightens his sweater and crosses to the door, running a hand through his hair.

As he unlocks the door, I start moving books frantically along one of the shelves.

'The door is locked because the library is closed,' I hear him say. And then a familiar voice rejoins:

'Well, it shouldn't be, old son. It isn't quite four yet.'

Looking over my shoulder, I see Dixon enter the room. He sees me at once.

'Oh, dear!' he says. 'If it isn't little Nora! What are you two up to?'

'Judd was complaining about the order of the books,' Walker says, lounging back against the side of the desk.

'You been in a fight, Nora? Your hair's all tousled. Get it combed. Better still, get it cut.'

'Did you want a book, Dixon? It is on four and I don't want to hang about,' Walker says.

'You go off if you want to, old son. I'll keep Nora company,' and he grins at Walker, as though he's sharing some secret with him. I look away and continue to check the shelves.

'Really, Dixon! What have you in mind? It sounds quite sinister.' Walker's voice is amused, as though the two of them are sharing some joke. 'I think I'd better stay to protect Metcalfe's honour!' he says, and strolls over to the windows, looking out.

I can feel a blush creeping up my neck, on to my face.

Dixon hesitates, his hands in his pockets.

'No, I don't want a book,' he says. 'I've read all the good ones.'

'I wonder why you came, then?' Walker asks, stretching and yawning as he speaks. 'God, I'm stiff from yesterday's squash.'

'I was just passing,' Dixon says with another grin. 'Thought I'd see how Nora was getting on. Haircut by Tuesday, Nora. Short back and sides. Report to me after evening prayers, so that I can check it. What d'you say?'

'Yes sir,' I answer.

He walks out, glancing at his watch as he does so.

'It's only just on four now, you know, old son. No wonder the library doesn't pay, if it's locked before time.'

Walker follows him to the door, saying:

'It's a long way to come just to check on a fifth-former, Dixon. Very odd behaviour.'

And I hear Dixon call, as he walks away along the corridor:

'I have a special interest in Nora, old son. I told you. Like to keep her up to scratch!'

Walker closes the door. I lean against the shelves. I feel sick.

'What did he mean?' I ask, not looking at him. 'What were you two saying? You seemed to be sharing . . . a joke about me. What was it?'

'Don't pay any attention to Dixon,' Walker says, quietly, remaining by the door.

Suddenly an awful thought occurs and I turn slowly to look at him.

'D'you talk about me? Is that it? Have you . . . told Dixon about us?' The sickness rises in my throat.

'No, of course I haven't,' he replies. But he is too quick, too glib.

I stare at him in disbelief.

'You have. How could you? You have. You've told Dixon.'

I'm fighting back tears now. I want him to go. I don't ever want to be with him again. If he's told Dixon – then they'll all know. All talking together in the Senior Common Room. All laughing together. About me.

'Metcalfe, listen to me,' I hear him say in a low, tense voice.

'No,' I spit, hot tears stinging my eyes, 'I won't listen to you. I don't want to hear you. Just go away. Go away . . .'

He crosses the room swiftly and grabs my arm again, turning me. With his other hand he holds my chin, forcing me to look at him.

'Of course I haven't talked about us.' He sounds intensely angry. 'What d'you think I am? How could you believe that? You don't understand anything.' And he stresses the final word as though there is a whole world beyond my knowledge.

But I am still angry and hurt and I won't let it go.

'What was it about then? You were joking about me. I'm not a fool, Walker . . .'

'Listen to me,' he says again, urgently. And, when I try to look away, he pulls at my chin, forcing my head round again.

'Dixon fancies you. He's always talking about you. He makes jokes about it. He says every prefect should be allowed to have a slave, like the Greeks and the Romans had.'

'How revolting,' I start to say. 'What does he think I am . . .?'

'Shut up and listen. I have to let him say those things. If I were to protest too much, he – or one of the others – might start to suspect. But it's meaningless. He wouldn't know where to begin with you. That's why he punishes you. He hates you, because he fancies you.'

'But what can I do?' I say, sudden fear gripping me.

'Just keep out of his way.'

'How? If he's got it in for me? How can I keep out of his way? He's a prefect. I have to do whatever he tells me. My hair isn't longer than anyone else's. Reading after lights out doesn't usually get six strokes. How can I keep out of his way?'

Walker puts his arms round me, holding me.

'I'll stop him. I promise you. I'll stop him. He won't hurt you.'

His hands slide down my body. But it isn't safe here. We've already nearly been caught twice.

'No, Walker,' I say, fighting free of his embrace and pushing back away from him, my fists up as though I want to hit him. 'Leave me. Leave me. It isn't safe here. Leave me alone. I don't want all this complication. Just . . . get someone else to . . . to play with . . . or whatever it is you want. Only, please . . .' and I'm sobbing now. The fear and the tension have overwhelmed me. I only want to be safe and free and away. '. . . please,' I implore him, 'oh please, Walker. Leave me alone.'

He grabs at my fists. I try to lash out at him, but his strength is far greater than mine. He forces my arms apart, gripping my wrists and preventing me from moving them. We are standing face to face, arms outstretched, like two crucifixions, and I see a look of such utter anguish on his face that I become more afraid for him than I am for myself.

'You don't want that,' he says. 'You don't want it to stop. Please say you don't.'

'I'm frightened, Walker,' I cry out in a hoarse whisper.

'I'll look after you, I promise you. But I can't let it end. I can't.'

'It isn't safe,' I wail. 'It only needs someone to come through that door and discover us and we're finished. Expulsion. I don't know what'll happen to you. But I know I'll never survive it. Facing my parents. Going to work in the business. Ruining my life. Our lives . . .'

'I know,' he says, and his voice sounds desperately sad. 'I know. Not here. I'll find somewhere else. You're quite right.' He crosses to the door. But as he's going out, he looks back at me.

'I love you, Kit,' he says. His voice is gentle and he uses the unfamiliar name as though it has always been mine. 'D'you understand? I am in love with you. I'm sorry. I can't help it. I've tried to. I can't stop it.' He vaguely smiles; a sad, sorry smile. 'I love you, Kit.' He says the words again, slowly and quietly and with absolute conviction. Then, with a nod of the head, as though in final affirmation, he goes out of the room and I am alone here.

# *Now*

I drove as far as the lay-by and then pulled off the road. I switched off the engine and the lights and sat in the dark. I was still trembling. I knew I'd behaved badly.

I'll phone when I get home, I thought. With any luck Angela and Dick will have gone by then. Or will they stay to comfort her and have a good gossip, all together, about how impossible I am and how cruel? Well, they'd be right. If I was with them, I'd join in.

I wished I smoked. I needed something to relieve the tension. I was gripping the steering wheel, staring out into the dark, scarcely aware of the beams of the oncoming traffic. I'd have to wait for a bit. I wasn't in control of myself. I would be a danger on the motorway.

The Prick-mobile had been parked in the drive when I arrived. That had started me off on the wrong foot. I hadn't realised that Angela was going to be there. Mother had simply said did I think I could come down for dinner, as there were things she wanted to discuss with me. She had phoned at the office, which always throws me. I'm not very good at thinking about two things at the same time and I was deeply engrossed in the plight of the South American rainforest tribes. Sam Terson has written a novel about them which has to be the best thing he's done and is certainly the best thing I've read in years. There are moments, in publishing, when you know you are on to something fantastic. They don't happen very often and when they do, you don't want your mother interrupting. Poor woman! It wasn't her fault that she chose such an inopportune moment. I phoned her back later and explained and she was full of apologies and we ended friends. It would have been churlish after all that to refuse her invitation, although Sevenoaks and back for midweek dinner isn't exactly my idea of fun.

But I hadn't been prepared for Angela and as I walked towards the front door I was thinking that Mother should have warned me. But then, if she had, I would probably have made some excuse not to come at all and Mother almost certainly knew that. Angela and I had never been the best of friends even when we were little. When I was eight, so the story goes, and she was an infant in her pram, I tried to push her into the sea at Margate. The story continues that I was 'taking her for a walk and I thought she'd like to be near the water, she being too young to paddle . . .' Not a bit of it. If a friend of Mother's hadn't intervened, I was heading straight on out until the waves consumed her. In my defence, members of the jury, I was having a godawful time at prep school by then, and I held her entirely responsible for my having been sent there. My action was therefore in the cause of self-preservation and her death would have been entirely justified. Had we not just spent seven years killing Germans in much the same spirit?

My dismay was consummated by hearing the Prick's voice droning away in the drawing room as I let myself in through the front door. I would, I think, have turned straight round, let myself out again and driven back to London had Mother not appeared in the hall and waylaid me.

'Here he is,' she called out in that voice that suggests that one is hours late and she gave me a meaningful look which conveyed that Dick was here. Mother and I share a kindred feeling about the son-in-law, best summed up as 'How on earth could Angela have ever done such a stupid thing?'

To which the only possible answer can be: 'Angela was born stupid.'

Dick was sitting in Father's armchair. Angela was on the sofa. They both had glasses at their elbows which could have been huge gins.

'We're on Perrier,' were the first words my sister said as I entered the room.

'How lovely,' I told her. 'I'm on a huge gin and tonic,' and I crossed over to the drinks table to pour myself one.

'You wouldn't be if you saw what we see,' Angela said behind me. 'I think the Government will have to do something about it.'

'About what?' I asked, genuinely puzzled.

'Drinking. They'll have to ban all advertising. And off-licences should only be open during pub hours. I mean, it is absolutely ridiculous preventing people from drinking in pubs when they can go straight into an off-licence and buy a whole bottle of the stuff at less cost. Absolute Alice in Wonderland.'

'Cheers,' I said and raised my glass.

Angela blinked and said nothing. The Prick changed the subject:

'Which way did you come, Chris?'

'The way I always do, Dick. A3, M25.' There's something cosy about familiar dialogue, like seeing *Gone With the Wind* again, or a Garbo movie; not too taxing and if you're a tiny bit bored, there's always some well-remembered purple moment up ahead to keep your sense of expectation. Oh, *Great Expectations* is another one. Martita Hunt's 'You can break his heart' is worth waiting a lifetime to hear again. I was just about to launch into the possible advantages of the Wandsworth-Croydon-Bromley route, when Mother, who has heard it all so many times she could be the projectionist, announced that maybe we should eat.

My family invented small talk. We have been doing it

all our lives. That is why the recent floods of emotion have been so unnerving. At dinner we covered the comparable desirability of supermarkets versus the local shop. 'Absolutely killing Canterbury stone dead. I won't go into a supermarket. The high streets of England are dying on their feet. Of course I know Safeway is very good and everybody raves about Sainsbury's but you don't get personal service. We went once, didn't we, Dick? – spent a fortune buying a lot of stuff that we didn't want . . .' 'Of course,' Dick chimed in, 'they're trained to lay out the shelves in a certain way. Brainwashing the public; forcing them to buy . . .' 'Maybe the Government ought to ban that sort of thing,' I suggested, just as my chin was about to fall into the chicken chasseur.

Then we had 'The Boys':

'Roger's going to have to pull his socks up. Got a brain. Won't use it . . . Rupert hates games, but I said to him: All boys play games, it gives you the right instincts . . . Ralph came out in these great big lumps and I thought, Oh, goody, mumps. Far better to get it over, particularly for a boy, and of course when Roger had them, Rupert got them and Ralph missed them.' 'And then, if you remember, darling, I got them.' 'Oh, crikey, yes. You were in an awful mess! But we won't go into that now.' 'I had them,' I offer, innocently. 'You probably don't remember? One of my balls got so big, I had to put oil on the scrotum to keep it from splitting.' 'Oh, for heaven's sake, Chris. We're eating . . .'

Then they got on to:

'No, I'm not saying the nurses don't have a case. But where is the money to come from?' 'Of course, when the Health Service was first conceived, no one envisaged how it would grow . . .' 'Like Topsy . . . I rather wish we were back to the old days. Richard would have made a wonderful family doctor . . .' 'That's what I am, darling.' 'No, but you know what I mean – like the supermarkets, you can't give personal service . . .' 'Well, I do try. And there are the private patients . . .' 'Well, I think they finance the whole shooting bag. I mean, of course it's right for poor people to get things for nothing, I'm not saying that, but it's ridiculous the way things are. Half Richard's patients are in the upper income bracket. My God, you should see the cars outside the surgery and yet in they come, expecting free pills and what have you . . .'

By the time we got to coffee in the drawing room their voices had fused into a cacophony of sound closely resembling those atonal symphonies that get played on Radio Three in the middle of the morning, when the DG thinks no one will be listening.

Actually, it didn't matter. It would have been far better if they'd just been allowed to rattle on until it was ten thirty and we could have all said good night and what a lovely meal and see you soon. But that's not why we were there. With coffee came the just deserts.

Mother, who had remained silent during the meal, brought the meeting to order by announcing that:

'The reason why I wanted you all to come tonight is that I have definitely decided to sell this house.'

'Well, I wouldn't do it now,' Dick said at once, practical to the last. 'Hopeless time for selling property. You wait till the spring. A sunny day will put another ten thou on to the value.'

'Obviously I am not going to rush out at once. But I thought that, as you will both one day inherit your father's estate and as I feel very much that I am only a shareholder, I should inform you of what I intend to do with one of the principal assets.'

'I see no problem there,' Dick waded in fearlessly. 'You should get a good price . . .' He seemed totally oblivious to his silent wife. 'Put it in the hands of one of the big companies; place like this deserves nationwide coverage . . .'

'Just a moment, Richard,' the wife said, sweetly.

102

'Sorry, darling?'

'We're going too fast.'

'We mustn't do that,' Mother said, warmly. 'As I say, that's why I asked you all to come. We must deal with this as a family, all together. I know, Angela, how much you love this place . . .'

'I was born here. It's always been home.'

'Yes, I know, darling.'

'I'd even hoped that, one day, Richard and I might live here. The boys so love it.'

'Well, if you wanted to buy it . . .' Mother said, seeming to be reasonable.

'Good heavens! I'm a doctor, not a tycoon. This place will fetch a fortune,' Dick declared, then added, with Prick-like precision, 'Angel meant after your death.'

An awkward silence followed while we all contemplated Angela's apparent disappointment at our mother's robust health.

'I see,' Mother said. 'Well, of course, that might have been possible. But your father's will leaves everything in trust to me, for my lifetime, and then it has to be divided equally between Angela and Chris.'

Angela glanced at Dick.

'I'm not sure how it would work, you keeping the house. You'd probably have to buy it back from the estate at the market value . . .' Mother continued, fine-tuning the situation that was evolving.

'Oh, please don't talk like that,' Angela admonished. 'I can't bear it. Daddy has only just died. I think it's far too soon to make plans. It's a well-known fact that after bereavement people have to move with extreme caution, otherwise they make the most ghastly mistakes. Well, I think what you're suggesting would be just that . . . No, Mother, let me finish,' as if anyone, or thing, could possibly stop her. 'This is your home. This is where you belong. All your friends are round here. We are just down the road and Chris . . .' She hesitated.

'I'm just up the road,' I said; I thought helpfully, but apparently not.

'Indeed you are, though we are a little disappointed to see how infrequently you have bothered to get into the car and drive down here. But that's another matter. Now, I quite understand, Mother, that at the moment you're lonely – good heavens, you've never lived on your own before. But you mustn't throw the baby out with the bath water . . .'

Once Angela gets going my head begins to spin and only alcohol will calm it. I rose to pour myself a brandy and immediately spurred her on to even greater heights of oratory:

'Give it a few months and you'll be redecorating, you'll see. And there's the garden to take in hand. You could even afford to have someone in to landscape it for you. We have friends who got a man in; now they've got a ha-ha and I don't know what else . . .'

'Do be quiet for a moment, darling,' Mother said, gently, patting Angela's arm. 'I can't hear myself think.'

Angela took her hand and held it. I realised then that she was probably full of genuine concern. But it didn't make me like her any the more.

'You must see that I'm talking sense, Mother.'

'I think you're talking your sense, darling,' Mother's tone was crisper, 'but not mine. You see, I don't like this house. I never have. We stayed here because your father liked it. And, as for the friends, as I've already told Chris . . .'

Angela looked at me accusingly.

'You mean, you two have already discussed this?' she said, her voice trembling.

'. . . As I've already told Chris,' Mother continued, over-riding this interruption, 'I wouldn't care if I never set eyes on any of my so-called friends again.'

'But that's an awful thing to say,' Angela exclaimed. 'They're good people. Betty Johnson and Marie St Just and . . . that nice little woman who lives in Beehive Cottage. Where would you have been without their support while Father was ill?'

'Darling, you're making me feel like a naughty child. Do, please, stop. I acknowledge willingly my debt to them all – but that doesn't mean that I want to end my days at their coffee mornings and their bridge parties and organising their fêtes.'

'All right then, what do you want?'

Mother looked at her only daughter and youngest child, trying, perhaps, to see the little girl who once must have inhabited the clear, unblemished skin. But it was bound to be a vain search. I suspect Angela became middle-aged with her first period and only survived the earlier years by playing 'Mothers and Fathers' in preparation for the life to come. Faced with the present domestic crisis she squared her shoulders and went to work. She knew exactly how to cope. There was, in her creed, a place for everything, including an aged parent, and an answer for every enigma known to man. Now, she simply waited, grasping Mother's hand, for the poor woman to explain what she wanted to get out of the rest of her life, rather like an organised housewife makes a shopping list.

When Mother failed to reply, Angela patted her hand and smiled.

'Don't sell the house,' she said, 'but go away for a while. Why not? Mrs Blake will keep an eye on things and Mills can keep the grounds tidy. You need a break. You looked after Father single-handed. It's only natural that you should feel depressed here. Good heavens, Richard and I marvel at the way you've coped. Spoil yourself. Have a holiday.' And, having, in her mind, sorted everything out very satisfactorily, she poured herself another cup of coffee from the jug on the table in front of her.

Mother frowned and glanced at me, as if for some support. But it was all way beyond me. I'd practically given up listening.

'A holiday?' she asked.

'Why not?' Angela beamed at her, as though she were Lady Bountiful dispensing favours.

'A cruise? Or a Saga tour?' Mother said the words with ominous clarity.

'Well, honestly, darling, I can't see you getting on with people on a Saga tour, they'd all be OAPs – but a cruise might be fun. The Caribbean, say. Why not? I'd go like a shot if I had the chance.'

'Then you go, darling. But please don't ask me to come along. I couldn't bear it. And besides, what would I do after? I can't go round and round the world like a Maugham lady! I'd have to come back sooner or later. And to what? The same old life? But that is precisely what I don't want. I want to start again. A new life. A new beginning . . .'

Angela glanced again at Dick, who had been mercifully silent, but who had the look of a man who knew the ultimate answer and would deliver same when the right moment arrived.

'How do you see this "new beginning" taking shape, then? I mean, I was only trying to help,' Angela said, cross because she'd been crossed.

'I want to go and live in London,' Mother replied.

'London?' Angela howled as though she'd just heard that her mother was going to Transylvania to live with a vampire lover.

'Well, it isn't so extraordinary, is it? That's where I had just started to live when I married your father.'

'You were eighteen then!' Angela chided. 'It was a different city. Have you any idea what London is like now? You cannot

106

travel with safety on the tube in the middle of the day,' she said, 'the middle of the day' in italics.

'I'll go by bus, then,' Mother answered.

'And besides, London is a lonely place. What would you do all the time?'

'I don't know, Angela.' At this moment Mother's temper was in the balance. She could either continue to keep it, or she could lose it. I think Angela sensed this.

'I mean, Chris, what do you say? You live there? Can you see Mother surviving there?'

'Why not?' the Prick cut in, deciding his moment had come. 'Mother can go and stay with Chris. Perfect. She can see how it suits her. A sort of trial run. We don't need to sell the house, and Chris and she can do the town together.'

'Well, I suppose that is an answer,' Angela said, appearing to mull the whole thing over. 'Yes, why not? That could suit rather well. What do you think of the idea, Mother?'

There was a fraction of a pause. Nobody was looking at me. I felt invisible. Mother smiled and the whole issue seemed to teeter on the brink of being a *fait accompli*.

'Well?' the Prick asked, beaming with goodwill.

'Well, yes, I think it's a perfectly lovely idea,' Mother said. 'But don't you think we ought to ask Chris what he thinks?'

The other two looked at me, apparently surprised at the suggestion.

'Good gracious, he's got a huge flat,' Angela said. 'How many bedrooms, Chris?'

'Three,' I replied.

'Three bedrooms – for a bachelor. Absurd! Don't you think it's a good idea? Then Mummy can have a look round, go to a few theatres. I'll come up one day, darling, and we can do the shops. I haven't for simply ages. I'd really like that. When did we last have a day in London, Richard? Oh, that time Rupert got lost in Hamleys. It was awful. He screamed the place down.'

'No, I don't think it would be a good idea,' I said, so quietly that at first I wasn't sure any of them heard me. 'In fact, I don't think it would work at all.'

'Why not?' Angela asked, clearly astounded by my statement.

'Because I live alone, Angela. That's what I have chosen to do. What you're suggesting is tantamount to me telling you to leave Dick and marry someone else instead. You have your life. I have mine. Sorry, Mother. I love you dearly, and by all means come for a couple of nights, if you'd like to – so long as you give me some warning. But as far as sharing the flat is concerned, then I'm very sorry the answer has to be no.'

Hell hath no fury like Angela scorned. I've always known that fact. It has stopped me in my tracks many times over the years. But any past reaction pales in comparison to what now took place.

'Have you quite finished?' she asked, with ominous precision. 'Because if you have, I'd like to say something now.'

'You'd like to say something, Angela?' I laughed. 'You haven't paused to draw breath since the moment I walked in here.'

'I think you are proving once again that you are the most selfish person I have ever met, Chris. We never ask you to do anything, because we know what the answer will be. But at least I thought that you might now, with Father only just in his grave and Mother desperate. But oh no. You go your own way, as ever. Whatever that way may be. What, I wonder, is so special about your little life that you aren't prepared to give up just a bit of it for the woman who brought you into the world, who cared for you and loved you and fought for you . . . Please God none of my boys turn out like you, that's all I can say.'

'Now, Angela, stop,' Mother said, rising and walking towards the fire. 'We're all getting overexcited.'

'My God, Mother! I can remember what he did to you and

Daddy when he was leaving school. I wasn't blind, you know. All we were asking – no, giving – him was the opportunity now, after all these years, to make amends. But oh no. Not Christopher, good heavens, no. He has his little bachelor existence that mustn't be disturbed. What, I wonder, does he get up to that is so special that even his own mother can't share a little of his life with him?'

'Would you really like to know, Angela?' I asked, rising also and crossing to pour myself another glass of brandy. 'All the details? Oh, no. I'd better not have another of these. I'm going to be driving, aren't I?'

'Huh!' the sister snorted. 'You're a wreck, Chris. Look at you.'

'I thought I'd kept myself in rather good trim,' I rejoined, turning to look at her.

'Oh, yes. You pamper yourself all right. You don't look your age, because you're not your age.'

'True,' I said, nodding vigorously and, as if to bear out her observation, I walked over to her and emptied the full glass of brandy over her head.

Angela screamed. Dick the Prick raced to her side, a clean handkerchief appearing as if by magic in his hand, and Mother, who had reached the fireplace and was in the act of switching on another bar of the electric fire, turned in horror.

'I'm going home now,' I said, and walked out of the room.

But I couldn't get far without pulling into the lay-by and sitting, trembling in the dark until the windows were all steamed up and the cold night air penetrated to the bones.

Of course it was worse for Mother. We had sat there portioning her off like goods in one of Angela's high street shops. How humiliating for her. I would telephone her as soon as I got in. And, come to think of it, I hadn't behaved nearly as badly as Angela. She was the one who should be sending round short notes of apology. She wouldn't, of course. Angela didn't believe in showing any signs of weakness; and to apologise was to be weak.

I became briefly angry again, but it didn't last and by the time I arrived back in Notting Hill Gate a gloom had descended. I parked nearly opposite the house and went in and up the stairs to the flat. Once inside my own front door, I paced from room to room, unable to settle to anything. It was nearly midnight. But I knew that I wouldn't sleep. I stood staring out of the sitting room window into the lamplit street. The railing of the private gardens opposite was still waiting to be repaired, where the tree had smashed into it in the October gales. The residents' association had put up temporary barbed wire to stop, they claimed, winos and drug addicts from using the shrubberies as a shelter. But there were no signs of either species prowling the streets, nor had there ever been in the Crescent, so far as I could recall. There was, at one time, a tart called Lil, who used to offer 'a cup of tea and afters'. But the residents' association were rather fond of her and thought she added character to the place; and, besides, the 'afters' took place in her basement flat and not where she could frighten the horses. But Lil had gone, perhaps to some great knocking shop in the sky, and yuppies had moved in who sank quantities of wine and snorted fashionable coke and had put up property prices in a most reassuring way.

The windows, I noticed, were dirty and one of the curtains was still burnt where Catherine had brushed it with a cigarette during an expansive moment. In fact, the whole place had a dreariness that I only noticed when on a down. Angela had referred to my 'bachelor existence'. Is that what it was? How strange. It was never meant to be. But then, I wonder, do any of us get the life that was meant to be? Does it ever turn out how we thought it would or think it should?

The phone started to ring. I crossed reluctantly towards

it. It was a depressing fact that there was no one who could possibly phone at past midnight who I would actually want to speak to at that hour. It was the hour for lovers. Not for messages or for news, but for saying nothing and everything to the one person with whom you wished you were sharing the night. Or is that just the romantic dream of a person who is out of love?

In fact it was Mother, whom I should have phoned. She was:

'Just ringing to see that you got home safely. No, darling, better not talk about it now. Apart from saying that it was ghastly. Well, Angela . . . got a bit out of hand. She means well. No, darling, don't say anything. I'm all right. Truly I am, Chris. Let's just pretend that none of it happened. Well, I'll go on for a bit longer. Richard is right, this isn't a good time to think about selling houses . . .'

She did all the talking and mercifully it didn't last long. She's a nice woman and, of course, I know how much she loves me and wants the best for me, but I was in one of those moods where I couldn't listen to any more words, or cope with any more sentiments. Eventually she must have noticed my silence, or been unable to ignore it any longer.

'Are you still there?' she asked.

'Yes. Yes, I'm here,' I replied. 'Sorry, I've sort of run out of words.'

'Are you lonely, Christopher?' the disembodied voice asked in my ear.

'I've always been lonely, Mother,' I replied.

'Always?' she asked, appalled.

'Almost always,' and, unable to say any more, I'm ashamed to admit that I hung up on her.

It is a strange fact that the voicing of a deep emotion can sometimes reveal it as if for the first time. I lived that night with a new awareness of my empty life. And by morning it was clear that nothing had changed, things were as they'd

111

always been. There was only one person who could possibly inhabit the space that I had always kept vacant.

When I reached the office, I wrote to the Blandfords Old Boys' Association, requesting, if it was known, the present address of Stephen Walker.

# *Then*

'If it were as you say, why did you write to me as you did at the time?'

'I could do nothing else. As I had to break with you, it was my duty also to put an end to all that you felt for me.'

'That may be so, but you had no right . . .'

'No. Sorry . . .'

'Oh, what's the matter, child?'

'Walker jumped two lines, sir.'

'All right. Break, all of you.'

TG rises, out in the darkened auditorium, and fumbles his way towards the platform.

'Is there any chance,' he says, 'that you will eventually know your lines, Stephen?'

'Sorry, sir,' Walker mumbles.

'Sorry isn't good enough. Is there something on your mind that is preventing you from concentrating?'

'No, sir.'

'Are you in dire distress? Are you in debt? Have you got one of the skivvies pregnant?'

'No, sir.'

One or two of the stage management boys giggle at this.

'Shut up,' TG yells. 'You have nothing to be proud of, any of you. Oh, go away, all of you. I can't stand the sight of any of you,' and he bangs his way out of the hall.

It is a thick night, with mist blowing in from the coast. Nigel and I leave the hall together and stumble across the

113

gravel towards the path to Ely. As we reach the first bank of rhododendrons, a figure appears out of the dark ahead of us.

'Kit?' a voice whispers. 'Kit, I've been waiting for you,' and I see Walker hurrying towards me. I realise that he thinks I'm alone.

I move forward quickly, hoping somehow to stop Nigel from hearing.

'Duff is with me,' I say, desperately.

'What's going on?' Nigel asks, catching me up and at once seeing Walker.

'You go on, Duff,' he says. 'I want a word with Metcalfe.'

Dimly, in the half-light, I see Nigel give me a puzzled look. Then he hurries away up the path through the shrubbery.

Walker draws me off the path into the bushes. We are both shaking.

'Damn,' he whispers. 'This fog. I didn't notice him. Would he have heard?'

'Bound to have,' I say.

'Will it matter?'

'Duff is my best friend, but – I didn't want him to know.'

'Are you ashamed?' Walker asks in a whisper.

'I don't know.'

He puts his arms round me. His duffle coat is wet with the mist.

'Oh, Kit,' he whispers, 'what are we going to do?'

I find that I am holding him and that, although he is taller than I am, he feels small and vulnerable. I can't bear the way he is suffering, not if it's my fault.

'I've found somewhere for us to go,' he whispers. 'Outside the school grounds. It's quite a walk. Will you come?'

'When?'

'This Sunday afternoon. Make some excuse. Please. It's our only chance . . .'

'Who's there?' we hear Heslop call from the path.

Walker puts a hand over my mouth and draws me further into the depth of the rhododendron bushes. The mist is too thick for us to see him, but we know that he is standing a short way off. My heart is beating fast and my body is tensed, ready to run further into the dense centre of the shrubbery.

'It's me, Cliff,' I hear Walker call, his voice loud because we're standing so close. 'I'm having a slash.'

'I thought I heard voices,' Heslop says.

Walker laughs, sounding so natural, but I can feel his tension in every part of his body.

'I was just going over those sodding lines,' he calls.

'I'm not hanging about, it's cold,' Heslop says.

Then I feel Walker's lips brushing my ear as he continues to hold me in front of him, with his body pressed against my back and his arms encircling me.

'Three o'clock, Sunday afternoon.' His voice is scarcely more than a breath. 'Go down towards the marsh and then take the lane that leads across Dun Bay. I'll find you.'

I feel his lips kiss my ear and the next moment he goes quickly and noisily through the undergrowth, calling:

'Cliff? Where are you? I can't see a thing . . .'

I lean against the branches, exhausted and trembling. Sometime soon we're going to be caught. We have had too many narrow escapes. And yet, caught for what? The most we have done, since that first day in the study, is whisper and plot and hold on to each other like drowning men. Yes, that's precisely right; like men drowning in a whirlpool, being sucked down into the dark, weedy bottom without any strength to swim clear of the current nor even the will to do so.

Blandfords Church stands in the school grounds. It is here that the school attends morning service every Sunday and on other religious festivals and significant school occasions; the beginning and end of each term is dedicated to the glory of God here, as is the Founder's Day and, for some obscure reason, the reigning monarch's birthday. (Cynics say that this observance is kept up today in the hope that the Queen will send Prince Charles here, instead of to Gordonstoun, where his father went, but so far she doesn't seem to have chosen so to do; or, if she has, word has not yet got round. The fact that there is a long waiting list and that Old Blandfordians put their sons down for a place before they are even born, would, it is supposed, be waived if Mrs E. Windsor made the right noises.)

The church is a large Victorian building, put up at the time when Blandfords Hall was made over to the Blandfords Trust in order that a school for young gentlemen could be created, where they would learn a basic education and a fine moral spirit under the watchful eye of Almighty God and the elected governors. The architect employed to design it drew heavily on other churches in the area, and one of its chief features is an angel roof, copied from the church at Blythbrough. But whereas the angels in the original are rough and vigorously spiritual, ours are stiff and harshly chiselled; looking more like a group of Wells Fargo delivery men than divine messengers; a fact that persuaded Nikolaus Pevsner to refer to them as The Holy Postmen.

Nigel and I are seated in a pew about halfway up the church. We had both been trebles in the choir together, then I had tentatively been shunted into the altos for half a term before it was realised that all the flat notes were originating somewhere at the back of my throat and I was asked to leave. Now Duff also is back in the main body of the kirk and we weave around the notes together. There is actually some question about us both playing women in this term's play. Neither of us is entirely in control of our voices and we sometimes hit all-time lows, which sound surprising coming out of Nora Helmer and Mrs Linde. Actually, I think

116

my husky sounds are a bit like Marlene Dietrich, but I'm not sure that she would have been cast as Nora either in a sane world.

Nigel has made no reference to the encounter with Walker on Friday evening and I think, perhaps, that he hasn't noticed anything strange. But I am nervous about approaching him with the request that must now be made:

'Are you going bird-watching this afternoon?' I ask him.

'Probably. I've got a pass signed. D'you want to come?'

'Mmmh,' I say. 'I'll get a pass from Heslop. Is that all right?'

Duff shrugs. It doesn't matter to him. If anything, he must be surprised at the request. I have often told him that I think bird-watching is only slightly less boring than watching cricket.

But when the time comes and we are walking down the drive together towards the school gates, where the duty prefect vets our passes and tells us to be back by five thirty, I am nervous again.

'We're going over to the sea lakes,' Nigel says as we proffer our passes.

'You can go to Zeebrugge for all I care,' the prefect tells him.

'We have to say where we're going,' Nigel replies, in a wounded voice. He, Nigel, will make a wonderful prefect when the time comes. He has a fine respect for The Rules.

The prefect looks at him through bored eyes and nods us on our way.

I wait until we are at the T-junction before I say:

'Actually, Nige, I'm not coming with you. D'you mind?'

He stops walking and turns and looks at me. But his expression is not one of surprise, it is more like concern.

'What are you up to, Chris?' he asks.

I shrug.

117

'Nothing,' I answer. 'You know I'm not really very keen on birds.'

'Why did you ask if you could come, then?'

I don't meet his eyes. I'm not a very good liar and he's my friend, which seems to make it worse.

'You could just have got a pass for a walk,' he says. 'Jenkins and Midgley were going down towards Orford . . .'

'I've got to go, Nigel,' I say, cutting him short.

'You're meeting someone, aren't you?' he says.

'Why d'you say that?' I ask, feeling myself beginning to blush.

'On Friday night, Chris, I waited for you up the path. I heard Heslop calling. I heard the reply. I couldn't understand why Walker would lie.'

'I really do have to go, Nige,' I say, backing away from him.

He watches me, sadly. Then he takes a few steps towards me.

'Chris,' he says.

'Yes?'

'Oh, nothing. Only – I think it's wrong what you're doing. I know it has nothing to do with me. Tell me to mind my own business. But I am your friend, and I have the right, as a friend, to tell you that. I think it's wrong, Chris. I'm not blaming you. I blame this place. But it is possible . . . not to give in.'

'I don't think you know what you're talking about,' I say, and I turn my back on him and walk away. When I reach a corner in the lane, I look back. He is still standing at the junction, watching me. He raises a hand, and waves.

'Chris,' I hear him call, 'be careful.'

Then I turn and run away down the hill towards Dun Bay.

Ahead of me the pale sea washes the long strand. It is a totally still winter afternoon; no wind; no colour even. A white and grey day; the sort of day that seems to be waiting to be finished off before it can be properly presented. Not cold, nor hot: not bright, nor dull. My footsteps on the narrow lane are the only sounds that I hear. The birds are silent. Even the distant swell brushes the shore without breaking.

The lane I am on reaches a long, narrow inlet which it crosses at its inshore end by way of an old stone causeway. At the high spring tides the water completely submerges it. But today the white line of the sea is beyond a flat expanse of mud and tangled weed. This is Dun Bay and here, as I reach the causeway, I see Walker waiting for me.

I feel horribly exposed as I walk towards him, as though eyes are watching me from every tree and bush. He holds out a hand to me as I draw near and he smiles, a diffident, shy smile; almost a weary smile.

'I thought you weren't going to turn up,' he says.

I glance at my watch. It is only just half past two.

'No, no. You're not late. I didn't mean that. It's just that I got here so early. Shall we walk?'

He leads the way along the causeway and then takes a path up the muddy side of the creek towards the low ground that forms the sea wall along this stretch of coast.

'If by any chance we should bump into anyone from the school,' he says, over his shoulder to me (for the path is too narrow for us to walk side by side), 'we can say we're going over lines. Leave the talking to me.'

Then he walks on in silence, round the side of the creek until we reach a place where a broad, weedy river slowly empties itself out on to the mud. The land beyond is sea marsh country through which the river curls like a languorous snake passing between stunted trees and stretches of low sea lavender; in summer a haze of violet and grey, now bleached white.

Our path has broadened out and we are able to walk together. But there is a shyness between us and we do not touch each other or even exchange a look until, after about a quarter of an hour, ahead of us I see the outline of a stone bridge across the marsh to our right.

'What's over there?' I ask.

'You'll see in a moment,' he says and this exchange seems to break the ice between us. He glances at me and smiles.

'Are you all right?' he asks. And, when I nod, he reaches out a hand and strokes the back of my head.

The bridge, when we reach it, turns out to span the winding river. We climb up a steep slope on to it and discover that its centre is overgrown with grass and weeds. In both directions a narrow weed-filled track disappears between banks of low, leaning alders and dark holly.

'What is it?' I ask.

'Disused railway, I think,' he replies. 'But it can't have been in operation for ages. We're nearly there.'

We pick our way through great clumps of nettle and sea thistle. I feel more confident now, because the plants and trees afford protection from both sides.

'How did you find this place?' I ask.

He looks at me and smiles.

'Oh, Kit. I've been searching for ages.' As he speaks, he moves closer to me and puts an arm round my shoulder, resting his weight on me and pulling me gently towards him.

We walk on in this way until, coming round a curve in the track that is leading us away from the coast towards the arable farmland that lies further inshore, I see ahead of us a wooden hut. It has a tiled roof, from which most of the tiles have at some time been stripped. Its walls are dark with pitch. It has a window that is boarded up and a door that is closed.

He looks at me again with a sad, questioning expression. I expect him to speak, but he shakes his head.

'What?' I ask. 'What's the matter?'

'Now that we're here, I'm afraid,' he says.

I feel sorry for him. I want to comfort him; to make it all right. I smile and touch his cheek. I realise at once that it is his sort of gesture, and I'm embarrassed that he may think I'm copying him. But he catches my hand and presses it against his lips. Then, still holding the hand, he leads me to the hut.

He puts his other hand on the door handle and raises one foot. With a sudden kick, he forces the door open. Then he looks back over his shoulder, scanning the surrounding trees and shrubs to see if the noise has alerted anyone to our presence. But only a few rooks flap out of the distant wood, cawing their disapproval.

The interior of the hut is bare except for a few packing cases and some empty drums. There are discarded rifle cartridges on the wooden floor and crushed dog-ends. The only light is from the open door, through which I am looking. He walks ahead of me into the room and turns slowly round, taking in the details. Then he stands looking at me.

'Will it do?' he whispers.

I nod, but I can't answer him. My throat is tight and I can't make any sound. He takes my reaction for disappointment.

'I know it isn't very nice. But it's the best I could find,' he says apologetically.

I shake my head and take a step towards him, crossing over the threshold. But I still can't speak.

The gloom of the interior settles round us like a comforting blanket. We stand, a little apart, shyly staring at each other.

'Are you cold?' he asks.

'No,' I manage to whisper.

He takes off his duffle coat and spreads it on the floor beside the empty boxes. Then he turns and looks at me again, reaching out a hand to me.

I, misinterpreting his gesture, take off my duffle coat and hand it to him. He holds it for a moment, then lets it fall to the ground and, stepping over it, crosses and puts his arms round me. I feel the warmth of his body and smell his clean, sharp scent. He buries his face down into my shoulder and I feel his cold cheek against mine. I lift my hands up, under his armpits, then slowly reach round his back, pulling him closer and closer. I feel his lips on my cheek and turn my face up towards them. At first our lips gently brush and then I feel his tongue against them. My lips open slightly, perhaps in surprise, and his tongue enters my mouth, exploring this new area. I feel a shock wave wriggle through my body and I gasp for breath, opening my mouth wider, admitting more of his probing tongue.

Still kissing me, he starts to pull my pullover up my body and to undo the buttons of my shirt. Then his hands are groping at the cotton of my vest. He stops and holds me away from him.

'Are you all right?' he whispers.

I nod.

'You want to?' he asks.

'Yes,' I reply and, as I speak, I feel a rush of excitement.

He slips a finger into my collar and starts to unfasten my tie.

'I'll do it,' I whisper. Then I look back over my shoulder out of the half-open door.

'We're as safe here as anywhere,' he whispers.

'If somebody comes . . .'

'Then we'll be caught. But no one will come, I promise you,' and, as he speaks, he passes me and pushes the door until it is just ajar.

He turns again and looks at me. Then he smiles.

'We'll be all right,' he tells me.

I start to unknot the tie. Then I take off my pullover and unbutton my shirt, but I don't take it off. He watches me silently from his position behind the half-closed door. Then with a sudden movement, he removes his own sweater and pulls his shirt off over his head. He is wearing no vest and I see the dark hair on his chest and the tight curve of his muscles. He crosses to me and slipping his hands over my shoulders, he pushes away my braces and removes my shirt. Then, as I raise my arms, he drags my vest up over my head.

I feel the warmth of his skin touching mine. I smell the sweat under his arms. My face and lips explore the hair between his breasts. His hands run slowly down my naked back, making me shiver, and his open mouth presses down on the side of my neck. My breathing is heavy; I keep shaking, but it isn't with the cold; it is the touch of his hands, his lips, his skin. I am not cold, but on fire.

Then his hands are at my stomach, feeling for the hook at the waist of my flannels, and, one by one, I let him unfasten the buttons and I feel my trousers slowly slide over my buttocks and halfway down my thighs.

He sinks slowly down into a crouching position in front of me and, as he does so, he gently slides my underpants down my legs, revealing my hard, standing cock. I look down at him, as if from a great height, and see him kneeling there, as though in worship, and as I watch, he puts his lips over the knob of my penis and gently takes it into his mouth.

The sudden, surprising, moist heat of his mouth surges through me and stabs at the base of my spine. I pull away, afraid that I will come to orgasm. He looks up at me, and reaching with his arms, he pulls me down beside him, then gently unrolls me on to his spread duffle coat.

He stands up, towering above me, and I watch in the half-light as he quickly unbuckles his belt and fiddles with the buttons of his flies. Then his trousers fall to the ground and he wrestles his feet out of them, his shoes catching on the turn-ups. His white underpants cannot contain his erection. It reaches up out of the waistband, hard and pressing. I run my hands up the sides of his taut legs and pull the pants

123

down to his knees, revealing the whole penis, surrounded by a vast fuzz of black hair. It seems so improbably large, with the tight sac of the balls at its base, that for a moment I am afraid of it. Panic seizes at my gut. What am I doing here? How did I get here? How can I get away? But then he lowers himself down on top of me supporting his weight on his outstretched arms and looking down into my open, startled eyes.

'I love you, Kit,' he whispers. 'I love every inch of your body. Whatever happens, remember that. I love you.' He says the last three words one after another with a pause between each of them, lightly, playfully and yet full of meaning. Then, sliding down on his side, he leans over and kisses me gently on the lips and I feel his hand caressing my genitals.

Even when he comes, kneeling with his legs on either side of my body and letting the hot sperm shoot across my chest, I don't feel revolted. I feel grateful, glad. And when our two orgasms mingle on my stomach and he lies once more on top of me, so that he also is covered by the sticky juices, it doesn't seem disappointing and sordid as it does in the private loneliness of my masturbatory bed. The sadness of after-sex is countered by the warmth of his body and the gentleness of his caress. I thought that, once we had done it, it would be over for ever. But it isn't. As he wipes my body with his handkerchief and kisses each of my closed eyes, I know that it is only beginning.

Is this what he means by love? Have I got it now? Will it be a lifetime of loving him?

'When we're alone,' I whisper to him, 'can I call you Stephen?'

'Oh, Kit!' he says, and he starts to laugh and to hold me and I feel my cock getting hard all over again.

124

# *Now*

Mother arrived at the flat just before lunch. She had telephoned the evening before to say that she was coming up to do some shopping, and could she take me out for a snack? But I thought it would be better and kinder if I cooked for her.

It was a Saturday in late November and there had been a ground frost. The air was sparkling and clear, one of those London days when the town looks clean and bright. I shopped at The Gate and walked back up Kensington Park Road and cut along the Gardens, entering the Crescent from the top end.

I'd bought fresh pasta and frozen prawns and was in the middle of preparing a salad when the doorbell rang. Drying my hands on a tea towel I went to answer it. Mother was standing on the doormat laden with bags and parcels and looking radiant.

We kissed and I divested her of some of the baggage before she staggered through into the hall.

'A drink?' I suggested. There was a bottle of claret breathing or Muscadet in the fridge.

'Unless, of course, you want a short?'

But no, she didn't or she would get sleepy and she wanted to catch the three-something train back to Sevenoaks. She was playing bridge that evening which meant that she wouldn't have to cook, but she wanted to get home in good time in order to bath and change.

I poured her a glass of red wine and she followed me into the kitchen.

I hadn't seen her since the family conference nor had either of us referred to it when speaking on the phone. I thought it was probably one of those things that was better forgotten about, like so many events in the Metcalfe family saga. Our history is stuffed with 'moments best not mentioned' and 'conversations that never occurred'.

'You're looking wonderful,' I told her; and she was. She was wearing her hair longer and in a looser wave, which suited her and made her look, I told her, ten years younger:

'Oh, good!' she exclaimed with obvious delight.

And her navy suit, with a pencil skirt and boxy jacket, accentuated her slim, upright figure.

'You don't think it makes me look like one of those cartoon women, do you?' she asked. 'Maudie Littlehampton or Mrs Gambol?'

We laughed and she settled down on one of the kitchen chairs while I got on with the salad.

I was doing a prawn and mint sauce for the pasta, which is a stand-by of mine and is instant cooking, so there were no hurdles to be surmounted. The only thing to remember is to defrost the prawns and that I was already doing, in a colander on the draining board.

She was gossiping about what she'd seen and which shops she'd been to, and I had just put on a pan of water for the pasta, when the doorbell rang again.

I pulled a face and glanced at my watch.

'Who the hell can that be?' I said, drying my hands once more and going out of the kitchen and along the hall to the front door.

I discovered a balding, middle-aged man wearing a City overcoat and a bowler hat. He looked at me and blinked.

'Mr Metcalfe?' he asked.

'Yes?'

'Oh, jolly good. I wasn't sure if this was the right place. You probably don't remember me. But I was at Blandfords with you.'

I was at once on my guard. I was aware that Mother was sitting in the kitchen, only feet away, and that she could certainly hear every word that was being said.

Since writing to the Old Boys' Association I had had no reply, but I certainly didn't expect someone to turn up in person.

'May I come in?' the person now said, trying to edge his way into the hall.

'Well, it isn't really very convenient at the moment,' I said. 'I have a lunch guest.'

'Oh, sorry, old son. How thoughtless of me. I should have phoned. I'm Gerald Dixon. We were in Ely together.'

Dixon the sadist. Really, if it hadn't been such an inconvenient moment I could have thoroughly enjoyed it. He was always ugly and round and the years had done nothing to improve him. His plump pink hand was longing to be shaken but I felt the moment had passed and I remained resolutely standing in the doorway, blocking off my mother's line of vision.

'No, I'm sorry. I don't remember. It was all so long ago,' I told him, pleased to see his look of disappointment.

'You wrote to the Old Boys. We were so delighted. We don't like the flock to stray. I do a lot of work for them. Being a solicitor helps. Perhaps, if I was to call at some other time? I live out at Virginia Water, but I'm often in town on a Saturday . . .'

'My schedule is so erratic,' I told him. 'I never know where I will be.'

'Yes, of course. Well, we have had the odd inquiry about you. You remember Duff? Fluffy Duffy? He wanted your address. I'll pass it along.'

'Thank you.'

'But I'm afraid that as far as your request is concerned, we can't be of any help.'

'Oh, well, not to worry . . .'

Mother appeared behind me at the door of the kitchen and called:

'Am I in the way, darling?'

'No, it's all right, Mother.'

'Oh,' said Dixon, taking advantage of this momentary distraction to get inside the hall. 'Is this your mother? I'm sure we must have met at some time.' He extended a hand which Mother dutifully shook. 'My name is Gerald Dixon. I was at school with your son.'

'Dixon?' Mother sounded vague. 'Were you friends there?'

'Well, not exactly, no. I was older. The older chaps didn't really make friends with the junior school, you know.' Then he turned his pink piggy eyes on me once more. 'That's why I was a little surprised to see your letter. Walker was my year. I didn't realise you knew him, Metcalfe.'

Strange how quickly one can slip back. Walker and Metcalfe and Dixon and Fluffy Duffy . . .

'I didn't know him,' I lied glibly and easily. 'I have a private matter which I needed to communicate with him. A work matter.'

Mother would know I was lying, but under the circumstances I couldn't be blamed for coping with one crisis at a time.

'Oh, I see, a work matter,' the sadist simpered. 'What is your work, Metcalfe? The Old Boys like to know how everyone is getting along.'

'I'm in publishing,' I replied. Then I added for confusion's sake, 'Amongst other things.'

You could see him toying with the idea of MI5 and Special Branch. I didn't really look SAS material. But it did the trick. He was nonplussed.

'Well,' he said with a shrug, 'we're sorry not to be of

more use to you. But Stephen Walker never registered with the Association and we have completely lost touch.'

'Thank you,' I said, forcing him back towards the door. 'It wasn't anything very important.'

'Oh, well, I'll let Duff know of your whereabouts. You two were great friends, I seem to remember.'

'So much as I can claim to have had any friends there I suppose that would be true,' I told him, holding the door for him.

'I remember you in the school play. Wait a minute – can't remember the name of the play, but your character was called Nora, wasn't it? We all found that a hoot at the time!'

'Come to think of it, I do remember you now, Dixon. You once caught me reading after lights out and had me beaten.'

'Oh, did I?' He looked at me, blinked and then laughed. 'Jolly good. Those were the days! Well, nice to have met you, Mrs Metcalfe. Cheerio. Thank you. Keep in touch . . .'

He continued to call cheerful phrases as he disappeared down the stairs into the entrance hall.

I closed the front door and followed Mother back into the kitchen. The pan of water was spitting and boiling on the stove. I turned it down and went back to finishing the salad.

'Shouldn't you have asked him in?' Mother asked.

'Certainly not,' I replied. 'He was a revolting individual and I shouldn't think for one moment he has changed.'

'How strange that he should just turn up out of the blue,' Mother said, pouring herself some more wine then holding up the bottle to me with an enquiring look to see if I also wanted my glass replenished.

'Yes, please,' I said. 'We'll be eating soon.'

'You'd written to the Old Boys' Association, is that it? Wanting an address?'

'Yes.'

I started to cook, busily, hoping the activity would distract her.

'Stephen Walker,' she said, staring at me, almost seeming to challenge me. 'But, surely, he was the boy who you had to stay?'

'That's right, Mother.'

'You told – what was his name? Dixon? You told him that you and Walker weren't friends.' She waited for me to react, but I said nothing. 'But of course you were friends. You had him to stay. Don't you remember? He's the boy I asked you about when we found those school photos in your father's desk. Chris?'

I could feel an odd mixture of irritation and apprehension possessing me.

'Yes. I remember. Of course I remember. It just . . . didn't have anything to do with Dixon. I saw no reason why I should tell him. That's all. There's no mystery, Mother. I simply wanted to get in touch with Stephen Walker and I thought the Association might have his address. They haven't. So that's all there is to it.'

There was too much passion in my voice. I was too shaken. She couldn't help noticing. But whatever she thought, she said nothing.

I wished she would go away; that she wasn't there; that I had received the negative news on my own; that I had time and space to assimilate the fact that I was no nearer to tracing Stephen.

'I thought he was very nice,' I heard her say quietly, as though she were a party to my thoughts.

'Who?' I asked.

She looked at me, thoughtfully.

'Stephen Walker,' she replied. 'I remember him clearly. I thought him a most charming boy. And handsome, terribly handsome. You want to be in touch with him again? Is that it?'

'Yes,' I snapped. 'Otherwise I wouldn't have asked for his address.'

She looked at me coolly for a moment, as though judging me and my mood, and then, quite obviously and without any pretence, she changed the subject:

'I do love this flat,' she said. 'It is so London. That food smells delicious . . .'

And we didn't return to it again, except that, as she was preparing to go, she suddenly introduced once more the theme of loneliness.

'I'm ashamed how lonely I am, Chris. And surprised. It surprises me. I didn't really think of your father as much of a companion – indeed, he wasn't one. We, in many ways, led separate lives. He at the business all day, and I at home. Then, when he sold up to Cutlers and Plates, I carried on much as before and he . . . retired, in the true sense of the word. Into himself. I never knew what he was doing in that study. I suspect, very little. Just as I don't think he did very much at the business, except checking that other people were doing things for him. I think the study was simply a business substitute. Somewhere to go between nine and five thirty: like a man who has his leg amputated continuing to feel the pain. So, really, although he was in the house, I saw no more of him than I had in the past. But he was, nevertheless, a reason. Do you know what I mean? A reason for cooking, and making the bed and . . . getting up, even. He was a pivot; a focus. Now that he isn't there – I still do all those things; but I question why. Why cook? Why make the bed? Why get up?'

'And yet,' I tell her, 'you look ten years younger.'

'I know. And I feel it. And you should see the dress I've just bought. But what am I doing it for, Chris? For whom am I doing it? I wonder, do you ever feel like that?'

For a moment I almost wanted to confide in her. No, I wanted to confide and for a moment I almost dared to. I

131

saw myself in her eyes and I knew she was seeing herself in mine.

'Yes, darling,' I told her. 'I understand.'

She nodded and said nothing. I was grateful to her. There was nothing to be said. We had simply, each of us, acknowledged our loneliness to each other, and there was a kind of bond in that. But whereas she, I think, was lonely for someone whom she had never known, I was lonely for Stephen.

After she had gone and I was clearing away the lunch, I thought again about Dixon's visit. It was extraordinary that he had bothered to seek me out in person. The non-information he had to deliver could have been easily communicated over the phone or by letter. But perhaps our chief characteristics never change, and Dixon was ever a nosy little bugger. If he wasn't careful I'd get Stephen to sort him out again.

# *Then*

As I close the hall door I can feel my heart racing. The children are staring at me, mute and stiff. They are supposed to run towards me, chattering and laughing. They did last night, at the dress rehearsal. But now, with that sea of faces staring at them, with the coughing and the giggling and the shushing, they seem to have given up completely.

'How fresh and well you look! Such red cheeks — like apples and roses. Have you had great fun?'

Not a sound comes from either of them. Pearson's brats are only babies. The boy is seven and the girl is five. It was madness thinking they could act. But they did at the dress rehearsal. What's wrong with them? They are supposed to be bubbling over with excitement. They are supposed to answer me; to question me. They are not supposed to stand stock-still, staring and blinking, and the little girl, Rachel in real life but Emmy to me, should not be crossing her legs as though she's peeing herself.

I can see Dixon in the second row. No one told me that I'd be able to see people, actual faces that I can recognise. Dixon has had a stupid grin on his face since the curtain went up.

'Have you?' I say again, a little louder. 'You have, haven't you? You've had great fun.'

But this is hopeless. I'm now shouting lines at them that they've never heard before. The boy, Hugo in real life (Hugo? Wouldn't you know Drippy Pearson would call his son Hugo? Or d'you suppose it was his wife. The Peach? 'Oh, darling, let's call him Hugo after the writer.' 'Which writer, my angel?' 'Victor, darling. Victor Hugo . . .), turns towards Smeddle, who is playing the Nurse, and looks as if he is about to cry. I must get rid of them before they ruin everything.

'Away, children. Away and play,' I tell them, rewriting Ibsen with abandon.

'Yes, yes, Mother will dance with you . . .' I can hear the prompter whispering frantically. I glare at him in his corner and push the children offstage, still bubbling and chattering to them, as though nothing is wrong. As if I'm glad that they've been struck dumb and appear to be also paralysed. As if, in fact, I love them and not, which would be nearer the truth, as if I could pull off all their little limbs one by one and throw them at the dazed and dreadful audience. One thing is for certain, I am not doing a dance with Hugo Pearson. Not tonight, not with Dixon grinning at me from the second row.

But now what happens? I've got rid of the children too soon. But never mind about that. I meant to do that. Now what? What happens next; after the children go off? What am I supposed to be doing now? In a terrible panic, I turn away from the nursery door and gasp with genuine shock. He is standing there. The man I most dread, the man I most fear. The man from whom I can never escape.

'Ah! what do you want?' I cry out, in genuine anguish.

'Excuse me,' he says, quietly, staring into me and through me. 'The outer door was ajar: I suppose someone forgot to shut it.'

'My husband is out, Mr Krogstad.'

'I know that,' he replies.

'What do you want here then?'

'A word with you.'

Now I should get rid of the children – but they have already gone.

'With me,' I say. 'You want to speak with me?'

Krogstad is staring at me. I am Nora, a doll, and this is my house and he has come to ruin me and I am powerless.

But of course none of that is the truth. I am really Chris Metcalfe and he is Stephen Walker and we are pretending to be people we are not. And we are doing it – making this pretence – for other people, for an audience. But not just tonight, not just for the play; it's what we've been doing ever since we parted on the causeway at Dun Bay after we'd been together in the railway shed. Pretending to be other people, ordinary people, the people we thought we were before that moment.

Then, as the dusk was pulling in over the flat horizon and sea birds were mournfully calling, he'd said:

'You go on ahead. It'll be better if we aren't seen together too much from now on.'

I'd nodded and started to walk away from him. We had been silent since leaving the shed. I was nervous and . . . sad. I didn't know why. But when he told me to walk away, I was disappointed. I think then I realised how hopeless it all was.

'Kit,' he'd called and I'd turned back to look at him. Mist was rising above the surface of the river and rolling in low bands over the clumps of sedge and sea lavender. The sky behind him was heavy with cloud, a thin breeze was blowing off the sea.

We'd stood at a distance, staring at each other through the darkening afternoon.

'I'm sorry, Kit,' he'd said. I hadn't understood what he meant.

'Why?' I'd asked him. 'For what?' And yet, in my heart, maybe I'd known what he was saying.

'You go on now,' he'd said. And I was surprised to see

135

him produce a cigarette from his duffle pocket and cupping his hands, he struck a match. The spurt of flame lit his face for a moment and I saw his sad blue eyes, staring at me.

'Stephen?' I'd said, crossing back to him.

'It's gone too far, Kit. My fault. I couldn't help it.'

'But it doesn't matter. I won't tell anyone. No one will know.'

'We'll know, Kit. You and I. We'll always know,' and he'd glanced at his watch. 'If you don't run, you'll be late.'

'When will I see you?'

'All the time, Kit. That's what's going to be so awful. You'll see me all the time.'

Of course he was right. We have seen each other every day since. And we've been playing two roles, each of us. We are Nora and Krogstad at rehearsals. We are Metcalfe and Walker the rest of the time. But inside: inside I am Kit and he is Stephen, and that's what hurts. Because Stephen and Kit don't exist, or if they do, then it must always be in dark corners and under cover. People mustn't know about us. Because what we are doing is wrong. It's sinful. It's unnatural. It's filthy; perverted; the worst thing that any boy can get involved in. I gaze at myself in the mirror and try to see traces of this new me. But I look the same. I feel completely different, but it doesn't show. I've started praying again, asking for forgiveness. Not because I've seen the light, but because any luck would be welcome now. HELP ME HELP ME HELP ME, a voice clamours inside Kit, while Metcalfe answers questions and sounds quite normal, and writes essays, and completes exam papers, and does exercise runs, plays fives and squash and rehearses and rehearses and rehearses, always with Walker there, but never with Stephen.

Last night, before the dress rehearsal, while Mrs TG was making me up, I caught sight of him staring at me in the mirror. He seemed so far away and there was an unfamiliar expression on his face. But I couldn't ask him what was wrong or why he was looking at me so strangely, because of the other people who surround us all the time.

TG himself does all the men's make-up and his wife does the females. TG had, briefly, worked as an actor in his younger days, touring with a company that did Shakespeare in village halls. His idea of stage make-up is heavy on the eye lines and a lot of reddish-brown greasepaint. Stephen looks almost more like Othello than Krogstad. He has been allowed to grow his hair longer than usual and it curls down on to his collar at the back. Glossop wears a terrible wig that makes him look more like Old Mother Riley than Dr Rank and Heslop combs his hair into a centre parting, but one side keeps falling forward, so he clips it back with a grip, which glints in the lights and looks ridiculous. Why, people will wonder, does Torvald Helmer wear a kirby grip? All the men have dark, greasy complexions. Why do they have to look as though they've spent twenty years working on a chain gang? Mrs TG's technique, in contrast, is peaches and cream. So that we – Nigel and I and also Smeddle, who plays the Nurse – look as though we are dying of a strange wasting disease. We are very white-skinned, with bright spots of rouge on the cheeks and thick black lines round our eyes, with white blobs in the corners. She also, on TG's instruction, paints a scratch-thin line of red down the ridge of our noses. When I ask her why, she smiles short-sightedly at me and tells me that she always does what she is told, but that she thinks the idea is to make the nose look slimmer. I stare at my apparently overweight nose and think I look like Madame Butterfly preparing to do a Cherokee Indian war dance. Is this the impression we are after?

The dress rehearsal had gone smoothly. TG said it was a very bad sign. When we were back in the green room, stripping off our costumes and putting cold cream on our faces to remove the greasepaint, I once more saw Stephen staring.

Now, here we are, in the middle of our first scene on the opening night and that same look is on his face again. We go automatically through the lines. We move to the right spots on the stage, we get through. He goes. The children appear at the door:

'Mother, Mother, the stranger man has gone out through the gate . . .'

The Maid brings tea. Torvald returns, and, at last, the rattle of the curtains and a bit of polite applause indicates that we've made it to the first interval.

TG is fuming. Why the muddle before Krogstad's entrance? Hugo Pearson screams that it was: 'all Nora's fault. She didn't say what she was meant to. She didn't do the dance . . .'

During the second interval TG is plunged into gloom. I think it must be something that I've done wrong. But it isn't.

'They hate it,' he tells us all, as if to reassure us. 'But what is worse, I hate it. It's boring. You're all bloody boring . . .'

'I've got a packet of biscuits here,' Mrs TG tells us, unmoved by her husband's tirade. 'Anyone want one?'

But I can't eat one. I'm too depressed.

Act Three begins with a scene between Krogstad and Mrs Linde. During it we discover that once, before the beginning of the play, they have had a relationship. I stand in the wings, waiting for my entrance with Heslop, listening to Stephen and Nigel Duff speaking on the other side of the canvas flats. They sound so intense, so intimate. The voice I hear is Stephen's voice, not Krogstad's.

'That may be so,' he is saying, 'but you had no right to throw me over for anyone else's sake.'

He speaks with such anguish. How does he know how it feels? How can he act what he has never experienced? Divided by the thin pretence of a wall, unable to see him, I am overwhelmed by a sense of pity and of mistrust. I don't know this person whom I can hear speaking. It isn't the Stephen I was with in the railway shed. That was some strange, other being, with whom I shared the secrets of my fantasy world; who became the creature of those fantasies. But who is this man speaking now? And how does he know so much pain?

The sound of the tarantella warns me that our entrance is drawing near. Then:

'I will wait for you below,' I hear him saying.

'Yes, do,' Nigel Duff replies, speaking like Mrs Linde, which isn't how Nigel speaks at all. 'You must see me back to my door.'

Then I hear Stephen again and I realise that he isn't acting, he's being Krogstad.

'I have never had such an amazing piece of good fortune in my life,' he says and the doors open and he steps out into the passage and he walks straight towards us. Beside me, Heslop starts taking deep breaths, which he does, he told me, to calm himself. Onstage, Duff is speaking. Our cue is coming up. Stephen passes Heslop, then, seeing me, he falters and seems to trip. He reaches forward, and I, automatically, reach out to save his fall. His hand grasps on to my shoulder and our faces are so close that I am splashed by perspiration from his brow.

'Damn,' he says. Then, 'Sorry.'

Heslop, ahead of me, grabs hold of my arm, prior to pushing me by force into the room because I don't want to leave the party for fear of seeing Krogstad.

'I love you,' I hear a voice whisper. 'Oh God, I love you, Kit.'

'No, no, no – don't take me in,' I cry as Torvald drags me towards the lighted opening of the door. 'I want to go upstairs again,' I say, looking back over my shoulder to where I can see Stephen leaning against the scenery, watching me.

'Do you? Love me?' He mouths the words as I am pulled away from him.

'Yes! No! I don't know!' I cry, out loud, and then I disappear from his sight into the presence of the audience.

And so we're into the final act, the act that caused a riot in the theatre on the first first night. But it seems to me, as I tread lightly through the emotions and deliver all the lines, that Nora Helmer's troubles are minute in comparison to my own.

'But some day, Nora – some day?' my husband pleads with me.

'How can I tell,' Nora replies. 'I have no idea what is going to become of me.' No more have I, Nora. No more have I.

'Let me help you if you are in want,' the senior prefect of Ely House is pleading, kneeling in front of me.

'No. I can receive nothing from a stranger,' I reply. Is it me who is speaking? Or someone else? Did I say that?

'Can I never be anything more than a stranger to you?' Heslop cries.

'Ah, Torvald, the most wonderful thing of all would have to happen.'

'Tell me what that would be?'

'Both you and I would have to be so changed that – Oh, Torvald, I don't believe any longer in wonderful things happening.'

I can see members of the cast, Smeddle, the Pearson brats, Glossop, standing in the wings, watching. I search for Stephen.

'But I believe in it,' Heslop says. 'Tell me. So changed that—?'

Stephen is standing alone in the corner by the proscenium arch. I can see him clearly over Torvald's shoulder.

'So changed that—?' I hear my husband saying again and I realise that I should have answered him.

'That our life together would be a real wedlock,' I reply, and then I can't see Stephen any more because my eyes are full of tears. 'Goodbye,' I gasp, and I hurry away through the door and out into the merciful gloom of the wings, unable to control the tears that are quite wrong for Nora and spring from that place in the heart of Kit that always knew the impossibility of what was happening.

'Well done. Well done. Well done.' The words ring round the green room. The headmaster, Mr Wildeblood, seems almost to know who I am, which is a change, and TG is positively glad to be speaking to me.

The cast are taking off their make-up and queuing for the two showers in the washroom. I am kept talking by TG who, having praised, seems hell bent on destroying with so many notes that I won't be able to remember a quarter of them. Meanwhile Mrs TG is removing my wig and Hugo brat Pearson is staring at my underpants as though he either expected lace knickers or he has got a very premature lust for me. How early does it start, I wonder? How long does it last? Do old men lust? Will it go on like this for ever?

Duff has already showered and is getting dressed. His mother and father have come to the show, because they're not able to come on Saturday, the last night, which will be the official 'Parents' Performance', with a coffee party afterwards. Mine are coming then; bringing Angela. I told Mother she'd be bored to death, but then they all will be. It seems stupid them coming, when I'll be home next week for the Christmas holidays. But Mother wants to see me in the play and Father only needs the slightest excuse to come back to the school. He was happy here, or so he keeps telling me. It is about the only conversation subject that we can ever find: How Happy He Was At Blandfords. He could write a three-thousand-word essay on the subject, in fact he probably did once. I bet Father was a dab hand at essays.

I take my towel and go to the shower room. Heslop is coming out as I enter.

141

'Really well done, Metcalfe,' he says. 'I thought you were first rate. Oh, I didn't know if you'd forgotten your line, at the end, or if it was an extra-long pause.'

'No, I . . .' I stop speaking, because Stephen is showering, with his back to me, and I wasn't expecting to see him. My heart starts beating too loudly. Heslop is bound to hear it.

'That's why I repeated the question. I don't think it mattered though.'

Then he goes and we are alone. Stephen remains standing with his back to me, letting the warm water splash over his face and through his long black hair. I cross to the other shower and switch it on. Then I stand, facing away from him, so that we are back to back, and start soaping my body.

'Wash all that make-up off, Kit,' I hear him say, and I look over my shoulder. He still has his back to me. He is speaking to me, without looking at me. 'Every scrap of it. I hate seeing you pretending to be a woman.'

'I thought it went well,' I say, unable to disguise the disappointment I feel. I wanted him to be pleased with me.

I can't look at him. I am afraid of his naked body so close to me that I could reach across and touch it and yet so removed from me, so hopelessly forbidden and dangerous, that the pain of its nearness hurts. All that we did has made me feel like this. That's what he meant when he said it had gone too far. But he took all the blame and really it was equally mine. I wanted what happened and I want it again, now. But as I want it, so I fear it and know that I must fight it.

So we wash in silence and do not look at each other and seem to pretend that we are Walker and Metcalfe showering, by chance, at the same time. And I feel hot with the hurt of it. Then, when the pain is almost beyond bearing, I hear his shower stop flowing.

'You're not a woman to me. Remember that, Kit. To me

you will always be what you really are. I hated seeing you as a woman,' and he goes quickly out of the washroom.

When I come out, he is already nearly dressed. He doesn't look at me. He is hurrying to get away. Yet if he'd only wait, we'd have time together.

I dress slowly, feeling depressed. There has been so much build-up to the performance, and now it's over. Maybe that's why.

Stage management are sweeping the auditorium and setting the stage for Act One, so that everything will be in readiness for tomorrow night's performance.

I climb down off the stage and make my way towards the main entrance. The coffee urn is in the front foyer, for refreshments during the interval – though knowing the Blandfords fathers, I expect most of them would prefer a stiff drink. Not mine, particularly. But some of them are a very boozy lot and are inclined to get noisily drunk late on Founder's Day. Duff is sitting at a table with his parents. He doesn't see me, and I don't want to get involved with them, so I hurry past.

Outside the night is dark and a fine rain is falling. I walk quickly across the gravel towards the Ely path. Suddenly, ahead of me, I see a figure appear from the cover of the shrubbery. My heart leaps. I hurry forward, relieved and glad that he has waited for me.

'Well then, Nora,' a familiar voice that isn't Stephen's hisses at me. 'What a little spectacle that was, wasn't it?'

I hesitate, instinct telling me that Dixon – for that is who it is – is in a dangerous mood.

'Come here, boy,' he says, in a low voice, reaching out with his hand towards me. 'Or should I say "girl"? Huh? Nora? A little girl, are you? Prancing about in lipstick and a skirt. It's disgusting. You know that? Utterly disgusting. I had to control myself not to want to vomit at the sight of you.'

As he speaks he lunges forward and grabs my arm, dragging me towards him.

'Let go of me, Dixon,' I say, more angry than afraid.

'I've got a little proposition to put to you, Nora,' he whispers in my ear.

'Let go of me,' I say louder and, as I speak, I force his arm away from me. But he's too fast and, grabbing at me again, he twists my arm up behind my back and clamps his other hand over my mouth.

'Not so fast. Just listen. I'm going to leave you alone, Nora. I'm going to give you a good time right till the end of term. And, in return, you're going to do early-morning exercises with me. D'you understand? Every morning, from now until the last day of term. We're going to the gym. So that I can stop you being a little girl . . .' as he speaks, he twists my arm, punctuating his words with sudden spasms of pain, '. . . and turn you into a man. Is that clear?'

As he says the final words, he pushes me away from him. I turn, really not thinking what I'm doing, and charge straight back at him, knocking him over and landing on top of him.

'What are you doing?' he yells. 'You'll be beaten for this.'

But I don't care. I raise a fist and am about to pound it into his fat, damp face when another figure appears out of the dark bushes and I hear Stephen say:

'Stop that, Metcalfe. Get off him.'

I scramble away from Dixon, surprised and suddenly frightened.

'Now go back to house. Go on. I'll deal with this. Oh, Metcalfe . . .'

I turn and look at him.

'Best if you say nothing. Leave everything to me. Now go,' and he turns his back on me and stoops to help Dixon to his feet.

'Did you see what he did, Walker?' I hear Dixon say. 'He attacked me.'

'Listen to me, Dixon. If I see you tormenting that boy ever again . . .'

'Boy? Boy?' I hear Dixon say with a laugh. 'The boy's a fairy, Walker. A nasty little pansy. You should know. You're in the play with him . . .'

'All right,' Stephen says, and he sounds so calm, 'I can see you're not understanding what I'm saying. Get your coat off.'

'What are you talking about? My coat?'

'All right then, keep the bloody thing on . . .'

Through the dark I hear the sound of his fist hitting Dixon somewhere on his skin.

Dixon cries out in protest, but his words are winded out of him.

Then both of them are on the ground, squirming and turning and grunting and snarling.

I know he told me to go, but I stay in the bushes not knowing whether to try to stop them.

'Stop it, you idiot,' I hear Dixon say, and, as he speaks, I see him crawling away from Stephen and getting to his feet.

'You hear me, Dixon. Leave that boy alone.'

'Why? What's so special about him? D'you fancy him, Walker? Is that it? Want him for your bum-boy? I was only going to make a man of him, old son.' And he laughs, and then winces. 'If I get a black eye, how will I explain it, Walker?'

'Tell people that I did it, stopping you victimising a chap half your size. You're revolting, Dixon. You know that?'

Dixon laughs again.

'I was going to give him early-morning gym. That'd have made the bugger jump! Do you remember Gillespie? He used to make me clean out the prefects' bog every morning at seven. Never did me any harm. I had to use my bare hands.'

Stephen walks past my hiding place in the bushes and a few moments later Dixon passes me as well.

'What a boring play, Walker. You must agree,' he says when he is abreast of me. 'Personally, I prefer something with a bit more spice – and real women!'

And he chatters on, calling to Stephen through the darkness as though they haven't just been fighting, until he is beyond my range of hearing.

The next evening, as beginners are called for Act Three and I am making my way to the side of the stage, I see Stephen alone for a moment.

'Thank you,' I whisper. 'For last night. Thank you.'

'I'm ashamed I did so little,' he says. 'One day I may kill him.' He says it with such vehemence that I almost think he will.

Strangely I spend more time with Stephen in the presence of my parents than I have done since our Sunday together. I don't quite know how it happens, but he brings them cups of coffee and, somehow, he manages to stay on.

As I expected, Angela is in a poisonous mood. She is wearing a brace on her teeth, which gives her face an oddly 'constructed' look, as though she's a reject from the Frankenstein laboratory, and she's wearing her school tunic, although Mother says she tried to persuade her to wear a dress.

'I like my uniform,' she lisps. 'It shows I go to a good school.'

Mother is wearing a woollen coat-like dress with a long skirt. I expect it's very fashionable, but she does stand out a bit compared to the other mothers and I wish that she'd wear more ordinary clothes. She also looks too young compared to Father, as if they couldn't be married, and she laughs a lot and talks to all the boys. Father has a long conversation with the headmaster, probably about me – although it could quite easily be about him and his time here. I don't think he approved of the play. Though it's hard to be sure. He hasn't mentioned it since I joined them in the foyer. Mother seems to think I was good and Angela is horrible about the way I looked and the fact that I was playing a girl.

'Couldn't they get girls to play girls? That would be better.'

'You played Bottom the Weaver last year,' I remind her.

'Only in scenes, not the whole play. And I am only nine. And anyway, it isn't as peculiar as someone your age playing a girl. Why did you have a red stripe down your nose?'

I could kill Mrs TG. I knew it hadn't done whatever it was supposed to do because everybody mentions it. It must have looked just as ridiculous as I thought it did. I ignore Angela's question and am about to go and get them some coffee when, like magic, Stephen appears with a tray.

'Would you like some coffee?' he asks Mother. He sounds relaxed and grown-up. His hair is still damp from the shower and he's combed it back from his face.

'Now, you were in the play, weren't you?' Mother asks him, after I have muttered my way through introductions.

'I played Krogstad,' he tells her.

I'm glad he's here, and nervous at the same time. I would like, more than anything, to be able to touch him in front of them all; to hold his hand or to have him put an arm round my shoulder. But I think, if I'm honest, that I want this not so much because I want to feel him close to me, but because I want us to be allowed. It is all too clear, as we stand side by side talking to my mother, just how impossible our position is. We will never be able to behave like . . . I hesitate to use the word . . . like what we are: lovers. We can never be ourselves, ever again. All this he knew when we were parting at the causeway. He knew so much and I so little; but I'm catching up fast.

'Oh, I thought you were very good,' Mother is enthusing to him.

Stephen smiles and shakes his head.

'Well, thank you,' he says. 'But I think your son must get the acting award,' and, as he speaks, he smiles at me. I, at once, can feel myself blushing.

'Chris is blushing,' Angela giggles.

'And did you enjoy the play?' Stephen asks her.

Angela hangs her head and sucks at her bottom lip with her wire-clamped teeth.

Then Father returns from his conversation with the headmaster and I introduce him also to Stephen:

'Father, this is Walker. He's a prefect in Ely and he played Krogstad in the play.'

'Jolly good. Krogstad? A prefect? Ely? Jolly good.'

'Don't you have a Christian name?' Mother asks him. 'I simply hate the way Chris never mentions anyone's Christian names.'

'We don't really use them here, Mrs Metcalfe,' Stephen says, smiling again. 'I don't suppose your son even knows what mine is. It's Stephen.'

'Stephen? Jolly good,' Father says and helps himself to a cup of coffee off the tray that Stephen has put on the table beside us.

'And where docs your family live, Stephen?' Mother asks.

'In Hong Kong. My father runs one of the banks there.'

'How wonderfully romantic. Will you be going there for Christmas?'

'No. I only go during the summer holidays. I stay with an aunt near Pitlochry for the winter and spring.'

'Pitlochry?' Father volunteers, as though he's just dreamed the name. 'You remember Pitlochry, Laura. Pretty place.'

'Yes, I remember. We once had a family holiday near there. At Loch Rannoch.'

'The Road to the Isles,' Stephen says with a nod. 'Yes, I know it well.' He makes it all sound so natural, so relaxed.

148

As though he is being polite to a complete stranger and his family. I hate it. I hate the way he can lie so glibly. I want to tell them about us, if only to stop him having to pretend. But of course I don't. I remain tongue-tied. I can't think of anything to say at all and so I'm leaving it all to Stephen. 'I'm sorry,' he now says, 'I don't know where you live.'

'Well of course you don't, old chap,' Father says. 'I don't suppose you and Chris see much of each other.'

The crush in the room is getting greater as more members of the audience try to fight their way to the coffee counter. We are jostled and squeezed into a tight little group.

'Well, not really,' Stephen replies, and as he does so, I feel his leg pressing against mine.

'We live at Sevenoaks,' Mother tells him. 'One day, if you're not going to Pitlochry, you must come and stay. I'm sure you'd enjoy being near London. Pitlochry is rather a backwater.'

'I'd like that,' Stephen says, and I feel his foot stepping on mine.

'Talking of Sevenoaks,' Father says, looking at his watch.

'Well, it's been very nice meeting you,' Stephen says, taking the hint.

'Goodbye, Stephen,' Mother says, offering him her hand and looking him straight in the eye. 'I thought you were gorgeous in the play.'

I can feel myself blushing again, but this time it is embarrassment for her. She sounds so insincere, but I think she means to be kind. And now she's still holding Stephen's hand, long after she should have let go of it.

'Yes, do come and see us, and when you do, you can explain to Angela what the play was about!'

'Mother!' Angela wails and looks down, not at her own feet, I realise, but at mine, with Stephen still standing on one of them. I pull the foot clear and wait for her to comment, but she says nothing. Perhaps she didn't notice.

149

At last I see them to the car. They have a long journey ahead of them. I can't imagine why they came. Mother embraces me and congratulates me on my performance. Then Father shakes my hand and tells me that:

'Mr Wildeblood was very impressed. He says you did very well and that next term you must get down to some hard slog so that you can hurry into the sixth form. He seems to think you've got an intellect! I don't know where you got it from: neither of your parents, I think. Jolly good. Keep up the good work. See you next week.'

Then Angela winds down the back window of the Bentley and says:

'Chris, will that dreamy boy really come to stay?'

'Good heavens, no!' I tell her. 'He's a prefect.'

After they drive off, I turn to see the 'dreamy boy' waiting for me by the door of Hall. As I look at him, he turns and walks deliberately away from the lighted gravel towards the darker path that winds through the Side Wood towards the san. I know he wants me to follow him, but I feel as if eyes are watching me from every tree and all the lighted windows of Hall.

I walk in the direction of Ely and then, when I am clear of the gravel area, where people are still getting into cars and calling their farewells, I double back, across the War Memorial Lawn and below the wall of the basketball court. I cut down into Side Wood part of the way along the rough path and then pause, listening, wondering where he is.

After a moment I hear an owl whistle. It is a strange, haunted sound. It makes me shiver. I look over my shoulder in the direction of the sound and, moments later, I hear it again, closer this time. A long reed-like whistle, followed by a series of shorter, staccato notes in a mournful falling scale.

Stephen steps out from behind a tree. He lifts his hands to his lips, cupping them round his mouth, then he blows through them the same, sad owl whistle.

I run into his arms. For some reason I'm crying. He holds me to him and I feel the heat of his body warming me. We move round behind the tree and I lean back against it. The night wind is cold. It moves restlessly in the branches above us.

I feel his hands tearing at the buttons of my trousers.

I know all the reasons why we shouldn't do it here, do it now, even do it at all. But I don't listen to the reasons. I push him away and start to unfasten my flies. In the half-light I can see him releasing his hard cock from his open trousers. I hold it in my hands. It is as big as I remembered but now it seems more eager, more demanding. I remember the feel of his mouth round mine. I want to give him the same pleasure. As I slowly slide down the trunk of the tree, I feel his hands pushing down on my shoulders and when my lips find the hot tip he puts his hands on the back of my head and forces my mouth to take in the full length until I gasp and think I will choke. I can smell sweat and urine mingled with the Lifebuoy soap from the showers. My face is crushed against the thick black hairs above the shaft. I pull back gently and feel him press once more with his hands on my head. Backwards and forwards, in and out, his cock moves in my mouth. At last I sense him coming to his climax. I pull away, afraid to take the semen into my mouth, but he holds me firm and thrusts his groin once more towards my face and grips great handfuls of my hair as he pumps his orgasm against the back of my throat.

I think I will choke, but somehow I manage to swallow.

I have swallowed him whole, I think. A moment of nausea turns to wonder. He is inside me. However wrong it may be, however sinful; he has given himself to me and I have taken him.

Then, when I think there can be no more sensation left, I feel him lift me up until I am standing once more, and he kisses me lightly and gently, and a moment later I feel his hot tongue on my prick and he is doing for me what I have just done for him. But I can't last out for long, because in my mind I have already reached my climax. He drinks me dry and then, with his lips still moist with my come, he rises and looks into my eyes.

'We're one now,' he whispers and, when I shiver, he puts his coat round both of us, shutting out the night cold.

'Stephen,' I whisper. 'Will we be damned?'

'Almost certainly,' he tells me.

'Aren't you afraid?' I ask him.

'Horribly.'

'Then – what can we do?' I ask him. 'I'm afraid, Stephen. What will happen to us? Tell me.'

'I don't know, Kit. I don't know any more than you.'

'Somebody must tell us. Somebody must help.'

'Who?' His voice is sharp with sense. 'Who can we talk to about this? Who can advise us? All they would do is separate us. Is that what you want?'

'No,' I sob. 'No. It's bad enough that the holidays are coming.'

'But there's all next term for us, and the next one,' he gently whispers.

'And then you leave. And then what? I'll have another year here, maybe two, without you.' I can't stop silently sobbing. It is as though the cold has got into my heart. 'What will happen to us, Stephen?'

'We'll think of something.' He says it with such conviction and yet his words fill me with dismay. The cold in my heart is like ice.

'I'm afraid,' I say and my voice is suddenly calm. The calm that comes when we face the inevitable.

'Yes,' he whispers in my ear and I feel his head nodding. 'But what could we do, Kit? Had we any choice?'

The calm makes me sane. The calm makes me reasonable.

Perhaps he had none, I think. Perhaps he had no choice. But it wouldn't be true to say I hadn't. That first day, in the study, I chose to go back to him. I chose to meet him at Dun Bay. I could have said no. I chose to be here now. I didn't have to follow. Perhaps he really is driven by some terrible urge. I can't claim that I am. Well, not until now. But now, Stephen, now. Now, I don't know.

'I'm so afraid,' I whisper; but not to him, to myself.

# *Now*

A group of singers, some of them carrying lanterns, were belting out 'Hark, the Herald Angels' beneath the statue of Ulysses and rattling collecting boxes. It was a cold, crisp evening. The trees in the park stood motionless in the frozen air. I followed the broad path away from the lights of Park Lane towards the Serpentine. A few joggers and several lurking shadows were the only sign of life.

I walked quickly. Having decided on the route, I almost immediately regretted it. There was something sinister and potentially dangerous about the dark open spaces and the distant rumble of the rush-hour traffic. Under ordinary circumstances I would be on a 52 bus by now and halfway home to the first drink of the evening. But the circumstances were not ordinary.

Mother had come to stay. She had asked if she could, in order to do some Christmas shopping. I had, at the time, seen no reason why not. I thought it would be for a couple of days, and had made enormous efforts to make her feel welcome and comfortable. But her departure date had remained unspecified and she had already been in the flat for the best part of a week. I was unable to ask her when she would be leaving without making it sound as though I wanted her to go – which I did, but I didn't want to hurt her feelings. She had arrived on Monday and now it was Friday. I had Catherine and Bill coming to dinner the following evening for the long-overdue introduction. It wasn't that Bill was deliberately avoiding me, I think; more that he wasn't really interested in Catherine's friends. I had already formed an impression of an insufferable youth – if mid-twenties is still youth? – who was, for the moment, enjoying screwing an older woman on the side. I rather think Catherine must be good in bed; she's been practising for years. If only she would stop getting romantically hooked on every penis she encounters. But that's Catherine and, come to think of it, it's probably what makes her so irresistible to the Bills of this world. I've noticed that liberated womanhood has created a sinister closet chauv; this man champions their right to freedom and equality and then enjoys banging the hell out of them with an added *frisson*. Poor Bill, he hardly stood a chance with me! I'd heard so much about him in endless phone calls and midweek binges, when he was with 'the other woman' and Catherine was forced to be with me, that I was heartily sick of him. However, I'd promised to behave when they came to dinner.

But when I'd told Mother about the dinner, implying that it was a private party and, consequently, that she ought to be thinking about packing her bags, she had said how lovely and what would I like her to cook? I already felt threatened by her presence. Things were beginning to be done her way. The washing-up didn't stay on the kitchen table until morning any more. Eggs were kept in the fridge. Rubbish was wrapped in newspaper and taken down to the bin each evening instead of being pushed into the pedal bin and emptied when it was full. But her reaction to the dinner confirmed my worst fears. It was obvious that she was moving in. She was going to have her way after all about sharing my flat – and my life. Either that, or we were due for one hell of a bust-up.

It'd been a pig of a day, mostly spent placating an author and avoiding phone calls from his agent. The last thing I wanted was another cosy evening with Mother, swapping domestic small talk and drinking too much wine. Walking home had seemed like a good idea.

The surface of the Serpentine was oily and black in the pale lamplight. I paused for a moment near the boathouse and looked out over the flat expanse of water towards the island, with the Lido dimly discernible on the far bank. It was cold, and I dug my hands deep into the pockets of my coat to keep them warm. A movement along the rows of benches attracted my attention. Two dark figures were sitting closely together. The movement had been one of them striking a match. In the spurt of the flame I saw that it was an elderly man, wearing a City overcoat and a bowler hat. Holding the match in his cupped hands, he reached sideways, allowing his companion to light a cigarette from it. This second person was a young boy with a shock of blond hair. He looked no more than a teenager and was wearing a leather bike jacket. The match went out. The boy drew on the cigarette so that it glowed in the dark. Then he passed it to his older companion, sharing it with him. Perhaps it was a joint, I thought, or just an innocent low-tar tipped. Either way, there was something disturbingly intimate about the scene that made me want to escape from it.

Reaching the carriageway I turned my steps towards Lancaster Gate and after a few minutes flagged down a taxi and directed the driver to take me home. Sitting back in the seat, I was surprised to find that I was trembling.

'You don't mind my saying, guv, do you?' the driver said, sliding back the dividing window and speaking over his shoulder as he drove. 'But it isn't really safe, walking in the park after dark. You get some funny types. Perverts, muggers. You didn't mind my saying? Only with you just flagging me down. Lucky, really. I'd just dropped a fare at the gallery – you know where I mean? – and I thought I'd head for Paddington. But I didn't expect to pick anyone up that quickly. Only you look as if you've got a bit of money and there are junkies and immigrants, you know what I mean? Don't know what London's come to. You didn't mind my saying, did you? Cor, I can remember when you didn't think twice about walking anywhere . . .'

If I lean through the opening now I can strangle him, I thought. Or would that be too quick a release? Maybe if I slowly strip in the back of the cab and then yell 'rape' through the window? Or speak in a foreign language and refuse to understand him? Or burst into loud and unruly tears? Why not? Anything to stop him giving me his far from potted philosophy of life; based loosely on 'Blacks out, poofs out and bring back the death penalty.'

I asked him to drop me on Kensington Park Road, at the corner of the Crescent. I paid him the fare and was about to add a tip. Then instead, on an impulse, I returned the change to my pocket and said:

'I won't, if you don't mind, give you a tip. I'm rather short at the moment. My homosexual black lover needs every penny I earn to pay for his drugs. Besides, why should you get a tip? I never do.' Then I turned and walked away from him, back up the road, thus preventing him from following me without first turning his cab.

I could hear him shouting something about 'diabolical liberty' and using a lot of 'fucks' but I didn't care. I turned into Kensington Park Gardens. I'm becoming an eccentric, I thought. How did that happen? The cab drove past with the driver yelling invective. I thought he might stop and attack me. But he'd taken on another fare and possibly he wasn't sure that he could count on whoever it was for support. I ignored him and he drove on down the road stabbing two fingers up and down in the air. As he turned the corner into Ladbroke Grove I imagined him sliding open the divider again and regaling the new, innocent punter with his version of what had happened.

'That geezer . . . that geezer . . . I practically save him from the hands of a bleeding mugger . . .'

'Oh, Chris. There was a phone call for you,' Mother called from the kitchen as I let myself in through the front door. 'What a pity, you've just missed him. I've written the name on the pad.'

In her neat handwriting she had written 'Nigel Duff phoned' and a string of numbers. It was like a moment of divine intervention. I dialled the number straightaway, without even bothering to take off my coat. I didn't want to risk missing him.

The phone was answered by a girl's voice.

'May I speak to Nigel Duff?' I said.

'Hold on,' she said and then I heard her calling, 'Daddy, it's for you. He's just coming,' the voice said to me and then there was a pause.

'Hello?' a man's voice said a moment later.

'Nigel?' I asked.

'Chris? How wonderful,' he said, and he sounded pleased.

He and the family were coming down to London for New Year, to get away from the dreaded social round.

'We're staying at some crummy-sounding place in Earls Court. All we can afford, I'm afraid. But there are five of us. I just thought, maybe we could get together. Not all of us, unless you'd like that. Mine are a bit of a handful *en masse*. How about you, Chris? Are you a father? Or just a wildly successful man?'

'Why don't the two of us meet for lunch?' I said. 'We can catch up on all the news then.'

We arranged a date for just after New Year and I suggested L'Escargot, because they know me there. He said it sounded frightfully grand and he hoped he wouldn't disgrace me. I said it wasn't grand at all and that he mustn't be silly.

'It'll be really good to see you, Chris,' he said, sounding as though he meant it.

It was like talking to my youth. He used once to be my best friend. He knew Stephen.

Mother was cooking supper in the kitchen and had already poured me a gin when I went in to her.

'I was thinking,' she said, with her back to me at the stove, stirring a white sauce for a cauliflower cheese, 'of course you won't want me at your dinner party tomorrow evening. I don't know what possessed me to suggest it. I'll get a train back in the morning.'

'Won't that be rather dreary?' I said. 'I should go back on Monday and we can do something cultural on Sunday. A concert maybe. I'll see what's on.' It didn't matter any more. The conversation with Duff had brought the past a little closer and the future a little clearer.

So she stayed on and the following day we cooked the authentic cassoulet de canard à la Languedocienne according to Claudia Roden. Except that her recipe is for ten people and we got in a horrible muddle over quantities so the authenticity was questionable and we still ended up with enough food for a battalion. But shopping for the ingredients took most of the morning and preparing it took most of the afternoon, and neither of us can go anywhere near the kitchen without feeling duty-bound to open and consume vast quantities of wine, so there was a kind of therapy in it and we ended up laughing a great deal and the best of friends.

We'd decided on a fruit salad to finish and no starter. There are limits to what four people can put away at one sitting and I didn't fancy cold cassoulet for the rest of the week. Mother took charge of the fruit salad and I laid the table in the third bedroom, which I use as a dining room, should Angela get any ideas about moving in as well. Then, at six o'clock, the phone rang and it was Catherine, in tears, saying that Bill was getting married and yes, bugger it, she would still like to come. What the hell? It was a relief really. And what a bastard he was. She'd be round by seven. Which hardly gave me time to give Mother a crammer's version of the sex life of Catherine and the present débâcle.

Mother was wonderful with her. We munched through cassoulet until it was coming out of our ears and she kept up a bright line in conversation, asking Catherine about books and the shop and where she had her hair done and did she know Spain because some friends near Sevenoaks had moved to a village in the hills somewhere above the Costa del Sol and below Granada and she had an open invitation and why didn't we all go sometime? It would be fun and the friends were perfectly civilised. Then, when Catherine obviously couldn't keep up the façade any longer, Mother leaned across the table and said to her:

'You don't want to talk about any of this, do you? Chris has told me about . . . Bill, was it? I'm so sorry. You must be feeling absolutely wretched.'

The conversation changed in tone as we refreshed our palates with fruit salad and mourned, in a fairly drunken way, the shittiness of life (me), of men (Catherine) and of old age (Mother).

'It is the waste of time,' she kept on repeating. 'I've left everything too late. Please, promise me, Catherine, that you won't do that.'

'Haven't I already?' Catherine said, manfully refilling her glass as though she was at a German bierfest.

'No. You still have time.'

'To do what?' Catherine challenged her.

'Whatever it is that you most want to do. You have youth and you have health. The Inca Trail is still a possibility for you. Or sitting a degree with the Open University. Writing the Great British Novel. Working for lepers . . . I don't know. Only you know. But you've still got time. Both of you have,' and as she drew me into the conversation, she reached out across the table and took my hand. It only needed me to grab hold of Catherine and it would look like the first act of *Blithe Spirit*.

'I'm all right, Mother,' I told her, patting her gently on the arm and disengaging my hand.

'No, Chris,' she said with sudden, uncontrolled power. 'Of course you're not all right. You haven't been all right since you were a child. I'm tired of you brushing me off with trite assurances. D'you think I can't see with my own eyes? You're a mess. I want to help you. I must help you. Maybe I even know what is wrong. Please, please, Chris. Talk to me. How else can we hope to . . .' she seemed to search for the right words, 'to . . . put things right?'

There was a horrible pause. Catherine was blinking across the table at me, as though she knew she should come to my rescue but didn't know what form the rescue should take. Mother dabbed at her mouth with her napkin and cleared her throat. I stared at my plate.

'Too much alcohol! It's fatal,' Mother said at last. Then she turned to me again. 'Sorry,' she said, 'that was unforgivable.' She smiled and looked at Catherine. 'Poor girl, I almost had you halfway to Machu Picchu then, and I'm sure that that's not your style at all, is it?'

We were silent once more and Catherine lit a cigarette. I couldn't think of anything to say and Mother seemed to have burned herself out. The fruit salad was hardly touched and the wine bottle was almost empty. I shared the dregs between the three glasses and, as I did so, I glanced at Catherine. She was wreathed in a haze of cigarette smoke and staring at the tablecloth.

'Is there another bottle?' Mother asked, draining her glass.

Why not, I thought. Let's get really plastered. I went out of the room to collect a bottle from the hall cupboard. I took it with me into the bathroom and had a pee. The image of the two shadows on the bench from the evening before flashed

161

into my mind. I don't want to be an old man sitting on a bench lighting cigarettes for boys, I thought. Is that what Mother means by old?

And then I realised that Stephen wouldn't be seventeen any more. And that he might be alone on a bench; not an old man yet, but, like Mother had said, with time running out.

I opened the wine in the kitchen and poured some into a glass. It was like discovering a piece of country in a well-known area that you had no idea existed; a hidden valley or a secret wood. I had never, in all the years, thought about him not being as I remembered him. I hadn't allowed him to grow older. Well, he'd better have grown older or he wouldn't give me a second look now. He was always the older one. In fact, I couldn't imagine relating in any other way. Like Peter Pan, I thought, I never grew up. The origin of the derogatory phrase 'a pansy'?

Was I a pansy? A queer? A poofter? Bent? Gay? Nancy? A faggot? A queen? A fairy? Homosexual? Perverted? Unclean? Damned? Should I really have any more wine?

Focusing my attention, I tried to assess myself. The best I could come up with was that I was faithful. I always had been. I almost certainly always would be. In some ways the faithfulness was like an old coat, familiar and warm; like a favourite book, no longer surprising but always there to be relived and rediscovered. The fact that I was faithful to the only person I had ever loved and the fact that that person was a boy would brand me in the eyes of the world no doubt. But when we loved, we didn't know about such things.

'Oh, Kit,' he had said, 'did we have any choice?'

Then, I denied him. But have I had any choice ever since?

'Your friend has fallen asleep,' Mother said, coming into the kitchen and helping herself to my bottle. 'What are you thinking about in here, all on your own?'

'Choice,' I told her. 'Do we have any choice?'

162

Mother sniffed and sipped her wine, thoughtfully.

'Probably not, after the event. But at the time – yes. Why not? I think there is a choice. Between letting it hurt or not. What I don't understand is why so often we choose to let it hurt. Do you?'

I got up, suddenly, and walked away from her into the sitting room. She followed me in as I was leafing through the dictionary of quotations.

'Ernest Dowson. Why don't I ever remember his name?' I said, putting down the book, open, on the coffee table. 'I'd better attend to Catherine. Poor Catherine. She's not usually like this.'

'Nor are any of us, Chris,' Mother said ruefully. 'She's a very nice girl. You should go together up the Inca Trail.' And she looked at me and smiled a crooked smile.

When I looked in again, on my way to the kitchen to make some coffee, she was sitting on the floor by the table, reading the dictionary.

'I'm making reviving coffee. D'you want some?'

She shook her head.

'I rather like your Ernest Dowson,' she said. Then she read slowly from the book: 'They are not long, the weeping and the laughter, Love and desire and hate: I think they have no portion in us after We pass the gate.'

She ran all the lines together, so that at first I couldn't discern the difficult rhythm. I pulled a doubtful face.

'Bit gloomy, isn't it? Does that mean we'll all be the picture of sobriety once we get to heaven? I'm not sure that I want that. Here's to laughter and tears, I say. You know why? They allow the possibility to hope. Here's to hope. A good man for Catherine and a canoeing holiday for you. How about that?'

'I'd settle for a fortnight in Spain,' she said, and we looked at each other and smiled.

'I've never really fancied Spain,' I told her and then, as

163

I went into the kitchen, I heard the lie. 'Oh, fuck!' I said out loud.

'What's the matter?' she asked, following me in once more.

'Oh, nothing you need worry about, Mother. I was once thinking of going to Spain. But it came to nothing.'

'You were?' She sounded surprised.

'Why not?' I said, playfully. 'You don't know everything about me.'

'No. That was precisely my point at the table.' Then she held up a hand, as if declaring pax. 'Will you come for Christmas this year, Chris?'

'Oh, Mother,' I groaned. 'I hate Christmas – and you always have all Angela's brood.'

'Please.'

'Angela and I haven't spoken since I poured brandy over her head, and the boys are so noisy.'

'Christopher Metcalfe, you sound like an old man!'

But before I could protest, Catherine emerged from the dining room, looking for the loo.

'She's been drinking most of the day,' I said by way of excuse and explanation, and hurried to help her.

# *Then*

'From Greenland's icy mountains, From India's coral strand, Where Afric's sunny fountains Roll down their golden sand . . .'

The Holy Postmen reach out rigidly above us, as though attempting to join in with the singing of the five-hundred-strong congregation.

'What though the spicy breezes Blow soft o'er Ceylon's isle . . .'

That bit is probably specially for the Kyton brothers, whose parents live in Colombo and are rumoured to be VRI – or Very Rich Indeed – which makes them socially acceptable in the predominantly White Anglo-Saxon Protestant company of Blandfords Hall.

This is the hymn that is always sung at the first evensong of term. It has become a tradition. Perhaps in the distant past some Blandfordian padre thought it contained a suitable message to join the sons of the far-flung families of the Empire into a Christian unit. But although I enjoy the travelogue, it always seems to me that the last lines are a bit suspect:

'In vain with lavish kindness The gifts of God are strown, The heathen in his blindness Bows down to wood and stone.'

What about the cross on the altar? Wood. And the Holy Postmen? Stone. What about the, admittedly few, Catholics, who go to mass in Ipswich, and the seven Jews who attend

165

a synagogue? Don't they get any of the lavish kindness? Certainly there have never been many of either species at Blandfords (nor any Buddhists or Hindus, so far as I know). I suppose they are all frightened off by the syllabus, where it clearly states that: 'At Blandfords all boys will be expected to take part in Christian worship both in their houses and in the school chapel where the emphasis will be upon the worship of God and the tenets of the Anglican faith. (Episcopalians, Catholics and Jews will be catered for as much as is possible without inconveniencing the normal running of the school curriculum but will be expected to offer simple worship at the end of each day in the company of their fellow housemates.)' Generous! I certainly wouldn't send any little Hymie of mine to such an establishment. Nor the blessed fruit of my Holy Roman loins.

We finish the hymn, more or less in unison, with a protracted 'Amen'.

Mr Wildeblood, the headmaster – who can be both bloody and wild but has somehow escaped a personal nickname apart from 'the beak' which has a touch of 'the Owl of the Remove' about it and is seldom used – climbs the steps to the pulpit and proceeds to dedicate his words, and later all of us and our works, to the glory of our exclusive Anglican God. He begins, as always, with the rousing – but, by many of us, dreaded – words:

'We have come to the beginning of another school term . . .'

I can't see Stephen. I am sitting with Nigel Duff on the end of a pew about halfway up the church. Stephen should be with the other house prefects in the front rows. I can see Heslop and Morrison sitting together. Van Burghen is in the choir. Dixon is at the far end and Wickstead is, for some reason, sitting with a group of prefects from Lincoln. But where is Stephen? I sat on the end of the pew because I thought he would be able to pick me out easily when the service ends and the school stands waiting for the prefects to leave. I got through the Christmas holidays simply by knowing that this moment would come. Now, when it has, he isn't here. A terrible panic grips me. What if, for some reason, he has left? Supposing that, somehow, we have been discovered and he has been expelled? But in that case, surely I would also have been 'asked to leave'? A letter would have arrived addressed to Father summoning him to a meeting with the headmaster. Is that how they do it? Or would they wait until I returned for the new term and then tell me to my face that my 'presence was no longer acceptable'?

But of course, I'm being overdramatic. There could be any number of reasons why he isn't here. He could have flu. The weather up in Scotland has been hellish since New Year's Eve. He could be snowed in. He could simply have arrived late and be sitting at the back of the church. He could be looking at me at this moment, without my knowing it. I turn slowly, scanning the rows of faces on either side of the aisle behind me, searching for him. Then I hear Mr Wildeblood's voice raised in anger from the pulpit:

'Pay attention. You, boy, in the middle of the church. I'm not here for my own amusement.'

Later, in the dormitory, as we're getting ready for bed, I ask Nigel if he knows what has happened.

'Any idea where Walker is?' I say, trying to sound innocent. Nigel shrugs and looks away.

'No,' he replies. 'I expect he got delayed.'

'Heslop's on dorms tonight. Will you ask him, Nigel?'

'I don't want to know. You ask – if it's so important to you,' Nigel says, still not looking at me but busying himself tidying up his drawers after unpacking.

'Please,' I say. 'I can't . . .'

'Chris,' he says, looking at me, 'you're not still . . .' He looks over his shoulder, making sure that none of the others is listening to us.

167

'Just ask Heslop,' I cut in, my voice shaking. Suddenly, from nowhere, I'm close to tears.

'No,' Nigel replies, almost savagely.

I turn to look at him, surprised by his response, and find him staring at me defiantly.

'Thanks,' I say bitterly. 'I thought you were my friend.'

'It's because I'm your friend,' he whispers urgently, 'that I won't let you go on like this.'

'Friends don't make judgements. Not in my book,' I tell him angrily. And I turn my back on him, ramming pyjamas and underclothes into my drawers.

'Oh, Chris!' I hear him whisper. 'I am your friend, honestly. But . . . . this is no good.'

'You don't know anything about it,' I tell him. It's like having Mother in the dormitory with me, telling me what I should do and how I should think, just the way she has been behaving all through the holidays. That was bad enough, but I don't have to take it from Duff. What right has he to behave like this? He's not even related to me. He's nothing to me. What has it got to do with him who I see, what I do, how I behave? I don't question what he does. I don't tell him if his behaviour is 'good' or not. 'Good'? 'No good'? Who the hell does he think he is?

'All right, you lot,' Heslop says, coming into the room. 'I got delayed so we're running late. Finish off what you're doing and into bed; fast!' He saunters along the centre of the room, his hands in his pockets, a bored expression on his face.

'Heslop,' I hear Nigel saying, 'hasn't Walker come back? Only I didn't see him in chapel and he wasn't in house.'

'You may as well know, all of you,' Heslop says, commanding our attention. 'Walker will be a few days late coming back. He had to fly out to Hong Kong, unexpectedly. I'm afraid his mother was killed in a riding accident. Obviously he won't want any of this talked about, but it's probably best if you all know. He'll have taken it pretty badly and may

168

not be up to much when he gets back, so just . . .' Heslop shrugs and seems almost embarrassed with the sentiment he's suggesting, '. . . treat him with respect and go gently with him. It's tough losing a parent. I know you probably think that we're hardly aware of you lot. But we're responsible for you and – well, all I'm saying is, Walker won't be up to much for a while and I'm looking to Ely House to give him silent support. All right? Thanks, Duff – for asking. But I was going to tell you all at house prayers tomorrow night anyway.'

In bed, in the dark, I pull the covers over my head and wish I could pray. I've never known anyone important die before; apart from an aunt, my mother's sister, to whom we weren't very close. I can't imagine how Stephen feels. What will it have done to him? I know so little about him. It's only by chance that I discovered that his parents live in Hong Kong. We haven't ever really talked. Not about ordinary things. Now, when I know that this has happened, when I want to feel sympathy, when I want to be concerned only for him, I can't stop bringing myself into the picture. Instead of compassion, I feel fear. Fear that this change may affect us in some way; that his father will want him to stay out in Hong Kong or that he, himself, will be so upset that he'll forget about me and only feel this new grief. Fear that the grief will have overridden his love for me and somehow trampled it away. When he heard the news, did he think of me? Did he wish that I was there to comfort him? Did he need me?

I try to imagine Mother dying. What does it do to me? We had nothing but rows over the holidays. I don't know what's the matter with her but she seemed to pick on me all the time. Father, of course, was hardly there. He's always at the business; first of all the excuse was the build-up to Christmas and then preparing for the New Year sales, so apart from the few days over Christmas itself I hardly saw him. If Father died, I don't think I'd really mind; except it would be very difficult for Mother. But if Mother died? It would be awful

169

at home without her. Just me and Angela and Father. It'd be impossible. Not just because of all the things she does for us – running the home and looking after us and everything – but the way she fills in between us and Father and between Angela and me. Yes, that's what she does. If she wasn't there, there'd be huge gaps between us all. Angela and I never get on, and Father . . . he doesn't let any of us near him. Is that what it's like for Stephen? Are all families like that? I had nothing but rows with Mother from the moment I got home until the last few days when I felt guilty that I was behaving awfully and started making an effort to be nice to her. Because I knew it was as much my fault as hers. I was in a mood the whole time because I didn't want to be there. I wanted to be with Stephen. But if Mother were to die – suppose suddenly, now, I heard that she'd died – what would it do to me? I think I'd need Stephen more than ever. That's all. Just that. If my mother died, the only person I'd want to share the fact with, and the pain and the confusion, would be Stephen. Please, please let him feel the same. And please let me know how best to give him – what was it Heslop said? – silent support. Just let him come back and I don't even care if we can't get to see each other very often. I just want him here, so that he doesn't forget about me and so that I can show him that I still care.

Just before I drop off to sleep, I realise that Nigel asked Heslop specially for me. I know it was a gesture of friendship and I feel grateful to him, but I know it doesn't mean he has changed his mind. I'm surprised that he feels so strongly about Stephen and me. Why should the fact that we love each other be of any concern to him?

'Because, Chris, it's wrong. It isn't natural. It isn't even real.'

'How would you know?' I say, feeling angry and hurt at the same time.

We are returning from the dining hall on the way to Ely. It's a cold, raw Saturday afternoon. The sky is heavy with clouds and gusts of wind cut through the bare branches of the trees. We have half an hour of free time before assembling in Hall to be given our afternoon activities.

Nigel brought the subject up. He says that I've been dreary ever since term started and that I should snap out of it. He got quite worked up about it. I tried to make a joke of it, but he wouldn't let me.

'It's Walker, isn't it?' he said. 'You've still got this ridiculous crush on Walker.'

Crush? I tried not to lose my temper.

'It isn't like that, Nigel,' I told him. 'It isn't a crush. Because he feels the same.' Then, hating my own doubting, I added: 'Or at least he did. I wish he would come back. I mean, how long can he stay away? This is a critical year for him – with his exams and everything . . .'

Nigel walked beside me silently. I could feel great waves of resentment and injured morality coming from him. Maybe that's what prompted me to say:

'You refuse to understand, don't you? Why? Why? What is it about my feelings for Stephen that you find so hard to accept?'

And he replies:

'Because, Chris, it's wrong. It isn't natural. It isn't even real.'

Not real? If it isn't real, why am I actually losing weight? If it isn't real, why did I fail to get my first essay of term in on time? If it isn't real, why do I want to kill Nigel now, for speaking about Stephen and me like this? Not natural?

'How would you know?' I spit at him.

He walks on in silence, a step or two ahead of me, almost as though he's hurrying to get away from me. All the time he clenches and unclenches his fists. I think, perhaps, he wants to hit me. Well, let him try. I'm ready for him. I'm ready for anything.

171

'You know what it is, don't you?' he says at last, and, as he speaks, he stops walking and turns to face me.

'You tell me,' I say, hearing the danger in my voice.

'It's perverted. It's dirty. It's against God, Chris.' He spells out the sentence as though desperate for his words to penetrate into me.

'God?' I say. 'Since when did you care about God?'

'The Christian teaching is based on sound moral sense. We may not hold with organised religion, but we can't deny the sense of the message.'

I walk past him and away from him up the path.

'You know I'm right,' he calls after me. 'If you thought otherwise, you'd at least argue with me.'

'Argue?' I say, turning on him. 'Why would I bother? You don't know what you're talking about, Nigel – because it's never happened to you. You don't know what it feels like, and yet you dare to judge? I didn't choose to feel the way I do. It happened. How can it be wrong? Is it wrong to love someone? Is it wrong to care for someone?'

'No,' he replies. 'Of course it isn't. But don't tell me it's right for two people of the same sex to allow their feelings to . . .' he hesitates, blushing and searching for a halfway-decent phrase to describe the unspeakable lust that he imagines, '. . . to get out of control. That's wrong. He created men and He created women so that, together, they could create other men and women. That's what sex is for. That's how it's meant to happen. It's God's law. But what you do . . .' He stops, blushing and stammering and shaking his head.

A group of boys pass us. One of them is Hobbs. He is a year younger than Nigel and me. He's in the upper fourth. He hurries up the path and then looks back at us. Catching my eyes, he smiles at me – almost as though he knows what is going on. Then looking away again quickly, he runs out of sight round a corner in the path.

172

'I don't believe this,' I say, lowering my voice to an angry whisper. 'God's law? Which God? Whose God? Don't tell me you've suddenly turned into a religious freak, Nigel? That you believe all that balls?'

'I believe in right and wrong,' he answers, matching my anger. 'And what you two get up to together is obviously wrong. It's horrible and disgusting and I don't like to think about it.'

'You don't know what we do.' I lower my voice, realising that we're surrounded by people on their way back from lunch.

'Can you honestly tell me that it's something you're proud of, Chris?' Nigel challenges me.

I don't answer him because his question seems barely relevant. Besides, how could he ever understand what I feel if he has never been through it himself?

'Have you never wanted to?' I challenge him. 'Can you really tell me that it has never entered your head?'

'Yes, of course it has.' He sounds near despair. 'I expect it has for all of us. That's not in question. But we don't give in to it . . .'

'Look, excuse me,' I say, stopping him. 'You're jumping to conclusions here. We have never, so far as I can remember, discussed this together. So how the bloody hell do you know anything about it anyway?'

'That Sunday, last term – when you used me as an excuse to get out of the grounds. What d'you suppose I think you did? Went over your lines with him? I'd seen you together in the shrubbery. I knew what was going on. You used me as an excuse to do that. You made our friendship dirty, by using it for your lies. You didn't even ask me. You used me . . .'

'Listen,' I say to him, catching hold of the sleeve of his jacket. 'What Stephen and I did that day wasn't dirty or any of the other things you want to call it. It was the most important moment of my life. And now, without him here,

173

I feel only half-alive. I don't care whether you understand. I don't care if this finishes our friendship for ever. If it does, then it wasn't worth keeping anyway. Besides, what do I want with friendship now? In fact, I'm glad this has happened. You've done me a favour. You've made me see just how much Stephen means to me. I'd lay down my life for him. He's the first person who's ever meant that much to me. And what we do together has got nothing to do with you or anyone else. Don't quote your religion at me either. Because I can't believe in a God who makes me feel the way I do about Stephen in order simply to punish me for feeling that way; as if life was some sort of obstacle race. What sort of compassion is that? What sort of mercy?'

'All right then,' he says, his voice changing from anger to triumph, like a tennis player hitting an ace. 'Tell me; has he written to you?'

I'm surprised by the move and wary of it.

'Written?'

'Walker. If he cares so much and you care so much,' he can hardly keep the sarcasm out of his voice, 'and it's all so perfect, then surely he'd have written to tell you what's happened? He wrote to Morrison about it, so why not to you?'

'He didn't know my home address,' I reply, realising that I sound defensive.

'He knows the address here. It's nearly a fortnight since the beginning of term. He could have written.'

'It's too much of a risk. Letters go astray.'

'Yes.' Nigel nods, seeming reasonable. 'Or – what if it's all over for him, Chris? That's what usually happens. These things don't last. What if he's not thinking about you any more? What then?'

I'll kill myself, I think. But to Nigel I say:

'He will be. You'll see.'

We walk in silence up the final stretch of the path and reach the house just as the first big blobs of snow start to fall out of the heavy sky.

'I don't want you to be ruined by it, Chris. That's why I'm doing this.' He seems to be pleading with me now. He looks sad and desperate. 'You're my best friend. I can't stand by and watch you destroy yourself.'

'Friendship?' I say, enjoying feeling bitter. 'I didn't ask for your friendship. I don't accept it. I don't want your so-called friendship.'

'Oh, Chris!' he says, filling the words with volumes of frustration and disappointment. He hurries away into the house ahead of me. I feel cold and trembling, angry and humiliated. I want to believe that right is on my side. I want to know that all he has said is prejudiced nonsense. But, most of all, he has left me with a knot of fear in my stomach. Supposing he were to be right. Supposing Stephen has tired of me. Supposing it is true, what I most fear, that his mother's death has in some way parted us. What then of Kit? I ask myself; and the bleak prospect is too desperate to contemplate.

Then, at house prayers, totally unexpectedly – when I've given up even hoping – Stephen walks into Hall with the other prefects. He looks perfectly normal; as though nothing has happened to him at all. The only sign of the tragedy he has suffered is the black band he is wearing on the arm of his sports jacket.

Mrs TG plays 'Onward Christian Soldiers' on the grand piano and the house sing the hymn loudly.

TG and the prefects face us across the refectory table.

'Let us pray,' TG says. We stand with lowered heads. 'Lord, bless this kingdom, that religion and virtue may season all sorts of men . . .'

Stephen is back, my heart sings. He's here in the room. If I lift my eyes now, I'll be able to see him. So far our eyes have not met but I know he knows I'm here. I'm standing in

175

the third row and Clegg, who is taller than I am, is standing immediately in front of me. But if I move to the side and open my eyes I will see him . . .

'. . . peaceably seek Thy Kingdom and its righteousness, the only full supply and sure foundation . . .'

His eyes are closed and there are deep frown marks between his brows as though he is forcing himself to listen to TG's words. I'd forgotten exactly how he looked. I'd forgotten that he is tall and that his hair is very black and the way he combs it back from the forehead and that it falls forward and he pushes it back with his hand spread open like a comb. I'd forgotten that just seeing him makes my heart beat faster and my knees feel weak. I'd forgotten how frightening it is and how exciting and how impossible to give up. If I think his name, really concentrate on his name, he'll open his eyes and he'll see me. Stephen! Stephen! I think, silently calling him. Stephen! Stephen! . . .

'. . . so that we may continue a place and people to do Thee service to the end of time. Amen.'

'Amen,' we all repeat and Stephen opens his eyes and he is looking straight at me. My heart stops. He stares at me. Then he frowns and looks away.

The following three weeks must be the worst of my life. I hang around the corridors of the house, hoping to bump into him. I leave rooms late or early, just so that I'll be in the right position to see him. And although we do, many times, see each other, he's always with other people or I am, or he's hurrying and appears not to be aware of my presence. He does dormitory duty once a week, but apart from saying 'Good night' to me as he does to all the others, we haven't exchanged a single word. Then, one Thursday afternoon, when I think I can bear the nearness and the distance no longer, I see Mrs TG waiting by the house door as I return from an incomprehensible maths test.

'Have you seen Morrison?' she asks me.

'No, Mrs Gerrard.'

'Do you think you could find him for me? I am supposed to be taking him in the car to the dentist in Saxmundham.'

'He may be in his study,' I say.

'Could you look, dear? Tell him we shall be late.'

As I go up the stairs to the Games Room landing, I can hear Morrison talking as he comes out of his study. He is saying something about 'the number of points required . . .'

'Morrison, sir,' I say, meeting him on the narrow stairs, 'Mrs TG is looking for you.'

'Out of my way, sprat,' he says, taking the stairs three at a time. 'I'm horribly late. Thanks for finding me,' and he's gone and I can hear his footsteps echoing away into the depths of the house. I stand in the half-gloom, my heart pounding. The sound of Ping-Pong alerts me to the fact that there are people in the Games Room. But no light spills out on to the dark landing, so they must have the door shut. Stephen is in the study. I heard him answer Morrison when he first opened the door. But what if there are other people there? Dixon or Wickstead? I'll make an excuse. I'll say I'm looking for Morrison. I could have missed him on the lower landing. It's quite reasonable.

I go quickly along the corridor, passing the Games Room door, and round the corner to the study door. Now, out of sight of the main passage, I pause. I can't stop trembling. I listen. There is no sound from the room. I take a deep breath and, raising my hand, I knock quietly.

At first there is no response, then:

'Just a minute,' I hear Stephen call and, a moment later, the door opens and we are standing face to face for the first time since our night in the wood. He is so close that I can smell him, that I can feel the warmth from his body.

The light is behind him and I can't see if his face is smiling the same, inane, happy and scared grin that is on mine.

'What d'you want?' he asks quietly.

177

I don't believe the question. It stings like a slap on the cheek. I wish, suddenly, that I hadn't come. I'm confused, embarrassed, afraid. There was no gladness in his voice, no love. It wasn't Stephen's voice, but that of a stranger. I can hardly speak for the tension in my throat.

'To see you,' I whisper.

He stares at me, motionless. I think he will reach out and touch me. But instead, he half closes the door, so that the wood is between us.

'Clear off, Metcalfe,' he says. 'Leave me alone.'

The door closes and I am in the dark.

Strange what despair will make us do. It is a new experience for me and yet the moment it strikes it has an old familiarity about it. It doesn't make me want to cry. I feel too numb for that. I only lean against the wall beside the door and feel the cold stones burning through my jacket, turning my body to ice. I can't move and in time my legs won't hold me up any more. So, instead, I slide slowly down until I am crouching on the floor outside his room. The room where he seduced me. The room where he has now rejected me. Once I stepped through that door a free person. I told him I had choice. I told him that it was my decision that I came to him; that I was in control of my actions. But I hadn't reckoned with this. How could I know the end when I hadn't thought there was to be one? Now I am unable to take any initiative. I can only wait here until someone comes and tells me to move; wait until he opens the door or Morrison returns from the dentist, or someone unexpected comes, wanting to see him. He is in there, on the other side of the door, thinking thoughts that are not my thoughts, that I cannot even know. He is in there, existing without me; breathing and warm and alive. Without me. 'Leave me alone,' he said, as though in some way I was a nuisance to him. But how can I leave him alone when he has become the only reason for my life? How can I leave him alone since we've become one? He is inside me, part of my body, part of my mind. So – how can I leave him alone?

Later, I don't know how long after he closed the door on me, it opens again and he stumbles out into the passage, almost falling over me.

'What the . . .' I hear him say, as he reaches out and saves himself against the wall. Then, seeing me, he turns and goes back into the study.

'You'd better come in,' he says.

But I can't move, and he has to reach down and take my hand and pull me up. The warmth of his flesh against mine sends shivers through my body. I feel the ice melting and the tears forming.

'What were you doing there? I told you to go,' he says.

I shake my head, unable to speak for fear I start to cry.

He stands across the room from me, staring and silent. Then he crosses behind me, closes the door and walks back past me, over to the window. He turns his back, looking out. Black clouds are banking in from the sea, bringing the night and more snow and cold. I can hear the wind blowing and, distantly, seagulls screaming and calling.

'Stephen,' I whisper. 'Why? What happened to us?'

'We must forget about all that,' he tells me. 'We must go on as if it never happened.'

He won't look at me, but his words find their mark. It is as if he were cutting me with a knife; tiny stiletto stabs slowly killing our love.

'Why?' I say, but the question is only to voice my own disbelief. I don't expect him to offer an answer.

'Get out, Metcalfe,' he says fiercely, still without looking at me. His arms are outstretched, gripping the top of the cupboard against which he leans, clinging on with white-knuckled hands. His whole body is shaking. He is in such distress. I can't bear to see it. I cross to him and put my hand on his back, a light touch. At once he swings

179

round, his fists raised like a boxer. He punches me savagely in the stomach then brings his other fist down on the back of my neck. I stumble forward, winded and convulsed with pain, and fall heavily against the fireplace.

'Now get out,' he says, panting for breath. 'Please, before I harm you.'

I crawl towards the door, fear and confusion making me fast. I rise and turn the knob, then, as I am leaving, I glance back and see him hunched up on the sofa, the sofa where it all began, his hands covering his face, silent sobs shaking his body.

I close the door and hurry away along the passage. I start to run down the spiral stairs to the house landing and then on down the next three flights to the side door.

Snow is falling through the gathering dusk. I take the side path that leads through the woods between Ely House and Lincoln and then branch off towards the main drive. I am wearing no coat and only my house shoes. The cold is intense. But I'm glad of it. I run along the narrow paths through the woodlands, avoiding the broad walks. Ahead of me the church looms out of the thick light.

The side door is always open during the hours of daylight. I let myself in, the metal latch echoing in the stillness. Inside, it is almost dark. Christ on his crucifix looks down from the altar. The stained glass has faded to black.

'Why?' I shout to the God of our fathers and Nigel Duff. 'Why?' And the tears start to fall, hot and stinging. 'Why?' I sob.

But no answer comes from the dark, no comfort, no hope. I know now how it feels to be utterly and desperately alone, a half-person. I have lost my better self; lost Stephen. And I don't know:

'Why?' I sob to the uncaring void.

# *Now*

Mother had made enormous efforts to please us all. There were fires in both the drawing room and the dining room hearths, although the day was actually quite warm and muggy. There was a tree in the drawing room and holly behind all the pictures. The cards were strung on ribbons. There was a great bowl of chrysanthemums in the hall and an arrangement of poinsettias on the landing window ledge.

I arrived at midday, ahead of Mummy and Daddy Prick and all the little Pricklets.

'You look like Santa Claus,' Mother said, greeting me with a kiss in the hall. It was true that I was laden with parcels, but if Santa Claus had even half my reluctance then the spirit of Christmas really is dead and we may as well give up the whole charade.

'Put the presents under the tree, darling,' she said, 'and then take your case upstairs. Oh, I hope you won't mind, I've put Roger in with you, on a camp bed. Now that the boys are so huge, I don't think they'll all fit in the small spare.' As she spoke she was hurrying towards the kitchen door, whence steamy smells evoked instant memories of childhood.

'I don't mind,' I said. 'But did you check with his parents?'

'Good heavens, don't be so silly. You're his uncle.'

Actually the thought of sharing my room with anyone, let alone one of the children, was irksome, but I had made a solemn promise to Catherine that I would be good and I was disinclined to break it at the first little hitch in the proceedings.

I'd seen a lot of Catherine in the week since Mother returned home. She had written a very sweet note to both of us, apologising for her drunken stupor on the Saturday, which I had brought down to show Mother at her insistence, but which I assured her was not in the least bit called for.

'We were all well away. You didn't behave badly. You didn't say "fuck" or fart or fall over. In fact it was a rather dull party,' I told her.

Catherine is very good, usually, about bouncing back, but:

'It's got to me this time, Chris. I don't know why. Maybe I'm getting old and I don't have the optimism I once had. Maybe I really loved him.' Saying the words made her start to cry.

We were in her sitting room. We were supposed to be going to a film together but from the moment I arrived it was obvious that what she really wanted to do was talk. And so I'd let her, of course.

'I want to live with someone, Chris,' she sobbed, 'not just to sleep with them from time to time.' She blew her nose noisily. 'I want to do ordinary things; I don't know, go shopping with someone, cook with someone, wash up with someone. God, how pathetic. I want to be married to someone. I just don't ever meet the right someone.' She frowned, puzzled at her own apparent lack of luck. 'Or if I do, they're already married or they're gay or they're you.'

'Me?' I asked, surprised that I was suddenly included.

'Why shouldn't it work? Us being married?'

'Is this a proposal, darling?' I asked her.

'No. But seriously, why not? You're lonely and so am I.'

'I think it requires more than mere mutual loneliness to consummate a marriage. Besides, who would we have to run to when things weren't going right between us? We'd have to find new friends and that'd be much more difficult.'

'But you don't,' she said. 'You don't run to me.'

'That's because things invariably go right for me.'

182

'Do they honestly?'

I had wanted to answer her truthfully. I didn't want us to have a one-sided relationship. I knew that my monastic existence was a disappointment to her; that it lacked the stuff of drama and of mutual recognition. But in all the years that we had shared each other's confidences, I had never told her about what happened at Blandfords. I couldn't start now. It was too long ago; too involved and still, I was surprised to be learning, too painful.

'Well, I've had my moments,' I told her. 'But you know me, I avoid trouble by never allowing anything to possess me in the first place.'

'Or anyone?' she asked, frowning.

I shrugged.

'I like my own company.'

'But you must have sexual urges?'

'I'm not sure how the spotlight swung round on me, suddenly. I thought we were talking about you and your hell.'

'You don't like it, do you?' she said, looking at me with her head on one side.

'What?' I asked, feeling my back against the wall.

'Us talking about you.'

'Of course,' I replied, crossing back to my chair and trying to make light of it all. 'I'll tell you anything you want to know.'

'Have you a secret lover?' she asked.

I tried laughing, but it didn't sound very convincing.

'Is that what you believe?'

'Sometimes,' she replied. 'Sometimes I think that you have quite an active sex life, but that you think it might shock me.'

'You mean rough trade? Or cottaging?' I said, staring at her coldly. She was right, of course, I don't like the spotlight. I don't mind asking the questions and listening to the answers, but I don't want to be on the couch, submitting to someone else's probing.

'Why not?' she continued. 'Quite a lot of people like rough trade. Particularly if they went to a public school. *La vice anglaise*? Sado-masochism? Something like that? I don't see you as a transvestite – though I'm told that the most surprising people are in the privacy of their own homes. Cottaging? What a very gay expression for you to use. Yes, I can imagine that. I'd be sad if it was true. But even that – I am right, aren't I? Picking up men in public lavatories and fiddling with them? – even that is somehow more healthy than nothing. You are gay, I suppose? Basically? I've always thought that you probably were.'

'Oh, I must be, mustn't I, darling? Otherwise how could I have resisted your allure over the years?' The sarcasm wasn't worthy of me. But she was overstepping the mark; that unspecified line that is drawn in a friendship between what is acceptable and what is forbidden.

'You're angry,' she said, surprised.

'No. I just don't think this conversation is getting us anywhere. We'd have been better off going to a film.'

'Chris, I'm your friend. Good God, you know more about me than anyone. I'm not prying – well, if I am it's only because I don't want there to be anything unspoken between us. I trust you completely. I'm only asking you to trust me in return. I wouldn't mind if you were gay, or if, maybe, you're having a wild affair with someone so powerful that you're forbidden to talk about it; Mrs Thatcher or a pop star. It wouldn't matter to me. I'd still love you just the same.'

'In that case, Catherine darling, why would you be asking?'

'Oh, you're impossible.'

'Sorry. Now, shall we return to you and the lamented Bill?'

'What's the point? If you've never been in love yourself how can you possibly understand what I'm going through now.'

'I didn't say I'd never been in love,' I replied, speaking so calmly and in such an ordinary voice that it surprised even me. 'I was once so in love that when it ended, I decided never to go through anything like it ever again.'

She looked at me regretfully; like a young child who knows she's pushed her luck.

Fatal, Christopher, fatal. What made me say it? The years of silence shouldn't be broken so carelessly. Now, in a gentle, soothing voice, the voice of the mother in her, she wanted to know all about it; the details, the full story. She wanted me to name names, cross t's and dot i's. She quite forgot about Bill and her own misery and revelled in this newly discovered nugget from my past.

'I had no idea,' she kept repeating. 'I'm sorry. I somehow thought . . . Of course, how stupid of me. Of course you know what I've been through, because you've been there yourself. Oh, Chris! I can't bear the thought of you being made unhappy.' She sounded as though she really meant it. I could feel myself being drawn towards the warm comfort she offered. 'Tell me about it,' she said. 'Please.'

It would have been easy then. But once I'd begun, who knew where it would end?

'No. I'm sorry,' I said, rising. 'I don't want to.' How could I suddenly talk about it now, when I never had before, not in thirty years? Such revelations surely require preparation and courage and some deep need to be relieved of the burden of them. I couldn't casually reveal my innermost secrets and trade them for a few of hers. So, instead, I'd made an excuse to leave, promising that we'd meet the following evening and go to the film.

Which we did. When Catherine is between men, I see her most evenings. Walking home from her flat that evening along Westbourne Grove, I saw a man wearing a City overcoat and a bowler hat coming towards me. As we drew level I had a moment of double recognition. I realised that he could have been the man I had seen in Hyde Park, lighting the cigarette for the fair-haired youth, and that he was Dixon.

'Metcalfe,' he said, raising his hat, 'good to see you. I gave Fluffy your address.' He seemed embarrassed by our encounter. 'Been to see a client. Must dash. Extraordinary, old son. We don't clap eyes on each other in years and now two in a row! I'll give you a bell sometime. We can get together and have a good gossip. Any luck with Walker?' All the time he was speaking, he was backing away from me. 'I'll keep my ear to the ground. Goodbye, goodbye,' and, raising his hat again, he turned and disappeared into the night. 'Happy Christmas,' I heard him call. 'I nearly forgot. Can't stop. Train to catch.'

Catherine phoned when I got in. She was sorry she'd pried. Would I forgive her? I assured her that there was nothing to forgive. That I was fine. That I loved her very much and that all I wanted was her happiness. We're better on the phone, more sensible and more fun.

I told her I thought Bill had behaved like a shit – but that probably his main aim had been not wanting to hurt her and that that could make people do and say stupid things. An example, perhaps, of killing with kindness. Although what I said made her cry, I think she knew I was right.

'But all the same, Chris. He isn't here. And that's all I want. Him here, with me . . .'

Until the next time, I thought, and I realised that, unknown to her, that was the yardstick by which I measured her periodic hurts. I couldn't ever believe in the depth of her misery, because she had always, given time, recovered from it. It was a harsh criterion, but it was the only one I knew. It was, after all, the one by which I had lived my adult life.

The Pricks had arrived by the time I came down from dropping my case in the room and having a pee.

'But Mummy, for heaven's sake,' Angela was protesting, 'of course Roger can sleep with the boys.'

'There simply isn't room, Angela. There was when Rupert and Ralph topped and tailed in the bed but they can't do that now. There's plenty of room on Chris's floor. It's only for a couple of nights. What is all the fuss about?'

Angela was wearing a dark blue knitted dress on which I complimented her, although in fact it made her look big in all the places that she was big and wished she wasn't.

'Thank you, Chris!' she exclaimed, as though a word of kindness from me was worth more than a hundred years in paradise. 'It is rather nice, isn't it? A friend in Canterbury has a machine. She knitted it – but I told her what I wanted: nothing too fancy, a full skirt and a shawl collar. It's fun, isn't it?'

Fun? It was simply a blue knitted dress that made her boobs and her bum look enormous. That's fun?

Richard staggered into the hall, weighed down under a heap of coats and parcels.

'Chris is here already, darling,' Angela informed him, which seemed superfluous as we were smiling acknowledgement to each other at the time. 'When you've put those things down, I want a word with you,' she continued.

'Let me help you, Richard,' I volunteered, relieving him of several anoraks and a red coat with a fur collar.

Rupert, the youngest Prick, came in lugging a giant suitcase.

'Good heavens, Angela! How long are you staying?' I said, taking the coats through to the garden passage and not waiting for her answer.

When I returned to the hall, she and D the P were in whispered consultation in the drawing room. Ralph and Roger came in from the drive. Ralph was patting a football up and down in a rather aggressive way, which can't have been good for the carpet, and Roger, who was wearing tiny earphones, had a bored expression. He'd grown very tall and looked exactly how his father must have done at that age; quite handsome in a pink and gold way. The hair helped him, of course, but it wouldn't be up there for very long so I hoped he was enjoying it. How depressing for him to look at Daddy Prick and know that there but for the grace of God went he.

'Hello, boys,' I said. 'Happy Christmas.'

I don't think they were going to bother to reply, but if they were they were prevented by Angela emerging from the drawing room, looking hot and flustered.

'Roger, you're sleeping on a camp bed in Uncle Christopher's room.'

'Sorry?' he said, lifting an earphone and making his mother repeat the sentence.

'OK,' he said, with a shrug.

'I want to sleep with Uncle Christopher,' Rupert announced.

'Well you can't. You're sleeping with your brother in the spare room. Now, off you go, all of you. Upstairs and wash your hands. Roger, take the case, darling. Ralph, no football upstairs.'

As soon as they'd trooped out of sight, she turned to me and said in a low, confiding hiss:

'Roger's got a girlfriend. He's frightfully serious about it.'

I got the feeling that the information was dual purpose.

'Good Lord! But he's a baby,' I protested, sounding like every bachelor uncle in Christendom.

'I've just told Chris about Roger's girlfriend,' Angela hissed to Richard, who had finished stowing the presents under the tree and had come out to join us.

'Oh, yes. Good,' he said, blankly.

'I hope you're supplying him with condoms, Dick?' I said, I thought helpfully.

'You see what I mean?' Angela cried. 'If you talk like that in front of the boys, I shall be very cross, Chris.'

'Then I promise I won't, Angela. We don't want you cross, do we? Not on Christmas Day.'

She gave me a look that neatly mixed dismay and venom and went towards the kitchen.

'I'll go and help Mother,' she said. 'Stop racing about up there,' she yelled. 'Richard . . .' The saying of the name conveyed their entire relationship.

'Chaps,' he called from the foot of the stairs, 'you heard your mother. Calm down!' Then he looked at me and smiled. 'Bound to be a bit overexcited. Christmas and all that. How are you, Chris? Been here long?'

No, not long and I came by the A2 and the M25 and I thought about coming through Bromley and there's someone at the office who swears you can get to Budleigh Salterton via Andover and I wish I was at home and:

'You're looking well,' he tells me, without, mercifully, waiting for a reply. 'Something smells good.'

'Lunch in half an hour,' Mother said, coming out of the kitchen and taking off her apron. 'Are you two drinking, Richard? Or are you still on the wagon? Let's all go into the drawing room. Why are we standing in the hall? A gin and french, Chris, if you're making one.'

The ceremony of Christmas lunch passed in a haze of banality thanks mainly to Angela, who kept the conversation going with innumerable and varied topics:

'Well, I think they should stop the Notting Hill Carnival – when in Rome, do as the Romans. We don't go jigging about in the streets in fancy dress; not in this country, thank you very much . . . Well, of course the Chunnel will ruin the countryside and it'll be an awful pity our not being an island any more and the thought of all those ghastly foreign cars swarming all over our lovely country lanes; but, and it's a big but, just think what fun! Weekends in Normandy . . .' and so on, endlessly. Where does she get it all from? Why does she bother?

We had one major domestic tiff; over how the boys would spend the afternoon.

'I don't want to listen to the Queen's speech.'

Good for Roger; he didn't say much but when he did he exhibited a nice bolshie streak. I quite warmed to him.

'Why is it so important, Angela?' I asked her, when it had all simmered down and things looked as though they were turning boring again.

'Because it's England,' she said, with the emphasis of the drum roll before the National Anthem.

After lunch the afternoon sprawled away. It was too warm for the fire and too damp for a walk. Dick and the two younger boys watched television while Mother, Angela and I washed up.

'Roger will be writing to his girlfriend,' Angela explained.

'Why? Where does she live?'

'In Canterbury,' she replied.

'Then he'll see her in a couple of days.'

'Well, you know what it's like when you're young and in love. Or maybe you don't.'

'I'm surprised that you do. I thought Richard was your first romance.'

'Heavens, no. If you'd rather he slept in the sitting room, Chris . . .'

'Who?'

'Rog. We could put his camp bed behind the sofa. I don't suppose any of us will be late going to bed . . .'

I shrugged:

'It's entirely up to you. If you think he won't be safe in my room, then by all means move him.'

'I didn't mean that . . .'

'Actually, he isn't my type. But I don't expect you to believe me. I go for the older man. Now, if Richard was in my room, you'd have every right to be worried.' For a moment I could see that she was almost pleased. My words confirmed her unerring taste – even in men. 'I also, of course, go for the older woman,' I continued. 'No, not you, Angela, but Mother.

You really wouldn't be safe from me, darling, so don't dream of sharing a room with me. You know that incest is all the rage at the moment. I could be your toy-boy son. Would you have me?'

'Certainly,' Mother replied gaily. 'That's settled, then. Chris will sleep in my bed and Roger can have the room to himself.'

'What are you both talking about?' Angela said, looking and sounding bemused.

'Incest, darling,' Mother told her.

'I just meant that I didn't want Chris to be put out.'

'That's very sweet of you. But honestly, it doesn't matter to me one way or the other.'

During the evening we had several bad-tempered games of Monopoly. Everyone wanted the Boot and we had to toss for it and I won. But I gave it to Rupert and took the Bowler Hat instead.

Later, mortgaged to the hilt and having sold all four stations and the electricity and water boards to Dick – who always wins – I phoned Catherine. She was staying with her mother in Lytham St Annes.

'How's it going?' I asked her.

'Oh, absolutely wonderfully,' she replied. 'We're on our fourth game of Spite and Malice and the television hasn't been switched off since nine fifteen this morning. How about you?'

I told her about Monopoly and the sleeping arrangements. She laughed and asked me if I'd managed to keep my temper.

'So far,' I told her, 'but I can't promise. I'll probably go up to London tomorrow. I don't think Mother will mind.'

'Give her my love,' Catherine said, and I promised I would.

Eventually the day was over and the younger boys were packed off to bed.

'I should go too, Rog,' his mother suggested. 'Then you can be all tucked up and out of the way before Uncle Christopher comes up.'

I thought of suggesting that she personally locked him into his sleeping bag and took the key with her, but why prolong a perfectly awful evening?

Eventually the senior Pricks also went up, yawning profusely and making remarks about heavy food and red wine and late nights, and Mother and I were alone in the drawing room.

'God!' she said. 'I know you call poor Richard Dick the Prick, but honestly – he's a saint putting up with her.'

'Mother!' I said, laughing. 'She's your daughter.'

'I deny it. I never did like that ward sister. I think she swapped babies.'

'I thought I might go back tomorrow. Is that mean of me?'

'Dear Chris!' she said, smiling. 'It's beastly of you. But I'd come with you given half a chance.'

The light was on in my room and Roger was sitting on the floor, listening to his Walkman.

I hadn't brought any pyjamas, because I never wear them. But I was determined to be grown up and unembarrassed about it. I went along to the bathroom and cleaned my teeth, then came back and started to undress. He showed admirable and sublime indifference to me.

I got into bed and adjusted the pillows.

'Good night,' I said.

He smiled vaguely, pointed at the earphones and said:

'I just want to finish this tape.'

I realised that he probably wouldn't be able to hear me if I said anything, so I didn't bother.

Eventually he rose with a strangely studied languor and stretched his arms up above his head. He was wearing jeans and a cotton shirt. He took off the headphones and wound the flex round them. Then he pulled off his shirt and dropped it on the floor. His skin was white and pink and he had surprisingly good arm muscles. Bare-chested, he stretched and yawned again. He seemed to be doing everything in slow motion. Then he unzipped his jeans and slid them down his body and pulled his legs free. Under them he was wearing boxer shorts. I'd forgotten what a young body looked like: angular, almost fragile, but firm and spare. He walked over to the chest of drawers and combed his hair, looking at his reflection in the mirror.

'Are you in any of these?' he asked, looking at the school photographs hanging on the wall.

'All of them,' I replied.

'Oh, there you are!' he cried, with a smirk in his voice. Poor child, he couldn't help it. He's a chip off the Prick. 'How old were you then?'

'Sixteen.'

He laughed, peering at my face in the photograph.

'My age. Well, almost. I'm almost sixteen.'

'Yes,' I said. Then, 'Get into bed, Roger, aren't you cold?'

'Not really,' he said. But he crossed back to the camp bed and turning his back on me put on a pyjama jacket and then slipped quickly out of his shorts and into the pyjama trousers, as though his nerve had suddenly deserted him.

'Good night, Uncle Chris.'

'Good night, Roger,' I said, and reaching out, I switched off the lamp.

I lay on my back, looking at the dark. I was shaken by his behaviour. He'd openly flirted with me; played me like a fisherman trawling a catch.

But I hadn't wanted him and I don't think for one moment he wanted me. He just couldn't help himself. Is that the secret of that age? So much emerging sexuality that you can't help . . . flaunting it? Being a tart? Is that what usually has happened for all those sad old men had up for molesting

193

*William Corlett*

teenagers? Are they subjected to similar treatment? Offered something on a plate, then persecuted for accepting it?

Mercifully, I hadn't wanted him. But his body had disturbed me. His youth disturbed me; his arrogance.

I was once like that, I thought. I'd forgotten. I was sure of my body and eager to share it. Not vain, just newly aware. Perhaps he has a lover at school? Do they do that sort of thing now? Did they ever? Or was it just me? Me and Stephen. I remembered when he tried to make it end, and the terrible waste of time. I remembered crying myself to sleep night after night in the dormitory and tossing off into a handkerchief and hating myself and, in time, of course, hating Stephen as well. Hating him, but not managing to be free of him. Even now. Even now, not to be free of him.

194

# *Then*

'Squad, attention! Stand at ease! Attention! At ease! Squad . . . wait for it, wait for it; squad, 'shun!'

Cold, damp March weather. The first faint fuzz of green on the stark branches. Playing at being soldiers in preparation for National Service.

Stephen is Officer I/C Ely Squadron and I am a mere cadet.

It still hurts to see him, but it's different now. The love I thought I felt for him has turned to a spiteful hate. I can't stop watching him. I manage to be in the shower room in the early morning or near the gym when he's training. He seems to spend all his spare time punishing his body. Work-outs, runs, squash; Morrison and he play together usually. He's even had the odd game of fives with Dixon. Whenever he sees me looking, he frowns and looks away. I've stopped trying to talk to him. I don't even want to. I could have reported him for attacking me in the study. But what would be the point? I could get him expelled. Has he thought of that? I could tell all to TG. I could finish his career. Hart's parents' divorce is all over the Sunday newspapers. His mother is taking the old man to the cleaners according to my mother, who was full of it during the Christmas holidays and seemed to be enjoying every detail. Poor Hart. He must feel such an idiot while all the Blandfordian parents and most of their sons devour the seamy tangle of his family life. Hart? Who would believe it?

His father has a mistress! But he looks so ordinary, and Hart himself is such a drip.

Well, I could do the same to Stephen. I could take him to the cleaners. But would anyone believe me? And would I get any satisfaction out of it? It would be obvious that I'd let myself become his bum-boy. That's what the school calls people like me. Though God knows what it's got to do with the bum. I'd have thought 'cock-sucker' would be better. He made me do that. Why did he make me do that? Why did he use me and then just drop me? Yes, I hate him. Wouldn't anyone? But why can't I forget what he feels like? Why does he still haunt me? Why can't I fall for someone else? Or be like Duff, pure and happy: his only passion apparently being to sight a lesser-spotted woodpecker or an Arctic tern; bird-watching is his bag, Stephen-watching has become mine. I'm an avid follower of basketball, just because he's on the team. I go to the gym a lot. I watch squash games. Does he know? Is that why he wears shorter shorts than anyone else, and parades round the locker room wearing only a jockstrap? Is he doing it for me? Does he know I'm watching? Or is he looking for a new bum-boy? Is he hoping to trap a fourth-former? Have I grown too old for him? Is he tired of me? Or is he enjoying destroying me? Is that how he's getting his kicks now?

'Terrible, Metcalfe. Look at you.'

Yes. You look at me, Stephen. See what you've done.

'Have you blancoed this belt? Well, have you?'

'Yes,' I whisper.

'Yes, what?'

'Yes, Stephe . . . Yes, Walker. Sir.'

'That's better. On fatigues, Metcalfe,' and he passes on down the line.

For fatigues I am given:

'A week of early-morning study duties, Metcalfe. Our fag's in the san. And you'd better be sure there isn't a speck of dust and that the fire lights first match — or I'll have you doing it all term. You're a disgrace. What are you?'

'A disgrace, Walker, sir. I'm a disgrace.' Oh, I can hate and it sounds in my voice. Is that what he wants? To make me hate him. Well, I think he got the message. His eyes stayed on me for a second too long. Yes, I'm hating you, Stephen. You've made me do that, just like you made me love you. See what a slave I am.

'He's not supposed to give those sort of fatigues.'

'Then what should I do, Nigel? What d'you suggest? Write to our Commanding Officer? Get him court-martialled?'

'Why's he doing it, Chris? I thought you two were . . .' He hesitates, not knowing the words to use to describe what he imagines we were.

'I thought so too. But you were right. He's got over it.'

'All the same. He doesn't need to persecute you. He was as much a party to what went on between you. He's older and he's meant to be wiser. I really liked Walker. I'm disappointed.'

Dear Duff! Just when I seem to forget that he's my friend, he pops up beside me, staunch and supportive. I hope I'll do the same for him, if he needs me. I can't be sure, of course. I don't think I'm a very loyal person. Well, I wasn't. But I would have been to Stephen.

The first morning of the fatigues, I have to manage to wake myself half an hour before the first bell rings, at six. I have to shower, dress and have finished cleaning the study before the last bell, at seven. I kept waking all night, for fear that I'd oversleep.

The first job is cleaning out the grate. Last night's embers still glow, dull red. I put them into a metal bucket and am sweeping up the ashes when I hear the door behind me open. I look over my shoulder and see Stephen, wearing a dressing gown, standing in the entrance.

'Carry on,' he says, coming into the room and closing the door.

I continue to sweep up the ashes, nervously aware that he's watching me. I become clumsy. I catch the edge of the shovel against the rim of the bucket and spill some on to the carpet.

'Watch what you're doing,' I hear him say.

I sweep up the mess and start to roll paper into spills for the new fire.

The silence behind me is unbearable. Eventually I look again over my shoulder. He is sitting on the arm of the sofa, his hands in his dressing gown pockets, staring at me. His face has a look of such tragedy. Then he lowers his head.

'Stephen,' I whisper. 'Please. What happened to us?'

'I can't get it right, Kit,' he says in such a low voice that I can scarcely hear him. He looks up at me again, searching my face with his eyes.

'I don't understand,' I tell him.

'I thought it would all be over by now. I thought it would be finished. But it isn't, is it?'

'But why? I love you.'

He smiles, sadly.

'You're only a child, Kit.'

'I'm older than I was last term.'

'My mother died, did you know?' He says it in such a conversational way.

'Yes, of course. We all know. I'm sorry.'

He looks at me again, puzzled.

'When I heard, my first thought was of us. I thought: this is a punishment for our profanity. Does that make sense? What we did was sinful and, in this dreadful way, I was being punished for it. I vowed it would stop. Not that I thought it would bring her back to life or any shit like that. But because it didn't seem right any more. She was healthy, Kit. She should have lived another forty years. She was a very good rider. She never had an accident in her life. Why should it happen?'

'Because accidents do. They do happen. Stephen, I'm sorry. But nothing you do will bring her back.'

'So it's OK to go on sinning, you mean?'

'I don't know. I didn't know you believed in all that.'

'I don't. I don't believe in God, if that's what you mean. I just think it's odd that it happened.'

'Odd?'

'We having such feverish . . . lust for each other; and then her dying. The two seem connected.'

'And so – you want us to end?'

He nods his head, drawing the dressing gown closer round him.

'That's what I want. But will it? Can you let it?'

I try to think clearly.

'I don't know,' I say. 'If I thought what we did was killing you, if it was damaging you. If you really wanted me to . . . Yes, I'd try. Try not to look at you, to want you. Is that what I have to do?'

He stared at me thoughtfully.

'When I was in Hong Kong, the day before the funeral, Father and I went out to a meal in a hotel, with some of his friends. I think they were trying to give him support and to get him to eat. He's taken it pretty badly, you know. It was a posh hotel. The head waiter was an Indian; tall and coffee-coloured, with incredible deep eyes and black, shining hair. He kept looking at me all through the meal. I knew why, of course. After we'd finished eating, I left the others drinking coffee and liqueurs and I went for a swim in the hotel pool. I saw the waiter again, watching me from the service drive. I got out of the water and walked over towards him, still wet, wearing only my trunks. I knew what I was doing, Kit. I wanted it. He took me into the pool pump room and there . . . he fucked me, Kit.'

199

He pauses, waiting for my reaction. I feel nothing, no pain or shock or disappointment; nothing. I can't react. I'm in limbo.

'Have you ever been fucked, Kit?'

Now I'm puzzled.

'Only with you,' I tell him.

'No. I mean really fucked?'

'I don't know,' I tell him. 'I've only ever been with you.'

'Oh, Kit,' he says, and as he speaks, the words turn into a sob. Tears force their way through his tightly closed eyes and his body begins to shake.

I get up and cross to him. I put a hand on his back at the base of his neck. The dressing gown is warm and rough to the touch. He continues to sob silently. He is crouching on the arm of the sofa, his head in his hands.

'Stephen,' I whisper, 'whatever has happened, I do not believe that what we did was wrong. If it was wrong, why does it make me feel this way? Is it wrong that for the first time ever I care more about somebody else than I do about myself? Is it wrong to love? Please, please, Stephen, don't cry any more. I can't bear to see you crying . . . Please . . .'

I know it's no help my blubbing as well, but it's tearing me apart to see him suffering. I kneel down in front of him and force his hands away from his face. I wipe his tears with my own fingers. I touch his face like a blind person reading each feature with my fingers; his thick black eyebrows, the lashes on the lids, the bone of his nose, the soft breath from his nostrils, the stubble on his upper lip, his lips slightly parted, his chin, his neck, the V of chest at the top of his dressing gown.

He sits with his arms hanging limply at his sides, looking utterly exhausted. Then, straightening his back and moving his legs, his dressing gown falls open, revealing his limp cock in its nest of dark hair. I've never seen it limp before. I kneel in front of it, staring at it, not wanting to touch it, not wanting to arouse it, fascinated by its seeming indifference to me. As I watch, I see it move. At first the merest tremor, and then a slow, stealthy hardening and a gradual rise.

'You see what you do to me,' I hear him whisper, and looking up I discover him looking at me. 'Not here, Kit. I'll find somewhere. Somewhere we can go regularly. Somewhere safe.' As he speaks he rises and covers his body with the dressing gown.

'Are we . . . all right then?' I whisper, suddenly afraid.

'All right?'

'Back together?'

'Oh, Kit!' His voice is desperate. 'Is that what you really want?'

'It's what I really want,' I reply, and I think I will remember my words for the rest of my life.

The luggage loft is a long, low attic situated above the stable and garage block of Ely House. It is approached by a narrow staircase from the garage where the TGs keep both their cars. TG has an open MG sports model with spoke wheels, but he doesn't often use it and I think it belongs to his theatrical past. Mrs TG has a more suitably sedate Wolseley. There is a side door into the garage which is always kept locked. Stephen has managed to get a key. I don't know how. He could make a very good living as a burglar, if he fails his Cambridge entrance. There is also a door at the top of the stairs into the loft which, very usefully, has two bolts on the inner side.

'If we're caught, there'll be nowhere to run,' he tells me, 'but at least the bolts will give us time to "adjust our dress", as all the best conveniences say, before facing our adversaries.'

He tells me all this in the break when I'm on the way to a mock O level French oral exam, which does nothing for my concentration. All I can think about, when I should be watching my participles and remembering my genders, is that he wants me to meet him by the back door in the middle of the night; well, twelve thirty, to be precise. I know it's fraught with danger. Prefects' lights out is at eleven o'clock, but the TGs use the back door as a short cut to their quarters from the garage. From my dormitory to the back door is a journey that includes two flights of stone stairs, a long sprint down a dark corridor and a glass door, kept closed as a fire precaution, which squeaks.

Nor did he tell me whether to wear clothes or pyjamas. I decide on the former. If we are caught outside in our pyjamas, it's going to be even more difficult to bluff our way out of it. Clothed we could at least try concocting a story about star-gazing or a sudden fascination with bats.

I reach the back door with a few minutes to spare, but he is already there, hiding in the shadows near the cellar stairs.

'I did think of down there, but it's so damp,' he whispers. 'Come on.'

He leads me not to the back door, as I expected, but into the washroom.

'The TGs always bolt the door when they come in. Actually, I think they're both in tonight. But it would be hopeless to find we couldn't get back into the house. This window is usually open at the top.' As he speaks he is pushing up the lower sash.

We climb out into the dark, raw air and he closes the window. It's a short way across the yard to the door. Stephen produces the key and inserts it in the lock.

Suddenly, behind us, a light is switched on in TGs bathroom. The yard is brightly illuminated. We both turn, like rabbits caught in the headlamps of a car, staring upwards. I see Mrs TG, in a floral nightie, drawing curtains across the window. As she does so, she is talking over her shoulder.

The lock clicks and Stephen pulls me into the welcome dark of the garage. I'm shaking with fright.

'It isn't safe,' I tell him.

'It is now,' he says, locking the door behind us. 'Come

on,' and he leads the way through the dark towards the stairs.

I feel my way along the side of the MG with my back to the wall. We all have to take our own trunks up to the luggage loft at the beginning of term and collect them again at the end, so I know the way. But it's different in the middle of the night, with a heart beating so loudly that I'm sure it's being heard across the sea in Holland.

He's waiting for me at the foot of the stairs, with his hand outstretched. I find it and cling on as he pulls me up the steps and pushes open the upper door.

The loft has no windows, and once we are inside and the bolts are fastened the darkness is stifling. Only now does he produce a torch from his pocket. He's so expert, it's as though he's done it all before. We edge our way round stacked trunks and suitcases, following a narrow, twisting path towards the centre of the loft. Here, to my surprise, a clearing has been made and a rug is spread on the floor.

'I don't understand,' I whisper.

'I couldn't have you lying on the bare boards, could I?' he whispers, and chucks me under the chin.

'When did you do this?'

'The other night,' he tells me. 'I had to know that it was safe. We can't have the torch on too much, because the battery isn't very new. I forgot to get another. You all right?'

I nod and look around me at the dark shapes and the shadows. I can't stop my heart from banging against my chest.

He puts a hand on the back of my neck, pulling me towards him. But now the worst imaginable thing happens; I'm so scared that I don't want him to touch me. I pull away from him, looking about me nervously; listening for any little sound.

'Hey, loosen up,' he whispers. 'It's OK. No one knows we're here.'

203

'What if someone looks in our beds?'

'Who the hell's going to look in our beds in the middle of the night?'

'I don't like it, Stephen. I feel trapped. Please, let's go back. Please.'

'After all my preparations? You're kidding.'

He kneels down on the rug, and taking my hand, he tries to pull me down beside him.

'No,' I say, pulling my hand free. 'I don't like it here. I'm going,' but as I speak, he switches off the torch, plunging us into darkness. I back away, panicking, and bump up against the wall of trunks.

'Kit, don't be an idiot,' Stephen hisses, and a moment later I feel his hands on my arm. He pulls me towards the centre of the dark space and then I feel his strong arms round my shoulders, forcing me down on to the ground. It's like sinking into black water. I fight myself free, gasping for breath. The warm, stale air presses in on all sides. I think I will suffocate.

I try to crawl away from him, but he finds one of my legs and grips it with both his hands, dragging me across the floor towards him. Then, releasing his hold, he dives for my shoulders and pins me to the ground with all his weight on top of me.

'What's the matter with you?' I hear his voice hiss in my ear and I feel his breath fanning my cheek.

I'm gasping for breath. His weight is squeezing the air out of me. I'm so tense, I feel I might break.

'Let me go,' I gasp.

'No. Not now. Not now you're here,' he says, and his voice sounds sharp and angry.

I try again to wriggle out from under him and, as I do so, I turn to face him, hitting out with my arms into the darkness. He sits up across my legs and I feel his hands pulling at the waist of my trousers. I can't reach his face, but I beat with my fists on his chest.

All the time I can hear his breath rasping as he grunts and pants and tears the buttons on my trousers. Then, with a jerk he pulls my trousers down below my knees. He sits back across my thighs and I know he's unbuttoning his own clothes. The weight of his body is pressing down on my legs, cramping them. He puts a hand on my underpants and tears them away. As he does so, I hear the cotton ripping. Then, with a sudden, vicious grunt, he rolls me over on to my face and I feel his fingers spreading the cheeks of my arse.

'No,' I whimper. 'Stephen . . .'

'I want to fuck you,' he whispers, his voice tense with anger and pleading.

I can feel his prick trying to find a way into my tight arse. I think I'm going to be sick. I want to get away. I want to escape. The tears start up into my eyes.

He spits on his hand, trying to lubricate the hole. But I'm too frightened and too ashamed to let it open.

'Please, Kit,' he implores.

'You're hurting me,' I sob. 'Get off me. You're hurting me.'

I try once more to fight my way out of his hold. He grabs my wrists, slamming my arms back, spread-eagled, on the floor.

'Stay still,' he hisses.

I squirm round, under him, on to my back, punching at his body with my closed fists. Then, surprisingly, for a moment I manage to scramble free. I slither backwards, away from him. The darkness surrounds me. I don't even know which way it is to the door. I feel his hands reaching for me and grabbing at my feet. With a wrench, he drags me back towards him across the floor, making the rug crease and pucker under me. He forces my legs up into the air and pushes with his hands at the back of my knees until they are forced down on either side of my face. Laying one arm across my face and legs, forcing them down and pressing into my nose so that I can hardly breathe, I feel the fingers of his other hand searching for my arsehole and a moment later his cock penetrates into me with an explosion of pain.

I cry out in agony, no longer fearing discovery; wanting someone, anyone, to come and help me. But his hand quickly covers my mouth, stemming any further sounds.

'Shut up, Kit. For Christ's sake. Shut up.'

'You're hurting me,' I sob. All the pain and the shame mingles with the long weeks of frustration and misery. I can't stop crying.

Above me Stephen stops moving. He is half kneeling, half lying on me. I can feel only the pain. Then he releases my legs and I feel his cock withdrawing painfully, like a knife, from my body.

For a moment there is no movement, no sound. It is as though I am alone in a black cave with only his legs trapping me to the floor.

Later he climbs off me and I feel him lift me by the shoulders and hold me to him so that I'm surrounded by his arms and his head is buried in my shoulder.

'Oh, Kit,' I hear his muffled voice say, 'I wouldn't want to do anything to hurt you. I'm sorry, Kit. I'm sorry. I wanted to do to you what was done to me. I'm sorry.'

'But it was hurting, Stephen,' I sob. 'I'm sorry. It was hurting.'

He holds me gently, letting me cry. Later still I hear him sobbing beside me. I'm making him cry, I think, and I don't want that. I lift his face up and hold it close to mine, pressing my hot cheek against his. 'Don't cry,' I whisper. 'It's all right. I'm all right now. I was frightened, that's all.'

'Oh, Kit,' he says, moving me down on to the floor and lowering himself on top of me. 'I don't want to fuck you if you don't want it.'

'You can do anything, Stephen,' I whisper, reaching up in the dark and touching his face. 'I love you,' I tell him.

206

It is as though I've never told him before, as if I've never felt it before. Not this love. This is new and rare and exquisite. I've never known this love before. I didn't even know it could exist. It isn't to do with fucking or not fucking. It isn't to do with sex. That's part of it, but it's not all of it. Yes, we can excite each other, my darling Stephen, and yes, we can please each other, but just now, when you stopped hurting me and held me to you, when you were small and vulnerable and despairing, then I saw another world; another love. Not to do with bodies. To do with life itself. Our life. Together. One. Is this what marriage really is? If so, there can be no divorce. It isn't possible. Can rape end like this? For that's what you were doing; raping me. But all the time you were hurting yourself, Stephen. I made you hurt yourself. I promise now, in the silence of my mind, I never will again. I'm the stronger person. I'll be strong for us both.

'I love you,' I say again, trying to imbue the words with all my newly found strength.

'I love you too,' he whispers, 'and I will never love anyone else . . .'

I put my hand over his lips, stopping him from saying any more. Don't let's tempt that baleful God who watches over all things, I think. Let's just be glad for now.

# *Now*

L'Escargot was empty when I arrived.

I had left the office early and walked through to Regent Street and then cut across Soho to Greek Street. It was a cold, bright day; the best weather for London. It had rained heavily during the night and the streets looked scrubbed and sparkling in the sunlight. The New Year sales had started and there was a nice sense of 'off with the old and on with the new' in the air. Even the Christmas decorations looked less tatty than they had before, and anyway, one could bear them now, knowing that they would soon be dismantled. What happens to them, I wonder? Do they go into some ghastly subterranean cupboard to be exhumed for a future Yule? Or are they sold at a knock-down price to one of the Third World countries to be used to celebrate the odd coup or a visit by the Pope of the moment on a journey of peace? Really I didn't care, so long as they were removed from my sight as quickly as possible. Wrapping presents is bad enough, but wrapping London as well only adds to the absurdity.

Stephen had kept me my usual table in the corner of the ground-floor front room. I realise that sounds as though I live in the place. I don't, but whenever I have a business lunch or just want to give myself a bit of comfort, I usually go there; upstairs to the grander rooms (and more expensive menu) if I want to impress a foreign buyer or either encourage or soften the blow for an author; downstairs in the brasserie if I want to relax.

For Duff I chose the brasserie.

I ordered a kir and glanced at the menu. Stephen came over and we chatted for a few minutes, until he was called away to welcome some new arrivals. Odd how, until then, I had never thought of his name as being special or in any way significant. There was no connection between my Stephen and the adult world I inhabited. He belonged in a separate compartment and didn't link with any part of my day-to-day existence. It was as though there were two different names. There was my Stephen and all those other Stephens – from the first Christian martyr to Sondheim, via Spender, an English king and even bottled ink. But now all that was changing, as the only begotten Stephen insinuated his way back into my thoughts; or, more accurately, as I allowed and welcomed his return. Not, of course, that he would be aware that this was happening. There had once been a time when I seriously believed that if I concentrated on his name hard enough, then he would know. But I hadn't gone that far back yet. It might come to it, but at that moment I was happy to contemplate the memory of him with a detachment that I had rarely achieved in the past and also with a delicious sense of expectancy. Like the first days of the New Year, there was a hint of excitement and of the unexpected that had been lacking from my life for too long. I welcomed it. It was a relief, no matter where it might lead, to know that my future wasn't entirely mapped out and to be expected; that there was still the possibility of surprise and even of adventure. Whether I would actually meet him again didn't at that moment seem as important as knowing that I wanted to. He was back in my mind and maybe that was where he should stay. As a memory of pain and pleasure; of the only joy I have ever known and of the ultimate despair that such joy almost inevitably must bring.

As the restaurant became busier, I battled with the *Independent* crossword and sipped my drink. Glancing up for a moment, I noticed a middle-aged man coming into the room from the hallway. I saw Stephen speak to him and point in the direction, I thought, of the empty table next to mine. I finished my drink and returned to the clue I was trying to decipher: 'A friend's hesitation bungled his DIY', ten letters, A blank A, seven blanks.

'Chris?' I heard a tentative voice say and, looking up, I discovered the middle-aged man hovering at the side of my table. I stared at him blankly for a moment.

'It's me,' he said. 'Nigel. Nigel Duff. Don't tell me I've changed that much!'

'Nigel,' I exclaimed, putting down my paper and pen and rising with arms outstretched.

'How splendid to see you,' he said, avoiding a full embrace, missing my hand and ending up gripping my wrist and shaking it firmly.

He took the seat opposite mine and one of the waitresses appeared, asking if he'd like a drink.

'Why not?' he said. 'What are you having, Chris?'

'A kir,' I said. 'White wine and . . .'

'I do know what a kir is. I may live in the sticks, but we're almost civilised up there now.' He smiled and nodded. 'I'll have the same.'

'You're sure? You don't want a cocktail?'

'Good God, no! Cocktail?' and he laughed, self-consciously. 'I say, this is very nice,' he said, looking round. 'I suppose you're here all the time.'

'Not all the time. But I do use it quite a lot. I always was a creature of habit,' I replied.

He turned to face me, with a shy, diffident smile. His hair had receded, revealing a high forehead, and there were thin lines round his eyes. The result was rather unnatural; like a bad character make-up with the familiar schoolboy face peering out from beneath, anxious and waiting. I knew I should start a conversation but I was unprepared for this sense of unreality;

I felt as though we were both characters in some play, waiting for the curtain to rise and the performance to begin.

A small, thin girl appeared at the side of the table, carrying a glass of kir. She wasn't the waitress who had taken the order.

'You asked for a kir?' she said and I indicated that it was for my guest.

'You're Chris Metcalfe, aren't you?' she asked, looking at me as she placed the glass in front of Nigel.

'Yes,' I replied, staring up at her, puzzled, trying to recognise her.

'I'm Penny Stratton,' she explained, which didn't help me at all.

'I'm sorry,' I smiled. 'I'm obviously going senile.'

'No. We haven't met,' she reassured me with a smile. 'I'm a friend of Bill Armstrong's and he's a friend of your friend Catherine.'

'Sounds terribly complicated. My friend Catherine . . .' Then I made the connection. 'Oh! You're Penny! The future Mrs Bill Whatever-his-name-is.'

Now it was the girl's turn to look puzzled.

'Sorry?'

'I mean . . . you're getting married to him, aren't you?'

'Married to him?' she shrieked, and bellowed with laughter.

'Oh, I've probably got it all wrong,' I said. 'Didn't you once work in a shop in South Molton Street?'

'Yes. But I decided being a shop assistant wasn't exactly using my talents.' She smiled again. 'You could argue that being a waitress doesn't warrant a second-class honours degree either – but this is only temporary.'

'So you're not getting married after all?' She shook her head. 'And you never were?'

'Have you met Bill?' she asked.

I was forced to admit that I hadn't.

211

'He's not the sort of person you marry. Ask Catherine!'
she laughed again. 'Are you ready to order?'

I told her that we hadn't looked at the menu yet and that
I'd call her.

'Sorry about that,' I said to Nigel when she left us.

'It all sounded wildly exciting.'

'Not really,' I told him. I was about to explain, but decided
that Catherine's love life would be too confusing and too
depressing to go into then. And so, instead, I suggested that
we study the menu and decide what we were going to eat
before getting down to the real business of the day:

'Thirty years is a long time to cover on an empty stomach!'
I joked. He laughed diffidently again and, taking glasses from
his jacket pocket, studied the menu.

'It all sounds delicious,' he said dubiously and turned up the
*plat du jour* which was clipped to the main courses, searching
I presumed for something familiar. 'Sausages with onion
marmalade,' he murmured, almost to himself, imbuing the
word 'marmalade' with distinct disbelief.

'It's just a sort of thick sauce,' I said, realising that I
sounded almost apologetic.

'Delicious,' he said, glancing up at me and smiling. His
glasses made his eyes look big, like a solemn owl. Had he
worn them at Blandfords? I couldn't remember. 'But,' he
continued, 'I have sausage and onions at home!' and he
grinned. Maybe he was sending me up? For a moment he
certainly made me feel that my lifestyle was uncomfortably
recherché, which it had never seemed before. Then he
returned to reading the menu.

The room was filling up fast; a few familiar faces passed in
front of me. I waved to one or two, and tried hard to ignore
others. I saw Christopher Martin going through to the upper
restaurant accompanied by an editor from Hamish Hamilton.
I was glad. Since turning down his book, I'd worried quite
a lot about it. Maybe there was still a place for the honest

and the sensitive; for the slightly boring but thoroughly worthwhile work of fiction? I wasn't prepared to bet on it, but I didn't in the least mind if some other publisher wanted to take the risk.

We ordered our food; potted shrimps for Nigel, followed by calves' liver – not a particularly adventurous meal for a man who had spent his entire working life living on the outskirts of Leeds, he admitted, but apparently anything with garlic gave him indigestion and they never had liver at home because none of the children liked it. I went for the goat's cheese salad, followed by monkfish kebabs, which seemed positively effete by comparison.

'You'll have some wine?' I asked him hopefully.

He nodded and smiled.

'You choose,' he said. 'I'm easy so far as the colour is concerned.'

He gave me an absurd sense of being more grown-up than he was and I remembered that that was how it had always been at school. Although we were roughly the same age, it always seemed that I was older and somehow more daring than he. But now, with the benefit of age if not of wisdom, I realised that it was an illusion that he created himself and it had very little to do with me. He was one of those people who looked up to you, both physically – he couldn't be more than five eight in his socks – and also mentally – though, God knows, he got a string of O and A levels and a decent place at Durham, while I failed miserably at most things and ended up working behind the counter in Metcalfe's of Sevenoaks.

I ordered a bottle of Sauvignon and handed the menus and the wine list to Penny Stratton, who had appeared once more to take our order.

'You didn't mind my introducing myself, did you?' she asked. 'It's just that Bill mentioned you were Catherine's boyfriend, and obviously I was interested, because of them both working together on that committee. And, well, Bill never introduces me to any of his friends . . .'

'No, I didn't mind,' I cut in, impatiently. Bill's line in sexual subterfuge was beginning to irritate, possibly because I wasn't in a position to give it my undivided attention. 'Can we have the wine straightaway, please?' I asked her, terminating the familiarity with the rather curt request.

'Yes, sure,' she said, with that maddening unfazability of a pretty girl with youth and a second-class honours degree on her side.

'She's very talkative,' Nigel said, after she'd gone.

'Far too,' I agreed. 'Well, here we are. I can't tell you how good it is to see you.' I hoped it sounded sincere. I had suddenly gone off the whole thing and wished I was having a beer and a sandwich on my own.

'I look a terrible wreck, I'm afraid. But you, Chris; I swear you look exactly the same as you did at Blandfords.'

'There's a very doubtful portrait in the attic that tells a truer story,' I said, smiling.

'Portrait?' he asked, frowning.

'You've got three children? Is that right, Nigel?'

'No. Four,' he replied.

'Four? Sorry, I've got it all wrong. I thought you said there were five of you down here. I worked that out as one wife and three kids . . .'

'Yes. But we have to leave Sam behind. He's the youngest.'

'I see. Who does the baby-sitting?'

He shook his head.

'No. He's in a special home. Sam suffers from Down's Syndrome.'

'Down's Syndrome?' The unexpectedness of the revelation made me clumsy. I didn't know how best to react.

'Mongolism,' Nigel explained patiently, as though he'd been through it all before many times.

'Yes, of course. I'm terribly sorry,' I said, knowing it was inadequate.

'Yes, it's a shame. We'd love to have him down here with us. But it's a bit difficult when we're eating out all the time.'

He said it so naturally, as though that was the only problem – that Sam couldn't be with them on their family holiday.

'Oh, Nigel. I didn't know. How awful for you,' I mumbled.

'Dear Chris, how could you know? This is the first time we've been in touch in God knows how long.'

'How old is Sam?'

'He'll be ten next birthday. You know, he's the brightest of them all. And they know it. I wish you could meet him, Chris. He's a lovely boy. A loving boy. We all feel very lucky.'

'What about the others?' I asked. For some reason I couldn't take the intensity of Sam, although Nigel seemed quite relaxed and unfussed about it.

'Two girls and another boy. Two of each. I was always neat, remember? The eldest, Claire, is eighteen. God! To think of it. She's just started at York. Jamie is sixteen and Jenny is twelve. They're all shopping in Covent Garden. I won't have a penny left!'

'And your wife's name is . . . ?'

'Helen. Didn't I say that? She'd brain me. She always says the kids come first with me; which isn't true at all.'

'How long have you been married?'

'Twenty-four years. Can you believe that? Twenty-four years living with the same woman! You must come to the silver wedding. But only if you promise to bring something Georgian and extremely expensive!'

He was married when he was twenty-five; seven years after leaving Blandfords. He met the girl while he was doing his National Service. But they hadn't married at once because she was training to be a nurse and it was:

'. . . a bit of a vocation with her. That's why we waited so long to have children. She stayed on working after we were married, until the month before Claire was born.' He smiled. 'I think she thought that one of us should be doing something worthwhile!'

He was a chartered accountant. The firm had recently been taken over by a London group, but his place was secure and he was actually doing very nicely thank you. Once his initial shyness left him, he chattered away quite happily and I was glad to let him do so. The wine was followed by the food and he tucked in to both, enjoying himself with unselfconscious pleasure. Once or twice he tried to quiz me about my own life, but I was disinclined to talk about myself in the face of so much radiant normality.

His life story didn't take long to relate. They'd moved house three times; but never again. They now could see Ilkley Moor from their drawing room window, which had apparently been a burning ambition for them both since they were first married, and they had half an acre of garden with a stream running through it, which Nigel had created with his own hands and an electric pump. They took holidays either in the Lake District or Scotland and hadn't been abroad for ages. 'Not since before Claire was born. That's nineteen years. Can you believe that? And then all we could afford was a fortnight in Brittany!' However, he was, he told me, still a keen ornithologist. He was a member of the RSPB and most weekends he managed to get a bit of time out on the moors.

'Helen comes with me sometimes, but it always seems to rain when she does, which puts her off. None of the kids is very keen. Jamie goes rock-climbing but Claire and Jenny are definitely not the outdoor types. Little Sam sometimes comes out with me but he gets bored quickly, just like the others.'

He looked at me again, and grinned.

'Listen to me! I haven't stopped chattering since I sat

down. And really all I want is to hear about you. You never married, Chris?'

'No,' I answered with an upward inflection, as though I was going to say more. But I didn't, because I couldn't think of anything.

Nigel waited politely, then changed the subject.

'You don't ever go back to Blandfords?' he asked.

'God, no. Surely you remember, Nigel? I hated the place.'

'Yes.' He nodded and looked down at his plate. 'It all seemed less important afterwards though. Didn't you find that?'

'I stopped thinking about it.' I couldn't help sounding cool. 'D'you ever go back?'

'We do, yes. Jamie is there, you see.'

I was actually shocked.

'You sent him to Blandfords Hall? Nigel! Whatever possessed you?'

'Well, it's a very different place now, you know. It's gone co-ed. There are two girls' houses and a third one being built. Jenny is down to go there as well, God help me! The fees are now astronomical.'

'Oh, co-ed will make it all much better,' I said, pouring scorn on his words. 'Now they'll all be able to indulge in natural fucking!'

He glanced over his shoulder at the next table, checking if my obscenity had been overheard.

'Really, Chris,' he said, trying to make it sound as though he was joining in some joke. 'Not everyone was "fucking", as you put it, when we were there.'

'More fools they then,' I said with a smile. I felt sorry that I was causing him embarrassment, but really . . . 'I personally could never see the point of doing anything else while I was there. And anyway, those who weren't fucking were all either screwed up with frustration or wanking themselves blind and racked with guilt.'

'I wasn't, Chris.' He said the words with such simple sincerity, I almost felt ashamed. Good people make difficult lunch companions, I decided, and Nigel was, as he had always been, patently good. 'I don't think most of us were doing that sort of thing,' he continued. 'Times were different then, of course. Sexual obsession only came in with the seventies.'

'Oh, the poor old seventies! They get blamed for practically everything now.'

'No, really. I don't think we bothered about all that much . . .'

'Oh, Nigel!' I exclaimed.

'Oh, I know there were a few . . .' He hesitated and I sensed that he was avoiding any reference to my own behaviour at the time. 'That little tart Hobbs, for instance – d'you remember him?'

I frowned. Why, I wondered, had he singled out Hobbs?

'Oh, you must do,' he insisted.

'Yes. I remember him. I didn't know that he was notorious.'

'Well he is now. He's a big noise in the advertising world. You must have read about him?'

'What was there to read?'

'He was mixed up in all those revolting male prostitute revelations that the tabloid press had such a field day with a few months back. Maybe you missed it. He wasn't such a scoop for the media as the bigger names.'

'Poor Hobbs. I had no idea. What happened to him?'

'He weathered the storm, I suppose. I'm not in touch with him, obviously. Although, actually, I did vote for him.'

'Vote? Is he an MP?'

Nigel laughed uncomfortably.

'No. He was going to be struck off the register.'

'Which register?'

'The school,' Nigel replied, as though I were some kind of imbecile.

Apparently Hobbs was one of a number of prominent showbiz and political glitterati who had been set up by rent boys, who were probably already in the pay of one of the tabloids. I remembered the cases. There had been a rash of shock-horror revelations, all along much the same lines. Perhaps the Aids scare had reduced the pros' earning power and they had looked for other ways to keep themselves in the luxury which they had grown to expect and maybe even deserved, but only if they kept their mouths shut. Instead there had been a series of sad spankings and tellings gleefully revealed by the gutter press to their ever-eager readership, desperate for a bit of filth to go with their morning butties. I had refused to give the matter any attention. But I must admit that I might have been more interested if I'd realised that Hobbs was one of them.

'And the school was going to strike him off the register?' I said. 'Really! How pathetic!'

'I agree. As I say, I voted against the motion. Most of us did – apart from the old die-hards. But there was quite a fuss.'

'It's a wonder then that I wasn't struck off while I was still there,' I said lightly.

He glanced at me. I couldn't decide whether he was glad I had brought the subject up, or whether it embarrassed him. He sipped his wine and helped himself to some more vegetables.

'You remember all that, of course?' I said, pressing home the point.

'Of course I do. But, thank God, none of that ever got out. And really, it was altogether different. You were still a minor for one thing and, obviously, it's an acknowledged phase that some people go through.'

I smiled at him encouragingly. It was somehow comforting to have the whole episode reduced to a 'phase'.

'What happened to Walker, d'you know?'

I asked the question so calmly. It sounded no more than

a chance enquiry; like the price of peas or the wellbeing of a mere acquaintance. As I said the words, I lifted the bottle and divided the last of the wine between our two glasses. Ordinary, insignificant movements; polite, casual conversation. But as I waited for his reply, I wiped tiny beads of perspiration from my forehead with the back of my hand and the wine glass trembled as I lifted it to my lips.

Nigel shook his head and scooped the last of the liver juices on to a piece of potato, and, transferring it to his mouth, he chewed slowly.

'Now, I think I did hear,' he said, ruminatively. 'I rather think he got married and went to live in Australia.'

I suddenly wanted to giggle. It seemed such an extreme step to take in order to escape my attention.

'Or was it the other way round?' Nigel continued, now sipping his wine. 'Was he already living in Australia? I can't honestly remember. You knew about him and Hobbs, did you?'

I don't think my face betrayed the shock his words gave me and I was saved from answering because he continued almost at once:

'Oh, of course, I keep forgetting. You weren't made a prefect, were you? Because of your . . .' He hesitated. Sometimes relaxed, boozy conversations lure one into traps; Nigel had just put his foot into one. He didn't know how to proceed. He looked at me and blinked. 'You know,' he said, smiling weakly. 'When you were . . . in that bad way.'

'I think the official description at the time was a breakdown, Nigel,' I said, I hoped helpfully.

'Quite,' he agreed, uncomfortably, and seemed to want to leave it at that.

'You were saying? Something about Hobbs and you being a prefect?'

'Oh, yes,' he said, draining his glass. 'It was something TG let slip. God, I admired that man. He's still alive, you know.

You should go and see him. He lives near Symonds Yat, on the Wye. Having rather a tough time, actually, Mrs TG's gone a bit potty. Just old age, I think. They're both in their eighties. But all the same, I think TG finds her quite a handful. What was I saying?'

He stared at me and blinked.

'Something about Hobbs?' Even I was beginning to lose the thread.

'Yes, that's right. It was during our last year . . . Do you remember? Hobbs got into the First Fifteen. Funny that . . .' He paused again and blinked self-consciously.

'What?' I asked, half knowing what his answer was going to be.

'Well, a chap like Hobbs playing rugger!' he said.

'You mean his type would have been more likely to play a woman in the school play?' I chided him.

Nigel laughed.

'*Touché*, Chris. My God, do you remember? What was my name? Mrs Something-or-other. I had a dreadful wig. I tore up all the photographs, I was so embarrassed . . .'

'Nigel!' I cried. 'Tell me about Hobbs.'

'Sorry, am I wandering? I do that. It drives Helen crazy. Well, TG told me he was delighted that Hobbs had made the school team, not just because it was good for the house, but because he hoped it would mean the end of his queer period!'

'His what? That's a dreadful thing to say.'

'I don't think he meant any harm. He knew I wouldn't say anything.'

'TG was a dreadful old gossip and I'm not at all sure that his morals weren't suspect. They never had children of their own, don't forget. And I wouldn't be at all surprised if Mrs TG turned out to be a lesbian.'

Nigel grinned.

'Actually it was Mrs TG who discovered them.'

'Whom?' I asked, innocently walking towards my fate.

'Walker and Hobbs. Apparently she had come back late – it was at the end of the summer term, Walker's last term – anyway, she'd heard a noise, or something, when she was parking the car and apparently she'd found Walker and Hobbs going hammer and tongs up in the luggage loft!'

Nigel's lips continued to move, indicating that he was still speaking. But I didn't hear any of the words. He and the sounds of the room and the room itself all disappeared down a long, narrow tunnel until they were no more than a blur in the distance. My forehead was cold with sweat. There was an uncomfortable tightness in my throat. For one awful moment I thought I was going to throw up.

'. . . Why I say I admire TG is that he kept the whole thing under wraps. It would have ruined Walker's career, of course. He was all set to go to Cambridge. TG said that one youthful indiscretion shouldn't be allowed to prevent a brilliant career . . . Of course, Walker was rather a favourite . . .'

The words formed and flowed and broke like waves around me. I had to keep swallowing to hold back the nausea. I sat rigidly, staring at him, both my hands gripping the sides of the table. It wasn't true, a voice kept whispering in my head. Say it wasn't true. Not with Hobbs. Not in the luggage loft. No. It wasn't true . . .

'Are you all right, Chris?' I heard the voice say, as if it was calling through a cave. 'Chris? Chris . . .?'

I must speak. I must stop him. I must get away from his moving lips and the echoing cave and the roar of the water.

Then I saw him reach across and put a hand on my shoulder.

'I say, you look terribly pale. You feeling all right?'

'Yes, fine,' a distant voice, that I recognised as my own, replied. 'Now coffee? Or would you like a dessert? Actually, if you'll excuse me, I'll just slip upstairs . . .'

I don't know how I got up from the table, nor how I

crossed the room. But somehow I managed it. The Gents' is up on the first floor. I took the front stairs, passing Stephen, who was speaking on the phone by the desk.

I reached the lavatory and, finding it empty, leaned against the basin, letting the cold water run into the bowl and splashing it over my face. Then I stared in the mirror, taking deep breaths.

It was all unimportant. It was all in the past. It couldn't touch me. Not now. Not thirty years later.

'He took Hobbs to our secret place,' the voice whined in my head. 'Hobbs. He took Hobbs.'

Does everyone have a voice that goads and taunts and mocks? Or am I the only one?

'Leave me alone,' I whispered to my reflection in the mirror.

'Hobbs,' the voice whispered. 'All the time he was loving you, he was loving Hobbs as well.'

The glass ashtray on the shelf between the basins was smooth and round in my hand but it shattered into a thousand sharp, glittering fragments and my face splintered as the mirror cracked. The noise of the breaking glass echoed round the room. I turned and walked hurriedly away.

Stephen was entering a booking as I passed him.

'There's an awful mess up in the Gents',' I said. 'One of the mirrors has been broken.'

'What?' Stephen exclaimed. 'A mirror? It must have been an ugly customer looking in it.' Then, as he disappeared up the stairs, he added: 'What am I talking about? We don't have any ugly customers. It's a house rule!'

Nigel was looking at my crossword as I returned to the table.

'Amateurish,' he said as I resumed my seat. 'Eight across. It's Amateurish. A mate ur ish. Do you hate people doing your puzzles for you?'

'Please, finish it,' I replied, sounding bright and cheerful.

223

'Don't be silly. It's taken me this long to do one clue!'

'Would you like some coffee?' I asked him. 'Or a pudding?'

'A coffee would be nice. Are you all right?'

'I'm fine,' I replied.

'I thought, perhaps, that I'd upset you. Mentioning Hobbs and Walker.'

'Heavens, no. I knew all about that,' I told him.

But it wasn't the truth. I'd only known some of it, and never about the luggage loft. Never that. And if not that, how much more? And why, why did it still hurt so much?

# *Then*

It is one of those nights filled with lashing rain and thunder and lightning; dark and wild, pure Brontë weather or good for a Margaret Lockwood costume drama. It's our last night at corps camp, up in the Highlands at a rain-drenched place called Comrie. We're out on manoeuvres, learning to be proper soldiers, preparing for eventual National Service when we are expected to step straight from the ranks into the officer class, as befits a 'gentleman and a Blandfordian'.

Stephen and I have hardly seen each other while we've been here. But it doesn't really matter. We've become much more relaxed about our relationship since we started going to the luggage loft. Some nights we've spent just smoking and talking. Stephen is very well read. He's introduced me to writers like Steinbeck, Salinger and Waugh. He's particularly keen on Ernest Hemingway, so Spain has occupied a lot of our conversations. The Civil War has become his new obsession and all things Spanish are his passion. I think he'd like to live there if he could. He has a reproduction of the Goya painting of the firing squad – the one with the man with his arms flung up in a gesture of defiance in the face of the soldiers – pinned to his study wall, and when he won the Senior School Reading Prize last term, he bought a book on Picasso with the money, not because he likes the paintings, but simply because Picasso was born one of the chosen. Or do we really talk about Spain in order to avoid contemplating the summer holidays? Then all in a moment Stephen will become 'an Old Blandfordian' and I'll be alone with two more long years before I'm free of the place. Better by far to work out a route over the Sierra Nevada in the direction of the sea than to consider such a time.

The week here has focused on these last two days. All our training and preparation are now being put to the test. We are out on manoeuvres – which is the military way of describing charging about the mountains in the middle of the night playing 'escaping from the Nazis and fighting the fight for freedom'. Or at least that's how I've decided to play it. I don't think anyone actually mentioned Nazis but I find a bit of a scenario helps me along and have decided that it's a J. Arthur Rank war film – and I've got the Dirk Bogarde part.

On parade this morning we were divided into two groups – 'Guards' and 'Attackers' – then each group was briefed separately. Thank God I was made an Attacker. It's a much better part. The object of the exercise is pretty simple. Over a twenty-four-hour period we, the Attackers, have to get from a series of different drop-off points back to camp without being caught by a Guard. We have to carry provisions and, needless to say, our sodding rifles. 'And God help the little turd who reports back with mud up his barrel.' 'Thank you, Sergeant Major.'

The day has gone really well for me. I like maps and have a good sense of direction. But then, just as it was getting dark, one hell of a storm broke. The rain has been coming down in stair rods ever since. Thunder crashing, lightning flashing and so wet that Dirk would have gone home hours ago. I decided to stop for a rest and found some shelter under an overhanging rock. Then, digging into my 'essential supplies', I broke off a piece of Kendal Mint Cake and settled down.

The sound of a twig snapping somewhere close at hand makes me freeze. Carefully I pull further back under the shelter of the rock, listening intently. My heart is beating like a piston. I can see a light moving through the undergrowth about ten yards away from me.

Then I hear a voice call from higher up the hill: 'Anything?' And a moment later another, nearer, voice – a voice that I recognise – replies: 'There's someone here. I'm sure of it.'

It's Stephen. As I watch I see his torch moving towards me.

This is it! The camera is turning! The whole place is swarming with Nazis – and one of them is Stephen. I panic, pulling away, trying to get round to the other side of the boulder. As I move, I dislodge a shower of small stones that scatter down amongst the trees towards the distant brook. The torch beam swings round in my direction. I crawl backwards, dodging out of sight. My breath catches in my throat, making me choke.

'Stephen?' the distant voice calls. I think it may be Morrison.

'Just a minute,' Stephen replies. He's coming straight towards me.

I press back against the rock, not wanting to be found. But then he starts to veer away and at once I want to be with him. Taking a deep breath, I cup my hands to my mouth. The plaintive call of an owl cuts through the night. It's our call; the call he taught me to make.

I see the light down amongst the trees below me stop moving. Then it slowly swings round, probing the darkness. The beam swings across my face, dazzling my eyes.

'No, there's no one,' Stephen calls. 'You go on along the stream. I'll try along the top of the ridge and catch you up later.'

I watch the light slowly move up the steep bank towards me, dazzling my eyes. Rain is dripping and drumming through the trees all around me, the wind is cold.

'Hello,' a voice whispers and a moment later I feel a warm hand against my cheek.

He says there's shelter up at the top end of the valley,

a disused barn. We go there. At least it's dry. He has a half-bottle of whisky and a packet of fags. We build a fire from dry timber that we find in a corner of the barn and sit huddled together, sharing the whisky and the cigarettes, getting slightly pissed and not even talking very much. At some point I must have fallen asleep. Because suddenly there is light filtering into the barn through a crack in the door. It takes me a minute to remember where I am. Then I realise that Stephen isn't here. The fire we lit last night has gone out and the air is cold in the barn. I get up, stretching and bending. The damp uniform clings to my body and I'm aching all over. I go to the door and step outside.

The rain has stopped. Thin mist is wreathing the dripping woods. I see Stephen, with his back to me, pissing against a tree. He turns, doing up his flies, and seeing me, grins. It's such a familiar smile. I have grown so accustomed to it.

'We'd better be getting back,' he says, crossing towards me.

'I'll just go for a pee,' I tell him, and walk away, turning my back. Strange that no matter how intimate we've become there is still a shyness.

When I come back he has kicked over the ashes of the fire.

'Always destroy the evidence,' he says. Then he turns and looks at me and grins. 'At least you got some sleep,' he says.

'Didn't you?' I ask.

He shakes his head.

'I don't like roughing it. Wherever we live, I promise it's going to have hot water and a proper bed!'

It's the first time that he's mentioned our living together.

'Is that what we'll do?' I ask, and I feel tears stinging my eyes.

'Of course,' he says, sounding surprised. 'Let's make it somewhere sunny, Kit, can we? Sod this bloody climate.'

'Like Spain, you mean?' I want so much to sound light-hearted and unconcerned.

'Why not?' he asks earnestly. 'We could both get jobs.'

'What are you talking about?'

'I've only got one more term at Blandfords. We've got to make plans, Kit.'

'What sort of plans?' I can feel the panic leaping inside me. I may have longed for this conversation, but now that it's come I feel scared.

'For the future, of course.'

'You're going up to Cambridge.'

He looks at me and smiles.

'You mean I should get my degree first and then we can go and bum around in Spain?'

'I don't want to be a bum,' still trying so hard to keep my voice light and jokey.

'Then what do you want, Kit?'

I don't know. Or maybe I haven't dared think about it. Not really. Not until now.

'We must go now,' I whisper. 'We'll be missed.'

'Yes, of course,' he says, and pulling me closer he kisses me.

We are standing in the doorway of the barn. He has his arm round my shoulder. I turn towards him, looking up at him.

'You do still like it, don't you? I mean, you're not getting tired of me?'

'Of course not,' I tell him, meaning it, but lacking his intensity. This sometimes happens. He seems so filled with feelings that I can't compete with them and then I feel inadequate.

His arm tightens round my shoulder, drawing me towards him. I reach up, putting my lips to his mouth, feeling his tongue forcing them apart.

'I love you,' he murmurs and then, pressing his cheek against mine, he looks away across the valley. As he does so, I hear him gasp.

229

'What?' I ask and then, almost at the same moment, as we both turn our faces towards the light, I see a figure across on the other side of the narrow valley. Someone is standing there, watching us. I push Stephen away from me and turn as if I want to run. But he catches hold of my arm, stopping me. Then he forces me to turn.

'It's all right, Kit. Don't panic! I'll deal with it.'

We are both looking across the valley. Stephen still has his arm round my shoulders. I feel we should hide but he seems strangely calm. At first I don't recognise the face. All I am aware of is that we have been discovered. After all this time, and after all our care.

'Come here, Hobbs. Don't be frightened,' I hear Stephen say.

Hobbs! Of course, it's Hobbs. Now my brain is working again. Hobbs from Ely House. Hobbs, who is always staring and giggling. He doesn't move. He has his usual simpering grin on his face and an odd, greedy look. The look of a person who wants to . . . what? Run and tell? Is that it? Is this how it must end for Stephen and me? Caught by a half-witted fourth-former?

'What'll we do?' I whisper. Then, glancing up at Stephen, I see the same dangerous, hungry look on his face and I feel him pushing me away from him across the clearing towards where Hobbs is standing, still open-mouthed and watching.

'You go on, Kit. I'll deal with this,' he says gently. 'Follow the track down to the road. You'll find your way from there. Hobbs!' he calls. 'Come over here. I just want to speak to you for a moment.'

I have to climb over the gate and pass Hobbs. He's smiling all the time. He smells of sweat and damp uniform. When I reach the track, I look back at them. Stephen has crossed back to the barn and is leaning against the door frame. As I watch, Hobbs walks slowly across the glade towards him. Then he looks over his shoulder at me. Stephen is speaking to him, but

I can't hear what he's saying. Hobbs continues to stare at me. He has stopped smiling and has a puzzled, almost frightened expression. I think I should go and help. But instead I turn and start to run. I run away and leave Stephen to cope.

# *Now*

The bungalow was at the end of a track which wound through thickly wooded country. Rounding a final bend the trees came to an abrupt halt. Ahead, across a rough lawn and unkempt borders, the ugly thirties building seemed to cling to a precipice with beyond it a blue void, like the end of the world.

The name 'Wyeview' etched in poker-work on a piece of rustic plank told me that I had reached my destination. It was just after two fifteen. Perfect timing. I had been told 'not to arrive while we're feeding' and that there was 'a perfectly decent hostelry in the village that can do you a sandwich or a plate of chips'. Clearly I was not being invited to lunch.

The bell, an electronic chime, echoed through the house. No one came. I paused briefly then pressed the button again. The repetitive chime hinted at undue impatience. Turning my back I sauntered away down the path, affecting a nonchalance that I wasn't really feeling. Then I turned to survey the building and discovered the figure of a man gesticulating from a bay window that protruded from the side of the house facing the void. He seemed to be telling me to go to the back of the building. With an embarrassed wave and a nod I turned and followed his mimed instructions round the side of the house.

Passing a window, with a view into a kitchen, I approached another door. As I drew near it opened and the man I had seen at the window appeared, leaning on a walking stick.

232

'Never use the front door – it sticks,' he said. 'Well, come in! Come in! You're letting all the heat escape. We've only got our pensions, you know.'

I followed him in and closed the door behind me. The kitchen smelt damp and the air was almost as cold as it had been outside. The man was now perched against the corner of a table, leaning on his stick and staring at me through thick glasses.

'I can usually remember a face – not so good on names.'

'I'm Metcalfe, TG,' I mumbled, feeling hopelessly self-conscious under his unswerving glare.

'Are you indeed! And you're the one who telephoned? Right? Well, come in! Come in!'

As he led the way across a dark hall a woman's voice could be heard calling, 'Trevor! Trevor!' The sound had a querulous, mournful tone, like the cry of a peacock.

'You'll remember my wife,' TG said, pushing open a door and going ahead of me into a large, light room. Mrs TG was sitting, crouched forward in front of an electric fire. There was also a calor gas radiator alight in the big bay window. The atmosphere was hot and airless.

'Trevor?' she called, without bothering to turn.

'I'm here, dear,' TG said, his response as automatic as had been her call, and he crossed to a wing chair at the other side of the fireplace.

Between the two chairs stood a low table with on it the remnants of a cold snack – a loaf of bread, butter still in the packet, some cheese standing on a plastic wrapper and a bottle of pickled onions. Two glasses held the dregs of what looked like beer and an empty glass jug was smeared with foam.

'Home-brew,' TG said, raising a glass and downing the last drop. Then he smacked his lips and beamed. 'Have the poofter!' he said with a sudden bray of laughter and po̶i̶n̶t̶e̶d̶ towards the window where a mound of worn leather s̶

233

to be the object of his remark. I pulled it into the middle of the room between them and sat down.

'How are you, Mrs Gerrard?' I asked, sensing that some contact was required. The old woman turned slowly and stared at me with a look of chilling disdain.

'I am very well, thank you,' she replied in a haughty voice.

'She's lovely,' her husband said, ignoring her and staring at me instead. 'So you're Johnson.'

'No. Metcalfe,' I corrected him.

'It was a hell of a long time ago, you know,' he said irritably. 'I can't be expected to remember every little pipsqueak who passed through my hands.'

'Pipsqueak!' Mrs TG echoed, enunciating the words with relish. Then she put a hand over her mouth and tittered girlishly.

'What other claim to fame have you? Apart from a totally unmemorable name?' He took a handkerchief from his pocket and blew his nose savagely.

I couldn't think of any and we relapsed into silence. The interview was not going well. I decided to try a different tack.

'You have a fantastic view from here, sir,' I said, turning to look out of the window and sounding all of fifteen.

'Fantastic?' TG enunciated the word with a tone of distaste. 'You can't live on a view,' he growled, 'however "fantastic" it may be.'

He rubbed his knees and stared at the electric fire. His wife seemed to be nodding off to sleep. I decided to jump in at the deep end.

'I played Nora in *A Doll's House*, sir. You directed it.'

'Ah!' TG said and stared at me again. 'That Metcalfe. Yes, of course. Were you any good?'

'Not very, I shouldn't think.'

He stared at me thoughtfully and murmured my name to

himself. 'Metcalfe. Mmmh. And what are you up to now, Metcalfe?'

'I'm in publishing,' I replied.

'Are you really!' His voiced sounded derisive. 'I have always maintained that people who can't actually do anything go into publishing. If you can – be a writer; if you can't – be a publisher!'

I was tempted to suggest that perhaps it was similar to being a teacher, but decided against it.

'I saw Nigel Duff recently and he was talking about you. It was he who actually gave me your address. I thought I should look you up . . .' I was speaking too fast. Nervous, I suppose. 'I thought it would be good to . . . make contact.' Then the flow ran out and I couldn't think of anything else to say. An even longer pause followed. TG stared at the electric fire and seemed not to have been listening. His wife had flopped over sideways and was snoring rhythmically.

'Oh, do shut up, old thing,' he murmured, without looking at her. Then with a sudden flash of temper he yelled, 'Shut up, Muriel!'

The noise woke her with a start. She looked round fearfully.

'Trevor?' she whimpered.

'I'm here, old girl,' he whispered and looked at her across the cluttered table with an expression of such despair that I was embarrassed for him and wished suddenly that I hadn't come. I began to think of excuses to get me out of the bungalow and only noticed that TG was speaking again when he was halfway through a sentence.

'. . . remember you. Got it in my head that you were in some kind of trouble. Something to do with Stephen Walker? Splendid chap. And of course full of potential. But . . . threw it all away.' He shrugged and shook his head. 'Well, come on, remind me!'

I stared at him helplessly. His eyes behind the glasses were large and unblinking.

'Yes, I was at school at the same time as Stephen. He was a couple of years ahead of me . . .'

'You were his bum-boy!' TG exclaimed and clapped his hands delightedly. 'That's it, of course. Now I know you. You were the one who had all that trouble. I say, how splendid. This will lighten our darkness! Come to confess, eh, Metcalfe?'

'Metcalfe!' Mrs TG said with careful diction.

'You remember him, don't you, my lovely?' TG said, without looking at her. 'You remember our Metcalfe, Stephen Walker's bum-boy? We heard all about him, didn't we? Every little detail.' As he spoke, he grimaced and delicately rubbed the tips of his fingers together as though he had been dabbling them in something unpleasant.

'You heard all . . . what about me?' I asked. I felt a sudden surge of anger sweep over me. This ghastly old man, pompous and self-important. How dare he sit there making veiled remarks about me?

'Obviously I don't remember all the details. The boy, Hobbs, he told me. You and Walker . . . at it like rabbits? Wasn't that the gist? Something like that.'

'You knew about us?' I said. I think I sounded shocked. 'You knew – and yet you did . . . nothing?'

'What was I supposed to do? It was already too late to do anything. It was the end of term. Walker was leaving. The holidays were upon us. No point doing anything. It was my wife who discovered them. Didn't you, my lovely? Walker and – what was his name? – Hobbs. They were in the luggage loft. She heard a noise, went to investigate and just walked in on them. Gave her a nasty turn. All that heaving male flesh. She ran to me, face as white as a sheet, unable to form words, gasping and gesticulating . . . She needed a cracking great gin before I could get anything at all coherent out of her.

Personally I didn't see any cause to make a fuss. I mean, we always knew that sort of thing was going on. I simply thought Walker was celebrating. You know? End of term, freedom, Cambridge – that sort of thing. I interviewed them separately, of course. Told Walker not to be a stupid ass and that if he got up to that caper when he was out in the world he'd end up in gaol. Lot of fairies ended up in gaol in those days. "It's one thing sowing the wild oats," I told him, "but it's bloody damn silly being caught doing so." Then we dropped the subject. Always liked Walker. Sensitive chap. Had a lot going for him. Later I tackled Hobbs. Obviously that was more difficult – he had several years still to do at Blandfords. I told him I'd turn a blind eye but that he wasn't to bank on it. I expect I thrashed him. He was the sort one itched to thrash. I don't really remember. Anyway, that's when he said that he wasn't the only one. I suppose he was banking on safety in numbers. Told me you'd been at it for terms. Didn't surprise me. You were always too quiet, Metcalfe. The quiet ones were usually up to something. As for Walker – well, some chaps matured early, but I must say he appears to have been a bit of a Lothario! Still – what was the point of ruining his chances? He was leaving. He'd got a place at Cambridge . . . I told Hobbs to hold his tongue. Put the fear of God into him and sent him off not quite sure whether I was going to blab to his parents or not. I expect he squirmed for the entire summer. Poor little sod!'

TG sighed and rubbed his knees. An oppressive silence settled over the room. It seemed somehow to mirror the scene outside the window. There clouds chased across a white-blue sky and the trees at the edge of the lawn moved restlessly. But no sound penetrated the double-glazed window. It was like watching a silent film. Then TG started speaking again.

'Later, when you were having that ridiculous breakdown, I decided to do nothing again. Why upset your parents?

Why upset the school? We were still hoping for the POW. Wildeblood used to pray for the Prince every Sunday. Well, the Windsors weren't going to send their little darling to a school full of queers, were they? So silence was the best policy. These things blow over. No point making a fuss. We didn't want a scandal and as far as morality was concerned, well . . . Most of our elders and betters have a bum-boy or two lurking in their murky pasts. Not really surprising. Very unhealthy places – all-male establishments. If we had had tiny offspring and they'd been of the male gender I most certainly wouldn't have had them educated at Blandfords Hall. No thank you very much! All that erupting sexuality, all those questing sperm.' He shuddered and rubbed his hands. 'Far better send them to a day school. A bit of lust in the shower room. A few wanks behind the pavilion and then groping hands up a girl's knickers in the back row of the pictures and everything nicely sorted out for the best . . .'

I rose quickly and pushed the pouffe back to its place in the window. I wanted to go. I had a feeling that TG was settling in for an afternoon of reminiscence and prurient gossip.

'I mustn't keep you,' I said, turning and crossing back towards him, my hand outstretched. The old man looked up at me, not reaching to take the hand.

'Why, I wonder, did you come?'

'I am . . . trying to contact Stephen Walker. I wondered if you might have his address?'

'Ah!' TG nodded thoughtfully. 'And why, pray, would you want it?' he added, still staring at me.

I held his gaze, determined not to be intimidated.

'As you know – we were friends . . .'

'And now, thirty-odd years later, you intend . . . what? To drop him a line? Or maybe you'll turn up on his doorstep? Is that it? Mightn't he think that rather odd? Has he ever contacted you?'

Then I couldn't take his staring eyes any longer. So

238

I turned my back on him and stared out at the dreary view instead.

'Well, has he?'

'No,' I replied, but the word came out so quietly that even I couldn't really hear it.

'Let me give you a bit of advice, Metcalfe . . .' I heard him say after a moment, and to my surprise I discovered that he had risen from his chair and crossed to stand beside me. I turned my head, looking at him. I saw him now as a little, wizened man in a frayed sports coat and a shirt with a stained tie. I wondered why I had ever been afraid of him. He was staring out of the window and seemed unaware of my attention.

'I just want his address,' I said eventually, breaking the silence.

'Well, I'm giving you advice instead. Bum-boys,' he said, 'should be seen and not heard. You can't go making trouble for the chap, Metcalfe. It just wouldn't do. These things that happen . . . they're a part of growing up. No more nor less important than spots and the voice breaking.'

I realised that he was being kind. I remembered that he could be. But I wasn't grateful.

'If I knew Walker's address – which I don't – I wouldn't dream of giving it to you,' he continued. 'Good heavens, he's probably a grandfather by now. Now how would it be for a grandfather to have his youthful indiscretion thrown in his face? Absurd!'

'You don't know where he is?'

'Australia. It is rather a large country. I have no address. Be a good chap and leave things alone.'

I looked at him for a moment but he was still staring out of the window and wouldn't meet my eyes.

'I'll go then,' I said. 'Thank you for giving me your time.'

'Always glad to see chaps from the past. Happy times.'

'Goodbye, sir.'

He raised a hand in a gesture of farewell.

'Metcalfe,' he called as I reached the door.

'Yes?'

'Slam the back door as you go out, won't you? It also sticks
. . . It's the damp, you know.'

# *Then*

'God be with you till we meet again; By His counsels guide, uphold you. With His sheep securely fold you: God be with you till we meet again.

'God be with you till we meet again; 'Neath His wings protecting hide you, Daily manna still provide you: God be with you till . . .'

Evening sunlight slanting through the tall windows, casting dark shadows and bands of flying dust. Duff, standing beside me, is singing heartily. I wish I were Duff. I wish the height of my passion was the sighting of a crested grebe and that a forthcoming holiday in Majorca was the full extent of my desires. I wish I knew how I'm going to live through the rest of my life or at least the next two years at Blandfords without him. I have to get used to saying 'without him'. It is the end of the summer term. It is the end of Stephen's time here. It is the end . . .

'God be with you till we meet again; When life's perils thick confound you Put His arms unfailing round you: God be with you till we meet again . . .'

There is no God. There is only sentimental Victorian verse and cheap music. 'Strange how potent cheap music can be.' Who said that? Stephen will know. But Stephen won't be here. I wish I could cry. I wish the lump in my throat would dissolve and that tears would flow. I wish . . .

'God be with you till we meet again; Keep love's banner floating o'er you . . .'

What do they know of love? What do any of them know? They don't even like to use the word. They giggle and snigger and blush and stammer if they so much as come across it in a book or have to read it out in class. They pretend to be so grown-up; but when Nora kisses Torvald, they groan and puke. The 'love of God' is apparently something quite different from my love of Stephen. God doesn't fuck, for one thing – but then my feelings for Stephen are more than that . . .

'. . . Smite death's threat'ning wave before you; God be with you till we meet again . . .'

We won't meet, not Stephen and I, not unless we take courage in our hands and alter our futures. That's what he told me last week in the luggage loft, whispering it in my ear as he forced his cock into my arse and started the slow, painful motion that has become our usual way of loving. 'We have to be brave, Kit. We have to plan carefully. They'll all come looking for us. We'll have to cover our tracks. But most of all we have to have courage.'

The plan is a simple one. Early next term after he's started at Cambridge and I am back here, we'll both . . . disappear. I'll wait for him to contact me – he says it'll take a few weeks to get everything organised – then I'll get a Sunday pass (more bird-watching with Nigel!). I'll take a change of clothes with me, dump my uniform, and catch a bus into Cambridge. He'll be waiting at the bus station. Then we go straight to Harwich, probably by train. We'll cross on the first ferry to Holland then hitch our way through Belgium and France, cross over the Pyrenees and we won't stop running until we're south of Madrid.

He's shown me it all on a map. I think maybe he'll end up working for Thomas Cook and Co. I don't know how much of it I believe. I want to, but it seems so far-fetched. I said so to him in the loft. He stopped me speaking by pressing his lips against mine and forcing my mouth open. I can never fight him for long, probably because I don't want to. And besides, I want to believe him.

'It's no more far-fetched than our love, Kit,' he whispered. 'And you believe in that, don't you?'

Sometimes when we are making love I don't really enjoy it. Being fucked hurts. I told him once and he said if I wanted to fuck him instead, he'd quite like that. But I couldn't. I don't know why. I think he wanted it, but I couldn't. I was frightened after that. Frightened that I might lose him, but he never asked again.

'Lord, into Thy loving care we commend those of our brothers who are setting forth on life's long journey. May they fight fearlessly, act courageously and speak truthfully in Thy name . . .'

Oh God, if you are there and if you're listening, give me courage. Let me do what he wants. Let me not lose him. If it means running away and living in Spain, I'm happy to do so if only he stays with me. I don't think I can live without him. It's not just a case of not wanting to, it's that I won't be able to. I didn't know it was going to be as bad as this. This is our last night together here at Blandfords. I wanted us to meet, he says we can't. We've said our goodbyes. The next time we see each other we'll be on the run in his fantasy world, living rough in Spain. None of it is true, but our feelings are. Oh God, make me brave. Let me keep Stephen and I will do anything you ask of me. I will be obedient to you only please, don't take Stephen away . . .

'The grace of our Lord Jesus Christ, and the love of God, and the fellowship of the Holy Ghost, be with us all ever more . . .'

Amen.

The light is on in the Games Room and I can hear voices as I'm coming up the stairs. The door must be open. I hesitate, then quicken my step. The sound of table tennis reassures me. Whoever it is will be too busy playing to notice me and if they do I'll simply say I have to see Walker. There is no crime in that. I hurry along the dark corridor and pass the half-open door. Then I'm at the corner that leads to his study. This is where it all began, I think. How long ago? I can't remember; a lifetime or a moment.

I knock on the door and almost at once it flies open. Morrison is there, staring at me.

'What d'you want, Metcalfe?'

'Um . . .' I seize up. I hadn't expected Morrison – though why I don't know. He does after all share the study with Stephen.

'Hurry up, old chap. I'm late for TG's sherry party.'

'D'you know where Walker is?' I blurt out.

'Already there, I expect. Can I give him a message?' As he speaks he is hurrying past me and going along the corridor.

'No, it's all right,' I say.

'We'll all be doing the dorms tonight,' Morrison calls as his footsteps ring along the stone passage and down the stairs. 'You can see him then . . .' he shouts.

I lean against the wall outside the study door and slowly slide down into a crouching position on the floor. Strange how events repeat. Half of my life seems to have been spent outside this door and the other half within. Maybe one day, before I leave, this will be my study. I shall share it with Duff. He will cover the walls with pictures of birds and I with pictures of the Alhambra.

No! I shake my head. No! I won't be here. Stephen is right. Our only hope is to run away together. I have only to stay calm and wait.

Later, before lights out, the prefects who are leaving come into the dormitory to say goodbye to us all. Heslop wishes me well.

'I still have a photograph of us both in *A Doll's House*, Metcalfe! I expect the memory is rather embarrassing for you, but I'm proud of it. You were very good, you know.

Really. If you wanted to be an actor, I expect you'd do very well!'

'Thanks!' I say, and smile shyly when we shake hands.

Then it is Morrison's turn. It's like a royal progress or at least a command film performance. We line up, waiting for our moment, and the high and the mighty pass us by, bowing, making polite small talk, shaking hands and soon to forget all about us.

Dixon, who has scarcely spoken to me since the fight in the shrubbery, slimes up. 'Well, Nora!' he says with a leer – he is the only one who still calls me that – 'I hope you make good use of the rest of your time here. You should try playing games more. A little physical exercise would do you all the good in the world. Put some muscle on you.'

'Like it has done for you?' I enquire, staring him out. He frowns, not sure what to make of the remark.

'Good luck, old chap!' he says and moves on. I don't bother to wish him anything. I just continue to glare at him and when he is speaking to Duff he glances back at me and I notice that he swallows nervously. How fascinating, I think. He is about to lose the only power he is ever likely to have in his entire life. Even now, as the last night of term comes to an end, his glory is on the wane. Tomorrow he won't be a prefect any more! His brief moment will be spent. I hope and expect that he will spend the rest of his life being kicked from the proverbial pillar to the proverbial post. And while he is still watching me, I raise an eyebrow and freeze him with a look. He reacts as if shocked. It is a wonderfully satisfying moment. Feeling a lot better I turn my attention away from him and find Stephen standing in front of me.

I don't know how long we go without speaking. It seems like eternity. There is chattering all around us. Morrison is laughing with a group of boys at one end of the dormitory and TG and Heslop are holding forth at the other. Duff is saying something to Dixon and Stephen and I are alone together.

'Please let me see you,' I whisper.

'No,' Stephen says urgently. 'The loft isn't safe – not with all the trunks gone. And Mrs TG went out in the car as soon as the sherry do was over. She could be back late. It isn't safe.'

'When, then?'

'I'll find a way. I promise. So, Metcalfe,' his voice louder, 'I hope we meet again,' and stretching out his hand, he takes mine and shakes it vigorously.

'I love you,' I mumble, fighting back tears. Then I turn and scramble into bed.

I wake suddenly. It is very dark. There is no moon. Half rising, I brush my arm against a warm body. Then a hand covers my mouth.

'Come outside,' I hear a voice whisper, then a dark shadow crosses the window and disappears out of my cubicle. I pull on my dressing gown and tiptoe out into the centre of the dormitory. All around me I can hear heavy breathing. I hurry towards the door and slip out silently on to the landing.

A light is always left burning on each corridor. But it is a single bulb and throws a meagre glow. Stephen is standing at the far end by the steps up to the shower room and bogs. I hurry towards him and only as I get close do I notice that he is fully clothed. Before I have time to register my surprise he takes me in his arms. He is clinging on to me and his body is shaking. His grip is so tight that I am suffocating. I fight free and look at him. He looks away, breathing shallowly and still shaking.

'What's happened?' I whisper.

'I can't tell you,' he sobs. Then he starts to tremble again, reaching out to me for support.

We are in the dark recess where the stairs to the bogs begin. Anyone could come.

'We can't stay here,' I whisper.

'Go back to bed,' he says, his voice tense and shaking. 'I just wanted to see you.'

'What's happened, Stephen? Where have you been? Why are you dressed?'

'Not now, Kit. We can't talk now. It's dangerous.'

'When then?' I plead, my own panic coming to meet his.

'The holidays. We must see each other in the holidays.'

'How?' I am screaming – but inside. I dare not let my fear be heard.

'I'm not flying out to Hong Kong until a week on Monday,' he says. He is speaking fast, forming an impromptu plan. I have heard him do it before. He creates a scenario – and then we live it. That's how we first went to the luggage loft, I think. That's how we'll go to Spain. A series of quick, light strokes of his imagination; anything to create the world he wants. Then, no more questions. Once he has imagined it, it is as though the matter is finalised, as though it was always going to be. 'If I leave Pitlochry on Friday – we could have the weekend together.'

'Where?' I gasp. I know it's useless. I can't suddenly tell my parents that I'm going away. It's all right for him. He has freedom. 'Where?' I repeat. 'Where can we meet?' and I start to cry for the first time that night. All the tears of evening service, all the pain of goodbye, coming out now when least expected, when most inconvenient.

He looks at me wildly for a moment, then presses his cheek against mine.

'Invite me home,' he whispers.

'What?' I gasp, pulling away from him.

'Your mother once said I should come – when we met after the school play . . .'

I remember his foot on my foot and his leg pressed against mine. Standing there with Mother and Father and Angela in front of us, feeling his body and secretly proud. I was brave once.

'You must go back to bed. I'll telephone you at home. You tell them I'll be arriving next Friday. Wait for my call. Now . . . go.' And he pushes me away along the corridor.

The following morning when I am taking my hand luggage down to the station bus queue I pass Hobbs standing outside TG's study. For once he doesn't grin and simper. In fact, when he sees me, he stares for a moment with big, sad eyes. His face is puffy and red. He looks almost ill. I wonder if I should say something to him. But he looks away and saves me the trouble. As I go on down to the hall it occurs to me that he has been crying.

# *Now*

The sound of a horn blaring brings me to my senses. I swerve from the fast into the middle lane and cut in on a van that flashes its lights aggressively. The car that was on my tail passes me, the driver gesticulating crudely. I'd better stop for a while, I think, I'm not in a fit state, and I indicate that I want to pull into the slow lane. At the next service station I drive off the motorway and into the car park. Only when I switch off the engine do I notice that I'm trembling.

When Stephen came and woke me on the last night of his last term he had come from having sex with Hobbs. When he came to me, shaking with fear – or was it excitement? – he had been caught by Mrs TG. When he came to me, he had just had a 'fatherly talk, man-to-man' with TG. When he came and held me, gasping and frightened, he'd just been cheating on me. With Hobbs; stupid, brattish, simpering Hobbs.

It could have been us who were caught in the luggage loft 'going at it like rabbits'. I think I'd have been glad if it had been. Because then our – what do you call what we had? 'Affair' seems magazine-ish, 'secret' is too dramatic, 'love' too personal – well, whatever it was, it would have been out in the open. Or do I only say that now, with the security of age and the benefit of independence? Then it was the constant fear of discovery that made us cling to each other. Maybe it was the impossibility of it all that gave it such intensity. It seemed special and unique and . . . ours. But I didn't know he was also seeing Hobbs. And if Hobbs then maybe there were others. Maybe Stephen's 'Kit' was just one of a string of 'bum-boys'. What was it TG had said? 'He appears to have been a bit of a Lothario.'

I get out of the car and lean against the bonnet. The evening air is cold and I'm glad of it. I have just driven over a hundred miles to spend at the most half an hour in the company of a decrepit, self-centred old bore and in that time the delusions of my life have been shattered. And now I'm driving a hundred miles back again. Really, Christopher! Your emotional stability turns out to be quite as erratic as Catherine's!

I suddenly have a huge desire to phone her. To be comfortably at home in the flat with a drink to hand and the curtains drawn, safely chatting. '. . . Yeah, had quite an interesting day really. Saw my old housemaster and he told me that my lover was caught *in flagrante* with a fourth-former. Well, it's rather a long story and I don't have all the juicy details. No, Catherine, I don't know how long their affair had been going on. Yes, Catherine, all men most certainly are shits! I've told you that before. Well, I'm sorry if it isn't lurid enough for you. The only person who could dot the i's would be Stephen, and I don't know where he is . . .'

I must stop living in my head. It's like being drunk without the pleasure of gin. Can one be breathalysed for excessive mental activity? 'You are charged with driving without due care while under the influence of an overactive imagination . . .'

Then I notice that I'm cold. I turn and am getting back into the car when I realise there is someone else who could fill in the details. Hobbs.

I reach over to the back seat and take my address book out of my briefcase. Why do I always travel with the briefcase? It's somewhere to keep the address book. Why do I always travel with the address book? It represents stability in a shifting world. I am Christopher Metcalfe and these are my . . . acquaintances. Christopher Metcalfe. This Is Your Life . . .

I find a pay-phone and dial Nigel Duff's number. I imagine the call tone sounding in the hall of his house with the view of Ilkley Moor and the man-made stream in the garden. I imagine the children all watching a wildlife programme on television and Nigel and his wife-of-a-lifetime playing with their Down's Syndrome son and being fulfilled and joyful and complete. It's a vision out of hell; like the ad for Startrite shoes and the Bisto Kids and Katie with her Oxo cube. It seems too good to disturb and I'm just about to hang up when Nigel answers the phone. Oh, Nigel! You always sound so pleased to hear from me. Or is that your telephone persona? Are you always pleased to hear from everyone? Are welcome and pleasantness your natural bent? Almost certainly. Though this time your pleasure is tinged with a hint of surprise at my request.

'Why on earth would you want to speak to James Hobbs, Chris?'

Just get on with your bird-watching, Nige! You know me. I've always used you as a cover for dark and dirty doings. I tell him I think there might be a book in Hobbs' experiences with the rent boys. Nigel assures me that it would be much better to let the whole matter drop. But I insist. In the end he relents and says he'll find out Hobbs' number for me but that really, if I am going to take an interest in the school again, I should join the Old Blandfordians. There is a London branch.

Back in the car I fill up with petrol and pull out into the stream of traffic heading for London. I'll go and see Hobbs, I think, and then I'll let the matter drop.

As Stephen should have done. If only he'd had the courage of his duplicity. If only he'd ended it there, at the end of his last term. If only he hadn't invited himself home to Sevenoaks.

# *Then*

'Now, Simon . . . is it?'

'Stephen, John! You must forgive my husband. He always has his mind somewhere else. Do sit there next to Chris, Stephen. Angela, you can help me bring in the vegetables. Perhaps Stephen would like a glass of wine, John.'

'Yes, old chap. How about it?'

It is going to be a disaster. It should never have been allowed to happen. I want to run away. Father is using a strange, unfamiliar voice as if he is trying to appear more upper-crust than he really is. Mother is determined to be relaxed and is treating Stephen as too much of an equal; she makes insinuating remarks and laughs a lot and touches his arm. Meanwhile Angela is being a nightmare, staring at him open-mouthed, as if he were some unfamiliar alien creature, and blushing and giggling if he refers a single remark in her direction. Ever since we were waiting for him to arrive at the station she hasn't stopped asking impossible questions.

'But why is he coming to stay? How is he a friend of yours, Chris? How much older is he than you are? How did you get to know him? Why haven't you mentioned him before? Where will he sleep, Mummy? If he sleeps in the guest room, he'll have to use a double bed. Won't he feel odd in a double bed – I mean he isn't married. Only married people have a double bed. Where is Hong Kong, anyway? Has he got Chinky blood? . . .'

'Oh, do be quiet, darling. Here's the train now . . .' Mother was beginning to sound fractious. Angela has that ability. Even a saint would end up wanting to gag her with Elastoplast – which is what I once did, on one of the many times when Angela's ghastly behaviour ended up with me being punished.

'You'll have to watch out for him, Chris. He's your friend. We don't even know him. That's why it's so queer him coming. That's what Daddy said . . .'

'Angela . . .!'

'Sorry, Mummy. But I just meant that we don't even know what he looks like, so Chris will have to . . .'

'All right, darling. I know what you meant.'

He actually looked quite different. So much so that I almost didn't recognise him myself. You could somehow tell he was no longer a Blandfordian. It wasn't his clothes, it was the way he walked down the platform with a sort of swagger, a new-found confidence. That's the look of freedom, I thought; it's the way a prisoner would walk as he stepped out of gaol, or a patient emerging from hospital.

'Golly!' Angela hissed in a too-loud whisper, 'he's quite dishy!'

He was carrying a suitcase and a small overnight bag. He put them down and we greeted each other stiffly with a handshake. Then I turned and reintroduced him to Mother and Angela. Mother said how nice it was to see him again and that it seemed ages since the school play and, 'What was it called? Something about a toy . . .' Angela only giggled and looked at her shoes. He was relaxed and charming with them both. He said how grateful he was that he could come to stay. That he would have had to put up in a hotel because the journey from Pitlochry didn't fit in with the time of his plane. But that anyway he was really looking forward to seeing a bit of Kent. He didn't know the area at all. Mother said she hoped the weather held and we could go for a run sometime and show him the sights. It had already been arranged that we would drive him to Heathrow on Monday morning. 'But that leaves two whole days for exploring,' she said, in a bright, encouraging voice. Two whole days and three whole nights to fill in! Standing on the station platform even before we had set off for home I was overwhelmed by the dread of it all. We have not been alone together since the night on the landing. We won't be alone together now. Not unless I can think of excuses for us to get away. But Mother will feel it her responsibility to entertain him, and even if I could persuade her that we could manage without her, Angela can be like a limpet when she sets her mind to it.

We put his luggage in the boot of the car, then just as he is about to climb into the back so that at least we'll be sitting together, Mother tells him to get in beside her and I have to share the seat with Angela instead. She immediately leans forward with her arms on the back of Mother's seat and stares sideways at him throughout the entire journey, while pretending to watch the passing scenery and humming tunelessly.

Once at the house I show him up to the guest room but Mother follows us and brings him clean towels and takes over, showing him 'the geography of the place'. I wince at the remark, knowing Stephen will consider it suburban. But Mother chatters on obliviously. It is as though she doesn't want to leave us alone. Maybe she half suspects his reason for being there. If so she needn't have worried. Stephen seems as determined as she that we won't be alone together. When she eventually goes – saying: 'I expect you'd like to wash. We'll be eating at seven thirty. Nothing special, quite informal' – and we are left standing on the landing, he tells me at once that he's going to change out of his sports jacket and goes into his room, closing the door after him, without looking back. I wonder if I should follow him, but then decide against it, which is probably just as well because Angela is standing in the hall looking up the stairs as I come down them.

'I don't understand how he can be your friend, Chris. We only have friends of our own age at Swanning. Older girls and younger girls are not encouraged – because of pashes. Do boys get pashes?'

'Oh, do shut up,' I say, pushing past her.

'I don't suppose they do,' she continues, following me into the sitting room. 'Pashes are for girls. Boys fight and smoke cigarettes.'

But I wasn't listening. I went straight across the room and out on to the terrace to get away from her, and when later I returned I found her sitting on the sofa with Stephen, showing him the photographs of our holiday at St-Malo.

Dinner passed in a welter of small talk and long silences. A small relief was to be had when Angela was packed, protesting, off to bed at the end of the meal. It was long past her bedtime and she'd only been allowed to sit up because Chris's friend was arriving and we were having an evening meal. As she was going, and as a final vicious jab, she turned in the doorway and said:

'At my school, Swanning Court, older girls and younger girls aren't allowed to be friends – because if they get a pash on each other it can be very bad for them.'

'Go to bed, Angela,' Mother said, sounding severe.

'I think it's much the same at Blandfords actually,' Stephen said, smiling easily. 'But Chris and I got to know each other when we were doing the school play and we kind of kept in touch.'

I could feel my cheeks burning. We had certainly kept in touch, I thought.

'And besides,' Stephen continued, 'your brother is much more grown-up than most of the chaps of his age. He and I reorganised the library together. We had a lot of fun, didn't we, Metcalfe?'

'Jolly good,' Father said. 'You didn't tell us about that,

Christopher. It is a splendid library. Of course the school has a long literary tradition.'

I can't believe that Father has ever used a library in his entire life. And for long literary tradition read one romantic novelist and a clutch of extremely dull religious tracts by the only bishop ever to have worshipped beneath the Holy Postmen. But I don't say any of this to Father, now not being the time to get into an argument. Once Angela had finally gone, Mother suggested that we might like to watch some TV. There was a repeat of a *Danger Man* which I'd seen but which Stephen said he hadn't. I couldn't remember much about it anyway and it passed in a blur before my eyes. As soon as it was over Stephen said he really ought to go to bed as he'd been travelling most of the day and he felt ridiculously tired.

'Nice chap,' Father declared as if passing sentence, once he had left the room. 'You can always tell an Old Blandfordian: easy in society and charming manners.'

Mother and I went to finish the washing-up. At one point I thought she might be going to ask me something, but whatever it was she thought better of it.

Eventually I went up to bed. No light showed under the bottom of the guest room door and I decided against going in, with Mother and Father still up and Angela no doubt with her ear pressed to an inverted tooth-glass against the wall. When Angela grows up she should apply for a job with MI5, or better still the Thought Police – if Orwell proves to be right.

The following day dawns wet and dismal. Father goes into his study soon after breakfast, saying that he has some business to attend to. Angela, bliss of bliss, has Pony Club and although at first she tells Mother that she doesn't think she'll go if it's still wet at ten, they fail to get hold of her friend's mother on the phone and she turns up to give Angela a lift, regardless of the drenching conditions. 'But we'll get soaked!' Angela squeals. 'Nonsense!' her friend's mother retorts. 'It's only a shower and besides, it's good for the skin!' God bless the English and their stoic endurance in the name of fun and a good complexion. Angela has to scramble into her jodhpurs, which make her bottom look huge, and her riding hat, which does ditto to her cheeks, and she goes storming off in a filthy temper which delights me, though I do have a twinge of sympathy for her friend and the friend's mother – Angela crossed is like a woman scorned, they both out-fury Hell.

So Stephen, Mother and I are left to fill in the morning and in spite of the rain I suggest to him that we should put on macs and go for a walk – knowing full well that Mother wouldn't dream of going out in so much wet. She says she can get her complexion out of a bottle and that it's the kind of rain that precludes even gardening – the only activity that can persuade her to make certain concessions to our abominable climate.

'But if you really want to, darling,' she says when I tell her our decision, 'though I can't think it will be much fun. I'd be quite happy to drive you somewhere if you'd rather . . .'

I decide to take him along the bridle path beyond the View of Eternity. As we are crossing the lawn I glance back at the house and see Mother watching us from her bedroom window. She draws back out of sight instantly, as if not wanting to be seen, but I am still aware of her shadowy form behind the net curtains. It makes me nervous. It's as though we're under constant surveillance, like criminals.

'Sorry,' I say, involuntarily.

'For what?' He strides along, making me almost run to keep up with him.

'I don't know. It's all so dreary here.'

'Dreary? How can you say that?'

'I think it is.'

'It's home, Kit. I'd give anything to have it.'

'You have a much more exciting time – flying out to Hong Kong . . .' Then I stop, seeing the trap I am entering.

257

'To an empty flat in a tower block, with Father at the bank all day and servants for company,' he says, finishing my sentence for me.

'I'm sorry. I wasn't thinking,' I mumble.

He looks at me and smiles, then lays a hand on my shoulder. 'I love you,' he whispers.

The hand felt heavy and dangerous. What if someone came past and saw us? What if it was somebody I knew? But I didn't want to move away, for fear of offending him. So we walked on, he with his hand on my shoulder and me rigid with nerves and staring ahead until we reached the low stone wall with the drop beyond.

The distant view over the valley was obscured by the scudding rain. The trees dripped and the grass soaked the bottoms of our trousers.

'This is hopeless,' I say.

'Nonsense!' he rejoins. 'It's good for the skin!'

I glance at him then, thinking he's twitting me. But he's staring at me with a smile on his face and when our eyes meet he bursts out laughing.

'What?' I ask.

'I'm already soaking!' he splutters, and he puts his arms round me and kisses me on the lips.

'No, Stephen!' I say, pushing away from him. 'Anyone could come.'

'Anyone who comes out here in this weather deserves to be shocked!' he says, and taking my hand he looks round, searching for somewhere to go to shelter from the rain. 'What we need is a disused railway shed,' he says.

'Or a luggage loft,' I add, and I feel a wave of desolation sweep over me. School, us, our entire being together seems a million years ago, in another country, in another world. I think at that moment I know how over we have become, how past tense, how once upon a time.

'Don't look sad,' he says and draws me away from the

stone wall in the direction of clumps of rhododendron and sapling birch.

We push our way into the heart of the bushes but they give little shelter from the weather and scant protection from possible prying eyes.

'Isn't there anywhere we can go?' he asks, sounding exasperated. I shake my head miserably. It is all too frightening. It's worse than being at school. The thought of being discovered here, at home, is infinitely more alarming. I push past him and make for the path once more.

'We'd better go back,' I say.

'No, Kit! Let's find somewhere.'

'I couldn't do anything if we did,' I tell him and hurry away towards the path through the spinney. After a moment he follows and catches me up and we walk together back towards the house. We spend the rest of the morning drinking coffee and listening to records in the sitting room, with Mother popping in and out and Father in his study next door.

In the afternoon the rain lets up a little and we all, with the exception of Father, go to a fête in a nearby village. Stephen plays all the games and wins most of them except when he and Angela have a competition at the quoits stall and he lets her win instead. At least I think that's what happens. She does anyway – win – and she squeals with glee and chooses a bag of mixed sweets as her prize, most of which she eats herself, in a steady stream from packet to mouth. But occasionally she remembers to offer one to Stephen, her new-found friend. I understand about the pashes of Swanning Court. They are certainly bad for the girls! They make them simper and cling, or at least that is what it is doing to Angela. She trots round after him, laughing at his jokes, prodding him enthusiastically, even on one occasion linking arms with him, and all the time she is persuading him to guess the weight of the pig or to 'Come over here, Stephen, I want a go on the crazy golf.'

Mother and I watch them from a distance, both a little bored. Villages fêtes hold scant appeal for either of us.

'Well, she's certainly taken a shine to him!' Mother observes.

'I hope she isn't driving him mad,' I say, morosely.

'Oh, I think he can cope,' she replies. 'He's a sweet boy. I can see why you're fond of him.'

I want to tell her then. I want to share with her all that has happened between Stephen and me. But I don't, of course. What would be the point? She wouldn't understand, and besides, my reason for wanting to do so is more about his behaviour now than anything that may have taken place between us before. I'm jealous, I suppose. I feel as if he is deliberately excluding me. There's no reason why he should spend all his time with Angela. It's as though he's doing it on purpose. We've had hardly any time together nor has he addressed more than the odd remark to me. To make matters worse, Angela keeps glancing at me with cold eyes and a superior smile, letting me know that she has commandeered him, that he's her friend now. I bide my time, seething inwardly, and wait for my chance.

It comes, delightfully and unexpectedly, in the cake and tea tent. Mother and Stephen are ahead of us in the queue. Angela, next to me, is piling a plate high with nourishment. She is leaning across the trestle-table intent on a slice of chocolate cake to round off her anticipated feast. (She already has three sandwiches, a flapjack, a sticky bun and a fairy cake on her plate.) As she stretches, she has to lean to the side to reach past a large woman and a little boy. It is an ungainly, awkward position, a dangerous position. All I have to do is accidentally trip her, the merest flick of my foot in front of her straining toes . . .

With a loud 'OOOOH!' of alarm my little greedy sister overbalances, crashing forward, hurling her piled plate high into the air and then coming down SPLAT! amongst the piled-up cakes and crustless, dainty sandwiches.

'Angela!' I shout out, the *coup de grâce*, drawing attention to her predicament. She even looks over her shoulder as she falls, an expression of muddled disbelief on her face. Then she is sprawling amongst the wreckage and it is only the swift thinking of the large woman and, I am forced to admit, myself that prevents the entire table from toppling over.

'Angela! What on earth are you doing?' Mother exclaims.

'I slipped,' she wails, picking herself up and wiping crushed chocolate cake off her face.

'You've ruined these cakes!' one of the women behind the stall thunders.

'I couldn't help it,' Angela wails. 'I couldn't help it.'

'You didn't need to push and grab,' the large woman declares, brushing imaginary crumbs off her floral frock. 'She was pushing past me, that was the trouble.'

'These cakes will have to be paid for. A lot of effort went into them. The proceeds are for the Village Hall . . .'

'Angela, stop snivelling and help clear up this mess,' Mother snaps as she removes squashed sponges and scattered sandwiches from the table.

We go home soon after, the débâcle in the tea tent having rather dampened our spirits. Angela sits in front, next to Mother. She is fretful and querulous. 'I don't know how it happened,' she keeps repeating.

'Oh, do shut up about it, darling,' Mother says, driving irritably. 'It was an accident. Caused by greed!' and she slams the car into another gear and corners too fast.

In the back of the car Stephen and I have our macs over our knees and after we've been driving a little way I feel his hand on my thigh. I stare out of the window and pull away from him as he reaches over towards my crotch. 'Never mind,' he says. 'I really enjoyed the day!' And he removes

261

his hand with an easy nonchalance just as Angela turns to look at us.

I see her frown and wonder if she has noticed anything.

'Are you two cold?' she enquires. 'Sitting there covered up in your macs.'

'We have to put them somewhere,' I protest, too quickly and too loudly. Fear is making me panic. 'Unless you'd like to take them,' I add sarcastically.

'No thanks!' she shrieks. 'I'm boiled!'

I wish he was leaving tomorrow, I think as I'm getting into bed that night. I wish he had never come. The anguish and the futility seem to be spoiling everything.

The following day a misty sun struggles out through the low clouds and at least it isn't raining. Mother spends the morning preparing lunch. Sunday lunch is a sort of ritual. We have it week in, week out. It is always a roast joint and these alternate with boring regularity – beef, lamb, then pork – with an occasional chicken thrown in to surprise us.

'Jolly good! You're here on a beef Sunday!' Father announces, as he sharpens the carving knife. 'Lovely grub! Nothing quite compares to good old British beef!'

'Oh, do be quiet, John. I expect Stephen eats far more exotic food in Hong Kong.'

'Exotic? Quite so. There is nothing very exotic about roast beef, I'll grant you that. But I still maintain there is no finer food to be had anywhere on this globe. Arise, Sir Loin,' and he knights the joint, with a delicate tap of the knife.

It's like eating under the auspices of Egon Ronay: 'My companion had the roast beef, a perfect dish for an English Sunday lunch . . .' I feel ashamed of them all and can't even look at Stephen. I know he'll be condemning us as unsophisticated and middle-class. He tells them about Chinese food and makes Angela hoot with his stories about baked poodle and flied lice.

After lunch is over I suggest that Stephen and I should go

for another walk. Angela wants to come with us but for some unaccountable reason Mother suddenly seems to be on my side. 'No, darling,' she says firmly. 'The boys will want to have time to themselves. You can stay here and we'll have a game of tennis.'

'I don't want to play tennis with you, Mummy. You always win.'

'Nonsense! We neither of us win. Now, off you go, boys. We only have a snack on Sunday evenings, Stephen, so there's no need to hurry back.'

'Take him along the ridge, Chris,' Father says. 'He'll like that.'

It is a warm, sultry afternoon. The countryside steams after the rain. A thick haze envelops the land and branches and undergrowth hang limply in the torpid air. The path we are on winds along the crest of a hill, with gently sloping ground to one side, with a main road down in the hollow, hidden by a line of elm trees, and a steep drop on the other, followed by miles of rolling orchards interspersed by hedgerows and dotted with stands of beech and oak.

We soon remove our jackets and have the bore of carrying them. Stephen isn't very talkative and my mind is in too much of a turmoil to attempt to make conversation. After we have been walking for about half an hour we come to a place where there is a park bench, with a small plaque explaining that it has been placed here by the loving relatives of some dear departed.

'Let's sit for a while, shall we?' he says, crossing to the bench. Then he feels in his jacket pocket and produces a packet of cigarettes and a box of matches. 'D'you want one?' he asks, holding the box towards me. Seeing me hesitate he produces a roll of Polo mints from the same pocket. 'To disguise the breath!' he adds and, relieved, I smile and take a cigarette.

'You can read my mind,' I tell him.

'I always come prepared!' he laughs.

We smoke in silence for a few moments, then he reaches out and ruffles my hair. It is a strangely uncharacteristic gesture. Or, no; the gesture is in character, it is the distracted way that he does it that is unfamiliar – as though his mind is miles away but he feels duty-bound to try to involve me.

'What are you thinking?' I ask at last, when the silence seems as if it will go on for ever.

'About us,' he says. Then he falls silent again.

'What about us?' I ask.

'Oh, just everything,' he says with a shrug.

'We will go away, won't we?' I ask, a sliver of fear beginning to unwind in my stomach.

'Away?'

'To Spain.'

'Oh! Yes, of course we will,' he replies easily. Too easily. I sense his mind not concentrating but wandering somewhere where I am not admitted.

'Stephen,' I plead.

He turns and looks at me. I don't recognise the expression. He seems distant and puzzled, almost as though he is seeing me as a stranger.

'What?' he asks.

'This is our last chance.' I stammer the words, desperate to make him focus on us, to help me, to at least make him see the enormity of what we are proposing to do.

And it works. There in front of me I see his mood change and with it his face and even the movements of his body. He becomes eager and animated, younger-looking, more the Stephen that I recognise from school. He reaches out towards me and takes my hand, throwing away his cigarette as he does so.

'I suddenly thought,' he says, 'have you got a passport – or are you on your parents' one?'

'No,' I tell him, catching his excitement, 'I've got my own.

They had to get me one when I went to stay with friends in France.'

'Oh, thank God. Where do they keep it?'

'In Father's study.'

'You will be able to get it? You'll need it to get across the Channel . . .' And instantly we are back like we used to be, Stephen and Kit, working out the details of the plan, going over everything, checking and double-checking.

'I waited last night for you to come to my room,' he suddenly says, changing the subject. 'I was all horny and waiting and you didn't show up. I had to wank into a hanky.'

'You didn't!' I exclaim, for some reason feeling shocked.

'It's all right! It didn't go on the sheets and I was thinking of you, so I wasn't being unfaithful!' and he laughs and grabs me in a hug. 'Oh, Kit! We're going to have such fun.'

'Shall I come tonight?' I ask, as we're walking back towards home.

'Dare you!' he says and he looks at me with dark eyes that seem to know everything that there is to know about me.

It is a challenge that I'm determined to meet. He keeps telling me that all we need is courage. What better place to put mine to the test than in my parents' house? But when I steal out of my room, long after everyone has gone to bed, I discover that Mother has left their door ajar and as I tiptoe across the landing I make a floorboard creak.

I reach his door and get inside, shaking with fear.

'Stephen,' I whisper when I reach the bed. I kneel down and put my lips near his ear. 'Stephen!' I say again. My heart is beating so fast I'm sure everyone must be able to hear it. At first he doesn't move. But I don't think he's asleep. 'Stephen!' I whisper for a third time and, as I do so, he moves his head and kisses my lips. 'We can't do anything here,' I whisper. 'Mother's left their door open.'

He takes my hand and pulls it down under the sheet until

it touches his erect cock. I hold it for a moment and, as I do so, it begins to go limp.

'Go back to bed.' He breathes the words. Then he kisses me lightly, finding my lips in the dark with his other hand and touching them gently like a blind man. 'We will have all the time in the world, Kit,' he whispers in my ear. 'The next time we make love will be under a Spanish night and the air will be heavy with the scent of jasmine. Go back to bed. You're right, it isn't safe here.'

'But I dared to come,' I tell him. 'I did dare to come.'

'Go on,' he whispers. 'Scram!' and he pushes me away from the bed.

As I reach my bedroom a lamp is switched on in my parents' room. I close my door and lean against it, breathing fast – not with fear, but with elation. I dared, I think. I really dared!

# *Now*

The phone was on an answering machine when I first tried
Hobbs' number, and as I have an aversion to speaking to
machines I hung up. But later, receiving the same recorded
message again, I decided to overcome my prejudice. 'It's
Chris Metcalfe,' I said to the airwaves. 'You probably won't
remember me. We were at Blandfords together but that was
years ago and we didn't know each other well even then.' I
realised that I was talking too much and tried to come to the
point. 'It's just that I wanted to ask you about . . . I'm in need
of a piece of information . . . It's rather difficult to explain. I'd
be grateful if you'd call me . . .' and, gabbling like an idiot, I
rattled off my number and slammed down the receiver.

I had waited until the weekend to phone him although
Nigel had contacted me with his number and address on the
Tuesday evening, only three days after I'd put in the request.
'Oh, by the way,' he'd said, 'the Association will automatically
contact him as well, telling him about your enquiry. So he
may try to get in touch with you. The Old Blandfordian
Association has a mania about associating! They want us all
to be in touch with each other all the time!' 'Unlike when we
were at school!' I merrily quipped, but he didn't take it up.
'I made the enquiry through Gerald Dixon,' he continued.
'You remember Dixon? He was in Ely with us. He does a
lot of work for the Association. I think it compensates for
the fact that he still misses school!' I told him that I wasn't
at all surprised, that school must have been the last time

that Dixon had had the least vestige of power or authority and that he now would have no one apart from himself to abuse. 'Oh, really, Chris!' Nigel had protested. 'He wasn't as bad as all that!' I assured him that he was, had always been and remained '. . . a fat little creep!' Nigel had laughed then, a trifle nervously I thought, and assured me that the poor chap really had changed, was quite good fun now and that he was extremely well thought of in the legal profession. 'Which says all you need to know about the legal profession,' I'd rejoined.

Poor Nigel! By then he was beginning to sound quite exhausted – or maybe even irritated? – so I told him how grateful I was to him for getting the information for me and we ended the conversation with him saying yet again that if ever I was in the Leeds area Helen longed to meet me, there was always a spare bed, and it would really be good to catch up on everything. Quite what the things are that we're supposed to catch up on I don't know. A chartered accountant can't have all that much to tell and although I think it a triumph that he's produced four children, there isn't a lot of in-depth conversation that one can have about that. Maybe he hopes that my life has been full of incident and that we could while away the hours on Ilkley Moor (with or without t'ats) as I regaled him with my conquests and he tried, gently but firmly, to coax me back to the straight and narrow – if indeed I had ever walked on that enviable but claustrophobic path in the first place.

But by Saturday there had been no call from Hobbs. So that afternoon I left the message on his answering machine and then forgot all about it as the prospect of an evening with Catherine took over with all the connotations of cosy intimacies and too much alcohol that that entailed.

She had phoned soon after I'd finished with Hobbs' answering machine. She said she was having a pig of a day at the shop, that she didn't feel like going home to a lonely flat and that anyway there was something she wanted to talk about. So, if she brought the booze, and if I hadn't anything more spectacular planned . . .

'When do I ever do anything spectacular?' I protested. 'I am a middle-aged recluse. Besides, it's Saturday night. On Saturday nights I always stay in and drink and I'd much rather do that with you than on my own! Only I warn you, there isn't much food in.' 'Good,' she said, 'I'm on a diet anyway.' 'Oh God! Not again,' I groaned. 'Which one this time?' 'Gin and radishes,' she replied. 'Oh, that one!' I cheered up at the thought. 'It really works,' she protested. 'It certainly does something,' I said. 'The last time you were on it, we got so pissed I had to take three days off work.'

I decided to clean the sitting room before she arrived and with the Hoover grinding away I only noticed that the phone was ringing just before it stopped. I picked it up, but knew I was too late. It could have been anyone, of course, and usually I'm quite happy not to answer it because it turns out to be Mother or Catherine and they can always ring back. But this time I was convinced it would have been Hobbs returning my call. I decided to ring him straightaway and went into the bedroom for his number which I'd left by the phone in there.

'Hello?' a voice answered almost as soon as the ringing tone began. 'May I speak to Mr Hobbs, please?' 'Metcalfe! It is Metcalfe?' 'Yes. Chris Metcalfe!' 'My dear! I'm so intrigued! After all these years. It's like an answer to a maiden's prayer. Look, I'm in a frightful rush. I have to visit someone in hospital. But I've got all your details from the ghastly Dixon. Are you in later?' 'I'll be in all evening. But tomorrow might be better,' I added hurriedly, thinking that I could be a tad inhibited speaking to him, however briefly, with Catherine hovering nearby, radish in hand. 'All right! Don't you worry!' he said, his voice warm and humorous. 'I can hardly wait! I'll be in touch!' and he whispered the last line before the phone went dead and left me speechless. I'm not at all sure I didn't stare at the receiver like they do in bad movies. Then I shrugged and went back into the sitting room, glancing at my watch. It was after six. The shadow of the yardarm fell darkly across the sitting room carpet. 'To hell with the Hoover!' I muttered and dragging it back to the cupboard in the hall, I poured myself the first gin and tonic of the evening.

Catherine arrived in a swathe of grey serge. One can fairly accurately judge her moods by the colour of her clothes, and grey did not bode well. She had a bottle of gin, some tonics and a big bag of crisps in a plastic bag.

'I thought we were on radishes,' I said, emptying everything out on to the kitchen table.

'I couldn't get any. And anyway, I'm starving. You must have something in the cupboard.'

'Well, there's always something,' I said lamely and went to look. 'Pasta with sardines?'

'Is it legitimate?'

'It's delicious.'

'All right. But let's have a drink first. Let's have several drinks. In fact, let's get thoroughly stocious. Oh, God! Chris!' The words had a mournful tone. I glanced at her.

'Take off your coat,' I told her, adopting the positive approach and pouring a liberal gin. Sometimes, if one gets in quickly enough, Catherine's moods can be averted and I felt an evening of light *badinage* was called for and not the psychiatrist's chair.

'It's freezing in here,' she complained, pulling her coat closer round her. Then she ripped open the crisps and crammed a handful into her mouth. 'I've met her,' she said, showering crumbs.

'Who?' I asked, guiding her towards the sitting room.

'Penny Stratton!' She said the name with clipped diction. I couldn't think who the hell Penny Stratton was.

'She sounds like a village on the Cotswolds. Penny who?'

270

'Stratton,' she snapped. 'Bill Armstrong's friend.'

'Bill Armst . . .? Oh, Nautical Bill! You're not still thinking about him, are you? I thought that was over ages ago.'

'It was. It is. I simply thought you'd be interested to know that his beastly thin little waif of a child bride has been to see me.'

'She came to see you?'

'In the shop. "You're Catherine, aren't you?" she said, all simper simper.'

'What did she want?'

'To know where Bill was. He has apparently done a bunk. Just disappeared. I felt rather sorry for her. No, I didn't. Not really. I was quite glad that she was suffering and I was delighted that she thought he might be hiding from her with ME!'

'Bitch!'

'Realist. I can't be doing with forgiveness.'

There was a long pause while she stared at her gin moodily.

'Did she say anything else?'

'Yes, Chris, as a matter of fact she did. She said she'd met you.'

Ooops! Dim drums throbbing in the air half heard! She was giving me a piercing look, the look of trouble.

'Of course, I met her,' I said blithely. 'Didn't I tell you?'

'No. You didn't, actually.' She glared accusingly.

'Well, it wasn't really a meeting. More a serving. She was a waitress at L'Escargot. She introduced herself to me while delivering the meat and two veg. I was entertaining a client . . .' It was only a small lie. Now was not the time to go into Nigel Duff's role in my life.

'You're my friend. You should have told me,' she spluttered.

'And if I had – what would you have done?'

'Gone straight round to L'Escargot and pulled both her

thin little legs off.' She paused for a moment. Then she giggled. Then she frowned. 'D'you know. He was never going to marry her. It was a lie he told in order to get away from me. That is the most extraordinary thing. He had to lie to me.'

'It's never easy ending a relationship . . .' I said and then I stopped in mid-sentence, hearing my words. Another person's pain is so much more clear than one's own. Nautical Bill leaving Catherine was a dead cert from the first day he hove into view over the horizon. But Stephen and Kit? Was there somewhere a Chris waiting to say 'I told you so' to me? And if so would I take it with the same good humour that Catherine always did? I doubt it – but then Catherine has had years and quantities of experience; Catherine has spent half her life getting over people and the other half getting on top or underneath them depending on the phase of the moon.

Now in the sitting room she had found her way to her usual chair, had slipped off her shoes and was curled up, gin glass in hand, frowning and deep in thought.

We really might just as well be married. Our lives have achieved the right amount of habit, we have that capacity to talk to ourselves in each other's presence, we even share our unspoken thoughts, change the subject in unison, laugh at little inconsequentials and disagree forcefully about films and plays while enjoying the same music and exhibitions. There could even now be a string of little Christophers and Catherines running about the place, demanding new shoes and trips to Battersea funfair. Or, to be more accurate, waiting for their exam results and sniffing glue behind closed doors, so fast and unnoticed has tempus fugitted.

'What are you thinking about?'

'Our children!'

'Have you already been on the booze?'

'No. I was thinking how long we've known each other and how often we've been through all this . . .'

'All what?'

'Us sitting here, glasses in hands, while you mull over a recently past affair and I get steadily sloshed.'

'How boring I must be for you.'

'No more boring than I am for you, I'm sure.'

'All right then.' She shrugged. 'I shall finish this drink and go.'

But she didn't, of course, and eventually we went into the kitchen together and cooked a doubtful pasta which we ate at the table, washed down as Miss David would say with a rough red wine.

I was opening a second bottle and Catherine had gone into the sitting room to fetch her cigarettes when the doorbell rang.

'Who the hell can that be?' I muttered, crossing to the hall, bottle in hand. But Catherine was already there.

'I'll get it!' she said cheerfully, and she turned her back on me, opening the door.

'Catherine!' I heard a man's voice exclaim.

'Oh, Jimmy! How extraordinary! I haven't seen you for ages.'

'Is it someone for me?' I called, trying not to sound peevish.

'I don't know!' Catherine said, without looking round. 'Why are you here?'

'To see Christopher Metcalfe,' the disembodied voice replied.

'Then you have come to the right place,' she said, and stood to one side, revealing a tall, well-built young man in jeans and a leather flying jacket. He looked at me and smiled. I smiled back, bottle in hand, and stepped towards him.

'I'm sorry. Can I help you?' I asked.

'Metcalfe! Don't tell me you don't recognise me? I'm Hobbs – Jimmy Hobbs!' And he smiled again and I recognised the smile and I knew him at once. It was simpering,

273

brattish, giggling Hobbs – but the grown-up, five-door version, with sun roof and power-assisted steering. He looked, I thought, fifteen years younger than me. Slim, brown and revoltingly healthy. His sandy-coloured hair was cut short and he wore a moustache.

'Hobbs!' I exclaimed, sounding, I fear, appalled. 'I didn't expect you to call round.'

'I was in the area,' he said.

Why, when I contact anyone from Blandfords, do they have immediately to be 'in the area'? It is exactly what happened when Mother was here and the ghastly Dixon took it into his head to appear on the doorstep. Now it was the Catherine and Hobbs variation. I must get rid of him, I thought, smiling a welcome.

But I had reckoned without Catherine, who now completely took the wind from my sail by putting her arms round him and giving him a noisy kiss.

'It is ages. I thought I was never going to see either of you again. How is Mark?' As she spoke she was ushering him into the flat – *my* flat – and closing the door behind her with a flick of her stockinged foot. 'Chris, you remember Mark?'

'Do I?' I asked, nonplussed. All the time Hobbs was staring at me, smiling like he always used to smile.

'. . . Well, you must at least remember me talking about Mark,' Catherine continued. 'Pretty Mark. Mark who wanted to be an actor. Who *is* an actor, I beg his pardon. He worked in the shop for ages and then got a long tour of some ghastly play. You and I, Chris, we went to see it in Bromley. Oh, what was it? Actually it isn't a ghastly play at all – it's the one with the spastic girl in it. Is she spastic . . .?'

'Catherine?' I cut in, fighting my way between two words. 'Is any of this relevant?'

'Yes!' she cried. 'This is Jimmy. Jimmy lives with Mark. Or did. You haven't split up, have you?'

'No. Still together,' Hobbs replied, glancing at me again and smiling apologetically.

'Come and have a drink,' Catherine said, putting her arm round him and sweeping him into *my* sitting room. 'Chris has just opened another bottle.'

'I'm sorry,' Hobbs said, looking back at me as I followed them into the room. 'For some reason I thought you meant you were on your own tonight. I could call back another time.'

'That might be better . . .'

'How do you two know each other. D'you still smoke, Jimmy?'

'I'm afraid I do, yes.'

'Thank God!' she said, offering him a cigarette. 'I spend my time feeling a pariah! Which at least gives me something to feel!' and she gave him a dazzling smile. 'Mark and I used to share every cut and thrust of our turgid love lives over instant coffee in the stockroom. Then one day he announced he'd found the real thing. How long ago was that?'

'We've been together just over ten years,' Hobbs replied.

'There is a God!' Catherine exclaimed.

Meanwhile I was pouring wine and bringing a bowl of Catherine's crisps and generally behaving like the manservant. I was returning with an ashtray for Hobbs when Catherine suddenly seemed to remember my presence.

'But how *do* you two know each other?'

Hobbs stared at me, waiting.

'We were at school together,' I replied.

'Metcalfe was the first love of my life,' Hobbs said.

'Did you have an affair?' Catherine asked, leaning forward both out of interest and also to help herself to crisps.

'No! Worse luck,' Hobbs said. 'He was too busy elsewhere and never gave me a second look.'

'Chris! You sly puss! He never will tell me anything about his private life. Busy with whom?'

'Stephen Walker!' Hobbs replied, caught up in her exuberance. 'You remember Stephen Walker, Catherine.'

'Do I?'

It was like being a character in a Hieronymus Bosch painting. *The Garden of Earthly Delights* or *The Last Judgement of the Souls in Purgatory*. Catherine, my long-time and possibly only friend, was sitting in my sitting room, drinking my wine and talking about Stephen. *My* Stephen.

'You know Stephen?' I blurted out, unable to contain the words, surprise making me almost incoherent.

'I didn't know that I did,' she said. 'How do I know him?'

'Well, know is putting it rather high,' Hobbs said, sipping his drink. 'He came into the bookshop a few times when Mark was still there. I remember you and he having a conversation about one of the Booker lists . . . I remember because Mark said you fancied him and that you had the same taste in books.'

'Well, I'm sorry. He doesn't spring instantly to mind. But then if I had constant recall of all the men I've fancied and lost – I did lose him, did I? We didn't . . .?'

'No. You didn't! He went home to Australia . . .'

'Australia! I think I do remember him. Lean and handsome and built like a lifeguard?'

'Aren't they all, dear!' and they both laughed.

Their intimacy was beginning to infuriate. Catherine was at her vulgar worst and was already waving her arms about, making extravagant gestures, although she'd hardly had anything to drink, and Hobbs didn't seem to have changed a jot from when he was at Blandfords and he drove me to distraction even then.

'I was sorry to hear about your troubles,' I said, with a voice of open hostility and no sympathy whatsoever.

'Troubles? Oh, you mean the case!' He smiled at me and shrugged. 'I've forgotten all about that really.'

'What case?' Catherine asked, sloshing more wine into both their glasses and ignoring minc.

'Catherine! Where have you been? Don't you read the tabloids? It was my one moment of fame. "Top Advertising Exec in Love Nest Scandal with Male Stripper!" I'm told the guy made ten thousand pounds out of my name. But the MPs and pop stars made him much more! Mark said I should have told him I was an archbishop. The child was so thick he'd probably have believed me. Thick — but a lovely mover.'

'You were involved in all that scandal? I hadn't realised. But, poor Mark . . .'

'Mark . . . gave me his blessing,' Hobbs said, and for a brief moment he lost his high spirits and bright smile.

'So you're not faithful? I think that's probably very sensible. An open relationship. That's what I want . . .'

'I can't believe I'm hearing this!' I exclaimed. 'When Nautical Bill told you about Penny What's-it you went into cardiac arrest.'

'I was going to marry Bill,' she said severely.

'But surely it is within marriage — or the permanent equivalent — that the open relationship is supposed to function.'

'Chris, as you never have any relationships at all, I don't see how you can comment,' she snapped.

'Don't you?' Hobbs said, turning to look at me once more.

'What?'

'Have any relationships?'

'No,' I replied, rising and going to draw the curtains for want of something to do.

'Not ever?'

'Not as far as I know,' Catherine said, almost speaking in a whisper as though exchanging classified information.

'Oh, Kit!' Hobbs said, his voice filled with regret. I looked round quickly, surprised and angry. But not by his tone. By the choice of name he had used.

'What did you call me?' I gasped.

'Sorry. Stephen always called you that. I never think of you any other way.'

There was an awkward silence. Hobbs obviously felt he had overstepped some unspecified mark. Catherine was lighting another cigarette and trying desperately to keep up with events. And I – I was in a strange limbo world; a world of moving shadows and evolving emotions; a world as unfamiliar to me as the world outside Eden must have been to those two poor innocents who transgressed only because it had been made possible for them to do so and then were doomed to suffer the consequences for the rest of eternity. Eventually, like them, I found a sort of bolshie bravado. To hell with Catherine sitting there, I thought. To hell with what the odious Hobbs may think.

'Are you still in touch with him?' I asked, trying to keep my voice from shaking.

'Stephen? Yes. From time to time. He doesn't come over very often. When he does, he sometimes phones.'

'I wanted his address,' I said.

'I'll write and tell him.'

'No need. Just give me his address.'

Hobbs smiled.

'Unlike the Old Blandfordian Association. I never give addresses without first checking with the other party.' He shrugged. 'He might not want to hear from you, Kit. He is after all thirty-odd years older, wiser and twice divorced!'

'He really is married?' I don't know why I was surprised. Anything was possible. But I was and I showed it.

'He's on to his third. And he has two children. Both girls.'

I walked slowly back and sat down. I felt incredibly tired.

'Can I have some more wine, Catherine?' I asked, holding out my glass. My hand was shaking.

'Sorry,' she said, pouring the bottle unsteadily and holding my shaking hand at the same time.

There was another silence.

'No. I don't suppose he would want to hear from me, then!' I said, trying to make it all sound light and joky and unimportant – as it should be.

'Well, you know Stephen! He wasn't nicknamed "The Tool" for nothing.'

'Were there a lot of us?' I asked, clearing my throat nervously.

'It depends who you believe. He claims there were. But I only ever knew about you and me. I used to fantasise that we'd end up having a threesome. I didn't really fancy him, you know. Not as much as you.'

'I'm sorry. I had no idea,' I mumbled, feeling embarrassed and aware of Catherine's eyes on me.

'Well, I tried to make it obvious enough!' Hobbs exclaimed, then he laughed. 'Were girls' schools hotbeds of lust and lasciviousness, Catherine?'

'God, no! Anyway I was a day girl. We just talked about boys the whole time and ran screaming if one so much as looked!'

'Now I really must go,' he said, getting up. 'I feel awful having intruded like this. Thanks for the wine. It was delicious.'

'Oh, not yet!' Catherine cried. 'It's ages since we saw each other.'

'I really must,' he said, bending and stubbing out his cigarette. 'I'll let Stephen know you were enquiring about him, Kit, and I'll give him your address.'

'I don't think there's really much point, do you?' I said, standing beside him.

'Oh, Kit!' His voice had that note of regret again. 'It wasn't something I did, was it? It wasn't because of us – Stephen and me?'

'I'm sorry. I don't know what you're talking about,' I said, trying to move him towards the door.

'Your breakdown. I've always worried that it was because you knew about Stephen and me.'

'Good God, no. I had no idea,' I said, being light, so light.

'I hoped that you'd talk to me. The following term. I wanted . . . to say I was sorry. You see, when TG was going on and on at me . . . I told him about you and Stephen. I thought there'd be safety in numbers – no, I didn't! I just wanted to halve the blame. Christ, what a ghastly place that was. It's a wonder we didn't all end up psychological wrecks. But in a way you did, didn't you? At least at the time. I am so sorry.'

And I believed him. I actually stood there, with Catherine – my other life – sitting and watching and listening, and I wanted to comfort him, to reassure him.

'Don't worry,' I said, putting a hand on his arm. 'It had nothing to do with you. It was my fault really . . .'

'Stephen didn't know what happened . . . about the breakdown, I mean. But then not many people did. The official line was that you had glandular fever. But I knew. I felt as if we were linked and . . . I knew what was wrong with you. But I did nothing. I've always felt bad about that. Really I have.'

'There was nothing to do,' I told him, forcing him towards the hall. 'It was just . . .'

'I know what it was,' Hobbs said.

'What?' I asked, confused.

'You were suffering from a broken heart. I knew that at the time. I watched you all the time. I even knew what you were up to the day you ran away. I expected it. I knew you were going to do it. I knew where you were going. I sort of . . . lived you. But I did nothing to help you.'

'It's all right,' I said. 'It's all right.'

'But now, Kit, all these years later . . .?'

'Oh!' I said, with a mocking shrug. 'I never think about it.'

'Really?'

'Not much. D'you know the poem . . . "I have been faithful to thee, Cynara! . . ."'

'". . . in my fashion."' He ended the quotation for me. 'Ernest Dowson!'

'Where were you when we needed that information! Well, that's me, you see, faithful unto death!' I smiled and opened the front door. Then Catherine appeared behind us.

'*The Glass Menagerie*. That was the play we saw Mark in. He played the story-teller. He was very good. You will give him my love, won't you?' she said, pushing past me and embracing him.

'Yes, of course.'

'How is he? Tell him I expect to see him soon.'

'He's . . . he's all right,' and that sad, lost look came over his face again.

'You tell him he owes me a visit,' Catherine said, noticing nothing.

'I will,' Hobbs said and kissed her on the cheek.

'Goodbye . . .' I said, holding out a hand.

'Call me Jimmy, please. Hobbs sounds so Blandfordian.'

'All right,' I said, taking his hand, 'but only on condition that you call me Chris.'

He looked at me and nodded.

'Yes, Chris,' he said and then he put his other arm round me and gave me a hug.

As soon as we were alone Catherine was bursting with questions but I managed to get her to go by saying I had to be at Sevenoaks early the following day and that I had things to do. She was disappointed, of course. She had hoped to pick over every juicy fragment of the evening's revelations. But for once I was firm.

'There is nothing more to say about it,' I told her. 'It was all a long time ago. Just kids' stuff and really not very important.'

After she'd gone I went into the sitting room and drew

open the curtains. Then I switched off the lamps and sat in the semi-dark, with only the streetlights' yellow glow spilling into the room from outside. At some time after midnight it started to rain; faint, gentle drizzle drenching the panes with tiny sliding diamonds of light.

The church clock up on the Grove chimed the passing of the hours. Strange how time slips by and with it our youth, our middle age, our life, almost without us noticing. Could any of it have been spent differently, I wondered? Was there, as is often suggested, a crossroads, and did I take the wrong turning? Or is it all laid out in a blueprint before we ever emerge, screaming our resistance, into this world? Will we know the answers when we die? Will it all become clear then?

And I heard his voice echoing down the years, young and striving, desperate to have me gone, to be free of me, to not have to face me any more:

'Just let it go, Kit. Please, for me. Please. We must. You must. It has to be over. Just let it go . . .'

# *Then*

The wind off the sea is bitter. I hadn't realised how cold it would be. I stamp my feet and walk up and down, willing the bus to come, as a pale dawn glimmers up over the flat horizon.

I am doing exactly what we planned – but with one big difference. I haven't heard from Stephen. I was supposed to wait for him to send for me. There were plans to be made – he would arrange about tickets on the ferry, find out about bus times through Belgium and France, work out which route we would take. He would enjoy all that, the planning was half the fun for him. Then, once everything was organised, he'd write and tell me when and where to meet him. But no letter has come. I've written repeatedly to King's and have twice telephoned and left a message but there's never been any reply. We've not exchanged a single word since Mother, Angela and I drove him to Heathrow to catch his plane. About a fortnight after he left, Mother and Father received a letter from him; a funny, formal note thanking them for their hospitality and sending his best wishes to Angela and me. Best wishes? He had to put it like that, I know, but the impersonal tone made me apprehensive. Sometimes I wonder whether he remembers me at all when I'm not with him. Even when we're together I've seen a faraway look come into his eyes and have caught him staring at me as though I were a stranger. When he's in Hong Kong he probably forgets about me completely.

But that way madness lies! I've learned that it's better to live in hope, even delusion, than allow myself to dwell on such thoughts.

So this time I worked out that as no letter had come for me at home it was obvious that he'd write to Blandfords instead. He'd have been worried that at home someone else might find a letter and read it. Which was more than likely – Angela wouldn't hesitate to read my private mail and I suspect Mother would find it hard to resist. Yes, of course, it was much more sensible to write to Blandfords! There'd be a letter waiting for me when I got back at the beginning of term. Only there wasn't, nor has there been. Each day I have been at the rack when the post arrives and each day I have gone away empty-handed and increasingly desperate.

Eventually, when half the term had passed and I could bear it no longer, I plucked up the courage to phone him at Cambridge. I made the call from the public box on the corner near the Shell garage while out on a Sunday walk with poor, long-suffering Duff. The man I spoke to said that Mr Walker couldn't come to the phone but that he would give him a message. I said to tell him to 'get in touch with Kit'. Then I waited. I knew he wouldn't phone the school, so each day I went to the rack, expecting a letter. None came. Two weeks later I phoned the college again. 'Can you tell him to get in touch with Kit. Will you say it's urgent, please. Say I really need to hear from him . . .'

By now I was desperate. It was already November and I knew that the Cambridge term ended before ours – that soon he'd go away, probably to his aunt in Pitlochry, for the Christmas vacation. Once he left Cambridge I'd have no address or way of contacting him. I was still allowing myself to believe that it was all some horrible mix-up; that in some way he would probably be as worried as I was. There had to be a reason for what was happening. A change of plan, maybe. But if so he should have let me know. Eventually I'd hear from him and he'd be surprised that I'd been worried. After all, we'd never set a specific time when we'd run away . . . But there were nights when I cried myself to sleep, hating him for what he was doing. Then, with the dawn, I found some new excuse for him, some reason for it all.

Meanwhile the anxiety was beginning to make me ill. I couldn't concentrate on anything. My work was suffering. My half-term marks were terrible. I wasn't sleeping or eating. People were beginning to notice. I've twice been sent out of class for lack of attention, the second time during French dictation when I was gazing out of the window and not writing down a single word. On that occasion I was reported to Wildeblood, who gave me a long and boring lecture about effort having its just rewards. I felt like telling him about me and Stephen just to shut him up. But of course I didn't. The poor man would only get in a terrible state about the sins of the flesh. Then he'd probably have prescribed some stuff called bromide – which is rumoured to be given to boys who wank to excess, though I've never actually known anyone who has been given it and I can think of several chaps who need it. The sound of pumping bedclothes in the dorm at night gives away those indulging in 'excesses of carnal pleasure' – which is how tossing off was once referred to in a sermon given by a visiting Anglican monk, much to the delight of the lower school.

Everything finally came to a head when I was waiting in TG's study one morning. I had gone there to speak to him about having time off for a dental appointment, and while I was waiting for him to arrive I saw a letter from Stephen lying open on the desk. I recognised his writing at once. I even had time to read some of it. He's enjoying his first term at King's. He's got a set on the second floor and the view from his window is over the Backs and they're looking magical in the evening light – straight out of Rupert Brooke. He has a lot of time on his hands with supervision every two weeks

– but he's enjoying the work . . . I didn't understand half of what he was talking about. All I knew was that he'd had time to write to TG and yet he hadn't written to me.

And so I decided to put our plan into action without waiting any longer for his go-ahead. I made sure I'd got my passport. I packed my small case with a few clothes. I took the money I'd saved – almost fifty pounds, thanks to birthday presents and holiday pocket money. Then I climbed out of our window, the one Stephen and I used to go to the luggage loft, and set off long before anyone was up and about.

Now the cold dawn is turning into a bright winter's day as I slowly progress across the rolling East Anglia countryside in a number of different buses interspersed with interminable, nerve-racking waits at wayside stops. It's late morning when I reach Cambridge. The streets look washed and clean after rain and the buildings sparkle in the bright sun. The sky is high and blue above the rooftops and a sharp breeze blows the branches of the leafless trees.

At the bus station I ask the way to King's College. There's nothing suspicious about that, I tell myself. It's only like a tourist in London asking the way to Buckingham Palace. But I'm getting very twitchy. It's almost lunchtime. I'll have been missed hours ago. I'm not sure what they'll do. At some point I suppose they'll phone home. But maybe not at once. The school always likes to keep any crisis from the parents until the last possible moment. They certainly won't inform the police before they have to. When we had the burglaries, Wildeblood tried to deal with the whole thing internally and was ticked off by the Inspector in front of a room full of senior prefects. Stephen told me that. The last thing the school wants is any hint of scandal and a boy on the run will be seen as that. Unless of course they think I've been kidnapped! There was a case recently at one of the other schools and it's thrown the authorities into a bit of a state. Not that any kidnapper would be likely to pick on me. There are kids from much richer families at Blandfords. But if they do think that I've been taken by force then they might panic and go to the police at once. What would the police do? Put a watch on all ports and airports? I don't know. If only my clothes didn't make me look so obviously like a schoolboy. If only we were already safely in Spain. They'd never find us there. But here in Cambridge every policeman could have my description and be on the lookout for me.

My growing panic makes me run the last short distance and in at the college gate. The man in the lodge seems unconcerned by my sudden arrival. He directs me across a big open square towards distant buildings. To one side of the square is a long, narrow chapel built of pale stone that shines like gold in the crisp light. There is organ music coming from within. I realise it's King's Chapel – where the carol service comes from on Christmas Eve. At home we always listen to it on the wireless while wrapping our presents and placing them under the tree – it's part of the family ritual. In fact the organ is playing a carol now – 'Once in Royal David's City'. The middle of November seems a bit early for carols, but the music is strangely fitting, like the background score for a big Technicolor film. I slow my steps down, trying to calm myself. My heart is beating too fast and my mouth is dry. Now that I'm here I feel scared. All at once I feel small and young and unsure of everything. All I want is to be with Stephen. Just to see him will make me feel better. Apart from all the worry about not hearing from him, I've been missing him. But now, when we are about to be reunited, I feel . . . almost shy.

After a bit of searching I find the appropriate door and climb the stairs to the second floor. Then I walk along a dark, narrow corridor until at last I am outside his room. I raise my clenched fist. Then my courage fails me.

Suppose he doesn't want to see me?

I stand outside the door, willing myself to knock. I

remember other times outside other doors. Once again I am going to him. It's always me who reaches out. Except in the very beginning of course, all those light years ago, when he first put his hand on me, taking me totally by surprise and sealing, I think for ever, my fate.

'Come in,' I hear him call in answer to my tentative knock.

He is lying on the floor in front of a small coal fire. The room smells exactly like his study at Blandfords, sooty and dank. He has his back to me and is reading a book. He is wearing grey flannels and a white woollen jersey. As if in slow motion he gradually turns his head and looks over his shoulder at me. I see his expression of indifference turn to surprise, then shock, then disbelief. I stand in the doorway, holding my suitcase in one hand, silent and staring.

'Christ!' he whispers.

'No. Chris!' I say, making a joke, and I grin foolishly, waiting for him to register pleasure at my unexpected appearance.

He lays the book down on the floor in front of the fire and slowly rises. His hair is longer than I remember but otherwise he looks the same. He pushes a lock back from his eyes and stands staring at me, his mouth slightly open. I wait for him to speak. The relief of being here, of seeing him, washes over me. Tears slide down my cheeks. But I don't feel sad. It's more a sense of achievement, like reaching the top of a high and difficult mountain or the other side of a wide and choppy sea.

'Can I come in?' I say, my voice a whisper.

My words have some effect on him. He strides across the room and pulls me into it, shutting the door behind us.

'I don't understand,' he says. 'Why are you here?'

'I couldn't wait any longer. I haven't had any letters from you. Maybe they went astray . . . I don't know. I waited as long as I could.'

288

'But – what are you doing here?' His voice has taken on an incredulous tone. There is no hint of pleasure in it, no sign of welcoming gladness.

I swallow hard. My tears have stopped. Even my heartbeat seems to have slowed down. I feel a chill shiver through my body. I gasp and take several deep breaths. Then I start to shake.

Stephen glares at me for a moment longer, then walks back to the fireplace and leans on the mantelpiece, with his back to me. I can't think of anything to say. So I wait. But even as I do so I know that something has gone terribly wrong. He isn't pleased to see me. The realisation comes as a shock. I can think of innumerable questions but am afraid now that any answers he may give will not be the ones I want to hear.

'Why didn't you write?' I ask at last, when I can bear the silence no longer. Then when no reply comes I try again. 'I telephoned twice. Didn't you get my messages?'

He says something but his voice is so low that I can't make out the words.

'What?' I ask, desperate for him to communicate with me, for him at least to turn and look at me. I'm still standing by the door. For some reason I haven't even put down my suitcase but hold it hanging heavily from my clenched hand. 'Stephen!' I plead. 'What's happened? You said you'd send for me. I waited . . . I waited for you to tell me to come . . .'

I fight back the tears that are rising again and as I do so I feel a sudden flood of anger. I've dared everything for him. 'You could at least look at me,' I say, my voice filled with disappointment and resentment.

Then he's speaking again in a low voice but still without looking round. I strain forward, desperate to hear what he's saying.

'I can't hear you!' I cry.

'Go away, Kit!' he says, raising his voice and turning at the same time. 'Go away. Are you mad? Go back to Blandfords before you get us both into trouble. Go away. I didn't tell you to come. *Go away!'* He emphasises the last words, spitting them out. And he glowers at me, a surly look, as though I have become somehow distasteful to him.

I have never seen him look at me like this before. And I'm not so stupid that I can't read the signs. This is the moment when I should just turn and go. Why, I wonder, do we so rarely listen to that sane, protective inner voice? Probably because it tells us things that we don't want to hear. Now it is saying that I should turn and walk away and get on with my life. Because at this moment I know why I haven't heard from him, why he hasn't responded to my messages and letters. At this moment, while he scowls at me from across a strange, alien room, I know that he never intended to contact me once he left Blandfords. Or maybe he did once – but now it's finished for him. It's as simple as that. Kit and Stephen, our love for each other, has come to a conclusion. It's ended, finished, dead and gone, never more to be so. That's what he's known while I've been waiting to hear from him. That's what this is all about. We're over. Only he forgot to tell me. Forgot? Or didn't dare? At home, during the summer, he should have told me then. He wanted to, I think. But he didn't. Maybe even last term – his last term – maybe even then, he knew. On that last night, standing in the dark corridor, holding on to me and shaking, I think he knew then. I think that's why he came to me, why he woke me.

'You should have told me,' I cry. 'You should have said.'

'What? Said what?' His voice is hard; a jagged, ugly sound.

'That it was over between us. That we were never going to Spain.'

'Spain?' He sounds surprised and with a note now of controlled irritation. I feel angry again; a great wave of hot, violent rage sweeps over me.

'Don't sound like that!' I shout. 'It was your idea that we

should go to Spain. You were the one who said we'd run away and live there.'

He looks at me for a moment and then takes a deep breath.

'Oh, please! You didn't think any of that was serious, did you?' he says. He sounds so contemptuous, so belittling, so superior and so cold. I want to kill him then. I want to smash his sneering face. I want to hurt him so that he feels even a little of what I'm feeling.

'Yes!' I say, dropping the suitcase. It falls on the floor and topples over. 'I did think we were serious. Yes!' I repeat, clenching my fists. 'Yes, yes, YES!' I shout, lunging forward. The case is in my way and I stumble over it, falling towards him. As I do so I raise my fists and start raining blows on his face and chest.

'Get off me!' he yells, lifting an arm and slamming it down against the side of my head. I stagger backwards, a stab of pain shooting through my brain.

'You bastard, Stephen!' I shout. 'You fucking awful bastard!' And I come at him again, arms flailing and kicking with my feet. My hands are spread now and somehow I reach his face, slapping and punching. He ducks away, concentrating on trying to grab my wrists. He manages to get hold of one and forces my arm behind my back, pulling me round. He is holding me in a grip, my back pressed against his chest. His strength is much greater than mine but my anger makes me wild. I struggle free and duck and turn, facing him once more. He catches my wrist again, but my other hand is free. I reach up, clawing at his cheek, dragging my nails down his flesh, making weals appear that ooze blood. At the same time I kick him hard on the shin and then bring my knee up into his groin. He gasps as I contact his balls. He yells out, doubling up in agony, staggering forward and clutching himself.

'You bloody bastard, Stephen!' I sob and I push him so that he falls forward, sprawling against a small table piled with

291

books. 'You bloody sodding bastard,' I repeat, then watch him as he turns slowly, still doubled up with the pain in his crotch. The sight of him stops me. I don't want to hurt him. I can't bear it that I have. I turn away and as I do so the door behind us opens and a man rushes in.

'What am I missing? Is it a game for more than two players?' Then he stops, seeing me. 'Well, hello!' he says and he holds out a hand and beams a smile. I ignore the hand and move away from him. 'I say, Stephen old fruit!' he says. 'I didn't know you were into child molestation. There's an amusing society I could introduce you to.'

'It's all right, Sam. You go on. I'll be with you in a minute,' Stephen says, straightening up and covering his bleeding cheek with a hand.

'Does that mean my presence is not required? Shame! Looks as though you've been having a lot of fun. I'm the Honourable Samuel Willoughby!' he says, turning towards me again. 'But you can call me my lord.'

I stare at him open-mouthed.

'And what about you? Don't you have a tiny little name that I could use?' he asks, putting his head on one side.

'Christopher,' I stammer. 'Christopher Metcalfe.'

'Well, Christopher Metcalfe, I do hope we meet again. But I somehow doubt we will. Now be a good boy and don't hurt Stephen. He's far too precious and far too beautiful to be damaged, don't you agree?' Then he turns, giving Stephen a final questioning look. 'You should be able to manage this on your own. But do be quick. We're late as it is. Martin's meeting us as soon as choir practice is over,' he says and goes out, closing the door after him.

After he's gone there's an awkward silence. Neither of us can look at each other. Stephen picks up the books from the floor and piles them once more on the small table. Then he straightens up, running a hand through his hair, pushing it back from his forehead. It is a gesture I have watched him make a thousand times. Its familiarity stabs at me. I feel like a stranger with him and yet I thought I knew him so well.

'I'm sorry,' I mumble.

'You've probably ruined my chances of fatherhood. Thanks to you there will be no little Walkers to follow in my illustrious footsteps! Not to worry. I daresay I'd have made a hopeless father.' Then, as if unable to meet my eyes, he crosses to the window and looks out. The bulk of his figure robs the room of light.

'I'll go then,' I say, crossing slowly to pick up the suitcase.

'No. Wait a minute, Kit,' he says. And he reaches out an arm towards me, without looking round. 'You can't just go. Not like this. Come here.' His voice is gentle, the voice I am used to, the voice I have longed to hear. I cross slowly over to him and he puts the arm round me, drawing me in beside him so that we are both looking out of the window.

The view is of carefully tended lawns dropping to a languid river with winter trees beyond. The sky is flecked with streaks of high cloud. The sunlight is muted. A few gulls flap over the ground, screaming distantly. They're a long way from home, I think, there must be a storm at sea. And I shudder, without meaning to. Stephen raises his arm round my shoulders, pulling me in more closely to him. I can smell the odour of his body. The sharp, tangy scent of salt mixed with raspberries. How do you describe a smell? The only possibility seems to be by comparing it, however inaccurately, with other familiar smells. But Stephen's smell is unique. He smells only of himself. It is a scent I know and recognise. Blindfolded and with my arms tied behind my back, I could pick out Stephen from a line of other people simply by his smell. That's how well I know him, I think. That's how much a part of me he has become.

'That man . . .' I say. 'Will he report us?'

'We're not at school here, Kit!' he says and turns in towards me, putting his other arm round me, holding me – but away from him, so that he can look at me. 'Hello!' he whispers. Then he smiles sadly. 'You look tired.'

'I'm all right,' I say. I reach up and touch his bleeding cheek. 'I drew blood. I'm sorry.'

He smiles and shakes his head. 'I should have written. I'm sorry.'

'We're both sorry then.' I feel suddenly weary. 'But, yes,' I continue, 'you really should have written. I've been waiting, you see.'

'I know. I understand. I'm so sorry. It's just . . .' He turns away from me and looks back out of the small window. Then he reaches for my hand. 'You and me . . . that was all then, Kit. This is now. You'll understand as soon as you leave. You'll know what I'm talking about. Everything seems . . . different now.'

'Yes, I expect it does for you,' I say, pulling away from him. If he's going to offer excuses, I think, I don't want to be close to him.

'But not for you, I know,' he whispers, turning to look at me. 'Please believe me when I say I'm sorry. I really don't want to hurt you but – it has to end, Kit. One day you'll understand. I mean, it was just fun at the time, wasn't it?' His voice grows in strength as he rewrites our past and believes what he's saying. 'It was never more than that. A way to relieve the prison years. A chance to indulge in a little "heavy petting" as the magazines like to call it.' He laughs, gently. 'We really went some, didn't we?' Then his face changes again to a look of sadness and pain. 'Oh Kit. Don't miss me, please. There are lots of other boys. I bet half the fourth form have a mad passion for you!'

'I don't want other boys!' I'm shocked by the suggestion. Does he really think it was only the sex that has brought us to this point? 'I don't understand you,' I gasp. 'You promised me so much . . .'

'That was all part of it, Kit. All part of our ... time together.'

'Why won't you say "love"?'

'Because that's a very big word for little boys to play with.'

I look at him for a moment.

'Take me to Spain,' I say.

But he only smiles and shakes his head.

'Just let it go, Kit. Please, for me. Please. We must. You must. It has to be over. Just let it go ...'

I stare at him and don't recognise the person in front of me. Stephen, my Stephen, has gone. This man is a stranger.

'Yes, of course,' I say brightly, not wanting to reveal my feelings to someone new. 'You're right. I'll try ... try to "let it go",' and I turn and walk away out of the room without looking back. He doesn't follow me as I retrace my steps down the steep, narrow stairs and out into the cold November air. But nor do I expect him to.

As I hurry back across the open square towards the porter's lodge a choir is singing in the chapel. 'The Holly and the Ivy'. 'But of all the trees that are in the wood, The holly bears the crown ...' I hear them stop and start again: 'The holly and the ivy When they are both full grown, Of all the trees that are in the wood, The holly bears the crown: The rising of the sun And the running of the deer, The playing of the merry organ, Sweet singing in the ...'

The first bus is going to Ely. So I take it. I suppose I am going back to Blandfords. There isn't anywhere else to go. I will go back and I will be punished. It seems irrelevant where I go or what happens to me. I've stopped caring, stopped living almost. I don't seem to be feeling anything at all. Nor does anything matter. There is nothing that is in the least important any more. Everything that was ... is over.

Then just as the bus is pulling away from the stop I remember my suitcase. I've left it on the floor in Stephen's room, back in the land of the living where I dropped it –

before the fall. I have a sudden surge of hope. He'll have to send it to me, I think. He'll have to send it and by doing so he'll have to contact me.

But such hope dies quickly and I shake my head at my self-deception. In my heart I know he won't send back the case. In my heart – is it really the heart that knows these things? Wherever – I know that I'll never hear from him again.

By the time the bus reaches Ely a ground mist has settled. The cathedral rises out of the plain like a galleon out of the waves. The sun is setting in a flush of rose-red and golden light. Even the ground is pink.

I walk up towards the cathedral in a daze. The streets are empty and the shops are closing. A sharp, damp wind is blowing. I am walking aimlessly, scarcely aware of where I am or taking in my surroundings. Only the cold is a reality. It cuts into me like a knife, turning my blood to ice. After a while I reach the open space in front of the cathedral. The great west tower soars above me, silhouetted against the darkening sky and wreathed in floating mist. It is a dream world of insubstantial shapes. Only the cold has reality; the sharp, cutting cold. I hurry towards the cathedral and push open the door.

The vast interior is dimly lit. I walk with echoing steps until I am standing beneath the high wooden lantern tower at the centre of the nave. All around me the shadows stretch into an infinity of dark. I feel as if I am the only living thing in the vast turning space of eternity. Alone. Single. Unconnected. As solitary as Adam in Eden. As isolated as the morning star.

Now, here in Ely, I will bury Kit and Christopher will live on without him, I tell myself. Kit is dead. But Christopher must go back and somehow he must survive. There is no other alternative. Except perhaps death itself. Back there I could have killed Stephen. Here I could kill myself. But how? And why? And to what end? I'm as good as dead anyway.

Because Kit is dead and it was only through Kit that I lived.

The light is fading outside the windows. Candles flicker in a side chapel.

Where am I? Why am I here? Where am I going?

I walk slowly, heavily, forward. It seems a gigantic effort to place one foot in front of the other. Around me the shadows leap and grow and the darkness solidifies into absolute black. Eventually my way is barred by the wrought-iron gates of the choir screen. Looking through, up the length of the choir, I can just see the high altar caught in the last glimmering light of the winter dusk.

If there are prayers to be said then this is my prayer: I, Christopher, will not allow anyone ever to do to me again what Stephen has done. I, Christopher, will never again allow my heart to be taken because I will never give it. In this way Kit will be faithful to Stephen and in this way I, Christopher, will never again be hurt.

There are no tears. Not now. There is almost no pain. That, I think, will come later. But for now there is only this strange icy coldness inside me.

I will never hear from him again, I think. It is over and it is finished.

# *Now*

*Dear Kit,*

*Jimmy Hobbs just sent me your address. I don't believe it! I've often thought about you and wondered what'd become of you. This is being dashed off on our way to the airport. I do a lot of travelling but won't be making the UK this year though I will be coming to Europe – Italy and Spain. Can't be bad! Any chance of you getting over? (To Europe I mean, not Oz. I know you Poms don't travel! God knows how we ever got an empire!) We'll be in Rome first, then up in the Pisa area. Then on to Barcelona and Madrid. Or – here's an idea! – we're going to the Granada festival, just a flying visit (17th through 19th June, staying at the Parador). How about it? We did always promise ourselves a trip. Remember? Anyway, I'll make contact when back from the land of the Kiwi ... Did I say? That's where we're off to RIGHT NOW – Car's at the door.*

The scrawled signature was just decipherable as 'Steve', with 'Walker' added in brackets.

There was no address at the top of the double-sided postcard. And although I waited, he did not 'make contact when back from the land of the Kiwi'.

# *Granada*

It probably says more about me than I care to consider but how has it come about that I am driving into the ancient citadel of the Alhambra with my mother sitting beside me? By a series of compromises – that's how.

It started in London when I casually told Catherine that I was thinking of taking off for a short holiday. She was thrilled! She had a couple of weeks owing and would give anything to get a bit of sun.

'Ah! Well, actually I was going to take Mother . . .' I said, grabbing at the name Mother rather like a drowning man at a lifebelt.

'The three of us then. She'd like that. She did once talk about us all having a holiday together . . .'

'Yes. But maybe not this time.'

'Why not? It'd be fun. Your mother and I get on really well . . .'

'I know you do, and under normal circumstances it'd be a good idea.'

'So what's abnormal about now?' Catherine can be unstoppable when she wants something badly enough.

'She has recently lost her husband, Catherine!' I protested, deciding shamelessly on emotional blackmail. 'It's been tough for her. I think she needs a bit of time with her son . . .'

It was unforgivable of me and Catherine had looked chastened or even mortified – but it did the trick.

'You are sweet, Chris,' she'd said with a tremble in the voice that made me feel particularly shitty.

I'd had to be ruthless though. Ever since Hobbs' visit she'd been at her most relentlessly prying. Like a louche Miss Marple puffing at endless Silk Cuts and downing wine by the gallon she'd beavered away every time we met – quizzing me about Stephen and my connection with him, about what we got up to at Blandfords, about 'sex in the dorm' and 'nights of debauchery behind the pav'. She somehow managed to imbue my schooldays with all the decadence of *What Katie Did, What Katie Did Next* and *What Katie Did After She'd Done That And Discovered That She Was Going To Have A Baby Which Was Jolly Awkward For Everybody Concerned* – which was fine except that she'd cast me in the role of Katie and it could be argued that playing the female lead was what had landed me in trouble in the first place. Sometimes I was tempted to tell her what had really happened between Stephen and me just to shut her up, but I didn't want to spoil her fun. She obviously thought she was on the scent of something really juicy and it seemed callous to ruin her sport by telling her the sad truth.

I had to be a bit firm however when she decided that we should get together with Hobbs and his friend Mark. 'It'd be fun!' she insisted. 'I really enjoy the company of gays. They have a great sense of humour and are usually very good cooks. Besides, with a gay you can be relaxed – you don't worry all the time that you're going to be pounced on!' This glimpse into Catherine's psyche would on another occasion have kept us occupied for hours. Did she really see every male of the species as a potential sexual threat? Discuss and develop. But I wasn't in the mood. 'You may not feel threatened,' I'd told her, 'but what about me? They might want to pounce on me.' 'And you in contrast might just enjoy it, Chris!' she'd rejoined, lighting another cigarette while the last one was still smouldering in the ashtray. 'Why not? Jimmy is frightfully attractive and he was mad for you when you were at school. You can have Jimmy and I'll play with Mark!' 'Oh, do shut up! You're getting on my nerves.' She giggled and shrugged. 'Why shouldn't he have fancied you? I think it's absolutely understandable, normal and healthy. I bet you looked gorgeous in shorts!' 'I did, Catherine, I truly did!' But I put my foot down and refused to budge about meeting them, and she, much to her annoyance, couldn't find their number and was forced to abandon the idea . . . 'Until they contact us again. Which I'm sure they will. Mark was really fond of me. I still don't quite understand why Jimmy called round to see you in the first place — if you haven't been in contact since school. I mean, that was ages ago. Why did you want Stephen's address . . .?' And the whole rigmarole started over again. Knowing Catherine can be an exhausting experience but at least she keeps herself amused and only really requires me there as an audience. Needless to say, I did not remind her that I already had Hobbs' address, having been given it by the Old Blandfordians. Nor did I tell her that I'd had a letter from him soon after he'd called to see me. A strange, short note which I'd put to one side, intending to deal with it later.

But at least I'd managed to squash the idea of her coming with me to Spain. Or so I thought until another variation on the theme presented itself. She happened to call round unexpectedly when Mother was up for an overnight stay. They welcomed each other like old friends — or actually like mother and daughter-in-law, to be chillingly accurate — and in no time at all the subject of when Mother and I were going away was introduced. Of course I had had no intention of inviting Mother any more than I wanted Catherine to be there, so I hadn't even told her that I was going away. Mother had looked increasingly mystified as Catherine droned on and on, making matters worse with each well-chosen sentence until eventually I was forced to interrupt her, complaining that 'It was meant to have been a surprise. Catherine.'

'What is all this about?'

'I thought we should go to stay with your friends in Spain. You know – the couple who bought that villa in the hills? The people you're always threatening to visit,' I extemporised glibly.

'The Andersons? Really?' Mother must have been stunned by my sudden care and attention after all those years of neglect. 'What a lovely thought. I had no idea. And . . . you're coming as well, Catherine? Is that it? What a perfectly splendid idea. We'll have fun . . .'

Oh shit! Here we go again! Why this sudden obsession with 'fun'? But I must have let my panic show because Catherine, after the briefest of pauses, leaned across and gave my arm a squeeze.

'No,' she said, with a dewy-eyed smirk of understanding. 'I think you two should have a bit of time on your own.'

This pronouncement was clearly beyond Mother's comprehension. But though she continued to look confused she shrugged and obviously decided to let the matter rest, turning the conversation to the safer realms of Catherine's love life – a dangerous topic but one always guaranteed to capture Catherine's attention.

Later, however, when we were alone, she did return to the subject, saying: 'Are you sure you want to drag me along with you, Chris? You so rarely go away. Do you really want your mother with you?' Of course I didn't. But by now I couldn't have put her off without being hurtful. So instead I protested too much and made matters far worse and had to ring her later in the week when she was back in Sevenoaks to reiterate my burning desire that we should go to Spain together.

'You are behaving very oddly! If I didn't know you better I'd think you'd been caught out arranging a dirty weekend with a mistress and this was your only way out!'

'If I was,' I'd replied tersely, 'I'd hardly be likely to invite my mother along, now would I?' Which under the circumstances had a nice touch of irony.

So new arrangements were made. I'd already booked myself into a hotel in Granada and had intended only going for a long weekend to coincide with Stephen's visit. Now the whole thing had to be rethought. We would go to Mother's friends for a fortnight and during the middle weekend I'd take off on my own in the hired car and go to Granada. Everything was set, everything was fixed, everything was fine. And really it was working out rather well – but then at the last moment, when we had already arrived at the villa, the Andersons were called back to London because their son had been in a car accident, and although we were free to stay on in the villa. Mother didn't like the idea of being left there on her own and insisted on joining me on my '. . . jaunt. I'd much rather anyway. I long to go to Granada. The gardens are supposed to be superb.'

'There probably won't be room in the hotel, Mother.'

'Oh, nonsense! I'm bound to get in somewhere. To tell you the truth I could do with a bit of sightseeing. Lying round a pool is all very well but I hardly feel I've touched the real Spain.'

When I'd done my original booking the Parador was already full. But my travel agent had managed to get me a double room at the Hostal American which I was assured was only down the lane within a stone's throw of the other hotel and was in an equally idyllic location, surrounded by the Alhambra grounds.

But as for accommodating Mother: 'There are no extra rooms. There's a music festival going on. I had a hell of a job to get booked in myself. I only managed it because a couple had cancelled just at the time I applied . . .' First rule of subterfuge, never divulge any more information than is necessary.

'A couple?' Mother cried, making straight for the chink. 'So – it's a double room . . .'

'We can't share a room, Mother!'

'Oh, pooh!' she exclaimed, downing the last of her drink. 'Don't be such an old man. I don't mind sharing a room with you. We did all the time when you were a baby.'

'You may not have noticed, but I am not a baby any more.'

'Then I promise not to look,' she had said with a mocking smile and had dived into the pool like a teenager.

That was two days ago and now here we are, Mother and I, driving through a Moorish gateway and on up a thickly wooded hillside with the sound of the cicadas heavy on the sweltering afternoon air. It is, I suppose, as near to the 'real Spain' as we are likely to get and she certainly seems to be enjoying herself.

Reaching a narrow street full of gift shops and restaurants I find a space and park the car under a tamarisk tree. Ahead of us the lane ends at the gates of the Parador, the buildings of which can just be seen through the trees. I wonder what time tomorrow he is due. I wonder if I'll recognise him, if I'll even contact him. He doesn't know that I've taken him up on his invitation to come to Granada, of course, and now that I'm here I'm already going off the idea – if only because having Mother around has rather complicated everything.

The Hostal American is a little way back from where I've parked. It's a pretty building with bright window boxes and once we are inside we discover a cool courtyard at the back with tables laid for dinner.

'Señor y Señora Metcalfe,' the receptionist says with a smile, taking my passport and the agent's booking slip. 'We have given you and your wife a room at the first floor.'

Mother beams at her and raises her eyebrows to me. 'Thank you,' she says. 'We'll enjoy that.'

'Oh, yes, it is very nice,' the receptionist assures her. 'You will like it. It has view.'

And it has – across the narrow road where we are parked to the buildings opposite with beside them a high, tile-topped wall. Fiercely bright swathes of bougainvillaea and clouds of white jasmine reach over, as if exploding from the gardens on the other side. The heat is intense and the light bright and dazzling although the sun is already low in the sky. My shirt is sticking to my back and my skin prickles with sunburn. Behind me I can hear Mother moving about in the room. The unreality is acute. Most of my life has been spent dreaming of visiting this place. Now I am here . . . with my mother?

'What a very nice young woman,' she says, opening a wardrobe and starting to unpack her case. 'I thoroughly approve of your being taken as my toy-boy! Or was she being polite, d'you suppose?'

'You're not going to unpack?' I say irritably. 'We're only here for two nights.'

'You even sound like a husband!' She laughs lightly and crossing to me gives me a hug, then leans on the sill beside me, looking out of the window. 'Isn't this fun?'

In Spain, we are told, dinner is served late. 'Perhaps señor y señora would like a drink first?' We decide to go to one of the bars down the street and discover sherry as if it has been newly invented. 'It tastes different here,' Mother declares. 'The Mothers' Union variety always seemed rather tame to me.' 'When were you ever a member of the Mothers' Union?' 'Never! But I did taste what we imagined to be their type of sherry – warm, slightly sweet and cloying and with a serious headache quota. We called it "Mothers' Ruin". Your father used to buy it from a wine merchant in Tonbridge. He would take an empty bottle and have it filled straight from the cask. He brought some back once in a whisky bottle and somehow got it muddled up with a bottle of VAT 69. We had those ghastly Bartons to dinner and Mrs B said she'd have a little sherry because she didn't usually partake. She then proceeded to partake like a convert and it was only as she swayed into the dining room that John realised he'd been feeding her schooners of neat whisky.' 'Really, Mother. You make home life sound almost amusing!' She looks at me wryly. 'Get us another delicious herreth,' she says, speaking like a native, 'and I may end up telling you the story of my life!' So I do. In fact we have several more and we're both rather tight by the time we stroll back to the Hostal and are shown to a table in the courtyard. Mother's relaxed, garrulous mood continues but by now I am growing increasingly tense and could end up bad-tempered. Drink sometimes has this effect on me. It makes me irritable within my skin; a sort of body-induced claustrophobia. I want to burst out of myself and fly – but know I can't, that we are forever trapped and earthbound. It's a kind of Icarus complex – and we all know how dangerous that can be.

Once seated we order the set menu and some wine. 'We may as well,' Mother says, 'we're already in line for a hangover!' Then just as the soup arrives – a cold, grey-looking concoction – she suddenly, out of the blue, asks me why we're really here.

It takes me completely by surprise and sobers me like a bucket of cold water.

'I've always wanted to come,' I reply after a startled moment, trying to make it sound light and dismissive and hoping that she'll move on to another subject. But of course she doesn't. Blame it on the sherry! 'For the want of a nail . . .' and all that.

'With me?' she asks, her inquisitor's eyes staring at me. 'You've always wanted to come – with me?'

306

'Not necessarily. But it's very nice that you're here.'

'And yet you didn't intend me to be.'

'Well, I thought you'd want time with your friends.'

'But you were already coming to Granada long before we decided to visit the Andersons. You booked this hotel months ago.'

'What makes you think that?'

'There's a festival on. You told me yourself the town would have been booked up ages ago. Anyway, I noticed the date on the docket from the travel agent.'

There's an awkward pause. She stares across the table, smiling and waiting. I suppose she can't help playing inquisitor; we are after all in Spain.

'Mother, dear!' I joke, hearing the panic in my voice, 'I spend most of my spare time fending off Catherine while she plays amateur sleuth. Please don't you start.'

I pour some more wine into my glass. Mother shrugs and holds out her glass for replenishment also.

'If you don't want to tell me what's going on, that's fine,' she says. 'But you could at least do me the courtesy of saying so. It's disconcerting knowing one is in the dark.'

'I don't want to tell you what's going on,' I say, meeting her eyes and holding the stare. Eventually she nods and dipping her spoon she lifts it to her mouth.

'This soup is delicious,' she says as though the previous conversation hasn't taken place. 'It's almond, isn't it?'

But there's a tension between us now that won't go away without some effort – and that must be up to me. Because now it has been acknowledged that something is 'going on', as she calls it. And of course there is and she has a right to know what and, yes! I can see that I do owe her some explanation. In fact maybe I owe her an explanation for the way I have been behaving for most of my life. Some reason is required to define her strange, reclusive son – all buttoned up and living on the surface of things. Is that really how I am?

307

I don't mean to be. I scarcely even recognise the description. Maybe I owe an explanation to myself as well. But it isn't going to be easy to start talking after all these years. I have kept silent for so long it's become more than a habit – it's my essential nature.

'Actually, it'd probably have been better if we hadn't come,' I venture, by way of an opening remark.

'Am I such a disappointment as a travelling companion?'

'I didn't mean that.'

She glances at me and smiles. 'That was an unworthy remark,' she says. 'I'm sorry. Now eat your delicious soup. You don't have to tell me anything if you don't want to.'

'I do want to,' I tell her, and realise that I'm speaking the truth. In fact, in a dangerous way, like the waters of a cracked dam threatening to submerge everything in their path, I have a sudden desire to tell her every minute detail and only hesitate because I don't know where to begin. 'Do you remember Stephen Walker?' I ask her, saying his name as though it were ordinary but feeling my heartbeat quickening.

'Should I?' she asks, breaking open some bread.

'He came to stay with us during the summer holidays before my last year at Blandfords.'

Now she's staring at me again, a half-smile on her lips and a frown on her brow, and I realise she's as apprehensive as I am.

'Yes. I remember him,' she says. 'Of course I remember him. A nice boy with dark hair. We drove him to the airport.'

'He's here.'

She looks round as though expecting him to be at one of the neighbouring tables.

'No! Not actually here in the restaurant with us, Mother! I mean here in Granada, at the Parador – or he will be tomorrow.'

'Oh! And you have come here in order to . . . see him?'

'That was the idea, yes. I'm not sure now.'

'I see.'

'Do you? No, I don't think you can.'

'Then – help me. I am trying . . .'

'Stephen and I were lovers at Blandfords.'

'Ah!' she says and she puts down her soup spoon.

I wait for her to continue, but she doesn't.

'Is that all you're going to say?'

'What else is there?'

'We were lovers, Mother.'

'Yes.'

'When he left . . .' I shake my head and can't go on. My throat is tight and I can't swallow.

'You were ill,' she says quietly. 'They phoned us at home. That headmaster, what was his name? Wildeblood. I never liked him. They said you'd disappeared. I took the call. Your father was out of course. Your father was always out. It was assumed that you'd run away. I promised them that if you turned up at home I would contact them at once. But I knew you wouldn't. Home was the last place to which you'd have run. You went to be with him?'

I nod, but can't answer. I wish I hadn't started now.

'But later – the same night – you returned to school?'

I nod again.

'Without seeing him?'

I shake my head.

'You did see him?'

I nod.

'Oh, Chris. I'm sorry.'

'Sorry? Why?'

'Because if, as you say, you were lovers and you went to be with him and you saw him and you then returned it can only mean that you were . . . rejected.'

I nod again. But this time I make a funny little sound, like a laugh. There is a pause and during it a waitress comes and takes away our soup plates, although I've scarcely eaten any of mine.

'We drove up the following day. I always enjoyed that journey. It felt exciting, as if one were really travelling. Once through the Dartford Tunnel and beyond Colchester and Ipswich there was that clear light in the sky and the feeling of driving towards the edge of the world. Your father went straight to see Wildeblood and I was taken over to the san by that funny secretary; the woman with the blue hair and all those different felt hats . . .' She shakes her head and then slaps her cheek. 'Mosquito!' she says, then she falls silent.

Remembering, I think. I suppose she's remembering.

I was dressed, but lying on my bed when she came in. I wasn't ill of course but they'd put me in one of the isolation rooms. What, I wonder, did they think was my contagion? Something dangerous that would spread like wildfire through the school if it wasn't checked. Manic depression, perhaps, or teenage hormonal eruption? They'd be bound to have given it a name if only to persuade themselves they knew what to do about it. If they'd asked me for symptoms – which they didn't – I would have told them that I was cold . . . frozen cold. The ice mists of Ely had penetrated so deeply that it felt as if nothing would ever warm me again.

A man had found me in the cathedral when he came to lock up and put off the lights. I suppose he was a verger, I don't remember much about him. I was holding on to one of the iron gates of the choir screen and seemed to have got stuck there. I remember he had to prise my fingers open. He asked me what I was doing. But I couldn't answer him. I'd lost the ability to form words. Or maybe it was just that I didn't see the point of communicating any more. Eventually he called the police and the police phoned the school. Then I was taken back in a squad car. It was after dark and all the windows in School House glowed with lights. They asked me a lot of questions. Mostly I just nodded or shook my head. Then they put me to bed in the isolation room.

Next day Wildeblood came and started his questions all over again. At some point TG popped in, took a look at me, shook his head and hurried away without speaking. A doctor came and the school chaplain. The door was forever opening and closing. It was a bit like being an exhibit in a zoo. I just lay on the bed with my back to them all and said nothing. It was amazing how easy it was not to react. Easy – and somehow safer. I was afraid that if I let go I might fall completely to pieces or implode into that frozen, still, silent centre that I'd found. So instead I just let it all happen around me and remained unresponsive, unmoved, unfeeling, really scarcely even there. Their voices echoed, their warm hands touched and probed. I think the doctor gave me a pill to take – maybe at long last I was getting bromide – and the chaplain preached a short but pithy sermon.

In the end they all went away and left me alone.

It was a grey and blue day, with a wind blowing and rain clouds banked on the horizon. I was so cold. I lay on my side with my hands clenched between my thighs for warmth. When Mother came in I was surprised to see her. She said that she and Father had come to take me home. She said that Miss Gibbon, the matron of Ely House, was packing my trunk. She sat beside me on the bed and put her hand on my head. I was so cold that I couldn't stop shivering. She kept asking me if I was all right . . .

'You looked completely different. I couldn't get over how quickly, how suddenly, your looks had changed. You weren't a child any more – but it was more than that. Your eyes were the same colour, the same shape, they were recognisably your eyes. But . . .' she shakes her head, crumbling the bread on the table and trying to find the right words, '. . . whatever was looking through the eyes, whatever it is that animates us, that *is* us – your spirit? I don't know about these things –

311

it had gone, or it had changed. The you I knew wasn't there any more . . .'

I don't ever remember seeing her cry. Oh, yes! Over Father she must have done. But not like this, not these tears; these tiny drops that have appeared in the corner of each eye and trickle down the sides of her face without her even noticing them.

'Don't cry, Ma,' I whisper. 'It's all right. Honestly it is . . .' and then mercifully the waitress returns with plates of chicken and the moment is broken.

'This looks good,' she says. Then she pushes the plate away from her and shakes her head. 'I don't really want to eat any more, do you?'

The night is dark and throbbing with life. Cicadas drone incessantly and bats skim in and out of the glow of the lamps. We have followed the same road that we drove up earlier but have now turned off on to a broad path that passes like a formal avenue, sloping down steeply amongst the trees. The sound of the traffic and the evening visitors is muted here. We come to a place where a fountain dribbles darkly into a reedy basin, surrounded by iron benches. There are lanterns hanging in the trees which give a pale, ethereal glow.

'Let's rest for a while,' she says, stopping by one of the benches. We sit side by side, staring into the distance with the sound of the water and the cicadas and the sudden, surprised hoot of an owl.

Across from us on the other side of the clearing a youth in white trousers and a white T-shirt is dimly lit by one of the lanterns. A spurt of orange light is followed by the smell of burning tobacco as he lights a cigarette. Then he leans back against the bench and lifts one foot up on to the seat beside him, sitting in a wide, indolent fashion, dragging on the cigarette and flicking ash away into the dark.

'What did you hope for?' she says.

'When?' I ask, but I understand her question.

'When you ran away from Blandfords to be with him.'

I smile and shrug and try to sound casual. 'You wouldn't believe me if I told you!'

'Try me!'

'We were going to come to Spain, make money washing up or waiting at tables and live as peasants under the cool of the vine veranda . . .'

'Never more, Miranda, never more . . .' She etches in another line of the quotation quietly to herself, as though talking in her sleep.

'I wonder who she was – Miranda,' I say, hoping to change the conversation. But we have gone too far and it wouldn't be right not to finish it now, and she is stronger and more determined than I.

'Is that why you are meeting him now?' she says.

'Why?' But again I know what it is that she's really asking. Perhaps I'm afraid of the question.

'Are you here because you want to live with him?'

'Mother! I haven't seen him for over thirty years!'

'But you have never ceased to think about him, never ceased to regret.'

Is she telling me or asking? I'm not sure.

'Not all the time,' I reply

A man in jeans and an open-necked shirt has appeared and is sitting at the other end of the bench from the youth in white. After a moment the youth rises, flicking his cigarette into the bowl of the fountain. Then he turns and walks towards us. For a moment I think he is coming to speak to us. I look up, surprised. But he moves on and as he passes me I catch his eyes and he smiles. His teeth are very white against his tanned skin. He has black hair cut quite short and parted to the side and his eyebrows are thick and arched above his dark eyes. His body is lithe and muscular. He moves like a dancer, prowling delicately on

313

long legs in the tight white pants. I can see the outline of his cock, straining against the thin cotton. I have a sudden strong desire to reach out and touch him. He saunters up the path away from me, back in the direction from which we have come, then he glances over his shoulder, looking at me again.

I turn away hurriedly, breathing too fast and perspiring. I notice that Mother is watching me.

'Are you all right?' she asks.

I nod. 'Not used to this heat,' I say, wiping my brow with the back of a hand.

'You will see him, won't you?' she says.

'What would be the point?' I ask. The man on the bench opposite has risen and is walking in the same direction as the youth. I glance up the path and see the youth at a distance look back over his shoulder as he hesitates under a streetlamp.

'You've come all this way. It would be a waste not to,' Mother continues. 'He's expecting you.'

'No, he isn't. He doesn't know I'm here,' I say, watching out of the corner of my eye as the man reaches where the youth is waiting and they both disappear together into the dark of the trees. I continue to talk, the inconsequential words coming out too fast. 'I had a letter from him, from Australia. That's where he lives. He said he'd be here. He suggested that we should meet . . .'

'Well then!'

'It was rather vague – the letter – but I think he'll be with his wife. His third, I believe she is.'

'And you're here with your mother.'

'That says rather a lot about our respective development over all these years, don't you think?'

'I think you should see him. That's what I think,' Mother says, and she gets up and crosses to the fountain, holding her hand under the dripping water.

'Why?' I ask. I'm surprised by her reaction.

She turns and looks at me. 'Because it's what you want.'

'Is it?' I can feel the worm of anger wriggling again. 'See him – and then what?' She continues to look at me, unaware of my change of mood. I want to deflate her, to shock her, to stop her taking my life and dealing with it as though it's a challenge at the bridge table. 'Shall he make passionate love to me under the trees, Mother? There wasn't an orifice that he didn't stuff once, we fucked for Britain, Stephen and I – well, for Blandfords anyway. We licked and sucked and rubbed and screwed . . . Hey-ho for the public school system! Is that what you're suggesting? A return match – here under the stars? Maybe you'd like to watch this time.'

I see her flinch, as though I've taken my fist and punched her. Then she straightens up and faces me.

'Isn't that behaviour still illegal here?' she says. 'I wouldn't want you to end up in prison.' And she turns abruptly and walks away from me up the path back towards the road and the hotel.

'I'm sorry,' I call, ashamed of the outburst, and when she doesn't look back I get up and hurry after her.

'I shall see about flying back to England,' she says, coming out of the bathroom wearing a nightdress. 'There's an airport here, though I'll probably have to go via Madrid.'

'Oh, Mother! I'm sorry. You know me. I always lash out when I'm threatened.'

'The bathroom's free now, if you want it,' she says, climbing into her bed.

'It was a dumb idea the two of us coming here,' I say.

'I think we've said enough for one night, Chris.'

They say things look different in the clear light of day – though quite who 'they' are I'm not sure, and anyway this time 'they' got it wrong. The light of day is decidedly clear but Mother is still at her most clipped, her most unforgiving. I suppose it's understandable. One shouldn't talk about fucking and orifices to one's mother. I did it for effect, so it could be considered to have been a successful operation. But having so recently decided to bare my soul, I don't seem to have got off to a very good start. Entirely my own fault, of course. I lost my temper and blew it. Put it down to too much 'herreth' and an unnerving sensation of being an outsider watching my own life being examined under a microscope. So far I don't think she's booking the next flight out but I can't be certain as she's been avoiding me all morning. She went out soon after breakfast and hasn't been seen since. However her case is still unpacked and she's taken her camera and sunglasses so I'm assuming that she's gone sightseeing.

Meanwhile I in my turn am avoiding the street outside the Hostal because Stephen should arrive sometime today and I've decided that he's the last person I want to bump into. In fact what I'd really like is never to have heard from him in the first place and I certainly wish he hadn't been sent my address by Jimmy Hobbs. This inept piece of timing is typical of me. The times I've set in motion a course of events and only later realised that the outcome would be the last thing that I'd want to happen has dogged me for most of my life. I expect that's how I felt on the bus journey to Cambridge when I ran away from school. Though maybe not. Then my overriding desire had been to be free of the anticipation of hearing from him – and the longing to see him and be with him. Now to see, hear, or be near him is about the last thing on my agenda. At the eleventh hour – no, at five minutes to midnight – I've rejected the plan and can see only its potential for total disaster. What could we find to say to each other? What have we in common? He's a thrice-married man, I'm a retarded bachelor. Where is the chemistry there? I certainly wouldn't buy the book for publication. It hasn't got a women's angle and we'd never sell the serial rights.

So I have decided to join the tourists as an excuse for going into hiding and, coming down into the hall, I leave a message with the receptionist. 'If Señora Metcalfe returns, will you tell her I have gone to look at the palaces?' I say, consciously avoiding referring to her as either my mother or my wife. Then I hurry out into the crowded lane wearing a sunhat and dark glasses for disguise and only relax once I am through the entrance gates and inside the Alhambra.

The heat is incredible. It has that sharp edge to it, like a knife. It cuts through my thin shirt, lacerating my back so that the skin feels as if it is cracking. My trousers cling against my perspiring legs and my straw hat sticks to my brow and releases beads of sweat that sting my eyes behind the dark glasses. I feel like an alien; I cannot escape this strange, detached, other-worldliness, as though I'm an intruder, a person in a dream.

In an attempt to get away from the searching sun, I make my way inside the buildings, where the shade is as welcome as an oasis in a desert. I wander, guidebook in hand, from palace to palace, slowly sinking into the alchemy of time, lulled by history and coaxed by the imagination. The Royal House, Mexuar, The Oratory, The Diwan Palace, The Hall of the Two Sisters, The Myrtle Courtyard, The Tower of the Comares, Abencerrajes Hall . . . Strange, exotic-sounding names drawing me deeper and deeper into an insubstantial world of light followed by shade, cold and intense heat, space then confinement as the gradually changing scene emerges and dissolves around me.

Pale golden stone is covered with intricate patterns and curling texts. Tiles in cool shades of greens and blues, blacks and a surprising dusty orange form geometric shapes as they line walls and floors with an abundance of vibrant expression. It's as if some impatient artist has been let loose on a blank canvas and wants to express everything in his heart all at the same moment, cramming in idea after idea in a glorious flood of exhibitionism. But the play of light and the extraordinary perspective of vistas and angled corners brings space and calm to even the most conflicting of images and the end of the endeavour is peace beyond imagining and beauty beyond compare.

Above me thin columns support encrusted roofs which drip stonework like regimented stalactites or erupt into clusters of stars as if the heavens have been caught in a great white net of gleaming marble. The sound of water is everywhere; cascading from lions' mouths, bubbling up into mirror-like pools, trickling and splashing from fountains and cisterns or sliding like a glittering snake through narrow open channels in the flagged floors of the rooms; the sound cooling and murmuring on the sweltering air with the onomatopoeic music of refreshment.

There are inner courtyards crowded with jasmine and oleander where the scent intoxicates the senses and sends one reeling towards dark stairways that lead to upper terraces, with shaded views of the lower town languishing in the noontime heat. Beyond are rooms with screens of pierced marble that filter the sun and capture the most gentle of breezes, revitalising the air and softening the harsh sun's rays to a glimmer of gloaming light.

What started out as an expedition to escape from the problems of the present has turned into a voyage of almost overwhelming sensations. And, as the tensions in me gradually relax, I feel the ice at the base of my spine, that formed one winter's evening long ago in Ely and has remained lodged there ever since, slip and move and jerk free as if sudden heat has started a thaw. The pain is excruciating as icy needles dart through my veins and to the ends of my

318

nerves, making me gasp and lean against a wall. The cool of the marble melts against my flaming back. My legs are trembling. I reach for a window ledge and grip hold of it for fear of falling.

Later – how much later I'm not sure, for I seem to have lost all sense of time – I pull myself forward and force my legs to carry me onwards through silent, echoing rooms and shaded courtyards until I find myself high up on a tower with open windows all around me. The breeze that is blowing is warm and scented. Below, in a garden of enclosing yew hedges and great pots of agapanthus lilies as blue as the sky, palm trees droop in the heat and cast their pale reflections on to the surface of a cistern brimming with water the colour of emeralds. For some miraculous reason I am alone here. Perhaps the other visitors have gone to their lunches or to the air-conditioned cool of their hotel rooms. The humming silence that encompasses the sounds of water and cicadas and even distant traffic encloses everything like a celestial dome.

Now I could believe in eternity, I think, for now there is no time and it is only time as it passes that admits change and destruction. Here, in this moment, the now and the then of existence seem to be joined into a creative, radiant present. There is no past, no future here. There is only this strange, recognised yet unfamiliar nowness. It is neither long nor short, high nor low, fast nor slow. I have arrived at a mystical centre from which all experience emanates and to which all eventualities return. I am neither young nor am I old; living nor dead; here nor there . . .

I'm breathing too quickly. I think this is hyperventilation. I may even be going to faint . . .

I take a deep, slow breath and then as I exhale I feel a renewed surge of energy up my back as though someone has taken a finger and run it from the base of my spine to the crown of my head. I gasp, enjoying the sensation of energy

319

flowing through me, like a welcome warmth suffusing my frozen body . . .

That's it, I think! That's precisely it! The cold has gone. At last, the cold has gone!

I turn my back on the view, resting against the ledge on which I was leaning. Footsteps echo, coming up the steps from the garden below. I see a man in a pale blue suit and with silver-grey hair slowly emerge on to the floor in front of me, rising up from the stairwell with slow, elegant movements.

As he comes out into the light, a lock of the silver hair falls across his brow and he pushes it back, using the spread fingers of one hand like a comb.

Then, as I silently watch, he turns and looks at me.

'Stephen!' I exclaim, knowing him at once.

'I've been searching this sodding place for two hours, looking for you!' he says. Then gradually his face breaks into an enchanting wide-eyed smile. 'Hello, Kit!' he says and he walks across and puts his arms round me, enveloping me in a bear hug that smells of raspberries and salt.

'When did you arrive?' I ask, pushing him away gently and moving at the same time so that there's space between us.

'We got in this morning. They gave me your note straightaway.'

This is obviously some dream that I've stumbled into and therefore it scarcely seems necessary to ask him what the hell he's talking about.

'Liz wanted a rest so I thought I'd come and find you,' he continues. 'They told me at the hotel where you were – I came looking on the off chance. It really is great to see you. I wasn't sure if you'd be able to make it . . .'

'You didn't give me an address, so I couldn't write.'

'No sweat! We're actually here on business – did I say that in the letter?'

'No.'

'Food and wine – that's my bag. I've got a restaurant in Sydney, a chain of booze shops and a vineyard – well, share of. We should start exporting in a couple of years. Keep your eyes peeled for Wannata Hill. "Fruity with an amusing little nose . . ." and all the other crap they like to spout. Actually the Chardonnay drinks like ambrosia. Anyway – that's why I'm here . . .'

'Don't they have quite a lot of their own wine in Spain?'

'Sure do – and I'm part of their export market.'

'Oh, I see. I thought you meant you were here selling.'

'Not yet – but watch this space!'

We're talking and behaving like acquaintances, I think. We're walking side by side through the gardens that moments ago I was seeing from above. We must look like any other middle-aged friends who've bumped into each other after years apart and are filling in the space between with small talk about their lives. He's taken off his jacket and is carrying it hooked to a finger and slung over his shoulder. At some point he stops to roll up the sleeves of his shirt. His arms are tanned and covered with a down of hair. I'd forgotten he was quite hairy. He's still tall and slim but his black hair has turned silver and there are little creases at the corners of his eyes.

'You look fantastic, Kit,' he says, glancing at me as if he's been reading my thoughts. 'You haven't changed a bit. Except . . .'

'I got older?'

'No. But you signed the note "Chris" and I couldn't think who it was from for a moment. Don't you call yourself Kit any more?'

'I never did. It was only you.'

Does he stumble for a moment? Does he cast a quick sideways glance? Most probably not. We read too much into the trivia of behaviour, I suspect – or at least I do.

'No, but people do change their names. Everyone calls

me Steve now. I guess that's living in Oz. They shorten your name and the lifeguards pad their bathers. That's really all you need to know when visiting the country for the first time!'

'So Big Jeff is really Jeffrey of average proportions? How disappointing!'

'It's really good to see you,' he says again, and he drenches me in that wide, open, sunny smile. 'What are you up to anyway? I always thought you might turn out to be one of the leading thesps of the West End stage.'

'Why?' I ask, surprised.

'Because you were so great in *A Doll's House*.'

He remembers, I think, and I'm pleased.

'No,' I say. 'I'm far too shy.'

'You are? You didn't used to be.'

'I was, you know.'

'Really? You?'

I nod and we walk on in silence. Is he remembering back, I wonder? Is he recalling how things used to be?

'So what have you been up to, Kit?'

The question confuses me. I'm not sure what he's asking. Does he mean my personal or my professional life? I feel suddenly uncomfortable and embarrassed. I continue to walk in silence, not looking at him. I hear him laugh.

'You look as if I just asked you to make general confession! What I meant was – how d'you make a living? I'm not asking for the steamy details of the last thirty years!' And he puts an arm round my shoulders and laughs again as he gives me a hug. 'Believe me, my escapades in that area take quite a lot of recounting!'

'So I'm told!'

'Who've you been listening to? It's lies, all lies.'

'No one really. Just Hobbs . . .'

'Jimmy? What's he been telling you?'

Do I detect a note of alarm? Probably not.

'Nothing much,' I reply. 'He mentioned that you'd been married . . .'

'And married . . . and married . . . I am a serial husband! Don't ask me why. Well – you can ask but I'm damned if I know the answer. You're going to meet the latest.'

'Am I?'

'If you'd like to. We're going to a concert tonight. She's a music freak – more than that, she's a performer. Concert pianist. Elizabeth Harker?'

He says the name as though I should have heard of it. I shake my head.

'She's only done one tour in Europe, though she's quite popular in the States.' He sounds almost disappointed by my negative response. 'She's really only just starting out. But Decca have her under contract and things are looking good. Anyway, this time she's just a member of the paying public. We actually hoped to be here for the Montserrat Caballe recital but that was last week so we're going to the Hilliard Ensemble in the Patio de los Arrayanes.' His Spanish accent sounds good. 'D'you have a ticket?'

'No.'

'It might still be possible to get one . . .'

'There are two of us, actually.'

'Great! Who're you with?'

'My mother.'

'Jesus!' and he starts to laugh.

I walk on stoically, trying not to be hurt by his reaction and knowing that I'm blushing.

'I don't believe it, Kit. You brought your mother – here?'

'Why not?'

'Because it's about the most romantic place I've been to in Spain. I mean, it must be! I bring all my wives here!' He laughs again. 'Sorry. I remember your mother. I liked her.'

'And she liked you. My father died last year . . .'

323

'Oh, I see. I'm sorry.'

'It's all right.'

'Look, Liz and I will be having dinner round about eight. At the Parador. Will you come – both of you?'

'That would be nice,' I say.

'My shout!'

Who is this man? My shout? Next he'll be telling me he doesn't give a 4X! I am tempted to challenge him, to get below his brash, unreal carapace. But we're near the exit now and he's glancing at his watch.

'I must run. I have phone calls to make. I've a man to see in Cordoba in the morning and I haven't managed to reach him yet.'

He walks with me as far as the Hostal and as we're parting he puts his hand on my arm.

'Maybe we could meet up after the concert tonight? Just the two of us. Please, Kit . . . I really would like to talk.'

I nod and feel my heart quicken. He's still in there, I think, the Stephen I used to know. Then I turn and hurry into the cool interior of the hotel.

Mother is lying on the bed when I come in. She isn't asleep. She sits up when she hears the door. I'd hoped that she wouldn't be back, that I'd have the room to myself for a while.

'I've behaved very foolishly. I'm sorry,' she says as soon as I enter. It's as though she's been waiting for me to arrive and has rehearsed the lines she will deliver. 'I've done something unforgivable, Chris.'

'I know,' I say, closing the door. The room is so small there is nowhere to escape. I edge round the side of my bed and sit down, with my back half to her. Then I take off my shoes.

'I can't believe it,' she says. 'I don't know what I was thinking about. I'll have to tell you. Promise you won't lose your temper?' I hear her breathing heavily. I glance at her and see that she is looking down at her hands, folded on her lap. She looks old, I think. Old and unhappy. I want to reach out to her but as I'm about to she starts to speak again. 'I left a note at Stephen's hotel this morning. What is even more unforgivable is that I wrote it as if it came from you. In it I said that you were staying here.'

'It doesn't matter,' I tell her.

Her face is tense and her hair untidy, as though she has slept restlessly. She does a nervous little gesture, which ends up with her scratching a shoulder. Then she shakes her head.

'I went back to retrieve it. But he'd already arrived. I'm so sorry, Chris. I really am.'

'And I'm sorry about last night – so now we're quits.'

'You've nothing to be sorry for.'

'I wanted to shock you.'

'Yes.'

'You mean – yes, I did?'

'I mean I understand why you wanted to. I'm an interfering busybody and you had every right to be furious with me.'

'And did I – shock you?'

'Not by what you were telling me – but the words were unworthy, I thought.'

'I'm sorry.' I suddenly feel incredibly tired. If I lie down I think I might just never get up again.

'It was my fault,' Mother is saying. 'I was interfering . . . I thought . . . that you should see him. I thought you were running away. I think you've been running away all your life. And . . . well . . . I wanted it to stop. But – what right have I to know for you? Did I do so well with my own life that I am in a position to tell you how to run yours? No – more than tell . . . I'm trying to do the running for you. Unforgivable behaviour . . .'

'It isn't. It's all right. Really it is,' I tell her, then rising quickly I cross to the bathroom. 'I'm going to have a shower,' I say, going in and closing the door. It is such a relief to be on my own. 'We're invited to dinner, by the way,' I call as I start to remove my clothes.

'Have you seen him then?' I hear her ask, having to shout to be heard. Her voice has a renewed eagerness in it. 'Is it Stephen we're to dine with?'

'Yes,' I call. Then I switch on the water, shutting off the possibility of any more conversation.

The first impression is of a child bride. Elizabeth Harker can't be more than twenty, I think. But once I'm talking to her I revise my opinion. Maybe twenty-five? Half his age. He always did go in for younger people. She also is clearly in love with him.

Mother is chattering away to Stephen and I am paired with her. I find it quite hard going. I am not wildly up on the music scene and really my appreciation stops somewhere round about Mozart with the odd sortie into the Romantics and an addiction for Vaughan Williams. So I let her do most of the talking, encouraging her to tell me about her career, where she trained, the concerts she has given, the competitions that she's won, her agent, her contract with Decca and even where she gets her clothes. Meanwhile I am able to sit back and take her in.

She's very pretty – beautiful almost. Her hair is what you notice first. It's blonde with a hint of red that makes it look like evening sunlight. She obviously thinks it her best feature; she wears it long and touches it a lot, drawing attention to it. She's not all that tall, nor even that slender. She has a rounded figure; sexy and cuddly. She's wearing a stunning white silk dress with a short skirt that shows good legs and very high-heeled white shoes. The neckline is cut low, possibly to reveal her cleavage or more probably to set off a wonderful necklace of opals and gold.

'It's a bit of a cliché, isn't it? An Australian wearing
But I do love them and as they're my birthstone Steve b
it for my birthday.'

'They're my birthstone as well,' I tell her.

'You're a Libran? Well! D'you know – all Steve's wives
have been Librans.'

I wonder if I am included in the list. Then I'm embarrassed. How much does she know? Not just about me, but
about his wives. Has he told her all the details or is she an
innocent? And if he has told her then why has she married
him? Being third wife must be a bit of a risk, and anyway,
he's old enough to be her father.

'Steve!' she's saying. 'Did you know? Chris is a Libran.'

'Well if I did, I've forgotten. It is quite a while since we
were together, you know. I hesitate to say it but – before
you were born!'

He is so easy, so relaxed. So smooth.

'Let's order!' he says, and we all return to studying
the menu.

'It is odd though, isn't it? The first thing I do when we
meet an available woman is check on her birth sign. He
married all those Librans! Mind you, it's fairly odd that
he's had all those wives. And they're just the ones we
know about!'

'Would you mind not talking about me in front of me,
darling, as though I were deaf.'

'Sorry!' and she laughs. 'What was he like at school, Chris?'

'Very good-looking,' Mother cuts in, I think in order to
help me.

'Was I?'

'You know you were.'

'So was Chris!' he says, giving me a dazzling smile.

'Yes. But I can hardly say that. I'm his mother.'

'He still is good-looking,' Liz declares. 'And he hasn't gone
grey like some I could mention!'

'Now you're talking in front of him as though he's deaf.'

'I don't mind,' I say. 'So long as she's saying nice things.'

We each order our food and Stephen takes a long time deliberating over the wine. Well, he would. He's an expert.

'D'you know what they used to call him at school?'

'Liz! Shut up!'

'The Tool! Can you believe that! Jimmy Hobbs told us. D'you know Jimmy, Chris. He's so nice. He came over last year, just after our wedding. I liked him a lot. He came to a concert I gave. I'm so sorry about his friend. I didn't meet him. Do you know him?'

'His friend? No. I've never met him.'

'He's so young . . .'

'Is he ill?'

'Didn't you know? He has cancer. Jimmy says the hardest thing is that everyone thinks it's Aids. But it amounts to the same thing, doesn't it?'

'Not necessarily,' I say, trying to keep up the conversation while my mind is flying in a circle. 'People can survive cancer.'

'I know. My brother's friend died of Aids. It nearly destroyed us all. It's such a cruel way to go. It was through Guy that I met Steve . . .'

'Liz!' Stephen says, breaking off a conversation with Mother and looking across the table at his wife.

Liz pulls a face and shrugs.

'He's telling me I'm talking too much. I do that when I'm with new people. You'll have to take over for a bit. What do you do, Chris?'

And little by little she draws me out, making intelligent remarks about publishing and talking about books while claiming that she's hardly read any. She asks me more about Blandfords and talking to her about the place makes it seem like a relic of antiquity.

'I can't believe you'd want to send him away when he was so young,' she tells Mother.

'I absolutely agree,' Mother replies. 'It was the fashion at the time.'

'But you wouldn't do it now, would you?'

'I don't suppose so.'

'Well, we won't be sending any of ours to that spooky place, Steve. So don't try to pull the old Alma Mater bit on me.'

'I promise you I wasn't going to!' he says, raising his hands in a gesture of surrender.

'I was happy there,' I say, and I see Mother glance across at me.

There's a moment's pause while Liz sips her wine.

'So was I,' Stephen says, and I look across the table at him and see that he is openly staring at me. 'In fact I'd go so far as to say it was one of the happiest times of my life . . .'

'Do you mind!' Liz exclaims.

'Until now, my darling. If you ever let me finish a sentence I would have said that without any prompting.'

'Damn! My big mouth!' and they smile at each other in such a private, intimate way that one feels like an intruder just sitting with them.

'I bet he behaved atrociously there,' Liz says. 'Screwing everything that moved!'

'You must forgive my wife. She's a daughter of Australia!'

'You didn't get called The Tool for nothing,' she says and then she giggles.

'Liz! You're embarrassing Laura.'

'Oh, I'm sorry!' She sounds so instantly contrite that she can't fail to melt your heart.

'You're not embarrassing me at all,' Mother says, obviously enchanted. 'I expect he was given the nickname because he was good at woodwork!'

And after a delicate moment we all end up laughing.

The meal passes quickly and then Stephen is asking, in impeccable Spanish, for a taxi to take them to the concert.

'We've got tickets for a Julian Bream recital tomorrow evening,' Liz says as we're parting in the grounds of the Parador. 'Why don't you come. Your hotel will fix seats.'

Mother says that sounds like a lovely idea and we arrange to meet at the concert hall.

'We won't be able to make dinner. Steve has to take out some business associates. And I will have to be the dutiful little wife. I get terrified. I let him down because I talk too much, as you will have noticed.'

'I didn't notice anything of the sort,' Mother says, embracing her.

As Stephen is getting into the cab he turns to me. 'See you later,' he mouths, and taking my hand he gives it a conspiratorial squeeze.

Surprised and embarrassed, I nod and commit myself to this subterfuge. Stepping back as the car drives off, I see Liz waving to me through the back window and feel a pang of guilt.

'What an enchanting girl,' Mother says, coming to stand beside me. 'I hope he's not going to ditch her like he usually does.'

I look at her and she smiles.

'Still,' she adds, 'he seems devoted.'

'Yes!' I agree – and I stop myself adding that maybe he always does.

I suppose the concert will last two hours. As it is due to start at the ridiculously late hour of ten thirty that means it will be after midnight by the time they return to their hotel. We haven't arranged where or when to meet. Am I supposed to hang about in the Parador grounds until I see him? And should I be in hiding or will he have told Liz? Almost certainly not, I decide. I feel another pang of guilt.

I like her. I don't want to deceive her. Meanwhile Mother is suggesting a walk before bed 'to settle our stomachs!' Am I going to tell her about our intended liaison?

We walk in silence back along the busy little tourist street. The restaurants are all packed and the sound of laughter and chattering voices is underpinned by classical guitar music.

'Isn't it festive?' she says. 'D'you suppose that music is live?'

Then reaching the wide area in front of the Palace of Charles the Fifth – a classical façade more closely related to the English Georgians or the right bank in Paris than to the exotic Moorish architecture of the Alhambra – we discover the source of the music. A young man is seated with a guitar on a bench backed by the box hedging of a parterre. His playing has attracted a small crowd round him.

'Is this impromptu, d'you suppose? Or is it part of the festival?'

'I don't know,' I reply. 'But it's rather nice.'

It is also heaven-sent, because it means that we don't have to talk. Mother finds a corner of a bench and I sit on the pavement beside her.

The music is gentle and not particularly taxing. Some of the pieces he plays are half-familiar to me. The only likely composer that readily comes to mind is de Falla – but they can't all be by him, if indeed any of them are. There is something intensely Spanish about the sound. It summons up pictures for me of the sad Don tilting at windmills and Goya-esque scenes of carnage and carnival. Wild, discordant images of stark beauty set against a cloudless sky. The notes fly and hover around us like moths round a candle, sometimes fluttering, sometimes diving to destruction, and when they end there is a heartbeat of exquisite silence. The next piece he plays is filled with erotic cadences and a sensual overabundance that enfolds and drugs me, as if pulling me down on to a great cool bed of desires and dreams. The

331

sound engulfs me, caressing and stimulating at the same time. I find a part of me wants to succumb and that another part resists; the puritan and the Sybarite as ever at war, thanks to the peculiar history of our peculiar island race and the added complication of middle-class respectability at odds with rampant lust.

I notice a boy in white trousers standing across the square from me. As I see him he turns and looks in my direction. I can't be sure that he's looking at me. But I recognise him at once as the youth who sat opposite us the previous evening on the benches near the fountain. Tonight he is wearing a dark shirt, unbuttoned to his navel.

The music stops abruptly and there is a scattering of applause. A gipsy child comes round with an empty paint tin, inviting us to put money into it. I have no change and have to stand to get a note out of my back pocket. As I do so I realise that my penis is semi-erect and that it is jutting out embarrassingly from the crotch of my linen trousers. That damn cock, I think. I never did have any control over it. I try to disguise it by putting one hand into my trouser pocket while fishing notes out of the back pocket with the other.

'I haven't anything small,' I say to Mother. 'Have you?'

'Then give him something big,' she says and as she speaks she looks up and gives me a sad smile.

This crude innuendo is certainly unintentional on her part but it does wonders for my cock, which shrivels with embarrassment. I take a note and when the child arrives in front of me I put it in the tin amongst the coins and small change.

'Bed for me, I think,' Mother says, rising as the crowd starts to disperse.

'I'll come back with you,' I say.

'There's no need. You're probably not tired yet. You're much more of a night owl than I am.'

'No, I think I will stay up. I've got a couple of cards I've

332

been meaning to write. But I'll come back. I need to get an address.'

I return to the same bench that Mother had occupied and sit writing the postcards I have just bought from a shop almost opposite the Hostal. I will send Catherine the lurid matador flouncing his cape. *'Thank God you didn't come!'* I write. *'These chaps are everywhere, stamping their feet, swishing their capes and doing unimaginable things with their hips! We are now in Granada and return to the villa the day after tomorrow. It's being good for us to have time together but I do miss you. No doubt I'll be back before this arrives. Fondest love, C.'*

I'm not sure that it's strictly true to say that I miss her – the thought of having to cope with her as well as Mother, Stephen, Liz, boys in white trousers and the erotic effect of guitar music might be the final straw – but there is something very comforting about knowing that she's there to be written to. In fact I do look forward to seeing her. At least with Catherine I am sure of forgiveness. Is that the essential quality of true friendship? The knowledge that your friend loves you in spite of yourself? Probably. In that case, what am I to say on the second card? It has been chosen with care and is a detail of the vaulted ceiling in the Two Sisters Hall – or so it says on the back. Why this card? Somehow I didn't want 'a view' and I certainly didn't want 'a joke'. It had to be something neutral, something beautiful but with no hidden agenda.

Taking the letter that I've just collected from our room out of the breast pocket of my shirt, I unfold it and read it again by the light of the streetlamp.

*Dear Chris,*

*It was good to see you the other evening but I'm sorry I butted in on your evening with Catherine. I'm not sure that I handled it at all well. I was surprised to see her there and was rather thrown.*

*Mark, my friend, is unlikely to get in touch with her but I didn't feel that was the time to tell her. In fact I doubt he'll be getting in touch with any of us for much longer – but why should I burden you with all this? I'm really writing to say that I have written to Stephen. I hope you didn't think me stuffy, not giving you his address. I always think what a nightmare it would be if people from my past just wrote (or worse still, turned up!) out of the blue! But I'm sure – in fact I KNOW – he'll be delighted to be in touch with YOU. Which I am. Funny. We weren't friends at Blandfords and yet I've often thought about you. The power of sexual attraction! Right now I sort of feel in need of a friend – so, if you feel like it, do phone me. We could go to a theatre together or just sit and have a drink. Anyway, if I don't hear from you I'll quite understand. It was all a hundred years ago!*
*Yours,*
*Jimmy (Hobbs!)*

When it had arrived, I'd read it once and then put it away. I don't know why I reacted to it in the way that I did. I think I had a sudden image of him as a young boy, always simpering and giggling when he saw me. I thought then that he was mocking me. It never entered my head that he could fancy me. It never entered my head that anyone would. That's why it was such a powerful experience with Stephen, I suppose. He wanted me. He went out of his way to get me. I was so . . . grateful? No. Thrilled. I didn't think that people noticed me – but Stephen had. And so, it seems, had the dreaded Hobbs.

I fold the letter and put it back into my breast pocket. Then I take the card and look again at the picture of the ceiling. It's actually quite difficult to work out what it's meant to be. It could be a magnified computer cell or an iced wedding cake. Or a Juliet hat perhaps? A weird formation of seashells? The close-up of a snowflake? An explosion in a white desert? The slow-motion recording of a drop of cream, caught as it breaks into a million particles . . .

I look up, stretching the back of my neck, and see the boy staring at me from across the square. It must be me he's looking at this time. Because I'm alone on the bench. I slip the two cards and the Biro into the breast pocket of my shirt and glance at my watch. It isn't midnight yet. I have almost an hour to kill.

The side of the hill is so steep that it's quite difficult to follow the narrow path through the trees without slipping and sliding downwards. We are surrounded by bushes and tall swaying fronds that interlace above our heads, forming nature's own version of the ceiling of the Two Sisters Hall. We come out into a small clearing. The dark woods surround us and the night sky presses down. There are so many stars and as I look up one of them slips away down the sky; a falling, shooting, dying world.

He takes my hand and leads me to the shelter of a tree.

'What you like?' he whispers, turning towards me and reaching out with his hand and placing it on my chest. I put my own hand over it and feel the bones of his knuckles and the smooth warm skin. His other hand touches my cheek and he steps closer, looking at my face with his dark, deep eyes.

'You like me?' he whispers.

I nod and press his hand harder so that I feel the warmth of it against my nipple. He pulls my face round, and kisses my lips.

Is this how it's to end? I think. Sex with a stranger? Will I have to pay him? Will I be able to function? Wouldn't I be better off back at the hotel in my room with Mother?

I giggle, making him pull away from me, searching my eyes.

'You laugh?' He steps back, releasing his hold on me.

'Not at you,' I whisper. 'I wasn't laughing at you.'

He glowers, as though he doesn't believe me.

'You speak very good English,' I whisper, putting a hand on his shoulder and pulling him gently back towards me. I feel him shrug and he makes a face.

'Foreigners do not speak Spanish. It is necessary.'

'I wasn't laughing at you,' I say, running a hand through his thick black hair. I'm surprised to find that it's covered with oil and as my fingers comb through it I can smell the sweet perfume of the dressing he has used.

'You a sad man,' he says.

I shake my head.

'I haven't done this for a long time.'

He shrugs again.

'That's why the foreigners come to Granada. They get their rocks off in the bushes and then go home to their wives.'

'What a desolate world you describe.'

'Why? They are content. I am content. The rocks are off.'

I smile again. I feel light-headed – light-hearted, even. I'm enjoying the warmth of his body and the sweet, cloying scent of his hair. I put an arm round his waist, drawing him in closer to me, feeling the flood of heat reaching through my veins. He places his hands on my shoulders, holding me, then slowly he slides them up the sides of my neck and round behind my head.

Shivers of sensation fizz along the nerves, reaching the surface of the skin in a shudder of anticipation.

'Don't be so scared,' he says, and I feel his moist lips brushing mine and I gasp and sob as his tongue enters my mouth . . .

The slightly metallic taste of the inside of his mouth as our tongues explore. His warm, soft hands pressing the back of my neck and probing up into my hair as he gathers it in his fingers and gently pulls it so that it strains at the roots.

'I like you,' he whispers. 'I like you very much.'

Like a cat he slides down my body, squatting on his haunches and unbuckling my belt. I lean over, towering above him, and encircle his shoulders with my arms. But he pushes me away impatiently. I lean back against the trunk of the tree, looking up at the dark velvet sky and the myriad stars, and abandon myself to his will.

I feel him struggle with my zip and then he is pulling my trousers down round my knees. He slips his warm hands up under my pants, dragging them over and down and releasing my cock from its lifetime sentence, from its solitary confinement.

For some ridiculous reason a picture of Mother flashes into my mind. She is lying on her bed at the Hostal – waiting for my return, I suppose. Then the vision fades and is replaced by Stephen. He is standing in the room in Cambridge and he's smiling at me. 'We're not at school here,' he's telling me . . .

Then, with a rush of light and heat and a high, piercing cry, I feel his warm, moist mouth envelop my cock and all the years of waiting surge out of me in one great expulsion of energy.

'Don't shout!' he whispers, rising quickly and clamping a hand over my mouth. Then he turns his face sideways and spits. I realise that my mouth is open wide and that the sound I can hear that seemed to come from somewhere deep beyond the Milky Way is my own scream. I feel his hand pressing against my open lips and the edge of my teeth.

'Don't shout! Don't shout!' he whispers urgently. 'We are not safe here!'

And I gradually relax into the soft centre of his palm. I lift my arm and take his hand in mine, kissing it gently.

'I'm sorry,' I whisper.

'You come so fast!'

'Not really!' I shake my head and start to laugh quietly. 'I actually took longer to come than you'll ever know.'

I put my arms round him and sink my head down into the hollow of his neck. But after a moment he pushes me away.

'I must go now,' he says.

'Yes!' I nod. I start to pull up my pants and trousers.

'You have enjoyed, yes?'

'Yes. Thank you. I have enjoyed.'

'But I, I think, have been working. You enjoy. I work . . .'

'Oh, yes, of course. How much . . .?' I unbutton my back pocket and take out the wad of notes. I hand him the first one I come to. He takes it, looks at it and hands it back.

'Is too much,' he says.

'No. Please take it.'

'You a rich foreigner?' he asks, slipping the note into his breast pocket.

'No,' I reply.

He shrugs, chucks me under the chin and turns to go.

'What's your name?' I call after him.

'Francisco,' he calls from the other side of the clearing.

'Thank you, Francisco.'

'You're welcome!' he says and he disappears into the dark.

'Thank you for getting my rocks off,' I whisper, and I lean back against the tree and start to laugh quietly.

I haven't been waiting long in the shrubbery outside the Parador when a cab pulls into the drive and I see Liz and Stephen climb out. Liz goes straight into the hotel and Stephen turns to pay the driver.

I cup my hands and place them to my lips, then, after taking a breath, I blow the long, swooping cry of the night owl.

I see Stephen look up midway through his transaction, a

startled expression on his face. Then he hurriedly finishes paying the driver and steps away from the car.

I blow the owl call again and he slowly turns in my direction, searching the bushes with his eyes.

As the cab turns round and drives back out of the gates, the headlights blind me for a moment and I raise my hands to shade them. Then, as the car goes, I see Stephen looking at me from the door to the hotel.

'Five minutes,' he calls and hurries inside.

Strange how familiar it all is! Waiting in the bushes in the middle of the night, snatching forbidden moments to be together, heightening the mundane with nervous anticipation. I wish I still smoked. Why did I give up smoking? I walk slowly back to the gates and stand outside in the dimly lit street. It is late now and apart from a few people returning from the concert the street is empty. The gift shops are closed, the restaurants are dark. A light is burning in the hallway of the Hostal. I hope they have a night porter, I think. I don't want to have to wake someone up.

'I officially have a headache!' he says, coming up behind me and taking me by surprise. 'I have said I'll try to walk it off!' And he puts an arm round my shoulder, hurrying me down the street. 'But I can't spend too long or she'll start to wonder!'

He looks at me and flashes that big smile. Then with a surge of energy he starts to run, pulling me with him, back along the lane and through the square outside the Charles the Fifth Palace.

'Where are we going?' I ask.

'Trust me!' he shouts.

We reach the end of the bluff on which the Alhambra is built. Here there is an ancient fort softly floodlit with orange light. He tells me that it is the Alcazaba. Who am I to question him? There are a few people sitting around on stone benches – the attraction being a kiosk that is still

339

open, selling cold drinks, ice cream, cigarettes and packets of nuts and olives.

'You want something?' Stephen asks.

I shake my head.

'I'm going to have a beer. You have one too,' he says and he goes to the kiosk. I sit on one of the empty benches.

The night is still warm and at the other side of the kiosk the boy with the guitar is playing quietly to himself. Two Spaniards are having a noisy, drunken argument but they stagger past me and away into the darkness from where we came before Stephen returns with the two open cans.

'Cheers!' he says and lowers himself down beside me, sitting astride the bench and facing towards me. He takes a swig of the beer and puts the can down in front of him. Then he leans across and presses with both his hands on the top of my thigh.

This openly intimate gesture takes me by surprise. I take a nervous swig at my beer and look away, wondering if anyone has noticed.

'Loosen up!' he says, gently mocking. 'You're not in the frigid north now! How are you, Kit?'

'You've already asked me that, haven't you?'

'Probably. I've wondered so often what we would say if we met – but I haven't got anything rehearsed.' He takes a breath and picks up the can of beer, swirling it in his hand before putting it to his lips. As he does so he looks round, away from me.

'I didn't know you were called The Tool at school,' I say, and I'm surprised to hear a complaining note in my voice.

'Neither did I – till Jimmy Hobbs told me.'

'Were there a lot of us, Stephen?'

'You jump in quick!' he says, and he turns and looks at me with a smile.

'I have to. You said you didn't have long. There are things I need to know.'

340

'Like how many kids I was screwing while I was screwing you?'

I swallow and don't reply. He takes another swig of beer and then produces a packet of cigarettes from his pocket and a box of matches.

'I'm not supposed to do this. Liz has a thing about smoking. Somehow it being illicit makes it all the more exciting!'

'Yes,' I say and I look at him as he strikes the match and see the thin lines on his handsome face and the mop of silver hair, and I want to shout out, to rail against time for passing and changing us and making us feel so ... different.

'Want one?' he asks, proffering the packet.

'I gave up,' I tell him.

He shrugs and puts the packet away.

'You can always give up giving up!'

'I'll have one then,' I say, forcing him to get the packet out again.

The taste of the smoke is sweet and goes straight to my head, like alcohol. I reel giddily for a moment then shake my head.

'I don't think I can take it,' I say. 'Sorry!' and I drop the cigarette on the ground and step on it.

'I did love you,' he says quietly.

I look at him coldly.

'Isn't that what you wanted to hear?' he asks.

'I don't want to hear what you think I want to hear.'

'So what do you want?'

'The truth.'

He shrugs. 'Ask me. Ask me anything.'

The boy is playing the Beatles song 'Yesterday' on the guitar.

'That's a bit corny, isn't it?' Stephen says after a moment. 'Cut the music!' and he leans across again and takes my hand

341

in both of his. I try to pull it away but he holds on firmly. 'Listen, Kit! Please! I did love you.'

I feel that lump in the back of my throat. He's always making it happen. I can't look at him. But I don't try to pull my hand away any more.

'It wouldn't have worked. We were children. No, that's not the only reason. It wouldn't have worked because it was too complicated. But that doesn't mean that I didn't love you.'

'Did you love Jimmy Hobbs as well?' I ask, finding the strength to retrieve my hand.

'Oh, God! Yes!' he exclaims, sitting back away from me. 'I love 'em all. Each of the wives. My two girls. Did you know I have grown-up daughters? From the first wife. She was Jill and we were at Cambridge together. Yeah! She followed you . . .'

'No,' I say, knowing I'm behaving badly, 'Jimmy Hobbs followed me.'

'Ah! If you're looking for chronology you're in for a hard time. The threads weave and interweave, cross and recross. Characters come and . . . characters go. I loved them all, Kit – at the time. Even the little bits on the side. Even the one-night stands. That's my problem.'

'Or ours.'

'Or yours. I think maybe it was that place, you know. Or is it too easy to blame school for everything? But it was there that I learned the overwhelming relief of sexual passion. Hey, Kit! We did do pretty well, didn't we?'

'But all that crap, Stephen – about running away and coming here and living on grapes and cheap white wine.'

'Absolute crap! Sheer shit! But it seemed like a good idea at the time and it didn't do anyone any harm.'

'What about me?'

'Jimmy Hobbs told me – a few years back – about your breakdown. I wanted to write to you but then I thought . . .

well, we're talking about a lifetime ago! He's probably settled down with a brood of children in Scvenoaks by now. He's hardly likely to want to hear from a vulgar dingo!'

'If you had written – what would you have said?'

He considers for a moment, scratching his thigh and staring into the distance.

'I guess I'd have said – come and meet me and wife number three in Granada one year and we'll drink a beer for auld lang syne. Jesus! I wish that guitar would stop that . . . He could have chosen something like "Yellow Submarine"! This is playing to the gallery, isn't it?'

I lift my beer can and hold it out towards him. He looks at me, questioningly, then he lifts his.

'For auld lang syne!' I say, and we drink a silent toast.

'I tell people that I started sex at the age of nine. It's almost true. My mother's houseboy showed me his cock round about then but I wasn't really interested. At school there were one or two furtive fiddles before you came on the scene. But you were the best, Kit.' He lifts a finger and stops my protest. 'No! I'm not saying what you want to hear – I'm saying what I want to believe. Jimmy Hobbs was an inconvenience – and anyway he really was far more interested in you . . .'

'Yet you went with him on the last night. Our last night.'

'And paid a heavy price. We were caught with our knickers down by TG's wife . . .'

'I know about that. But why did you go with him? Why not me? If I was so special why not spend the last night with me?'

'Because I wanted unadulterated sex. I didn't want cosy domesticity.' I turn away, shocked as if he's kicked me. 'Sorry!' he murmurs.

'Is that how it was?'

'It's how it got. It's how it always gets. Why d'you think I'm a serial husband?'

'Poor Liz!' I say and I am suddenly overwhelmed with pity for her. 'She doesn't stand a chance.'

'She does. I adore her. She's sexy and fun and feisty – and she has her own life going.'

'That's important to you?'

'Yeah. It gives me space.'

'For what?'

'Oooo! The sound of moral indignation! You're thinking I want space to screw around, aren't you?'

'Is that what it's about?'

He considers for a moment then he nods.

'Probably. It's a game and I love it!'

'Then why marry them – I nearly said us. But yes, I include myself. You were the one who spun the web of living together, of never parting, of running away. You were the one who forged the wedding bonds.'

'I always do. I suppose I live in constant hope that this time might last for ever . . . I'd better go! Or this one might end rather prematurely.'

He stands up, his legs still straddling the bench, his crotch within inches of my face. I get up and stand beside him. Then I smile at him.

'I'm glad we've seen each other,' I say, and I do mean it.

'Yeah!' He leans forward and gives me a hug. 'If you see Jimmy, tell him how sorry I am. Oh, did you know . . .?'

'Liz told me his friend has cancer.'

'No. He died – I heard just before we left Sydney. Tell him I will write to him.'

'Yes. I'll tell him.'

He lifts his leg over the bench and then still with his arm round my shoulder he turns us in the direction of the hotels.

'I loved you too, Stephen,' I say.

'I know. Was I your first love?'

'Yes,' I whisper.

344

'I'm glad. You were mine. I think we have impeccable taste and that there couldn't have been a better start for life!'

As we're nearing the Hostal he stops in the shadow of a doorway.

'I really want this one to work, Kit. Liz and me. I want to end up an old married couple. I want to have what you have and what Jimmy Hobbs has and what I expect most of the people in the world have.'

'What's that?' I ask.

'The capacity to grow old gracefully, to mature naturally and to be a good companion. Hey! It sounds like a superior bottle of wine!' and he laughs. 'Problem is, I may have to cut my cock off to attain it and I'm not sure I'm that brave!' and he pulls me against him and kisses me on the lips. 'For auld lang syne. Oh, and by the way – you were fantastic sex!'

'Fuck off, Stephen,' I say, for once having the last word.


'There's a note from Liz,' Mother said as she joined me at the table for breakfast. 'It's just been delivered.'

'You read it,' I tell her. I don't add that I'm sure I know what it'll say.

Mother puts on her glasses and looks at the sheet of paper.

'It appears that their plans have changed. They'll have to stay in Cordoba tonight, so they won't make the concert. Oh, what a shame!'

'Not to worry,' I tell her, sipping my orange juice.

'She promises that they'll see us the next time they're in London. Here, d'you want to read it?'

I shake my head.

'So, today . . .?'

'I very much want you to see the Generalife Gardens. I went yesterday and longed for you to be with me.'

'And you must see the Alhambra.'

'So – we'll rubberneck?'

'What an extraordinary, unlike-you expression, Mother!'
'Well! I don't feel like me!'
'Neither do I. It's quite a nice experience, isn't it? Before we go out I have one more card to write . . .'

*Dear Jimmy,*
*I'll be back from here in a week and will contact you. I am so very sorry to hear what has happened. If there is any way that I can help I would like to. If not — and you can bear it — it would be just good to see you for that drink.*
*Fondest wishes,*
*Chris (Metcalfe)*